Finally they pushed out of the forest and there it was—the yawning, spectacular Grand Canyon with its layers of rock and the glitter of the Colorado River flowing like a silver thread far, far below. Professor Sutherland froze in his tracks and threw his arms toward Heaven.

Dunn and Josie left their flock and hurried over to join him. The three stood poised on the rim, feeling the hot wind sweeping up from the depths of the canyon. To the east, Dunn could see the great union between the big and the Little Colorado rivers. A pair of golden eagles, dwarfed by space to the size of sparrows, soared effortlessly over immense stone cathedrals. Straight across the ten-mile chasm was an excellent view of the South Rim. And beyond, perhaps a hundred miles away, Dunn could see snow-clad peaks, probably created by centuries-old volcanoes.

Dunn took Josie's hand and they walked away, leaving the professor to his musings. "What are you thinking?" Josie asked.

"I was thinking that I no longer have any desire to go back East. I'd like to stay right here . . . to build our flock, to catch wild horses, to raise cattle, perhaps even mine for gold . . ."

"And I'd like to have our child born in Havasu Canyon."

Dunn nodded. It would work out. They just had to have faith, hold on tight . . . and *always* stick together.

GRAND CANYON

GARY McCARTHY

PINNACLE BOOKS
KENSINGTON PUBLISHING CORP.

PINNACLE BOOKS are published by

Kensington Publishing Corp.
850 Third Avenue
New York, NY 10022

Pinnacle and the P logo Reg. U.S. Pat. & TM Off.

First Printing: June, 1996
10 9 8 7 6 5 4 3 2 1

Printed in the United States of America

The finest workers in stone
are not copper or steel tools,
but the gentle touches of air and water working
at their leisure with a liberal allowance of time.
                                                    —Thoreau

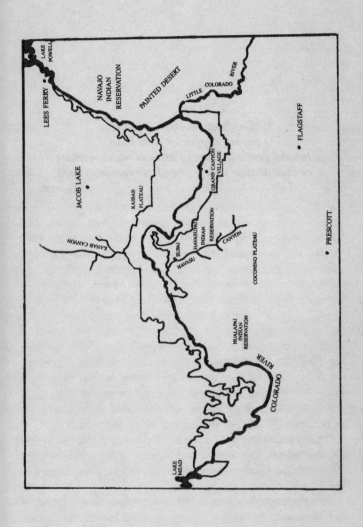

Prologue

South Rim, Grand Canyon, September 1540

Antonio Madrid was dreaming of a peasant girl with flashing eyes and hair the color of a raven's wing shining in the sun, a girl whose hips swayed seductively as she strolled through his dusty Spanish village. Her name was Maria Casteneda and she waited for Antonio to return from the New World a very rich man, like the earlier soldiers under Hernando Cortez, who had plundered the wealth of Mexico and brought to the natives the Virgin Mary and the Christ.

Maria, I am coming! Antonio breathed through his cracked and bleeding lips as he reached for the vision of her lovely hand and whispered his well-remembered promises. *I am coming back for you. We will be married by the kind old padre, Fr. Sebastian. And then we will do nothing but eat, sleep, and make love for one whole year while I hire men to build us a casa grand enough for all our children. And we will never be poor again. We will be the envy of all in our village.*

"Antonio, wake up!" Captain Pablo de Melgosa urged, sharply tapping his young infantryman with the toe of his boot. "You and Juan Galeras must get ready to follow me down into hell."

Antonio's sweet vision of Maria dissolved and, instead of her loveliness, he saw the pocked, bearded face of his captain, a man twenty years older than he, who treated him more like a son than a soldier. Antonio blinked, then squeezed his eyes shut again, desperately attempting to retrieve the vision of Maria. But this time, Captain Melgosa booted him harder.

"Antonio, listen to me. I have chosen you and Private Galeras to help me reach the deep canyon river. I have told our leader that the three of us have the best chance of finding a way down to the bottom so that all his men can be saved."

"The Hopi scouts should go instead," Antonio groaned, rubbing his back.

Pablo Melgosa shook his leonine head. "No! Cardenas needs the Indians and, besides, they will not go down into the canyon because they believe it is the home of demons.

Antonio groaned and rubbed the sleep from his eyes. More than anything—even more than Maria or a mountain of solid gold—he desperately wished an end to this accursed expedition. If only their leader, Francisco Coronado, would face the truth that there were no lost cities of gold in this hellish land but, instead, only despair, and then death.

"We can do honor today for Spain!" Captain Melgosa of Burgos whispered passionately. "Antonio, if we can somehow reach the water and find a way down for everyone, we will be greatly rewarded."

"And what if we fail and cannot reach the river?"

"We *must*," the captain said, clenching his big fists. "Our lives depend upon it. Get ready! I will lead the way."

"To our open graves, my captain."

In reply, Captain Melgosa leaned so close that Antonio could smell his foul breath. "If we fail to reach the river, we might die of thirst anyway. Is it not better to die fighting like Spanish soldiers than to lie up here panting like whipped dogs?"

Before Antonio could answer, Captain Melgosa grinned wolfishly in the waning moonlight, his teeth whiter than polished ivory, his eyes blacker than obsidian. "And think of this, Private Madrid! If we reach that river and return to save this suffering company, our fame will be assured. The great Coronado himself will remember us when we return to Spain as heroes."

"If we go down into that hole and die," Antonio argued, "will our sun-bleached bones care if they are famous? And will your sweet wife, Candid, or your six children? Will it matter even a little to my family or that of Juan Galeras if we foolishly die beside some stinking river in an abyss so deep and hot that even vultures dare not fly down to pick our stupid bones?"

Captain Melgosa scowled. He was a tall, powerful man with the beak and temperament of a hawk. He was fair but fierce, and Antonio believed there was no finer soldier alive, but Melgosa was too eager to martyr himself for God and country.

"My captain," Antonio whispered, "even if we reach the bottom of that chasm—which we cannot—we will never climb out alive."

"Yes, we will!" Melgosa argued. "We will have water and weapons. There must be fish in the river and things to hunt and eat down there. Our lives will be saved by that river."

Antonio disagreed. For three days, they had searched for a way to the river far, far below but had failed. The canyon simply was too immense, an unholy and open tomb large enough for every living thing that had ever existed.

"The orders have been given that the three of us should go at first light," Captain Melgosa was saying. "We will wear the armor of Spain and we will find . . ."

"In armor!" Antonio protested. "On top of all else we must wear armor!"

Now Melgosa would not meet his eyes. "It was ordered so that the men we leave behind will not lose their spirit. To do otherwise would be a sign that we expect to fail."

"But . . ."

Melgosa's big hands shot out and he grabbed Antonio by both ears and shook him like a puppy. "No more argument!" the captain hissed. He released Antonio's right ear and drew his sword. "Private Madrid, do you refuse my order?"

Antonio's heart began to hammer and he choked, "No, my captain! I will prepare myself at once!"

"Good! I expect us to reach the river by noon and to carry as many empty boda bags as we can fill with water for our thirsty company."

Antonio dared not remind his captain that the Hopi believed not only that the great canyon was filled with demons, but that it was even larger than it appeared from high up on this South Rim. Captain Melgosa's immediate superior, Major Garcia Lopez de Cardenas, judged it to be only a few leagues across, but the Indians thought it much, much wider. Their Hopi scouts also claimed that the river was very big, as wide as fifty men were long. But in this Antonio thought them mistaken, for the river appeared only a few yards wide and it was red with mud, thus earning it the name of Rio Colorado.

"Hurry!" Captain Melgosa growled as he went to awaken Juan Galeras.

Antonio reached into his tunic and clutched a wooden crucifix suspended by a leather thong. The crucifix symbolized both his poverty and his Catholic faith. Someday, he hoped to replace wood and leather with gold and then to become a wise and wealthy man who gave much to his village and to the Church. But now, as Antonio faced the prospect of almost-certain death, those dreams tasted as bitter as ashes. His only solace was that an all-knowing and merciful God would take into account that poor Antonio Madrid had already spent time in this wilderness purgatory and, therefore, was qualified to pass directly into Heaven.

Antonio whispered a quick but fervent Hail Mary and Our Father, then climbed to his feet. His shirt and underwear were stiff with an irritating mixture of red dust and dried salt so that every crease of his flesh burned. Like all the other soldiers on this ill-fated expedition, he was thin, insect bitten, scratched by the harsh Sonoran vegetation and a bit feverish. His brown eyes wept constantly under the blazing sun. And, even though Antonio was among the youngest of this company and the most fit, weariness had seeped into the very marrow of his bones. On top of that, wearing the hated Spanish armor was a personal torture, despite the fact that it had been reduced to a rusting helmet and a dented breastplate that stewed his heart like a cooking chicken.

Antonio struggled through his morning prayers. To the east, he could see the first faint beginnings of sunrise. Warm, un- bidden tears slid down his dusty cheeks. He scrubbed them away and breathed deeply of the sage and high desert piñon and juniper pines. The sky would soon turn the color of roses. It was a miracle that something so beautiful could bless these badlands each day at sunrise and sunset, like a desert flower that bloomed and then all too quickly died. Antonio found it impossible to comprehend how anything of such delicate beauty could exist where every living thing fought savagely for survival with tooth, claw, or thorn.

He pulled on his shoes and threaded his way past the slum- bering infantrymen until he stood highlighted beside the great chasm. Yes, it was still waiting down below, silent but alive and with colors ever mutating. How, he wondered, could a loving God have created this cruel monstrosity?

As the light grew bolder and the edge of the rising sun topped the mountains, the shadows shrank back from the chasm like cowards. Now he saw the Rio Colorado crawling like a frightened worm between the towering walls of silent stone. During the past three days as Cardenas's poor soldiers had searched for some way down to the river far below, An- tonio had found himself wondering if perhaps the Hopi were right, and this canyon really was the kingdom of demons. The very thought of entering such an unholy place caused Antonio to fumble for his crucifix while making a hurried sign of the cross.

You must not think such thoughts! It is only *a canyon. Noth- ing more. Go down with the captain and that fool Galeras until we can go no farther, then find a way to get out quickly.*

"There he is!" Galeras exclaimed, hurrying over to Antonio and roughly grabbing his arm.

"Let go of me, damn you!" Antonio swore, yanking his arm free.

"I thought you might have gone off," Melgosa said around a mouth stuffed with biscuits.

"To where?" Antonio asked, looking around. "Where could I go to hide in such a place as this?"

Galeras actually looked around in search of a hiding place but the captain extended a handful of biscuits. "Here," he said, "eat these before we go so you will have your strength. As I have told Private Galeras, I have a trail in mind that holds promise of reaching the Rio Colorado."

"I remember it well," Galeras said. "I think it *will* take us all the way to the river!"

Antonio resisted the urge to scoff. He and Juan Galeras were about the same age, but Juan was a model Spanish soldier. No doubt, when informed by their captain that he was one of only two chosen to make this impossible descent to the Rio Colorado, Galeras had felt very honored.

As they hurriedly prepared to leave, Garcia Lopez de Cardenas himself came to wish them good fortune, saying, "I do not need to tell you that you do this for the glory of God and Spain. I believe that you will reach the water and, from that vantage point, determine how I can deliver my soldiers to the river far below. And who knows? Since no man has ever gone so deep into the earth, perhaps we will discover that this Rio Colorado is filled with gold!"

They bowed their heads and Cardenas gave them a hurried blessing before he yawned and returned to his bed. Antonio had the impression that he had been given the last rites, but that stupid ox Juan Galeras now appeared euphoric, too ignorant to realize they would likely die this day. And then Captain Melgosa marched them straight into the rising sun. No words were spoken during the next hour until the captain halted and turned to gaze down into the abyss.

"There is the path," he said, pointing at the faint mark of

a game trail that ran down several hundred yards of crumbling limestone to end on the lip of another cliff.

Antonio followed his leader's gaze, not daring to believe that they were about to attempt this mere rabbit track leading over the South Rim.

"I think here," Melgosa said, peering into the great chasm, taking a deep breath and then plunging over the edge and down the game trail. Galeras, however, waited.

"Go on!" Antonio urged. "Since you are so eager for praise and glory, run after him!"

"My orders are to follow *you*," Galeras said, not bothering to hide his contempt.

Antonio understood. Captain Melgosa, fearing that Antonio might lose his nerve and flee back to camp, had ordered Galeras to kill him if he balked.

For an instant, Antonio considered pulling his sword and attacking Galeras. Perhaps he could get lucky and even slay the idiot, but then what? Captain Melgosa would return and would have no choice but to kill Antonio or march him back to camp, where he would be tortured to death as an example to the other soldiers.

"All right," Antonio said, despairing of escape.

But, an hour later, with the captain out in front picking their way down the rabbit track, it occurred to Antonio that perhaps he had been wrong. This really was a game trail, and it was not altogether inconceivable that animals might have used it to reach the water far below. The trail faithfully brought them down to the base of the first cliff.

"See," Melgosa proudly announced as they removed their helmets and drank a little water. He craned his head back and pointed toward the rim, which was a good five hundred feet above. "Look up to where we started. It's a good start, eh?"

"A good start, Captain!" the simple Galeras happily agreed.

"A good start," Antonio heard himself saying. "But just a little way ahead, there is yet another cliff."

"Where we will find another trail," Melgosa promised.

"You will see. This day we not only will have water, but gold! God would not bring us so much suffering without a great reward."

"His reward is said to be in Heaven, not at the bottom of a canyon," Antonio dared reply.

Melgosa's cheeks blazed and Antonio knew that he had erred. The captain was desperately attempting to build hope and optimism. He would brook no more sarcasm and, if the trail ended at the top of the next cliff with nowhere left to go, God help them.

The captain hurried down the slope toward the rim of the next cliff. Antonio lingered, waiting for Galeras to forge ahead but the soldier refused, causing Antonio to cry, "Go on! I'm not going to turn and run back to camp after coming *this* far."

"Too bad," Galeras said, "because I would enjoy killing a Spanish coward."

Antonio hurried after his captain, who now stood leaning over the second cliff. Even before he reached his superior's side, Antonio could see that the captain's confidence had eroded.

"Well?" Antonio asked, peering over a vertical drop of at least eight hundred feet. "What do we do now?"

"I don't know," the captain admitted. "But surely we can find a way."

"Where?" Antonio demanded, looking both to the left and the right.

Melgosa made the mistake of pointing toward some real or imagined path but his hand shook, perhaps from weariness but more likely from fear. Antonio could see no trail, but when the captain stubbornly insisted on its existence, Antonio said, "Look! What about over there? Perhaps we could descend that narrow chute. It drops all the way to the next terrace and I see plenty of handholds."

"Yes!" Captain Melgosa licked his cracked lips. "I see what you mean, now. That *is* a better way, Antonio. You . . . you start out and we will follow."

Again Antonio thought to protest, until he saw Galeras's faint smile and how his hand edged toward his sword. "All right."

The chute had been carved by falling water fed by the same violent summer storms that created flash floods capable of destroying everything in their path. Antonio had never actually seen such a flood, but he'd seen the aftermath, trees torn up and even boulders as big as houses rolled down into arroyos and canyons. And, long after these powerful floods, gentle streams would bleed over the rim in a thousand places, raking the cliffs until they appeared like plowed fields standing on end.

Antonio led them over to the vertical chute. He was not unreasonably fearful of great heights but, as he leaned far out and peered straight down to where the jagged chute ended several hundred feet below, he found himself struggling for breath.

"What is wrong?" Captain Melgosa asked, his face bathed in sweat, his eyes bloodshot and bulging as he also gazed at the rocks resting far, far below.

"My captain, what is wrong is that, even if we make it to the next slope," Antonio said, easing back from the edge and working hard to breathe in deeply, "I do not think we can climb back up this chute."

The captain thought about this for several long moments. Antonio listened to his racing heart and tasted the hot, rising wind. He silently whispered a prayer that his captain would realize that, starting right now, to go on was to die.

"Maybe," Melgosa finally offered, "we had better remove our armor and leave it here, taking only our weapons."

"But . . ."

"Do it!" Galeras spat, throwing his helmet down so hard it bounced off the rocks and rolled a long way without stopping.

Unwilling to prolong such insanity, Antonio tore off his own helmet as well as his breastplate and hurled them to the ground. He also ripped off his stinking undershirt so that he was bare-chested before he attacked the long, narrow chute of rock. Heed-less of his peril, Antonio descended in a shower of rocks and dirt, not looking past his own two feet. He grabbed anything and everything he could, often tearing away shrubs and crum-bling red rock, which fell hundreds of feet, rattling and bounc-ing off the narrow walls of the chute. He tore his fingernails and ignored stickers and barbs that pierced his flesh. Twice, Antonio lost his footing and almost fell to his death but man-aged at the very last minute to jam his sword into a crevasse where he dangled, kicking and clawing for purchase, until he managed to wedge himself into the safety of the rocks like a crab fighting the surf. Cursing and grunting with exertion and fear, both Captain Melgosa and Galeras were having their own difficulties.

"Antonio, look out!" Melgosa shouted as he dislodged a large rock that dropped like a missile and nearly broke Anto-nio's shoulder.

Antonio was drenched with sweat. An almost-constant shower of pebbles rained down on him and he expected that his skull would be crushed by a falling rock if he did not first lose his grip and tumble to his death. But it never quite hap-pened and then his feet were planted once again on solid ground and he was staggering forward to drop on his hands and knees at the base of the cliff.

"We made it!" Captain Melgosa choked as he tumbled for-ward to collapse beside Antonio with Galeras soon to follow. "We really made it!"

It took several minutes for Antonio to find the strength to raise his head. Melgosa was praying but Galeras was crying. His face was ashen and his body trembled as if he had the ague.

"How many more cliffs?" Melgosa finally asked, ignoring Galeras.

"Just look across to the other rim," Antonio said. "If it is the same as this, there are three or four more cliffs, but none so tall as this."

"Three or four," Melgosa whispered, shaking his head and letting sweat pour from his black beard. "Lord have mercy on our poor souls!"

Antonio pushed to his feet and staggered down the sloping terrace to the next low cliff. He closed his eyes for a moment, feeling the rising air caress his cheeks and then he looked down at the river again. It was still far, far away. Impossibly far, but he could now see that it was a very large river, like the Hopi had told them from the beginning.

Antonio unstrapped his sword and let it fall. Somewhere, he had already lost his dagger. He sleeved a river of sweat from his brow and took a little more water. The sun was almost directly overhead and the air was now very, very hot. His eyes burned with salt and he saw ghostly visions floating in this terrible abyss that reminded him of a great, bleeding sword slash across the belly of the earth.

Dear God, he thought, *we really have come to the end. We have no way left to go down, and lack the strength to climb back out. This will be a bad, bad place to die.*

Antonio sat down and cradled his head in his hands, praying for God's infinite mercy and deliverance. Deliverance not only from this terrible canyon but also from New Spain. He desperately wanted to go home to his little country village where, still a poor but much wiser man, he would fall to his knees and beg Maria to marry him anyway. In return, he could promise her only a humble home, but many strong and loving children. He would be true to her and do everything in his power to make her happy.

"Please, God," he whispered, "I am too good a servant to die so young! If you do not show me the way, I fear that I will go crazy from thirst and lose my faith. And then, I could not help throwing myself off the cliff." Antonio shuddered but forced himself to continue. "Dear God, the old padre said that to kill oneself was a mortal sin. Please Lord, protect me!"

Antonio could say no more so he listened and listened until, far away to the north, he heard something, maybe only after-

noon thunder, but maybe the voice of God. He decided to take
it as a sign that his prayers were to be answered. Antonio felt
a new strength fill his body and he raised his eyes to Heaven,
then to the North Rim. With God's help, he would find a way
to save them all and marry Maria.

One

*We are now ready to start on our
way down the Great Unknown. . . .
We have but a month's rationing . . .
We have an unknown distance yet to run;
An unknown river yet to explore.
What falls there are, we know not;
what rocks beset the channel, we know not;
what walls rise over the river, we know not.*
—Major John Wesley Powell

Mouth of the Grand Canyon, August 13, 1869

The great Colorado River flowed strongly but William Dunn could no longer hear its voice. Dunn was uneasy. He much preferred a boisterous river glorying in a collision of rock and water. For three months, the mighty Colorado had roared with defiance and the nine-man, four-boat Powell expedition had been humbled by its immense canyon creation. But now, just as the Colorado was about to enter its deepest, most secret canyon, the water had fallen silent and Dunn was worried. He stared downriver toward the melding place where the thin, red stream of the Little Colorado flowed distinctly for several hundred yards before being swallowed by the big Colorado, now as thick as a huge brown snake.

William Dunn was a tall man in his mid-thirties. Like the

other members of the expedition, he was gaunt and crusted with a film of red river mud. He wore a matted beard to protect his face as much as possible from the blistering summer sun, but his lips were cracked and perpetually bleeding. Dunn's shoulder-length hair was thick and wavy, and his buckskins, once as fine as any ever made by a Ute woman, were stiff and as cracked as his lips. Squatting against a warm rock beside the river and draped in his worn-out buckskins and moccasins, Dunn seemed as old and yet as ageless as the canyon itself. Only his eyes moved, though they were red, swollen, and constantly weeping. He was a restless man, happiest on the move or when occupied by work or engrossed by a good book. Now he had neither, and his watery brown eyes were fixed suspiciously on the river which flowed quietly into the waiting Grand Canyon—the great abyss, the Great Unknown.

Dunn made himself look back toward their camp, hoping to see a task yet undone, but everything was in readiness. During the past three days, they had been beached at this junction of the two Colorado rivers, captives in this immense amphitheater of multicolored lime and sandstone. Their boats were caulked; fractured oars either replaced or repaired; the lumpy, moldy flour sifted through mosquito netting and dried . . . again. Yes, Dunn thought, everything and everyone was ready except Major John Wesley Powell, who remained lost in his notes and scientific observations, unmindful of the expedition's mounting tension, the punishing heat, and the Colorado River's quiet treachery.

Dunn could no longer remain still, so he climbed to his feet. It was time to speak with the major. He had an idea that required the man's help.

"Major Powell?"

The one-armed Civil War hero stopped writing and looked up, his bearded face pleasant and untroubled. "Yes, Mr. Dunn?"

"May I speak to you for a few minutes?"

"Of course."

Dunn sat down and crossed his legs, Indian style. "Major, I know it may sound crazy, but I'd also like to write a journal of this expedition—especially of what we'll face in Grand Canyon."

Powell frowned. "I had no idea you wanted to write."

"The idea just came over me the last few days we've been here," Dunn admitted. "I've been feeling the need to put whatever becomes of us into my own words, maybe even to be recorded in print someday."

"I didn't imagine that you were the least bit interested in that sort of thing," Powell said, laying down his pencil and smiling, "but then, you, more than any of the others, are an enigma."

"Why do you say that?"

"You're a loner and an experienced mountain man, but you are obviously well educated."

"I have always had a fondness for the written word. But the truth is, I've profit in mind."

"Don't be ashamed of profit," Powell told him. "It is a great and worthy motivator. Many of the world's greatest accomplishments have been realized for no other reason than money."

"I'm glad to hear you say that," Dunn said. "I have no literary illusions, but I think I can write well enough to chronicle whatever lies ahead and to sell a highly readable account."

"I don't doubt that for a moment. When did you come up with this idea?"

"When Oramel Howland lost all his notes in the river and gave up his own writing project."

"Yes, the man was devastated. I offered Mr. Howland an extra journal so that he could rewrite his experiences while they remain quite fresh, but he declined."

"The truth is, Major, Oramel is preoccupied with other, darker thoughts."

Powell leaned forward, suddenly intent. "Such as?"

"Since that day when he almost drowned, Oramel has decided that we'll never make it off this river alive. I'm afraid that Seneca also shares this view."

"Seneca has become your closest friend here, so talk sense to him," Powell urged. "After all, every one of us has had his desperate moments on this river. Still, that doesn't change the fact that we are going to emerge safely through these canyons."

"I believe that, Major. If I didn't, I wouldn't be here right now asking for the same journal you offered to Oramel."

"Then you shall have it," Powell said, reaching into the oil-skin shoulder bag he carried with his latest notes and all of his writing materials. "Here, use it profitably."

Dunn accepted the journal. "Major, there's more to this than money."

"So I suspected. But you don't have to explain."

"My real motive, sir, is to win the hand of a most beautiful young woman."

"Excellent! Do you plan to marry her?"

"Yes. But her father is a very rich and powerful Philadelphia banker. He has refused me Cynthia's hand."

"Why?"

"He doesn't think I measure up. And, to prove that I was unworthy, he even gave me a position at his bank."

"As a clerk handling figures and money?"

"Yes. Mostly it was ledger work. Adding and subtracting figures without end, hour after tedious hour."

"And I suspect you did not excel at that type of work."

"I was a complete failure," Dunn admitted. "Cynthia's father berated and humiliated me every day. Finally, I snapped."

"Did you strike the tyrant?"

"No sir! But I did lose my temper and quit the bank. I was about to be fired anyway. Mr. Holloway—Cynthia's father—forbade me ever to call upon his daughter again. But we found ways to meet and our love grew even stronger."

"Bravo!"

Dunn forced a smile. "But we finally were caught and I was arrested."

"On what charge?"

"Kidnapping."

"How could that be! If the girl . . ."

"Mr. Holloway is a very powerful and influential man. He told the authorities that I had tricked and confused his daughter, then drugged her into . . ."

"Drugged?"

"Yes, you see, we were caught sharing a bottle of champagne. Two, actually."

"So, you were intoxicated by love *and* liquor."

"Yes, sir. I was quite boisterous and gave the authorities quite a battle before I was subdued."

"You assaulted the authorities."

"Yes, and I have no one to blame but myself."

"I have a feeling things got much worse for you."

"They did," Dunn admitted. "After spending several weeks in jail waiting to be sentenced, possibly even to prison, I was visited by one of Mr. Holloway's vice presidents."

"I assume it was not a social call."

"Hardly."

"I'll bet that gentleman made you what seemed like a rather easy offer to accept—go West and disappear, or go to prison."

Dunn was amazed. "How could you know that?"

"Because," Powell replied, "had I been Mr. Holloway, I would have done the very same thing."

"But, sir, my intentions were . . ."

"Honorable. Entirely honorable. I know that, Mr. Dunn. You are a fine man and Mr. Holloway judged you wrongly. I have no doubt that one day you will become very successful."

"Up until now, I've been searching for some way to make my fortune so that I can return to Philadelphia a successful man, worthy of claiming Miss Holloway."

"It is good to aim high." Powell scratched at his thick, brown beard. "You haven't said anything about your parents."

"My father was a country schoolteacher. My mother died when I was very young. My father was heartbroken and never remarried. Teaching was his only joy. He very much wanted me to become a teacher also and was extremely unhappy that I was blackmailed into leaving Philadelphia. He begged Mr. Holloway to intervene on my behalf, but there was no mercy in that man."

"Of course not! It was his own design to get rid of you forever. But your father's vocation does explain your love of books and superior education."

"He loved great literature. However, he had little interest in science. In fact, almost all of what I've learned of geology, astronomy, botany, and archeology I owe to you, Major."

"Mr. Dunn, since we have confided on a very personal level, allow me to share something about my own father, who was a Wesleyan preacher. Like your father, he also wanted me to take up his life's work. When I finally summoned the nerve to tell him that I was determined to become a scientist—more specifically, a geologist—he became irate. He ridiculed my worthy aspirations and vowed me no help or encouragement. So I left home and never returned. But the pain and disapproval I received is still a painful memory and one that I cannot excise."

"Then you really *do* understand."

"Yes. And I continue to believe that we are all uniquely shaped by our many and varied experiences and circumstances. No two individuals are alike. God has given us a free will and unique talents. I believe my talent is to do scientific explorations. I know that this is true because it is what I enjoy doing most."

"It shows."

"I hope so. But the real question is, what do *you* most enjoy?"

"Books, adventure, the great outdoors."

"Then you *should* write about the West. Perhaps even a novel."

Dunn waved his hand. "Oh, no, I have neither the talent nor the patience for that. But Oramel has convinced me that

I might well be able to sell an account of this journey—perhaps even to his former associates at the *Rocky Mountain News*."

"I should expect so."

"And I would also send my published accounts back to Philadelphia to show Mr. Holloway that I am not the failure he thinks."

"Yes," Powell said. "That would be sweet redemption."

"One I would give anything to see," Dunn whispered, eyes bright with anticipation and new hope.

They were quiet for a moment, savoring the image of that banker poring over Dunn's well-written and widely read accounts. Then Powell broke the silence when he asked, "How long has it been since you saw Miss Holloway?"

"Three years. But I have written to her many times. I send the letters to a friend, who smuggles them to her."

"Have you heard from Miss Holloway in all this time?"

"No," Dunn sadly admitted. "I have never been in one place long enough to receive letters—as I've been in the wilderness searching for gold and good hunting."

"I see." Powell stretched and gazed back to the cliffs before pushing himself to his feet. "We shall soon continue this conversation."

"Yes sir. And thank you for the journal and the sage advice."

"Think nothing of it." Powell retrieved his pencil to indicate that the discussion was drawing to a close. "So, how else may I be of assistance?"

"I suppose I need a pencil."

"Of course!" Powell found one immediately. "I advise you to keep both the pencil and the journal in a waterproof oilskin and secured to your person at all times. That way, if you are pitched into the river, you would keep them dry and they will also be handy. That works best for me."

"Good advice."

"And, by the way, anything you can do to calm the unreasonable fears of your friends would be most appreciated."

"I'll do my best," Dunn promised, "but I have lived among

the Utes. They really do believe that, after the Green and the Grand join, this Colorado River plunges straight down into the earth."

"Nonsense! If everyone who went into the Grand Canyon of the Colorado were swallowed up, how could anyone—even a Ute—know that it dives into the earth?"

"I can't say," Dunn admitted, "but the Utes generally know what they're talking about."

Powell patted the oilskin pouch filled with his scientific observations as well as hundreds of astronomical readings and calculations defining their daily longitude, latitude, and elevation.

"Mr. Dunn," he began, "please remember that I'm an able scientist who also has done his historical homework. We know from records that there is a lower Colorado that emerges from the deep canyons just ahead. We know this because, only twelve years ago, Lieutenant Joseph Ives and his men ascended the Colorado River for more than two hundred miles above the Gulf of California in a steamboat. And centuries before that, Spaniards left written records and descriptions of this river as it traveled through the very deepest of canyons. Maybe even the one we now face."

"But, Major," Dunn countered, "it is not uncommon for a river to suddenly plunge underground and then reappear. In that case, we'd all perish."

"If you're so convinced that we are all going to die," Powell said, "then why even begin to write—or dream of your triumphant return to Philadelphia to claim the hand of Miss Holloway?"

"Because we're seasoned boatmen now, experts to a man. You've taught us to read the rock—the harder and more upthrust, the worse the rapids—and we have become one with the very pulse of this great river. Saying that, I believe that we will be forewarned. I am betting that we can save ourselves."

"And then what would we do?"

"Why, we'd have little choice but to abandon our three boats and scramble out of this great earth trench. I presume that you'd order us to locate a good trail and hike up to the top and make our way to the nearest Mormon settlement or army post."

"Never."

Dunn blinked with confusion. "Sir?"

"We are going *all the way,* mapping what never has been mapped and charting the full length of this river. I won't allow us to fail. I *swear* that we'll make it. So write your account well and may it profit you greatly when we return to civilization. My suggestion is that you write from your heart as if you are writing a love letter to your dear Miss Cynthia Holloway."

"A *love* letter?"

Powell chuckled. "Of course! It will make things much easier and . . . if an editor finds that the letters are too intimate to be published, then they can be altered slightly. But a very personal touch makes for the best reading."

"Do you really think so?"

"Certainly. My scientific notes and journals are quite dry. But my letters to dear Emma are far more interesting. Although I am sure Emma would not consent to have them published, they would prove far more popular to the public."

"I see."

"Bare your soul a bit, Mr. Dunn. I find there is no better listener than a blank page, ready to receive my deepest fears and greatest ambitions. I also promise that such writing will become a source of comfort and joy for you."

"I will try that, sir!"

Dunn's eyes rose to the mouth of the canyon that awaited, dark and forbidding as a giant sarcophagus lying open at the gates of hell. He saw mist, boiling up from the canyon's black maw, playing colors like piano keys back and forth between the towering stone temple walls. He could not help but shiver with dread.

"And Mr. Dunn . . . Mr. Dunn, are you listening?"

He snapped his attention back to the major. "Oh yes, sir!"

"Good. Then, the next time the subject comes up, please tell the Howland brothers that we are less than a hundred miles upriver from the Mormon settlements and that they wouldn't stand a chance up on the rim."

Powell's voice dropped but took on a grim edge. "We both know that they'd either die of thirst or be killed by hostile Indians. You and I might stand a chance, but those two are not nearly experienced enough to survive in the wilderness."

"That's why I expect they'd like me to lead them out."

"Refuse! For their sake as well as your own, refuse!"

"I will," Dunn promised before leaving.

Powell repositioned his journal on his knee and collected his pencil. The major's hand seemed to have a life of its own and he was thinking of his own dear Emma Dean as he wrote:

> *We are three-quarters of a mile in the depths of the earth, and this great river shrinks into insignificance as it dashes its angry waves against the walls and cliffs that rise to the world above; they are but puny ripples, and we but pygmies . . . lost among the boulders.*

Two

When Dunn rejoined the rest of the men, he poured a cup of coffee, grabbed two dried apples, and sat down by himself so that he could think of a good start for his journal. He leaned against a rock, opened the first page of the journal, and wet the lead of his pencil. Beginnings, he knew, were always the hardest.

Seneca ambled over to join his friend. He was of medium height, sandy-haired, with a pleasant disposition and an easy smile. "So, the major gave you a journal. Have you ever written anything before?"

"Letters."

"It's a lot harder to write for publication."

"Yes, I know. But I'm going to write as if I were sending it to my fiancée, Miss Holloway."

"What!"

"It was the major's idea, and I'm going to try it."

Seneca scowled. "Oramel won't be pleased."

"It's not his account. The major convinced me that writing as if to Cynthia will be much easier and a comfort."

"But my brother says that newspaper readers are most interested in the facts."

"I'm sure that's true," Dunn said, pencil hovering over the page like a hawk seeking prey. "Listing the boats and men will make an easy beginning."

When Dunn still hesitated, Seneca offered another nugget

of wisdom. "Don't try to write finished copy. Just record the facts and worry about polishing it up later."

"That makes sense to me," Dunn said, taking a deep breath. And so, in his best penmanship, he began to write.

My Dear Miss Holloway: I apologize for not writing sooner but I have been very, very busy making history! You see, I am one of nine men honored to be chosen by Major John Wesley Powell to be the first to explore a several-hundred-mile stretch of the Colorado River and a canyon so immense that it can scarcely be imagined. This canyon has had many names, but the Major calls it GRAND CANYON because he says that there is probably nothing to equal either its size or grandeur anyplace else in the world.

We began our journey after our boats were unloaded from the new Union Pacific line at Green River, Wyoming. After several days of preparation, we launched our four boats on May 23. At first we were easily intimidated by rapids and cataracts, but no longer. We have seen some very beautiful country in the Utah Territory and have had some close brushes with disaster these past three months. We have become an expert team, each helping all the others. Our leader is Major Powell, who, having lost his right arm in the bloody battle at Shiloh, continued to fight and command Union troops until the end of the Civil War. He is a great man and a great leader and sits in a chair atop our boat, the Emma Dean, *named after his beloved wife.*

And now, I shall provide you with a short accounting of each vessel and its brave crew.

BOAT #1—Emma Dean—Our lead boat is just 16 feet long. Besides Major Powell and myself, this boat carries Jack Sumner, Civil War veteran and trapper. The Emma Dean, *built of pine rather than oak, is smaller and lighter than the other boats and we use her speed and maneuverability to scout ahead for bad water and other dangers.*

BOAT #2—Kitty Clyde's Sister—She is manned by the Major's younger brother, 27-year-old Captain Walter H. Powell, who served in the 2nd Illinois Artillery but was captured and spent most of the war in a Confederate prison. Captain Powell is moody but dependable, and a good singer. Also aboard this 21-footer is George Bradley, another Civil War veteran, who served with the 19th Massachusetts Volunteer Infantry and who was wounded at Fredricksburg. Bradley reenlisted after the war and served at several different army posts until the Major got him honorably discharged for this trip. He is a good man, nearly as strong as myself.

BOAT #3—No Name—This vessel carries Oramel Howland, former editor of the Rocky Mountain News, *and his younger brother, Seneca Howland, a veteran of the 16th Vermont Infantry, who was wounded at Gettysburg. The third man on this boat was Frank Goodman, an Englishman, who almost drowned and abandoned the expedition at the Unita Indian Reservation on the Fourth of July; Goodman might have been the smartest of us all.*

BOAT #4—Maid of the Canyon—She also is 21 feet and is manned by "Billy" Hawkins, who served with the 9th Regiment, Missouri Cavalry. Billy is the expedition's cook and a crack rifle shot. His companion is Andrew Hall, a 19-year-old Scot. Everyone likes Andy because of his good nature and willingness to work hard. I know you would like him too, my dear, for Andy shares your wonderful sense of humor.

"There," Dunn said, "that part is finished, what next?"
"Did you say anything bad to your beloved about me?"
"Enough to make your ears burn."
Dunn smiled and then reread the beginning, pleased with his first attempt at writing. It would need plenty of polish, but

he could do that with the help of a seasoned editor. He supposed he ought to go back in time and tell Cynthia about some of the magnificent places they had visited and even named, sites like the rich red country they'd called Flaming Gorge, where the Colorado cut deeply through the great Unita Mountains. Or he could tell her how thrilled they'd all been to discover the faded letters: ASHLEY 1825, revealing where that famous early fur trader had abandoned the Green River after spinning down it in nothing more than a bull hide boat.

Or how they had shot the rapids in a canyon they'd named Ledore in honor of the famous poem by Robert Southey, which seemed so appropriate to their desperate circumstances at the time.

> *Advancing and prancing and glancing*
> *and dancing, Recoiling, turmoiling,*
> *and toiling and boiling. . . .*

Shortly after that, they'd lost the *No Name,* smashed to kindling on a great boulder that had reared out of the boiling white water. That was when the Howland brothers and the Englishman named Frank Goodman had been capsized and nearly drowned. They had never been the same stalwart adventurers again after surviving that watery terror.

He closed his eyes, pencil poised over the journal, seeing images—good and bad—of the things they'd done on the long river's run down from Wyoming. He recalled how they'd left the river for a few weeks to hike up the Unita River to the Ute Indian Agency for mail and to replace their lost and water-soaked provisions. That's where Goodman had left them and where the expedition party had suffered from very low spirits.

"Did you talk to the major about abandoning this river?" Seneca asked, pulling Dunn out of his reverie.

"Major Powell doesn't believe that this river goes underground."

"Oh, that certainly makes me feel better," Seneca quipped. "Then I assume that the major can see into the future?"

"Don't be ridiculous!"

"I'm not! We all know that the Ute Indians believe this river plunges into the earth somewhere up ahead. And we also know that those Indians have probably lived in this canyon country for at least a few thousand years. But if the major can see into the future . . ."

"Drop it," Dunn ordered.

But Seneca would not. "My friend," he said grandly, "there is a ray of good news here. Can you guess what it is?"

"No," Dunn replied, "but I'm sure you're about to tell me."

"That's right. You see, after we are swallowed up by the river and completely vanish from the face of the earth—we'll become one of the great mysteries of American history! Someday, someone will probably erect a monument to us and we'll be assured at least a paragraph in future history books."

"I'm not listening to you anymore," Dunn growled, thinking that he might describe to Cynthia how Andy Hall had convinced the expedition to loot an untended potato patch they'd discovered on an upriver sandbar. Famished for greens, the entire party had devoured the unripe potato tops and almost immediately had been seized by violent stomach cramps. For about an hour, they had been so ill that they'd all expected to die of food poisoning. Finally, their vomiting and diarrhea had subsided and the expedition had continued, weaker—but far wiser.

No, Dunn decided, that was not the sort of thing to relate to his lady.

Seneca rolled his head sideways. "Mind if I read what you've written so far?"

"Yes."

Seneca had a devilish chuckle.

"If you find this so amusing," Dunn said, "then why don't *you* write a journal?"

"Because I've nothing to say. Oramel possesses whatever literary talent is to be found in the Howland family."

"Speaking of whom," Dunn said, "here he comes now—in a lather, as usual."

Oramel Howland was a tall, cadaverous man with a long, scraggly brown beard and a high, domed forehead topped by a receding hairline. He was intense and excitable, as opposed to Seneca, who liked to joke and fish.

"We spotted some Indian ruins!" Oramel shouted as he and Bradley hurried toward the camp. "Major! I promise that you're going to want to have a look."

"How far?"

"Not more than a mile or two up that bench," Oramel said, pointing up the terraced southeastern slopes of the canyon of the Little Colorado.

"Then lead the way." Powell was never one to miss an opportunity to document a new archeological find.

Seneca pushed to his feet. "Come along, Bill. This is fodder for your new journal. Maybe we'll even unearth some skeletons that you can describe for dear Miss Holloway."

"Not likely," Dunn said, shoving the journal into his pack, then hurrying after the others.

A few men grumbled and were reluctant to leave camp. They were the ones who objected most whenever the major went charging off to explore, map, and measure the river's intersecting canyons, its astounding geological features, or an occasional archeological site. Dunn had to admit that these unplanned and frequent side trips, in combination with very poor hunting and fishing, were the primary reason why the expedition was now running dangerously low on food and supplies.

But despite that, Powell's excitement was always contagious, especially in the matter of Indian ruins. Whenever the party inspected a new find, there was a shared sense of mystery and wonder, as if they were the privileged first to enter another dimension of time. When they entered the ancient rock and adobe dwellings, there wasn't a man in the party who did not strain to hear the Indian spirit voices.

A very strict protocol was followed whenever they entered an ancient ruin or dwelling. Powell's instructions were quite specific: they were not to damage or even move any artifacts or physical evidence, which Powell meticulously sketched for the benefit of a future archeological survey. Like the immense, overpowering, and seemingly immutable canyon geology which made everyone feel small and insignificant, every contact with a lost civilization was a sharp reminder of their own tenuous and flickering mortality. An Indian people with flesh and blood and dreams and desires had been in this very place. Untold centuries ago, they'd felt the sting of cold rain and panted in the suffocating heat, known pleasure and pain, and stared out at the same incredible vistas, undoubtedly humbled by the great mysteries of life.

Now, as they hurried after Powell and Oramel, anticipation replaced grumbling and they scaled the canyon's sides, climbing for nearly a mile until they topped a windswept sandstone bench, where they discovered a trail faintly etched in the soft, warming rock. They craned their necks and gazed up toward the rim of the canyon, sucking in deep draughts of the hot, rising air and feeling sweat trickle down their spines.

"This is a very old and well-used Indian trail," Powell told them in a hushed, eager voice as he ran his fingers lightly over the sandstone path. "And, if you observe closely, you can see where footholds have been cut into the rock wherever the grade becomes especially steep. Follow along, but watch your step."

The warning was unnecessary; they had only to glance over their shoulders to see that they were already a thousand feet above the Little Colorado. To slip and fall would be to die. Even so, they felt no fear or anxiety. After hundreds of such precipitous outings, they had become nearly as agile and daring as mountain goats.

Powell was especially fearless, even, they thought, reckless and foolhardy. On several occasions, he had gotten himself into such hazardous predicaments that he needed to be rescued off the face of a high cliff whose handholds had suddenly vanished, leaving him stranded against the sky and eternity. Having but one arm could be a serious handicap when edging up the near-vertical face of a canyon wall, but you couldn't tell that to the major. Dunn vividly remembered another tense occasion when, just below the place where the Yampa River joined the Green, the only way they'd been able to save Powell was to extend the man a pair of long johns a moment before he'd have lost his grip and plunged to a certain death.

"Up here!" Powell called, disappearing over a ledge.

When Dunn scrambled over the top, he joined the others standing before a lone cliff dwelling. They lapsed into silence, hearing only the warm, dry wind whispering hollowly through the canyons and feeling the rising heat tickling their beards. This Indian ruin was like several others they already had discovered, particularly the ones near Cataract Canyon. The exterior stone wall was well crafted, rising halfway up to a rocky overhang and enclosing an amphitheater-like cavern. There were many windows and doorways, some quite large, through which they could see inside where dim, silent compartments of dusty stone held the remnants of an ancient settlement.

"Look at this," Powell marveled, halting almost reverently before the main entrance. "As usual, the mystery is not only *who* these ancient people were, but *why* they chose this inhospitable site."

He swung around to gaze out over the vast chasm of three great merging canyons—the northern one they'd floated down, the deep canyon of the Little Colorado, and the Grand Canyon yet to be explored.

"Do you suppose," he asked rhetorically, "the ancients who built these cliff dwellings were every bit as impressed with the view as we are today and *that* is why they chose to erect their houses on this site?"

After a long, thoughtful silence, the always-irreverent Andrew Hall wisecracked, "Maybe the people who once lived here made very long fishing lines and cast their ancient bait into all three canyons."

Everyone, even Powell, enjoyed a laugh. "Come," the major urged, leading the way, "let's go inside. Just be very careful not to step on anything of archeological significance."

The ruins were cool and lightly coated with a soft patina of pale dust so that, when a man placed his foot down, the dust puffed up in little mushroom clouds. As always, they followed the major, keeping exactly to his tracks.

Powell began his usual lecture. "Gentlemen, you can easily see by the rubble that there were two stories to this cliff dwelling. And I suspect the decayed wood collapsed against that adobe wall was once part of a stepladder."

"Look, Major," their cook said, peering into the shadows. "Pottery."

There were three large pots, reddish in color with black markings and two smaller ones of the same general coloring and design. Each, however, was badly cracked and corroded by the ravages of weather and centuries.

Powell reached down and cradled one of the smaller pots. He raised it up to a shaft of sunlight that poured warmly in from under the rock overhang. "This would be welcomed at the Smithsonian Museum, my friends. It's an excellent example of the early Anasazi work and very similar to pieces found in the ancient ruins of southeastern Colorado."

"How long ago do you suppose these people lived here?" young Andrew Hall asked.

"A couple of thousand years."

"And why did they leave?"

"There are theories, but no one really knows."

Andy grinned. "Haven't found an Indian old enough to remember yet, huh?"

Powell was too absorbed by the object he held to appreciate the Scot's joke. He dug out a notebook and pencil and began to document this finding.

"Major," Oramel Howland said, "perhaps a couple of us

should go on up to the top and see if there is any game to be shot."

"Sure," Powell said, absently waving them away. "Good idea. And the others should go down and break camp. I'll be finished in an hour or two."

Excitement over the find quickly waned. The day was becoming very warm as the men prepared to descend to their river camp far below.

"William?"

He turned to see Oramel and Seneca moving off to one side. "Yeah?"

"Why don't you come along. You're a better rifle shot than either one of us and it won't take us more than twenty or thirty minutes to reach the rim. Might be a deer or antelope up there just waiting."

"Not likely," Dunn said, eager to get back to his journal and describe this new Indian find to Cynthia before Powell's return to camp.

"We really can't afford not to try, given that we're running so low on food, can we?" Oramel persisted.

When Dunn shrugged, Oramel came over, lowering his voice to say, "We *need* to talk."

"There's nothing to say."

"I think there is," the older man grated. "Seneca told me that you had a discussion with the major and might have expressed our mounting anxieties about what lies ahead."

When Dunn still resisted, Seneca stepped close and whispered, "We'll be gone less than an hour. My brother just wants to talk and, besides, we really might get lucky and shoot a deer."

"All right," Dunn finally relented.

They returned to the old Indian trail that snaked its way up to the mesa. Dunn climbed steadily, the only sound in his ears that of his labored breathing and the slight moaning of warm updrafts channeling agelessly through the stone corridors of these canyons. Occasionally, Seneca would glance back over his shoulder but Dunn ignored him, sorry that he'd not returned to camp with the other men.

"There it is," Oramel said, badly winded as he bent over with hands on hips and struggled for breath. "Go on ahead, Bill."

Dunn passed both men and, when he neared the flat top of the mesa above, he checked the rifle to make sure that it was in readiness, just in case there actually was something to shoot.

Dunn slowly raised his head over the edge of the rim and was both surprised and overjoyed to see a pair of sleek pronghorn antelope grazing about a hundred yards to the south. He ducked back out of sight and studied the dangerous footing he would have to traverse in order to bring himself into firing range. The edge of the rim dropped vertically about ten feet to a long, narrow ledge where even a rabbit might feel pinched for rib-room. And, after arriving at a place directly opposite the unsuspecting antelope, how would he scale that ten-foot drop without tumbling backward into the chasm below?

"So what is the plan?" Seneca whispered as he and his brother hovered nearby.

"They're too far down the rim to stand a good chance of shooting one from here," he told them. "I must get closer."

Both the Howlands surveyed the crumbling rimrock. "How?" Seneca asked.

"You could follow and give me a boost," Dunn said. "All I'd have to do is pop my shoulders and this Spencer over the rim and take a quick shot. We'd be within fifty yards of them."

"Too risky," Oramel hissed. "Way too risky!"

"We need the meat," Dunn insisted. "Besides, it was your idea to come this far, and I'm not of a mind to quit this close to a dinner of antelope steaks."

"I'll do it," Seneca breathed. "Let's get this over with before they wander off—or before I come to my senses."

"Let's go," Dunn said, easing onto the narrow ledge and flattening his chest against the rough wall.

"It isn't worth the risk!" Oramel grated. "Dammit, you could both fall to your deaths!"

They ignored him and inched along the ledge. The footing was solid enough. There was a wider place ahead where Dunn figured he could put a boot into Seneca's cupped hands and be hoisted over the rim for a good shot.

"Steady," he warned, holding the rifle out over the wall and moving slowly forward. "One shot is all I'll need," Dunn promised.

Ten harrowing minutes later, he reached a good firing position. "Come on!"

Seneca made the mistake of glancing down. His eyes widened and he paled but kept moving until they were side by side over a whole lot of air.

"How am I supposed to bend over in order for you to put your boot in my hands?" Seneca breathed. "This *is* insane!"

Dunn raised his boot and placed it into Seneca's interlaced fingers. "When you lift, go straight up—not out."

Dunn hugged the wall and slowly transferred his weight onto his suspended left foot. With the rifle in one hand, he didn't have the luxury of two handholds, but Seneca elevated him until Dunn could grab the rim. He managed to drag the Spencer rifle over the edge without a sound and take aim at the largest antelope. When he squeezed the trigger, the recoil knocked him backward. Dunn bellowed as he began to lose his balance and tilt outward. Arms windmilling, he dropped the rifle and clawed at the rim's edge while Seneca struggled mightily to retain his own balance.

Oramel wailed helplessly as Dunn's fingernails bit into the hard rimrock for purchase. For a moment, it could have gone either way but Seneca gave him a tremendous boost and he hauled himself over the rim to safety.

"Help!" Seneca cried.

Dunn reversed directions and peered back over the rim to see his young friend struggling to maintain his own footing. "Grab my hand!"

Seneca threw his arm up. Their palms struck, their fingers laced, and Dunn hauled his companion over the top. They were both drenched with icy fear-sweat, out of breath, and drained beyond the point of exhaustion.

"We were fools," Seneca finally managed to gasp. "That *was* insane."

"No question about that," Dunn wheezed.

"Did you shoot the damned antelope?"

Dunn's head rolled sideways. "Either that, or he saw us and died of fright."

Seneca didn't appreciate the joke. They pushed to their feet as Oramel came hurrying over to join them. "You dropped the rifle!" he shouted. "That was *my* rifle!"

Dunn did not bother to respond, but instead went over to collect the antelope. It was in good flesh and weighed about eighty pounds. Enough for at least a couple of meals. Dragging the animal over to the rim, he gazed down and saw the rifle where it had landed far, far below. Still ignoring Oramel, he picked up the carcass and tossed it over the rim.

"There," he said, turning to the former editor. "We'll collect them *both* on our way to camp."

Seneca began to giggle as Dunn walked heavily over to the Indian trail leading down to the cliff dwellings where the major was lost in his own world of discovery.

Three

August 13, 1869

My Dear Miss Holloway: We are almost ready to leave this confluence place of the big and little Colorado rivers. The Little Colorado is very red and muddy, also small and salty. We have spent three days repairing the boats and the gear while Major Powell has been primarily occupied with his geologizing work and inspecting a new Indian ruin. My dear, I would give anything if you could only see the exquisite Indian crockery we recently discovered. The bowls are all cracked and somewhat corroded by the centuries but have retained their great beauty. The Major says these Indian people knew how to fire their pottery in kilns and how to use roots to mix dyes for decoration.

We leave everything just as it is found but mark the location for future study. This is such a hard, lonesome land that it is difficult to imagine that anyone actually would choose to live here.

Yesterday, John Sumner carried a barometer up to the rim and we measured the cliff at two thousand feet. We have boiled the best of the bacon, thrown some away, and sifted our lumpy stores of flour through our mosquito netting. The apples have been spread out to dry—again—and everyone is anxious to proceed after feasting on roast antelope meat. Oramel is still angry about his rifle, whose stock was shattered when I dropped it off the South Rim.

Dear Cynthia, I know that your delicate nature could

never withstand the rigors of this canyon country, but I
wish you could experience it in a gentle way because you
have a much keener sense of beauty than I. There is so
much to see, so much to learn from Major Powell. No
matter what happens after we enter Grand Canyon, this
shall always be one of my happiest times. I love you and
pray someday to see you again.

They were on the river again, caught up in the roar and the spray as the swift current carried them down into the waiting maw of the canyon. They ran six miles at breakneck speed, then emerged into a more open part of the canyon, where the water, as well as their hearts, finally slowed. But soon they were back into swift water and the river corkscrewed past sharp angles of rock and over increasingly violent rapids.

Powell signaled the boats into the shore and, when they were clinging to the base of the cliff, he spoke. "We're going to have to line the boats over this next section of rapids. We can't afford to lose any more of our food or scientific instruments."

"Damn the instruments!" Oramel swore over the din of the crashing water as everyone set to work lightening each boat by hauling its supplies and provisions downriver and across the slick and treacherous rocks.

It was hard, dangerous work. Several of the men had lost their shoes, and the rocks cut and abraded the soles of their bare feet. Sometimes they had to tie lines to each other and swim around particularly large boulders that could not be scaled, then be dragged back into the shoreline below, half-drowned and clinging to their precious cargo. There was no other way when the cliffs dropped so steeply.

"I'll bet we spend more time out of the boats than in them before we get through this damned canyon," Bradley gritted after falling into the rocks and barking his shins. "We'll be lucky to make five miles today."

No one could argue that fact as they left a man below the rapids with their stack of provisions and crabbed the slippery rocks until they reached their waiting boats. Now, lines were attached to each vessel's bow and stern. Every man knew his job and there was no need for shouting over the thunder of the rapids as bowlines were carried to a point below the rapids.

With men below the rapids holding the bowline and men above holding the sternline, they pushed each boat out into the churning current and used both ropes to "line" or play her down through the rapids. Emptied and buoyant, the plunging boats could survive the rapids. Whenever they did unavoidably smash into rocks, the lesser force of their impact greatly reduced the damage. When the end of the sternline was reached on particularly long stretches of rapids, it was released and the empty boat would then plunge downward, where the men holding its bowline could haul it in to safety.

As the day wore on, they repeated this process over and over and they were exhausted by nightfall. In the fading light, they camped below a particularly bad set of rapids inside the shelter of a large cave.

"How far do you think we got today?" Andy Hall asked as they huddled on a thin stretch of beach.

"Four, maybe five miles," Powell replied. "I'm sure we'll do a lot better tomorrow."

"I hope so," Oramel said, "or we are going to run out of food."

Dunn saw Powell open his mouth to speak, then he seemed to change his mind as he turned away, probably deciding it was pointless to argue. Besides, Oramel was right. They *would* run out of food soon and die of starvation—if they did not drown first.

August 14
My Dear Miss Holloway: There is increasing concern because this river enters a stretch of hard granite and grows ever swifter. From the short distance we can observe ahead, the canyon narrows as spires of rock thrust directly out of the water, sometimes lying in wait just below the surface

ready to tear the bellies out of our boats. This morning, we almost went over a forty-foot fall but were barely able to pull our boats into shore and make a portage.

Later, around noon, we heard another great roar and, with Major Powell in the lead, we came upon a place where the river dropped eighty feet in less than a third of a mile and became a cauldron of white foam. Even worse, there were no footholds on either side by which we could effect a portage, and it was a thousand feet to the top of the granite so we could not carry the boats around this impossible stretch. There being no alternative, we were forced to run these rapids. The Emma Dean *filled with water and became unmanageable; we swamped, somehow made it over the rapids, and bailed her out. The other boats fared little better. Everyone was afraid as we glided down the deep canyon, straining and dreading to hear the rumble of the next waterfall or rapids. We were forced to make two more portages and line the boats several more times over rapids before we located a thin shelf of rock, some forty or fifty feet above the river, where we made our camp.*

We found a few armloads of driftwood lodged into the rocks and made a camp, but it began to rain. There was no shelter, so we huddled in our rotting ponchos, sleeping but little. Even Andy Hall lost his smile and my only comfort was the memory of your sweet face and how happy it appeared that afternoon as we skipped through the rain across Franklin Square . . . laughing and singing, hand in hand.

August 16
My Dear Miss Holloway: Things have been a little improved these past two days. Yesterday, we discovered a clear, sweet creek that bubbled down through a handsome red canyon. On a fine beach, we camped under a huge tree with willow-shaped leaves. We decided to name this

creek Bright Angel because it was so fine and refreshing. Some of the men tried all morning to catch fish in Bright Angel but without success. Despite that and being low on food, the Major decided that we should remain here to rest, repair the boats, and find wood to make new oars. No one complained, even though our food is bad and running low. Finding a large pine log up the course of the stream, we rolled it down to the Colorado on skids and then set about to saw new oars. They will be much stronger than the previous ones we have been forced to make of soft, usually water-rotted, cottonwood.

In late afternoon, the Major returned after hiking up a little gulch and discovering the ruins of several old stone houses. Only the foundations remain, their blocks scattered about by the ages. An old grinding stone was found, its grinding surface worn deep. When I saw it, my love, I immediately thought of how you would wrinkle your nose at the mere suggestion that it was once an important tool in woman's work.

We discovered a great deal of broken pottery and many old Indian trails worn deeply into the rock. As always, we pondered the mystery of why any people would come to such a desolate place. We saw little plots where they tried to farm, but could not imagine they had much success. Major Powell holds the theory that these ancient Indians were fleeing the Spaniards, who were bent on subjugating them as they had the Indians of Old Mexico. He says that the Spaniards came into these lands and destroyed many pueblos and villages to the east. I wonder how your father would judge those strict but well-intentioned Spaniards. Approvingly, I should think.

The next morning, Dunn was preparing to make another entry in his journal when Oramel came over to join him. "How is the writing progressing?"

Dunn slipped the journal into his waterproof oilskin pack.

He did not much care for this man but, since Oramel was Seneca's brother, he remained civil. "Well enough."

"If I can help you with some words, or whatever, I hope that you'll just ask."

"I will," Dunn said, knowing he would not.

"Just now, we had to throw out the last of our bacon because it was so rancid and rotten," Oramel said, looking almost pleased at this hard news. "And the major himself reckons that we have only enough flour left for nine or ten days. Yesterday, we made less than fifteen miles. I doubt that we'll do any better this day. We're running out of time."

"I know. But we still have plenty of dried apples and coffee."

Oramel ran his fingers through his thinning hair, not listening. "The major's barometers were damaged in the last portage. Even he admits their readings are now inaccurate."

When Dunn did not respond, Oramel added, "I'm sure you know that means that we have lost our reckoning in altitude and can't possibly know how much descent this river has yet to make before we reach the Mormon settlement on the Virgin River."

Dunn could barely contain his irritation. "And I understand that you lost some of our maps back at the falls."

"We're lucky we all haven't lost our *lives!* Of course I lost some maps. We've lost about everything else. Why point out my loss and not all the others?"

Dunn pushed to his feet. "I had better start helping the men prepare to leave."

"You saw the ruins and those Indian trails yesterday," Oramel challenged, eyes darting toward the rim. "Wouldn't they lead up to the top and probably on to water? We could follow Bright Angel and . . ."

"No," Dunn snapped as he marched over to help load the boats.

Throughout that day, intermittent rain showers alternated with a scorching sun that pushed the mercury in their thermometer to 115 degrees. Even worse, the rapids came so frequently that they were often forced to portage the boats. It rained again that night and they had no shelter. The next day, the *Emma Dean*, running several hundred feet in advance of the heavier boats, was caught in treacherous rapids and capsized.

"Hang on and ride it through, men!" Powell shouted.

Jack Sumner's head popped up and he grabbed the bow. Dunn grabbed the stern and clung to it, feeling his body being pummeled and his stomach almost ripped out by a submerged rock. But somehow, they passed on through and were finally caught up in a gentle whirlpool and overtaken by the others.

"Are you all right, Major!" Dunn shouted, as they slowly pulled their vessel to shore.

"A little the worse for wear, but nothing serious," the major replied. "Let's bail her out and get moving."

Dunn and Sumner pushed on through the rest of the day, constantly running rapids. That night, they made a big campfire and were finally able to dry their clothes.

"You're walking a little bent over this evening," Powell observed as he came over to join Dunn near the campfire. "I hope you haven't suffered any serious injury."

"I was dragged over a half-submerged rock and bruised a few ribs. Nothing serious."

"That was a nasty stretch," Powell said, his expression troubled. "I expect that we made only about twelve miles today but that we'll do better tomorrow. The rock looks softer up ahead and the canyon seems to widen a little."

"We could use a break, Major."

Powell leaned closer so that his words could not be heard by the others. "Is Oramel still wanting to abandon us?"

"He said something about it the morning we left Bright Angel, but nothing since then. I brushed the subject aside."

"Good."

Powell leaned back and gazed up at the stars. "I have a feeling that the next few days will be much better than the last few. Did your journal stay dry?"

"Yes."

"Glad to hear that," Powell said. "I've been so worried and busy that I haven't been writing enough. But I hope to catch up before long. How is your writing coming along?"

"Fine. Just as you suggested, I'm writing as if to Miss Holloway and enjoying it very much. But I doubt it's worthy of publication."

"Don't be so sure of that. Besides, it will sound better after we reach safety. Our states of mind are in such turmoil these days that nothing sounds very good."

"Even to you?"

"Yes," Powell admitted. "Don't tell anyone else, but at this point, I find myself regarding the Grand Canyon almost . . . almost as the enemy. I feel as if we are locked into a life-and-death struggle and the enemy is definitely winning. It's as though it has us in its jaws and we're fighting with all of our might, but we can't break free."

"Just as long as it doesn't devour us," Dunn said, forcing a grin.

Powell managed his own thin smile. "You're right, Bill. And thanks for your loyalty."

"Major," Dunn said, before the man could climb to his feet and walk away, "the Howland brothers still want to abandon this river, and they sound as if they'll do it with, or without, me."

"If things get bad enough," Powell said, "we'll all get out. But the majority will rule."

"Glad to hear that."

"Mr. Dunn, we *must* stick together. It is the key to our success . . . and our survival."

"Yes sir."

August 20
My Dear Miss Holloway: Today was an easier passage because the canyon broadened slightly, the walls having more slope. We saw many little alcoves under the cliffs

that looked shady and inviting. It was very hot, and we stopped early, making about ten miles progress. We camped on the right bank and discovered more ruins on a terrace several hundred feet above the river. There were little mealing stones, the usual broken pottery, and a faded globular basket made of fibers. When the Major attempted to carry it to better protection, the basket dissolved into shreds, which I know would have upset you greatly. We found many beautiful chips of flint and several fine arrowheads, so we knew that an ancient arrowmaker once lived in this place, but we could not imagine what his people could have hunted. We have not seen a Bighorn sheep in weeks, not a rabbit or anything but a few rattlesnakes. There are no fish to be caught and we see few living things other than birds, some of which are both colorful and in great profusion. Major Powell identifies them as bats, swallows, and, in the wooded side canyons, hummingbirds, goldfinches, and even yellow warblers. The hawks stay high near the rims, probably because it is better hunting up there.

Yesterday we saw a very large lizard sunning itself on a rock and thought to kill and eat it, but the lizard slithered into a crevice of rock and inflated itself! It was such a strange sight to see its body expand. We were so impressed that we decided to spare the poor creature. Major Powell said it was called a chuckwalla. We also see pink rattlesnakes, which are thought to be good eating but very poisonous. No one in the party wants to try their meat.

August 23
My Dear Miss Holloway: The last two days have been better and we have made good progress. Yesterday, we finally came out of the granite and the rapids were not so bad; the Major estimated that we traveled at least twenty miles, which was heartening. My ribs are still painful to the touch, but it is of no great consequence. We

also had to make a long portage and several times it was necessary to line the boats over rapids. While thus engaged, Major Powell climbed to the top of the canyon and learned that its course leads southwest. The walls rose very sharply from the river, some two or three thousand feet, and then fed into a gently sloping terrace near the rim. Today we made at least another twenty miles and passed a stream that dropped more than a hundred feet to the Colorado, forming a cascade with rainbows. The cliffs below the waterfall were covered by beautiful ferns and flowers. I found it impossible to believe such pockets of paradise could be found in this hot and hellish canyon, and I yearned to pick you a lovely bouquet.

August 24
My Dear Miss Holloway: My ribs are feeling much better today and the river was kind, allowing us another twenty miles. We all are very hungry and constantly searching the cliffs for signs of Bighorn sheep, but see nothing. Major Powell said, only half-jokingly, that we were in a race for dinner and not a moment of daylight was lost.

August 25
My Dear Miss Holloway: We saw monuments of lava standing in the river this morning, a few of them several hundred feet tall. Major Powell was excited and pointed out cinder cones which he said were extinct volcanoes. After passing over a difficult stretch of rapids, we passed a volcano which actually had a crater tipped into the very brink of the canyon itself. Being a fine geologist, the Major ordered us to pull for shore. With great excitement, he pointed out where vast flows of lava once poured into the river. The entire north wall was lined with black basalt rock and more could be seen in pockets on the south wall, appearing like black mud, thrown by mischievous children against a white wall. Major Powell also discovered a fis-

sure over which the volcanic cone stood, and we saw
streams which tasted of lime and which left a white en-
crustation on the surrounding rocks. Rarely have we seen
the Major so excited, and he spends this evening talking
about volcanoes and trying to impress us with the great
conflict that must have occurred millions of years ago
between the opposing forces of molten rock and water.
The Major says the river would have boiled and sent
steam rising clear to Heaven. But, when I think of boiling
water and steam, I can think only of food, perhaps a
chicken stewing in a pot—or lobsters like we both loved
to eat at that little Front Street café overlooking the river.

August 26
My Dear Miss Holloway: Today the walls again narrowed
and the river ran swifter with many rapids. The evidence
of volcanoes was mostly behind us, and our anxiety in-
creased until, at about eleven o'clock, we spotted an Indian garden near the shore where a small stream runs
down from a side canyon. We could scarcely contain our
joy as we furiously rowed to shore, calling for Indians.
The garden and the verdant little side canyon were
blessedly uninhabited and we discovered a field of unripened corn.

There was much discussion, and no one wanted to become a thief, but we were starving and so took ten or
twelve of the large, green squash that had already ripened. Hurrying away, we rowed only a short distance before we hauled for shore and started a fire and made a
great kettle of green squash sauce. We had no salt to season it but felt like kings at a feast as we gorged ourselves.
Everyone was smiling and happy and we resumed our
journey with bellies full for the first time since last we
were able to kill a Bighorn sheep up on the Green River.

In happy spirits, we made an incredible thirty-five
miles before darkness and again gorged on green squash,

which seemed to agree with everyone. Cynthia, I do hope you do not think less of me for stealing and eating Indian squash.

August 27

My Dear Miss Holloway: Our happiness soured like curdled milk today because the river clashed once more with hard, upthrusting granite. By this rock and the narrowing of the canyon, we know we are in for some bad rapids, and maybe falls. The growl of the canyon had never been louder and our first portage came before nine o'clock. Ahead of us, mist rose a thousand feet and we saw the dreaded white, foaming water up ahead.

At eleven o'clock, we struggled hard to pull into shore because the river was very swift and the current strong. The Major climbed a few hundred feet up the canyon wall and, when he returned, his expression told us that the river below was very, very bad. After much discussion, we decided to scramble up high rock pinnacles, but even at that elevation we could see no way either to portage the boats or to line them down because of the steep cliffs that plunge straight into the water. Furthermore, as far as we could see, there was a succession of terrible rapids that we doubted we could survive.

Far, far below, we could see where lateral streams long ago washed immense boulders into the river forming a dam, over which the water drops for perhaps twenty feet, more than enough to wreck our boats. Beyond the bad falls was another set of rapids, then more leading to the next bend in the canyon. The Major remained on the cliffs, trying to figure how these dangers could be run, for there is no apparent way around them.

The men returned to camp and yesterday's high spirits were gone. There being nothing to do but to wait until the Major returned with a plan, we made an early camp and watched the clouds play through the canyon. As you know,

*my love, I have always liked clouds, and there are none
more interesting than those in and above the Grand Canyon. Sometimes we catch them stealing like thieves down
through the side canyons, gliding silently and sneaking
around, sometimes thick and cold, sometimes just thin
ghostly wisps of vapor. Their shadows often follow us like
a giant cat ready to pounce. Many times since leaving
Green River, I have seen white, puffy clouds suddenly turn
angry like a pouting child, stabbing at us with bolts of
jagged lightning and then pelting us with hard rain.*

*The clouds in canyon country are big, bigger than any
I have ever seen, and I often dream of how it would be
to sit upon them and thus be able to observe and learn
in advance whatever danger awaits. I think of clouds as
fickle friends. I like days that have clouds better than days
that do not, even when they bring the hard, sudden rains.
Down here in the Grand Canyon, physical hardships are
real and punishing, but it is the mental anguish and un-
certainty that take the greater toll. Thinking of you and
the day we will be together again is my greatest strength
and comfort.*

Seneca and Oramel came over that afternoon while Powell
was still somewhere up above trying to figure out how to get
through the rapids.

"You know as well as we do that there is no way we can
pass through what we have seen up ahead," Oramel began.
"To go on is to die."

"It doesn't look good," Dunn admitted. "Seneca, what are
you thinking?"

"I don't know," the younger man confessed. "From where
we stood up on the side of the canyon, I can't imagine how
we could survive the rapids below."

"We've seen them look bad before and fought our way
past."

"Yes," Oramel interrupted, "because every time we could

either line or portage our boats when things were really dangerous. In this case, we can't do either."

"I know that."

"Then we've *got* to talk to the major and make him understand that none of us is ready to die tomorrow," Oramel insisted.

"And take our chances up on the plateau?"

"Of course!" Oramel scowled. "We've had enough rain lately so that we ought to be able to find water basins until we reach the Virgin River. And there should be game. As fine a marksman as you are, Bill, we'll have fresh meat by tomorrow night."

"You're making a lot of assumptions," Dunn told the former editor. "We might not find water. The rainwater filling rock basins will evaporate quickly in this heat. And, since no one has been up on top, we don't know about the hunting, much less the temperament of the Indians."

"They'll respect our weapons," Oramel confidently boasted. "One musket shot and they'll prostrate themselves, thinking we're white gods."

"I wouldn't want to bet my life on that," Dunn replied. "They might have met the Spaniards once and hate all white men while knowing the limitations of our weapons."

Oramel wiped his hand across his sun-blistered face. "What you're telling us is that you're not going to speak to the major about leaving."

"*You* speak to him!"

"All right, I will," Oramel vowed, looking disgusted. "But he doesn't care much for me, and so I don't expect anything from the man. I just know that Seneca and I are not going to go to our certain deaths tomorrow in those rapids."

Seneca leaned closer, his voice low and urgent. Almost pleading. "We need your support, Bill! You know Indians and the land. Our chances on top won't be as good without you."

"Talk to the major."

"I'll speak to him tonight," Oramel said. "After supper and in private."

Dunn looked to Seneca. "Are you also going to talk to him?"

"I'll let my brother do my talking."

"That's fine," Dunn clipped. "Just don't let him do your thinking."

Seneca flushed with anger, causing Dunn immediately to regret the remark, but there was no apology in him right now. He left the brothers and went off by himself to think and to write away some of his troubles.

My Dear Miss Holloway. This is today's second entry. I doubt that I will sleep tonight for I am very troubled about tomorrow. My loyalties are with Major Powell, but if Seneca is determined to go with his brother, I cannot in good conscience stay behind. And, in truth, I agree with Oramel that it will be foolhardy to continue on this river tomorrow, for we would surely all be drowned.

Maybe there will be water on the top, although it has not rained in three days. I know nothing about the nature of the Indians we could encounter. We would need to strike for the North Rim, for that would take us directly to the Mormon settlements located on the Virgin River. There is nothing on the South Rim except the distant lands of the Hopi and Navajo.

I hope that God is with us tomorrow and will guide us all to safety. There are times like now when it seems as if you are but a fantasy, a beautiful dream, my darling.

Seneca came over to sit beside him after dinner. They both watched as Oramel got up and went to speak to Major Powell. A moment later, the pair left camp to speak in private.

"Bill, do you think the major will listen to my brother and agree to leave the river?"

"No."

Seneca's broad shoulders slumped. "It's a waste of breath. The major has too much riding on this expedition to give up and be viewed as a failure."

Dunn glanced sharply at his friend. "What does that mean?"

"He'd be accused of being a quitter."

"And what about us? If we leave the others and hike out, will we also be judged as quitters?"

Seneca shook his head. "No. Frank Goodman was a quitter because he left us way up on the Green River. But we've stuck this out until it has become foolhardy to go any farther. We've proven that we're neither cowards nor quitters."

"I suppose there's no shame in wanting to go on living," Dunn conceded.

Seneca relaxed. "That's right! We're just trying our damnedest to be *survivors*. Nothing wrong with wanting to get through this and go back home. Is there?"

"No."

"Then you'll stick with us? Without your help, we'd . . ."

Dunn held up his hand to silence his friend. "Let's just wait and see what happens come morning."

Four

"Major," Oramel Howland said when they were alone, "I expect that you know what I'm about to say."

"I do," Powell replied, trying to calm his emotions, "but first, let me say that I've spent hours studying this bad stretch of water just ahead and I'm sure that we can ride it through. You see, if we can . . ."

"Major, we're *determined* not to proceed down this river because we believe it to be impassable. Our food is nearly gone and, even if we could run those rapids, the cliffs are growing higher and higher."

"Meaning?"

"Meaning that, if we should survive a wreck, we'd be unable to climb out of the canyon. In short, to go on is either to drown or die of starvation."

Powell took a deep breath. "Mr. Howland, we've come a long, long way and passed through many dangers. There have been times when I know we *both* expected to die, but we've always stayed and seen it through. If we stick together now, tomorrow will be no different. I implore you, don't abandon this expedition when we are so near to success."

"Success?" Oramel threw his hands up toward the soaring cliffs. "We are about to destroy ourselves! Directly above us appears to be a trail that will deliver us up to the North Rim. We still have enough food to make a land crossing and reach those Mormon settlements up on the Virgin River. It is the *only* rational choice, sir!"

"Does Seneca share your intentions?"

"Yes. And William Dunn as well."

"I'm sorry to hear that," Powell said.

"Major," Oramel said, managing a thin smile, "please consider making the overland crossing with us. You spoke of sticking together through adversities; then let us go *together* across country to the Virgin River. We've done more on this river than anyone could have expected. We have suffered and mapped all but the last small measure of the Colorado. Let someone else do that from the south end . . . or from the rim. Or . . . or petition Congress for more funds and do it yourself next year! But, sir, don't risk everyone's life because of your pride."

Powell stiffened. "Pride? That's why you think I insist we go on?"

"Good night," Oramel said, dropping his hands to his sides in a gesture of resignation. "We have both spoken honestly, and there is nothing to be gained by argument."

Powell glanced up at the stars. "It's a clear night. I'm going to use the sextant and take some celestial measurements to more precisely determine our position. If we are very close to the end of the Grand Canyon, would you . . ."

"No," Oramel interrupted, "because certain death awaits on the very next stretch of river. Major, good night."

Not trusting his voice, Powell simply nodded. He waited beside the river until Oramel had returned to camp, and then he went for his sextant and maps. He could feel the men anxiously watching as he began to take his measurements, but Powell ignored them as he made his notes and calculations under the light of a nearly full moon. It was a brilliant evening, but he was so filled with anxiety that his hand actually shook when he began to make his final computations. But, at last, his pencil came to rest and he stared at the final figure.

"Forty-five miles," he whispered, "on a direct line to the Virgin River, which we know is several miles *below* this Grand Canyon."

Powell's mind refused to compromise the figures in order to strengthen his own position. Forty-five miles direct line to the Virgin River meant about ninety miles on this Colorado. But if the last ten or twenty miles came after the Grand Canyon, then they could not have but seventy, maybe eighty miles of dangerous, uncharted rapids. Five more days, maybe less if they did not have to make too many portages. There *was* enough food to carry them to the Virgin River!

Powell gazed back up at the stars. Yes, he thought, there was enough food, but could they survive the terrible rapids that awaited just below this camp? And, even if they could, would there be even worse rapids somewhere ahead? Or a waterfall in a section of the canyon too steep to portage or line the boats around? Yes, he understood Oramel's concern. They were all much weaker than they cared to admit. To be swept down and wrecked in a corridor of rock that they could not scale would mean certain death. And yes, he too had seen the trail up to the North Rim and knew that it offered an escape—perhaps their final chance for escape.

Powell closed his eyes and prayed for an answer. A sign, perhaps a shooting star. Something! But all he heard was the incessant thunder of the river and the booming of the rapids. Shaking his head, he glanced back at camp and saw that everyone had fallen asleep. It was very late. He stared at the sextant and his maps. Climbing stiffly to his feet, he went back to camp and wakened Oramel.

"What is it now?" the man said with irritation.

"I've completed my observations. I want to show them to you."

"Can't this wait until morning?"

"No."

Oramel trudged sleepily back to the riverbank, where the maps and calculations lay spread on the sandy beach. "Look," Powell began, "I've done all the figures and measurements and I can assure you that we are less than forty-five miles from the Virgin River."

"On a direct line?"

"Yes, but . . ."

"Which means twice that distance on this river," Howland said curtly.

"Dammit, man, that still would be only ninety more miles and we have enough food!"

"None of that changes what we saw waiting to destroy us just downriver. Good night again, Major."

It was all that Powell could do to say, "Good night."

After the man had left, Powell realized that he had conducted himself badly. He had lost his temper and thus his argument. A real leader would have been far more dispassionate and persuasive. He began to pace back and forth on the narrow, sandy beach, examining and reexamining all of his stellar and mathematical conclusions, but one could not calculate the chances of surviving the rapids and falls that awaited. Powell's orderly mind was frustrated. Trapped by questions he could not answer, his thoughts batted around and around in his head, seeking a way out of his excruciating situation. He became so desperate that, once, he even determined to wake up Oramel Howland and tell him that he had changed his mind and also decided to abandon this terrible canyon. On top, and all together, they *would* somehow make it to the Mormon settlements. Dunn and Jack Sumner were excellent frontiersmen and they . . . stop it!

Powell rushed over to their boats and examined each vessel, as if he were a doctor and could judge their health. Their health was failing. His *Emma Dean* was in the most desperate condition. They had not been able to find enough pine pitch in the canyon to plug her many leaks. Her soggy pine timbers were scarred, patched, and abraded. Poor *Emma Dean* was nearly broken, unable to stand much more of this mighty river's incessant pounding. The other boats, being stouter and made of oak, were battered but solid and able to go on. However, their sterns rocked fretfully in the current and Powell imagined that they were trying to crawl farther up onto the safety of

land. It was almost as though they were afraid of the river . . .
as he was.

Powell remembered how it had been when they'd first begun, up at Green River, Wyoming. How strong and optimistic
they had been. And how careful. Rapids that they had portaged
on the upper Green River now would be considered mere rip-
ples compared to what they had faced in the Grand Canyon
and probably had yet to face.

There would be no answer this warm, starry night. There
would only be another day and then, soon, a conclusion—death
or the passage through this canyon. Powell stood knee deep
in the river and craned his head far back so that he could see
above the canyon's towering rock walls. They seemed to pul-
sate, like the spilled viscera of dying soldiers on a Civil War
battlefield.

He leapt out of the river and hurried back to camp. With a
hand that shook quite badly, he awakened his brother, the troubled Walter, and told him of the decision by the Howland
brothers and William Dunn to abandon the river. "What should
I do?"

"I don't know," Walter said, "but you'll do the right thing."

Walter's confidence steadied him. "All I want is your support, brother."

"I will not leave you, Wes. I'll stick, even if this river does
wash us down into hell."

"It won't! Now, go back to sleep, for there is still an hour
or two of night, and tomorrow we must all be ready for the
test."

After Walter, Powell awakened each of the others. Hawkins,
their cook, Bradley, young Andy Hall, and the other frontiers-
man, Jack Sumner. Every one of them vowed to stick with
him to the end, wherever that might be.

"Thank you," he told each before urging him to go back to
sleep.

But no one did. Dawn finally came stealing over the canyon
wall. Billy Hawkins started a fire and prepared their usual

meager breakfast of coffee, a few hard biscuits, and shriveled apples. No one spoke for a long time; the meal was uncommonly solemn. Powell noticed that Dunn, Oramel, and young Seneca had seated themselves slightly apart from the others.

"Well," Powell said finally, unable to avoid the moment any longer, "we all know the question that faces us right now."

He turned to Oramel, determined not to lose his temper again. "Mr. Howland, I have polled the others and, to a man, they are staying with me. I beg of you and your friends to do the same."

But Oramel shook his head.

Powell turned to Seneca, raised his head, and said, "I want you to remain with us."

"I can't leave my brother."

"I understand. And you, William Dunn?"

"I cannot leave my best friend."

"Then, for the unwise decision of one," Powell sighed, "two others commit a terrible mistake?"

Oramel's cheeks flamed. Before he could object, Seneca said, "Oramel, perhaps we *should* remain together. If you'll stay, I'll stay."

"No!" Oramel pointed downriver. "Look at those rapids and those waterfalls! There is no way that they can be run. And they'll get worse! Mr. Dunn assures me that we can make it across the North Rim plateau."

Everyone turned to look at Dunn. He fidgeted, then raised his eyes to Powell. "Major, there's no doubt that I *can* get them across."

"Oh, but there *is* a doubt. That's wild country, and you can't predict anything up there with certainty."

"I believe our chances are better up above than down here on this river."

"Ah, ha! You see!" Oramel cried. "Mr. Sumner, you know the wilderness as well as Mr. Dunn. You also must realize that we can reach the Mormon settlements."

"I'm stickin' with the major."

"There'll be a good hundred miles to cover and you might run into hostiles," Powell said, spitting his words at Dunn.

"I expect that there will be rainwater basins," Dunn said quietly, "and game enough to hunt. Four days hard marching ought to bring us to the Virgin River."

"Very well," Powell said with deep resignation, "take the rifles and what food you think is fair."

"Thank you," Oramel said, turning to make the last-minute preparations.

Powell turned to the others, wanting to thank them for their loyalty but realizing that he might be leading them to their deaths; thanks at this point were inappropriate. "Let's break camp and prepare to leave."

The men hesitated. They had shared so much hardship that they found it nearly impossible to believe that it had come down to this irreversible division of minds and bodies.

"Let's go," Powell said quietly. "Load up the boats."

"We'll not have enough men to . . ."

"I know," Powell said, "we'll have to leave one of the boats behind."

"Which?" Sumner asked.

"My *Emma Dean*," Powell said, having to clear his throat. "She is the obvious choice. Now . . . now, do as I say and load up. We have a hard day ahead of us."

"If you have any day at all," Seneca warned.

The three deserters accepted two rifles and a shotgun, but refused any food. Hawkins left them a pan of biscuits and a gruff parting. "You can eat those biscuits or leave 'em to rot— makes no difference to me."

They took the biscuits.

"What's the major doing now?" Dunn asked.

"He's writing a letter to his wife," Jack Sumner replied. "One he wants you to carry out in case we don't make it. And here, take my watch. It was my father's, and I want it to go to my sister, if I'm not heard from again."

"Why give it to me?"

"If it's bad up there, you're the only one who has any chance of coming through alive."

"We'll *all* either make it on top, or die."

"You say that now, but . . . well, take the damned watch. The major's wife can get it on to my sister."

Dunn took the watch and shook hands with all the men. The major gave his letter to Oramel along with a duplicate set of records and notes that he had kept for just such a sad parting.

"God speed us all to the Virgin River," he said quietly.

"We'll be waiting for you," Dunn promised, shouldering the rifle and his pack, which included his diary.

"Don't stop writing," Powell urged. "Until we meet again, you men are all still part of this expedition and the world, as well as your fiancée, will appreciate a full and detailed account of your overland journey."

"You'll have it as well."

"And a few sketches."

"I can't draw worth beans."

"Try," Powell ordered, no longer looking angry or disappointed, but only resigned.

"Yes sir."

Tears began to stream down young Seneca's cheeks and then Andy's. When the two young men embraced, Dunn thought he might also break down and cry, so he pivoted and charged up the faint trail that they believed would carry them to the North Rim.

Powell removed the few remaining supplies from the *Emma Dean*, then laid his hand on her bow, as if she were an old and faithful friend. They all watched in silence, turning now and then to witness the progress of the three who were trying to climb out of the canyon.

"Major, are you all right?" Bradley, the former soldier, asked.

"Yes, I'll ride the rest of the way in the *Maid of the Canyon* with Hawkins and Andy."

"Look up there! They're waving good-bye," Andy shouted.

"Dunn isn't waving good-bye," Sumner corrected. "He's trying to motion us to come on up and join them. Looks like they can see the way up to the top."

Everyone looked at Powell, who didn't even bother to glance up at the trio but instead climbed in the boat and started to push it off, even if that meant he'd continue alone.

"Let's go," Hawkins grunted as he and Andy jumped into the major's boat. "We should call this place Separation Rapids!"

"Let's just hope that it won't be renamed Dead Men's Rapids!" Sumner deadpanned as their boat gained momentum.

They were immediately seized by the powerful current and struggled to keep close to the north wall as they lined up on a chute a moment before their boat plunged over a six-foot waterfall.

"Hang on!" Powell shouted as water filled the open compartment of their boat and it wanted to roll.

Andy and Hawkins knew they were going to swamp if they didn't row, and so they pulled with all their might, aiming for the south wall and barely missing a huge rock as they blasted through another funnel of water and punched into a series of foaming rapids. Their boats almost stood on end, rearing and bucking like wild horses getting their first taste of the Spanish spur.

How long it took to shoot that stretch of river, they did not know. Perhaps only a few harrowing minutes, but then they were past the terrible stretch of white water and gliding deeper into the ominous shadows where walls three thousand feet high leaned over the Colorado, ready to topple and crush them like waterbugs. Powell yearned to take one instant to twist around to observe his other boats. He could not imagine that they also could have survived.

"Pull for shore!" he cried.

When they reached the south bank, they managed to leap to the rocks and drag the *Maid* into an eddy of water. The other two boats smashed into them as their occupants jumped out and secured their bowlines. Everyone collapsed on the dripping rocks.

Powell gazed across to the North Rim, but the three defectors were gone.

"We *made* it!" Andy breathed, looking astonished.

"Fire our weapons as a signal to Mr. Dunn and the Howland brothers," Powell ordered.

Rifles were retrieved and fired, though their retort was puny compared to the thundering water.

"Major, do you really think this will change their minds now that we've made it?" Sumner asked.

"No, but we'll wait a little while, just in case I've misjudged their stubbornness."

"Is that why you left the *Emma Dean* with a set of oars?" Hawkins asked. "So that they could change their minds and still overtake us?"

Powell pretended he did not hear the question, but everyone knew that he had.

They waited . . . and waited, feeling the rocks beneath them shiver beneath the pounding of the river.

"All right," Powell said, "they're gone. Let's go!"

They returned to their boats, casting farewell looks and prayers at the cliffs, then turned their minds and muscles to the challenges ahead. There were more rapids and falls, terrible ones, but they were determined and expert boatmen. They fought the river all day, lining the boats or gritting their teeth and flying over low waterfalls and then plunging into the deep, boiling pools of black water. Once, while attempting to line a boat, it broke free and George Bradley was swept downriver to vanish over a waterfall. Everyone was certain that he and the boat were lost until they saw it pop up like a cork, far downriver, with Bradley waving his sopping hat in triumph.

That night, the men were so shaken and battered that no one cared to eat or even talk. They found a small alcove where they could camp, but no driftwood, and, therefore, they had no fire.

"Tomorrow will be better," Powell promised them as he sat on a rock some fifty feet over the river. "Tomorrow will be much better."

"How do you know that, Major?"

He turned and spoke to Hawkins. "I have a very strong but unscientific belief that we are almost finished with the Grand Canyon."

"Or is it almost done with us?" Andy asked.

"Sleep," Powell ordered, and they all tried, wondering how they could possibly survive another day like this one and if the three who had gone were still alive. And then, Powell took up his own journal and began to write.

August 29—At twelve o'clock we emerged safely from the Grand Canyon of the Colorado. We are in a valley now, and low mountains are seen in the distance. . . .

Tonight we camp in a mesquite thicket. The relief from danger, and the joy of success, are great. How beautiful the sky; how bright the sunshine; what "floods of delirious music" pour from the throats of birds; how sweet the fragrance of earth, and tree, and blossom! Something like this are the feelings we experience tonight. Ever before us has been an unknown danger, heavier than immediate peril. Every waking hour passed in the Grand Canyon has been one of toil. . . .

Now the danger is over, now the toil has ceased, now the gloom has disappeared, now the firmament is bounded only by the horizon, and what a vast expanse of constellations can be seen!

The river rolls by us in silent majesty; the quiet of the camp is sweet; our joy is almost ecstasy. We sit 'til long after midnight talking of the Grand Canyon, talking of home, but talking chiefly of the three men who left us. Are they wandering in those depths, unable to find a way out?

Are they searching over the desert lands above for water?
Or are they nearing the settlements?

Powell could hardly keep from grinning like a love-smitten schoolboy the next morning, and the other men did not even try to suppress their elation. They ate extravagantly of their meager supplies and lingered over coffee before pushing off and running through a few low canyons. The river was tame, the sun very warm on their faces. The water sparkled. Here and there a thin stream trickled off the cliffs, creating quivering rainbows. Several of the men broke into song and used their battered paddles to splash each other, like children, as they had done up near Green River. It seemed, Powell mused, very strange to be able to look out to see horizons. Not that there was anything significant to observe. The land here was dry and harsh, the mountains purple and punished. He saw mostly the water-loving paloverde and occasional cottonwoods along the river and then sage and creosote brush beyond.

"Look, Major! Indians!"

Not having seen any other human beings since early July at the Unita Indian Reservation, even a few Indians were cause for great excitement. Too much excitement, because the Indians were frightened and ran to hide as the Americans whooped and hollered their hoarse greetings.

"We mean you no harm!" Bradley pleaded as the last Indian disappeared.

"Save your breath," Powell said, "for we'll not see that bunch again. I expect we'll see plenty of others soon enough."

He was right. Just a few miles later, they came upon an Indian camp.

"We are friends!" Andy yelled.

All but a man, a woman, and two children scattered headlong into the rocks to hide. Powell smiled, waved, and ordered his men to row for shore.

"Pretty humble," Andy said, eyeing their sage- and brush-covered huts.

Powell, who knew a few words of many Indian languages, jumped out to discover that he could converse with this family. The man wore only a flat-brimmed white man's hat, the woman only a strand of beads; their children were completely naked.

"Friends," Powell told them, making a little sign language and then motioning downriver. "We are looking for the Mormons at the Virgin River. How far?"

The Indian stepped forward, grinning. "Tobacco!"

"Sorry. No tobacco."

"Friends. Tobacco!" the Indian repeated.

"Someone find something else to give him," Powell ordered. "Something handsome that he can show off."

"We haven't much of anything to give," Bradley said. "Maybe some old apples."

"Here," Sumner said, marching forward with a piece of colored soap.

The Indian beamed with pleasure. He held the soap up to the sun, turning it very carefully one way and then the other.

"It's to wash yourself with," Andrew explained, making a rubbing motion over his body.

The woman and children began to giggle at the young Scot. The father struggled not to do the same.

"Mormons," Powell repeated. "Virgin River. How far?"

The Indian eased past him toward the boat, looking hopefully at the things inside. He started to reach for a rifle but Sumner stepped in front of him and the Indian retreated.

"Let's go," Powell ordered.

They climbed back into the boat and waved good-bye as they rowed for the center of the sluggish water and continued downriver.

"It's coming," Andy said. "I can feel that we've almost reached the Virgin. It's just around the next bend . . . or the next."

And, surprisingly, it was, as Powell wrote that day:

August 30, 1869

The journey is over! Shortly after noon, we see three white men and an Indian hauling a seine, and then we discover that it is just at the mouth of the long-sought river.

As we come near, the men seem far less surprised to see us than we do to see them. They evidently know who we are, and on talking with them they tell us that we have been reported lost long ago, and that some weeks before a messenger had been sent from Salt Lake City with instructions for them to watch for any fragments or relics of our party that might drift down the stream.

Our newfound friends, Mr. Asa and his two sons, tell us that they are pioneers of a town that is to be built on the riverbank. Eighteen or twenty miles up the Valley of the Rio Virgen there are two Mormon towns, St. Joseph and St. Thomas. Tonight we dispatch an Indian to the last-mentioned place to bring any letters that may be there for us.

August 31, 1869

This afternoon the Indian returns with a letter informing us that Bishop Leithhead of St. Thomas and two or three other Mormons are coming down with a wagon, bringing us supplies. They arrive about sundown. Mr. Asa treats us with great kindness to the extent of his ability; but Bishop Leithhead brings in his wagon two or three dozen melons and many other little luxuries, and we are comfortable once more.

September 1, 1869

This morning Sumner, Bradley, Hawkins and Hall, taking on a small supply of rations, are ready to start down the Colorado with the boats. It is their intention to go to

Fort Mojave, and perhaps from there overland to Los An-
geles. The rest of us are to return with Bishop Leithhead
to St. Thomas. From St. Thomas we go to Salt Lake City.

As the *Kitty Clyde's Sister*, the *No Name* and the *Maid of*
the Canyon floated downriver, Walter Powell waved, his face
anxious with worry for his departing friends.

The major patted his brother's shoulder. "Don't worry about
them, Walt. They've just survived the Grand Canyon of the
Colorado. I doubt that anything they could face the rest of
their lives will prove so difficult."

"I know," Walter whispered, "but we might never even *see*
them again."

"If not in this life, then in the next," Powell said as the
boats disappeared around the river's bend and he led Walter
toward the waiting Mormon wagons. "Just as I hope one day
to see Mr. Dunn and the Howland brothers."

"I thought they'd be here already."

"No," Powell said, turning to gaze into the desert wilderness, "but they're out there somewhere and they're still coming. I'm almost sure of it."

Five

William Dunn heard the faint echo of rifle shots from the depths of the canyon. He stopped, bent slightly at the waist, gasping for breath because they had been following an extremely steep and zigzagging trail. His eyes strained back down into the canyon and, for an instant, he saw the three boats.

"They all made it!" he said, grinning broadly.

"Or that might have been a signal that they capsized and are stranded below," Oramel suggested.

But Dunn knew otherwise. "No, the major told me that they'd fire their rifles to let me know they'd made it through the rapids. He said it would mean that we ought to climb back down to the *Emma Dean* and join them."

"The *Emma Dean* is ready to break apart at the seams."

"But *maybe* she could make it," Seneca offered, looking at Dunn for support. "The major left oars and, once we were through those rapids and rejoined the others, we could divide up in the other boats and . . ."

"No!" Oramel lowered his voice and sleeved perspiration from his brow. "We've chosen our course, let's not waver at this critical juncture. Right, William?"

Dunn nodded, studying the trail that he hoped would deliver them to the North Rim. They weren't halfway to the top yet.

"You all right?" Seneca asked his brother.

"Just winded. If we'd left the river earlier, as I urged, we wouldn't be suffering through this ordeal."

Dunn supposed that was true enough, and he was worried about the man. Oramel was thirty-six. Gray-faced and sweating profusely, he was having the most difficulty climbing out of the canyon.

"Oramel, maybe we should rest for an hour or so," Dunn suggested.

"We'd better not," Oramel said, taking deep breaths. "The day is getting hotter and we've only the three canteens. We're going to use most of that before we reach the top."

"The major says it ought to be a lot cooler up there," Dunn told him.

"And how would he know that?" Oramel demanded. "Or has the man some mystical power of observation that none of the rest of us enjoy?"

Dunn ignored the caustic remark. "You ready too, Seneca?"

"Yeah, but I sure hope we can find game on top. I'm so starved I'm feeling shaky."

"Then you ought to eat one of Billy's biscuits," Dunn said, taking the lead and starting back up the narrow, winding trail.

"I believe that I will!"

Dunn was hot, tired, and in very low spirits. He kept thinking about how the major and all the others actually had made it through those rapids and waterfalls. If he'd remained on the river, they'd all be gliding on down the canyon. He'd be in the front boat with Sumner and the major because they were the best and strongest oarsmen. Powell would be pointing out rocks and strata, calling off the proper names of bushes and birds, just as he'd been doing for months. Mostly, however, they'd be listening for the water to warn them of approaching falls or rapids. But up here fifteen hundred feet above the floor of the Grand Canyon, with an even harder fifteen hundred feet yet to climb, he heard only Oramel's gasping and the thud of his own heart. There wasn't even a song in the hot, rising wind.

They climbed for another hour and then Seneca called, "Hold up, I need to take a breather!"

Dunn was happy to stop, but he knew that this rest was really for Oramel's benefit. The man was pale and gasping for air. They'd climbed a good deal since leaving Green River, but nothing this high or steep.

"You'd better drink more water, Oramel," Dunn suggested. "Otherwise, your muscles might start cramping, and we'll wind up carrying you to the top."

"That'll be the day," Oramel wheezed, but he drank at least half the water in his canteen and almost immediately looked healthier.

"What do you think?" Seneca asked, glaring at Dunn.

"Think of what?"

"Hell, I dunno. The view."

They both let their eyes wander out across the great expanse of silent air. To the east, the canyon walls were immense, changing color moment to moment. In the morning, the mostly red, white, and brown rocks stood out in sharp relief but, by noon, they had softened almost to pastels, the bold contours blending and flattening into fewer dimensions. Later in the afternoon, as the shadows jumped off the high walls and began to shroud the canyon, the colors and features again became more pronounced. The sky turned a darker blue until sunset lit the red sandstone on fire, magnifying and highlighting everything even as talon shadows seized the highest rocks. It was then that the eye most clearly beheld the broken terraces, the slashing side canyons, pinnacles, mesas, and buttes that boldly stepped forward.

"Do you think this canyon will ever draw people?" Seneca asked.

Dunn shook his head. "Why would anyone go down in there?"

"I don't know. Maybe just to see it, out of curiosity or adventure—like us."

Oramel made a face. "We all saw the high-water marks hundreds of feet up the canyon walls. In early spring, after a big snowpack on the Rockies, this canyon must be transformed into a great gutter of muddy water, destroying anything and everything in its path. Anyone but a complete fool would realize that nothing could long exist in that canyon."

"There are birds of every description and maybe a few fish," Dunn said, feeling hot and argumentative. "And remember those pink rattlesnakes?"

Oramel scoffed. "Fish can swim in a flood and birds can take wing to save themselves. I don't know how the rattlesnakes survive other than that they must constantly slither over the rim and tumble to the canyon's floor."

"Big tumble."

"Serpents are tough. And besides, we were talking about human beings."

"Then what about those people whose green squash we stole?" Dunn asked.

"What about them?"

"They obviously lived and farmed on that canyon floor," Dunn said. "They had even planted a cornfield."

"They're probably seasonal farmers who stay up on the South Rim during the winter and spring floods, then venture down into that canyon each summer to plant. In this heat, things must grow very fast."

"We should have stolen a few more squash," Seneca decided. "I could eat a whole one right now."

"Well," Dunn said, "let's see if we can get an antelope or a deer up on top before it gets dark."

"In that case," Oramel said, "I'd suggest you stop talking and get moving."

Dunn clamped his jaw and attacked the trail, not caring if he left the older man far behind. Hour after hour he climbed, sometimes having to backtrack a few hundred yards in search of a better way to the top. By late afternoon, the river had become just a thin aqua-colored ribbon. The rising heat from the canyon floor grew more intense but, when they finally approached the rim, they tasted the sweet scent of pines.

"Not much farther!" Dunn gasped as he struggled the rest

of the way before scrambling over the rim and collapsing to his knees. "Would you look at this, now!"

Seneca knelt down beside him and they studied the landscape in amazed silence. Neither had ever seen anything quite like this. For about a hundred yards from the rim, there was what the major would have termed a distinct climatic zone, very dry and desertlike, much like the canyon's floor. Just beyond that, however, stretched a great forest.

"What do you make of it?" Seneca asked, head swiveling back and forth as he studied the amazingly thin and arid corridor.

"My best guess," Dunn said, trying to remember one of Powell's shorter lectures about how the Grand Canyon's flora and fauna was the result of a succession of those climatic zones, "is that the hot air rising off the canyon floor has dried the edge of this rim. The rising hot air pushes out only to the edge of the forest, beyond which extends a much colder and wetter zone.

"You were listening to the major more than I was," Seneca said, looking impressed.

"He predicted that there were probably forests and meadows up here. His worry was that there would be few streams or rivers."

"But there *must* be some," Seneca replied. "How else could it be so green?"

"Snowfall," Dunn told the man. "Deep snows that water the forest and the meadows through autumn.

"Snow, rain, or rivers," Seneca replied, "it's far more beautiful than I'd dared to hope."

Dunn felt the same way. What trees they'd seen on the South Rim had been mostly juniper and piñon pine, but these were spruce, fir, and ponderosa pine. Deep red rocks contrasted sharply with lush alpine meadows ablaze with colorful wildflowers of every description.

"This must be prime hunting country," Seneca whispered. "Crawling with deer and antelope."

"I agree," Dunn said, feeling the hollow in his own shrunken belly.

Oramel staggered over the rim and crawled to their sides, face lighting up at the alpine beauty. "We've climbed into another world," he exclaimed.

"We have," Dunn said, twisting around and gazing back down into the Grand Canyon. "And it's a world far more to my liking."

"And mine," Seneca added as he checked his rifle and took a measurement on the setting sun. "It'll be dark in an hour or two. Maybe we ought to wait right here for the deer to come out and feed."

But Dunn shook his head. He climbed wearily to his feet and began walking toward the Mormon settlements that they had to reach. His eyes missed nothing and, when the brothers overtook him, he said to them, "There are deer signs aplenty. I'd say this country is crawling with mule deer . . . and bear."

Seneca also had spotted the clawed pine. "Black bear or grizzly?"

"That was probably done by a huge black bear, but we'd be fools to rule out stumbling across a grizzly. They won't ever have heard the sound of a rifle, so they'll be bold and very dangerous."

"Then let's just hope that our luck has turned and we don't meet up with any," Oramel said, clutching his shotgun.

"Look!" Seneca cried, rushing across the meadow and collapsing beside a tangle of wild berries, which he began to tear from their vines and cram into his mouth.

Dunn and Oramel were right behind him. The berries were ripe and sweet. They stripped off handfuls and ate until the wine red berry juice flowed through their beards and stained their shirts.

"I'd forgotten how good berries taste," Dunn finally said after gorging himself. He wiped his hands on his buckskins and belched with contentment. "Oramel, I think you made the right decision after all."

"Of course, I did."

Dunn grabbed a last handful of berries and stuffed them into his mouth. "We've still got an hour of daylight, and we don't know exactly how far we have to go to reach the Virgin River. I say let's use the last of our daylight before we make camp."

Seneca wasn't happy. "What about that venison?"

"We'll come across deer before long now," Dunn promised, his spirits and confidence soaring.

But they had to skirt a deep side canyon and then chanced upon the remains of a large Indian camp. Dunn dropped to the ground and motioned his friends to do the same. They waited until Dunn was satisfied that there were no Indians about, then hurried to examine the site.

"What do you think?" Oramel asked anxiously as the sun was diving into the trees. "It's a pretty old camp, isn't it?"

"I'm afraid not," Dunn said. "The Indians were here only a few days ago."

"How can you tell that?"

"The moccasin tracks are still distinct and it rained not very long ago."

The Howland brothers digested that for a moment, then Oramel said, "Well, just because we had rain down in the Grand Canyon doesn't mean this place would have gotten the same shower. Maybe it hasn't rained up here in a month or so."

"Look around you," Dunn ordered. "What do you see?"

Oramel didn't like being spoken to that way. "What is that supposed to mean?"

"It means that this plateau gets a lot of summer rain and winter snow. It *has* rained in the last few days, but these tracks haven't been washed away."

"Can you tell which way they went?" Seneca asked, bringing his rifle up and turning completely around.

As the sky began to flame, Dunn hurried to read more signs. He quickly decided that the only thing thicker than mule deer in these parts were Indians.

"They've spent some time this week hunting here," he reported to the anxious brothers. "But I've no idea where they might be camped tonight or have a permanent village."

"Not to the west, hopefully," Oramel said, looking the way they had to travel to reach the Mormon settlements.

"Do you think you could speak their tongue?" Seneca asked.

"Probably not," Dunn said, "for I doubt they are related in any way to the Utes or any of the other tribes I've visited."

"But you'd at least be able to speak in sign language with them," Oramel said. "Isn't that true?"

"Maybe," Dunn hedged, not wishing to make any more promises . . . especially promises that could get them killed.

"Oh sure you would!" Oramel insisted. "And I'm certain these people would be friendly."

"We dare not count on that," Dunn warned. "The Indians native to this North Rim country might be Paiutes. They gave the emigrants and then the Central Pacific fits when they were crossing the Great Basin of Nevada."

"That's a long way from where we stand now," Oramel said, clearly displeased with the response.

"Let's just try like hell to be silent and avoid them," Dunn suggested. "With any luck, we'll reach the Mormon settlement in three or four days."

"We've got to eat before then," Seneca said quickly. "We've got to use our rifles and kill at least one deer."

"We just *did* eat!" Dunn protested.

"Berries won't give us enough strength to get to the settlements," Oramel argued. "There's no strength in berries. We *have* to have meat."

Dunn supposed this was true. If he'd been alone, he'd have been well satisfied with berries or whatever else he could find to eat without taking the risk of firing a shot and possibly alerting Indians to their presence. But he wasn't alone, and neither of the Howland brothers had the self-discipline to march through this wilderness on berries.

"All right," he conceded. "Tomorrow we'll get some venison and then we'll make do on it until we reach help. Agreed?"

The men nodded, but neither looked very happy with the arrangement. "I was counting on filling up with roast meat tonight," Seneca said. "A celebration."

"Celebration of what?"

"Of escaping the river and making it up to this paradise. Hell, we could have taken a tumble and died a half dozen times today. That was as bad as anything we've ever climbed."

"Yes," Dunn agreed, "it was. But, to my way of thinking, we ought to hold off celebrating until we reach the Mormons. *Then* we'll really have something to celebrate."

"Yeah," Oramel said, "except that those people don't know how to celebrate. There'll be no strong spirits when we arrive. You know that."

"That's true, but at least we'll be well fed."

"Let's get some wood and get a fire going," Oramel suggested, turning to leave. "We can build it right over the ashes of this Indian campfire. That ought to give you something colorful to write about in your diary tonight."

"I'd prefer to write about our climb out of the Grand Canyon and our adventures on this North Rim."

"How, by starlight?"

"If I have to," Dunn said tightly.

"Well, you *won't* have to because we're having a fire," Oramel snapped. "Dammit, man, we're wearing rotting rags, we've no blankets and it's getting *cold* up here on top since the sun went down."

Dunn looked to Seneca for help but his friend turned and hurried after his brother to collect firewood.

"Damned pilgrims!" Dunn muttered, worried far more about hostile Indians than food or warmth.

Over his objections, the Howland brothers built their fire. Dunn felt a barrier forming between himself and the pair, especially Seneca. He should have guessed that blood was thicker than friendship. Had he figured that out earlier, he'd still be riding the rapids with Powell, and the brothers could hunt this high rim country and build all the fires they pleased. Dunn had no interest in a celebration because he was sure that Indians weren't all that far away. To ease his mind, he began to write to his sweetheart.

My Dear Miss Holloway: Today we hiked out of the canyon and it was very difficult. Major Powell had it guessed right about what we'd find on top. Thanks to him, I can identify many of the trees and flowers. I saw a squirrel unlike any I've ever seen before and I know its sighting would give you and the Major a great deal of pleasure. The squirrel was dark haired, with tufts on its ears and a white tail. Handsomest little critter I've ever seen.

We had a big fire tonight, but there wasn't much talk among us. We hope to make good progress tomorrow and maybe get some fresh meat, for we are much weakened by today's climb out of the Grand Canyon.

Tonight I was thinking that I must start to make more of myself in this world and accumulate some wealth for the comforts of our old age . . . and for your security when I am gone. I desire that you never should want for anything. I am determined to give you the kind of life you were born to and I will not quit trying until that comes to pass.

"If you want," Oramel said, yawning, "I'd be happy to read over what you've written after we reach the Mormon settlements. Check for spelling and style. That sort of thing."

"No thanks," Dunn said, putting the journal into the oilskin pouch tied securely to his belt.

"You shouldn't begrudge us a little fire tonight."

"I don't begrudge you or Seneca a thing," Dunn replied. "I just think that we're taking unnecessary chances. An Indian can smell smoke for miles."

"What reason would they have not to think it's just lightning striking some pine tree?"

"There's not a cloud in the sky."

Oramel rolled over and went to sleep. Seneca was already snoring, but Dunn was too angry and maybe too tired to go to sleep right away. He sat staring into the flames and brooding about his decision to leave the expedition and get himself into this mess. Tomorrow, they not only would have to begin their hard trek, but they'd also be forced to search for water and refill their canteens.

Sometime after midnight, Dunn grabbed his pack and canteen, then walked to a point overlooking the Grand Canyon. There was enough moonlight to work on his diary, if he were so inclined . . . but he was not. He eased down in some rocks and studied the silvery thread of water far, far below. Gazing down into the great gorge brought him a measure of peace, probably because he'd gotten accustomed to sleeping there. Tonight was the first in a long time that he had not fallen asleep to the gruff lullaby of the river. Dunn realized that this forest stillness had become a bit unnerving. There wasn't a sound up here, other than the faint whisper of a breeze. It was an exceptionally quiet night. Almost *too* quiet. There should have been a rustling of night animals, the screech of an owl, the scurrying about of critters. Then again, he'd never been in this country; how could he possibly know what kind of wildlife abounded here?

Dunn was spooked by sitting alone on this North Rim instead of resting his bones on a sandbar way down there with the boys. With Powell's brave men all around, a man didn't have to worry about being attacked by Indians. There weren't any in the Grand Canyon, except the ones who'd raised green squash, and they obviously were just farmers. Up here, the Indians wouldn't be farmers because the growing season was too short and wild game far too plentiful.

Get some sleep, he thought, stretching his legs out, feet to the very edge of the rim.

* * *

Dunn awoke abruptly to the heavy boom of a rifle. His eyes snapped open and he blinked into the sun struggling over the eastern horizon. He had overslept and he knew that Oramel had probably seen deer grazing in the meadow and gotten them some meat for breakfast. Good. With venison in their bellies, there would be no more complaining and they could move faster.

Dunn stretched and wiggled his toes in his worn boots. He was thirsty and thought of the succulent berries. They would quench a man's thirst and . . .

"William!" Seneca cried, voice ragged with terror.

Dunn exploded to his feet.

"William! Help!"

Dunn's only weapon was his big hunting knife. He heard Oramel's shouts of alarm join those of his brother. And then Dunn heard the triumphant voices of Indians. A shotgun blasted. Dunn's spine turned to ice as the cries of more Indians filled his ears.

Dear God! The camp is being overrun! Dunn strained to hear Oramel or Seneca's voice. He scrambled into the rocks, peering this way and that. Their camp was less than two hundred yards away. Dunn squinted back toward it and saw dozens of moving shadows.

Go help your friends! Do something to save them! Don't just lie here and let them die without lifting a hand. You promised that you could get them to safety. You promised!

But when he tried to extract his Green River knife from its sheath and go to the aid of the Howland brothers, Dunn discovered that he could hardly breathe. And, when half a dozen Indians suddenly burst into view, he froze and his mouth went as dry as sand.

The Indians had the shotgun and the rifles. They had canteens and Powell's duplicate journal, whose pages they began to rip free and toss into the air, all the while laughing, shouting, and dancing.

One of them seemed to look directly at Dunn. He waited, heart in his mouth, until the warrior turned away and disappeared back into the forest where the others almost certainly were mutilating the Howland brothers or removing valuable arrows from their savaged bodies.

Dunn knew that he had to run for his life if he were to have any chance of survival. Sure, the heathens were celebrating now, but they'd quickly settle down and discover evidence of his presence. Then they'd be on his backtrail, howling for more blood.

"Seneca," he whispered, covering his mouth to keep from emitting an anguished sob. "I'm sorry!"

Dunn waited until the Indians disappeared for a moment, then grabbed his pack and dashed headlong to the east because the Indians blocked escape to the west. He would run and run until he left the murdering Indians far behind.

But where could he go?

Dunn hadn't a clue. All he knew was that the Howland brothers were dead and he was alive. And to stay alive, he needed to get as big a head start as he could before the Indians found his tracks.

Six

When he started to run, Dunn had no idea where he was going, only that he had to make the most of what little head start he could gain before the hunt began. He was furious that he had not thought to bring his rifle or canteen, another oversight that very likely would be his undoing. All he had, besides his hunting knife, was a small leather pack with matches, fishing lines and hooks, and a few other odds and ends, including his diary and pencils.

As he ran eastward, following the North Rim, Dunn kept flushing wild game. The forests and meadows were thick with quail, rabbits, and mule deer although he saw no Bighorn sheep or antelope. At this altitude, the mountain air was cool but very thin.

Dunn pulled up gasping when he came to the place where a stream had cut a deep side canyon feeding into the North Rim. He and the Howland brothers had skirted this obstacle only the day before and the detour had cost them better than an hour. Now, Dunn didn't think he had that much time to waste as he gazed into the several-hundred-foot-deep chasm. He turned his ear to the wind, listening and expecting to hear the excited cries of his pursuers. He expected that the last sound he might ever hear would be that of arrows in flight an instant before he was brought down. No, Dunn decided, he could not risk the luxury of circling this side canyon. It would take far too long and might even allow the Paiutes to get ahead of him and lay an ambush.

Dunn's lungs were burning and he thirsted for water. Well, there it was, a clear, cold stream waiting for him at the base of this side canyon. He had no choice but to make his way down the precarious west face, then cross the stream and quickly scale the opposite wall before he was spotted by the Indians. The decision made, Dunn began to search for a trail that would lead him down the nearly vertical wall. If he lost his footing and fell, or even twisted an ankle, he would be a dead man.

He began to hurry along the rim of the side canyon, looking for the best way to descend. The wall was composed of broken and crumbling sandstone, which always was dangerous footing. Between the broken rock lay fields of loose shale that flowed all the way down to the stream. Dunn trotted over to the nearest rock slide and began his descent. He sank nearly to his knees, trying to keep his footing as showers of rock began to bounce and roll to the canyon floor. Dunn felt as if he were becoming mired in quicksand. Then, he saw the slide begin to move just ahead.

"No," he grated, fighting to retreat but feeling himself being drawn inexorably downward as the slide gained power and momentum. There was no way to avoid being swept downward, so he kicked his feet up and sat down hard, arched his back, and went sledding down the canyonside, engulfed in a cloud of boiling dust.

Twisting and spinning, Dunn rode the slide to the bottom, praying all the while that he would not be buried or beaten to death by heavy boulders. He reared to his feet and threw himself toward the opposite wall, chased by rocks the size of melons. But the rocks came to rest, damming up the stream as clouds of billowing dust floated away on the hot, rising canyon wind.

Dunn was seized by a hard coughing fit as he staggered up the canyon a few dozen yards to collapse beside the stream. Dipping his head into the ice-fed water, he drank deeply, but then pulled his head up, knowing that he could not run on a full belly. He washed his eyes and took an inventory of himself. He was intact. No broken, cracked, or crushed bones. He had been extremely fortunate. Flopping backward, he stared up in amazement at the rock slide he'd just sledded down. Eyes lifting, his gaze came to rest on the rim; and that's when he saw the Indians. There were at least a dozen. Dark brown men wearing buckskins like his own. Dunn's heart started to pound. His hand reached for the handle of his knife as the Indians watched him as vultures do carrion. Then, one of them threw back his head and emitted a blood-chilling scream. Two of the Indians fired arrows, which arched slowly outward, then dived to narrowly miss him. Dunn grabbed one of the arrows and broke it in a pitiful gesture of defiance.

The Indians came storming down into his canyon, bounding like mountain goats, howling like wolves. Dunn began to scramble wildly up the opposite slope, engulfed in a hailstorm of arrows. When he finally reached the top, he twisted around to see that three of the Paiutes already had leapt over the stream and were halfway up this slope. Dunn grabbed a massive rock with both hands, raised it overhead, and hurled it down at them. The rock began to bounce, creating a small avalanche. The three Paiutes looked up and Dunn saw their fear. They shouted and tried to move but were bowled over and sent tumbling down to the bottom of the canyon. One managed to crawl a little way but the others lay like broken, half-buried rag dolls.

The surviving Paiutes flew into a rage.

"Come on!" Dunn bellowed, waving his arms and egging them forward. "Come and get me!"

Two more of the Paiutes attacked and Dunn raised another big rock, cradling it until the Paiutes had climbed twenty or thirty yards before he grunted and heaved it downward. The rock began to bounce wildly, airborne for twenty or thirty feet at a bound and breaking other rocks free. The pair below retreated, barely avoiding injury.

"Ha, ha!" Dunn shrieked, mocking them.

In response, the Indians fanned out and began to climb the slope. Dunn tried to hold them off but it was impossible; there were far too many. There being nothing else to do, Dunn turned and ran for his life. He had always been a swift runner and was certain that he could coax enough speed out of his long, powerful legs to outdistance his furious pursuers. But for how long? They might not possess his swiftness, but he had no illusions about their superior endurance. They were accustomed to this altitude and Dunn knew they'd eventually overtake him.

He had not run a quarter of a mile before he heard their angry yelps telling him that they'd already emerged from the deep side canyon.

Hold a steady pace, he told himself. *Don't panic and run yourself out in the first mile or two. This is going to be a long race, and you had better not fade before you find a way down from this rim.*

He slowed a little, but he was still breathing hard and already bathed in perspiration. Suddenly, a band of mule deer exploded from a stand of thick manzanita and Dunn's heart almost stopped in anticipation of an ambush. The deer sprinted away and he took a deep breath, wishing he could be one of them instead of a desperate white man running for his life across an uncharted wilderness.

How far ahead was the trail which he and the Howland brothers had used to make their foolish exit from the Grand Canyon? A mile? Five miles? Dunn's mind was in such turmoil that he found it impossible to think clearly. But . . . if he did reach the trail before he was overtaken, then he stood a chance. Maybe the Indians wouldn't bother to chase him down into the belly of the Grand Canyon. And even if they did, his salvation still lay in the waiting *Emma Dean.* Dunn could visualize the familiar little boat resting on the sand and waiting to deliver him from these heathen devils. Mouth hanging open, dragging hard for breath, he ran on and on, the vision of the

Emma Dean giving him hope and the strength to keep his long legs churning.

As he ran, Dunn searched for landmarks which he and the Howland brothers had noted only yesterday. And he also began to chant—*Emma Dean, Emma Dean, Emma Dean*—until the thought of that boat was as powerful as the Lord to an unholy sinner.

Yes, there is that lightning-struck pine, the one halved and splintered right down to its roots. And there is that curious-shaped rock that Seneca thought looked like an anvil.

And look! The berry patch where they'd first gorged until their hunger was satiated and their beards were purple and matted with sweet juice.

Dunn ran on and on as the sun finally reached and passed its zenith. He ran until he saw the twisted pine that marked the place where they'd finally topped the canyon.

There it is!

He had slipped into a trance and now his legs didn't want to stop churning. He very nearly ran over the edge of the Grand Canyon.

Dunn collapsed, body shaking with fear and fatigue. His head sagged and he panted like a winded dog, sucking in great gulps of air. After a minute or two, he twisted around to study his backtrail. He could not see the Indians, yet he knew they were no more than a mile behind, possibly even closer, because his pace had slowed during the last hour.

Dunn yearned for something to eat. His strength was gone, his body shook uncontrollably. If he had just ten minutes, he could find another patch of berries. He climbed to his feet and took a few steps away from the rim, eyes searching for berries. They were plentiful, if he just . . .

The arrow shot out of the trees on a fast, flat trajectory and its flint head sank deeply into the meat of Dunn's left bicep. He staggered, and it was well that he did, for a second arrow would have struck him in the lungs but instead only nicked his cheek before it sailed over the rim. He tried to tear the arrow from his bicep but it was embedded too deeply; he reeled with pain. Breaking away the shaft, he lurched toward the rim. When he reached it, Dunn momentarily lost his courage, certain that he could not possibly escape down the dizzying path to the *Emma Dean*.

"Yiii-yipp-ii!"

He plunged over the rim with his fingers and the toes of his boots digging for purchase. He figured he had less than a minute before the Indians reached the rim. His only hope was to reach a shoulder of rock which would shield him from danger. He leapt downward, almost falling at every bound, until he ducked under the rocky buttress a moment before arrows sought him like raptors.

Dunn pressed his shoulder blades to the buttress of rock and stared downward. He took comfort in the sight of the great canyon cathedral. This he knew and had grown to respect. Even these rapids and waterfalls that had driven him and the Howland brothers from the expedition now seemed benevolent compared to the murdering Indians. Besides, Powell and the others had run that stretch of bad water and, if he could reach the *Emma Dean*, he was going to try to do the same. Even drowning was preferable to being shot full of arrows or captured and slowly tortured. Dunn knew Indians, and he knew that they would not soon forgive him for the killing he'd done in that deep side canyon.

He inspected his arm, which throbbed mightily, but the bleeding was minimal. The sight of the broken shaft protruding from his violated flesh bothered Dunn almost as much as the injury, and he worried about how he could dig it out. These types of wounds often became infected and he had seen men die of lesser injuries. Well, he'd either live or die, but there'd be no amputation in this country.

Dunn pushed on, sure the Indians would not dare follow him down this trail. But he soon discovered that he was wrong. They *were* coming. He could not see them, but he could hear their voices. The only thing that gave him hope was that there were very, very few places during the entire descent where the Indians could mass and fire their arrows. Almost everywhere else, they would have to be single file and unable to risk using a bow.

Hurry!

Dunn lost track of time. The canyon was running northwest, and the sun was hanging low over the rim, hot and bright in his face. Once more, he felt the baking heat of the rocky walls, and the sting of salty sweat burned his eyes. But he kept going, heartened by the familiar and intensifying roar of big water in his ears. It drowned out the cries of his enemies.

Before he knew it, darkness closed on the canyon and there was only moonlight to guide him down to the river, and there, resting peacefully on a beach scarcely larger than a two-man tent, was the little boat.

He collapsed beside it, head resting against the stern. Had it not been for the possibility of Indians catching him in this place, he would have slept beside the *Emma Dean*, content with rest and the promise of daylight. But the Indians *were* coming, and so he climbed onto a high rock where he could at least see a few hundred yards downriver.

Powell had spent hours studying this most terrifying stretch of water and he'd calculated that, if a boat had any chance at all of surviving the rapids and waterfalls below, it had to run a very precise course. Dunn took a deep breath and felt the river's cool spray on his face. He could see that, from a side canyon, large boulders had washed off the rim down into the Colorado, thus causing all the difficulties ahead. These boulders had formed a partial dam, over which the water tumbled for what appeared to be almost twenty feet. If a man and his boat survived that waterfall, he would be swept over churning rapids into a second, but smaller fall. Should he survive that, there appeared to be no more waterfalls but at least two hundred yards of rapids and huge projecting rocks, any one of which would break the *Emma Dean* into kindling wood. And finally, after a short span of clear water, there was a huge rock that projected halfway out into the course of the river from the north side of the canyon. Dunn could see that, if he and the boat were still intact, he would have to row like crazy in order to get around that monstrous rock and enter the swift chute of water that funneled downward into a curve of the canyon. God only knew what lay beyond that immense boulder.

He eased the battered *Emma Dean* across the sand and gently into the water, feeling the dark, swift current swing her bow sharply around. The oars were in their locks and Dunn took a last glance backward. The Paiutes were almost upon him. He could not hear or see them, but he could *feel* their ominous presence and knew that every passing second was a precious gift not to be squandered.

"So long, you bastards!" he screamed, giving the *Emma Dean* a hard shove and throwing himself inside. "I may surrender to the river, but not to you murderers!"

His voice caromed off the rocky walls and he grabbed the oars, rowing hard and keeping to the north side. The boat slid fearlessly toward the edge of the waterfall. Dunn stroked with all his might, aiming for a clear chute over the falls, grazing some rocks and feeling others tear at *Emma Dean's* scarred underbelly.

"Ahhh!" he cried as she teetered for just a moment, then suddenly dropped.

He momentarily lost consciousness, then was slammed back into awareness as a wall of water cascaded over him, ripping away the oar in his left hand while the one in his right splintered and began to flop about like a broken wing.

Dunn grabbed the gunnels, locking his feet under the seat and gulping for air. The *Emma Dean* shook herself like a wet hound and then charged blindly ahead, striking rocks and racing madly toward the second waterfall. Dunn knew she wasn't going to survive when a rock spun them sideways into the falls an instant before they rolled and dropped into a cauldron of white water. A scream filled his throat and he was torn from the boat as she broke in half. Dunn's instincts took over and he fought his way to the surface. Something snagged his foot and he screamed as his leg was wrenched and nearly torn from his hip. Tons of water smashed him downward. He struck a submerged rock and the river tossed him into the air. After that, Dunn remembered nothing until he awoke to stare up into the cruel faces of more murdering Indians.

Seven

Dunn attempted to make a grab for his hunting knife, but with one arm stiffening around an embedded arrowhead and the other swollen around the wrist, he could do little more than grunt with pain. Everything hurt. He could not breathe through his nostrils because his nose had been broken. But all that meant nothing compared to the chill Dunn felt as he gazed up at the Indians, all of whom held bows, arrows, or sharp spears. There had to be at least a dozen of the impassive killers, who wore only buckskin breechclouts and moccasins. They were a uniformly muscular group with high cheekbones and long, flowing black hair.

"Go ahead and shoot," Dunn wheezed, his lungs rattling with river water. "I won't be tortured."

The Indians shifted uneasily and continued to stare. Dunn waited, his breathing shallow and labored. He thought of his family back in Philadelphia and how his bones would be lost in this wilderness while theirs would eventually wind up in beautiful cemeteries with great marble headstones. And, worst of all, he thought of how he'd abandoned the Howland brothers and shown his true colors as a coward. He should have died then, quickly and with honor. Dunn wanted to choke on this sad and ignoble end to his life. Full of hope and enthusiasm, he had ventured west to prove his worth to Mr. Holloway and Cynthia, but instead had confirmed himself to be a deserter, a coward, and a failure.

"What are you waiting for?" he asked, rising painfully to one elbow. "Kill me and let's be done with it."

But the Indians continued to watch him with their dark, expressionless eyes. Dunn was certain that they were hoping he would weep and beg for his worthless life.

Well, he thought, trying to muster up all of his courage, *I will not accommodate that kind of heartless perversity. Instead, I'll provoke them into killing me quickly.*

"I killed about five of you in that side canyon, didn't I!" he shouted, sweeping his five fingers across his throat so that there could be no misunderstanding.

Dunn raised his head and stared at the river, wishing it had already drowned him. Maybe the river could have him yet, if he could somehow reach it and rob these heathens of their perverse sport. He rolled onto his back and forced an eerie laugh. Then, he threw his eyes at the cliffs, pointing and shouting.

"Up there, look!"

They didn't understand his words but the ruse still worked. The Indians twisted around and gazed up the wall. Dunn rolled hard for the sweeter death of the river. He rolled three times and was in the water when they grabbed his legs and dragged him back out.

"Kill me!" he ordered, kicking and shouting. "Kill me!"

But instead, the Indians formed a solid wall beside the water, clearly unwilling to allow him that trick again. Dunn pushed himself to one knee, then swayed to his feet.

"Outa my way!" he ordered. But the Indians refused to budge.

Dunn wasn't sure what to do next. And while thinking about it, he suddenly realized that he was staring up at the *North Rim.* He must actually have crossed the Colorado and washed up on the opposite shore!

"Paiute?" he asked, dragging a shaky hand across his face.

One of the Indians pointed to the arrow shaft embedded in his bicep, and this caused a lively discussion. For the first time, Dunn noticed that the arrows these people carried had feathers of a different color from the ones he'd dodged on the North Rim.

"Who are you?" Dunn blurted.

The Indians did not understand his question, but they looked quite different from the murdering North Rim Paiutes. The most obvious difference was that those Indians had been warmly dressed in furs while these deep canyon people were almost naked. Dunn forced a smile.

"Who are you?" he repeated as he made sign language.

The Indians exchanged surprised glances until one, an old man with silver hair, began to respond. Dunn was pretty good at sign and, if he was correct, this old chief was telling him they were called . . . *"the people of the blue-green water."*

"Where do you live?" he asked.

The leader pointed up a deep side canyon which created more questions in Dunn's mind than answers. The old man could mean that they lived only a short way up the canyon or all the way up and beyond it down into Old Mexico. Thinking that these people might speak Spanish, Dunn clumsily repeated his question in that language, but elicited no response. It didn't matter. Dunn was now convinced that these were *friendly* Indians, and that he was unlikely to be murdered unless he committed some grave insult.

One of the Indians disappeared for a moment and then returned to extend a fat green squash to Dunn, then pantomimed a rowing motion which caused the others to erupt in giggles.

Dunn blinked and then exclaimed, "Why, you're the farmers whose squash we stole a few miles upriver!"

The Indians did not understand his words, but they *did* fathom his sudden revelation, which made them laugh even more. Dunn joined their laughter. These *were* good people, as generous and happy as children.

Dunn tried to bite a hunk out of the squash but his teeth failed to gain a hold; this squash was very large with a thick, knobby green skin. The Indians thought that absolutely hilari-

ous. One of them finally produced a stone club, which he used
to crack open the squash. Dunn began to devour it, seeds and
all. It was delicious, much sweeter than the unripened ones he
and Powell's party had hurriedly made off with. He was famished and he ate until he was full and very sleepy in the afternoon's heat. Unafraid now, he fell asleep before sundown
and slept until full daylight flooded the deep canyon the following morning.

Because of his considerable injuries, the canyon Indians
gently placed him on a litter of poles and woven river reeds.
Four of the younger ones began to carry him up a wide and
very deep side canyon choked with willows and cottonwood
trees, and fed by a beautiful blue river. Dunn remembered that
Powell had remarked on this *huge* oasis canyon but that they
had not taken the time to explore it.

Now Dunn saw small plots of corn, squash, and beans and
a number of Indians busy with weeding and irrigation. The
corn was tall and he had a powerful hunger for an ear or two.
The urge was so strong that he made sign language and so
the litter was stopped and the Indians tore off several ears and
handed one to him. Dunn peeled away the husk and ate it raw,
enjoying every juicy mouthful. As they went on, the canyon
narrowed and its high, broken red rock walls rose to over a
thousand feet. A short time later, they came to a surging cataract and it was then that Dunn realized that the water really
was an unusual hue that he could describe only as turquoise
blue, quite unlike anything he'd ever seen before.

"Such color!" he whispered with admiration, wishing that
Major Powell had seen this beautiful waterfall.

The Indians, realizing his appreciation of their canyon, were
pleased. They even stopped at the base of the waterfall so that
Dunn could admire how the river curved and flowed through
smooth, winding chutes of rock to tumble softly into deep,
inviting pools. Several of the Indians removed their clothing
and dived into the pools to splash in the water. Dunn envied
them, for the air was hot, well over a hundred degrees, al-

though the foliage was so thick that they were almost always in shade.

Once above the falls, Dunn saw more fields in cultivation. On many occasions, the Indians crossed irrigation ditches and deep, bubbling canals. It was clear that these people, probably over many centuries, had developed a very sophisticated irrigation system. Dunn saw other Indians digging out weeds and cleaning the ditches using paddle-shaped wooden tools. Once, he saw a band of horses, perhaps twenty, that were being herded by an Indian boy, who grinned and waved. The horses were shaggy and very small; they bolted and galloped away when they saw the litter and approaching men. The boy went yelling and chasing after them.

They had gone only a short distance when Dunn heard the sound of what had to be a very big waterfall. It grew thunderous as they approached. Despite his injuries, Dunn felt his heart quicken when the Indians rounded a bend in the trail and then set his litter down. He pushed himself to his feet and took a few painful steps forward to behold a truly magnificent waterfall, whose foaming torrent dropped almost two hundred feet before exploding into a deep blue pool ringed by plants and rock coated with a smooth and glistening substance that made it appear like hard rock candy.

Dunn rested while the Indians went swimming again. A shout brought his head up and Dunn saw three of his companions poised on top of the waterfall. Clearly, they were showing off, and Dunn held his breath as they dived, arms outstretched, backs arched to plunge over the waterfall and then cut cleanly into the great swirling pool far below. One by one, the Indians surfaced, grinning and laughing.

One of the Indians brought Dunn a handful of wild grapes. They were succulent, and he buried his bruised face into the cluster and let the sweet juice stream through his dirty beard. He ate them all and even sucked the last of their sweet juice from his sticky fingers.

They rested for several hours before it was made clear to

Dunn that he was to return to the litter. They indicated that he was to hold on tight and it was well that he did, for the climb up and around these majestic falls was tricky and not a little dangerous. At one point, Dunn simply closed his eyes and prayed that he would not lose his life. But, soon enough, they had circumvented the magnificent waterfall and were back under the thick canopy of cottonwoods. Here, the canyon walls seemed to lean in on them until there was only a thin slice of blue sky above. Dunn saw a pair of mule deer but no evidence of beaver nor any sign that these people were fishermen. The canyon was a haven for birds of every description and they swarmed after insects. Swallows swooped over the water like dragonflies, brightly colored hummingbirds darted from flower to flower, while the raucous echo of ravens filled the air between the high, narrow canyon walls.

There were two more waterfalls, one a thin, lacy veil of water that curled downward at the whim of the wind, the other more substantial, with several channels of foaming torrents. The canyon widened. A few minutes later, they were trudging into the outskirts of the village itself, surrounded by many acres of cultivated fields, all lying sun-washed at the junction of a second deep canyon branching to the southwest.

The village already had been alerted to Dunn's impending arrival. Several hundred curious Havasupai gathered to welcome him as he was carried down their dirt street between dozens of brush wickiups and small but neatly tended fields of corn, beans, squash, and what appeared to be tiny orchards of fruit trees. The young women were comely, the children and old men naked and well fed.

Dunn was in pain, and, now that they had lost the benefit of the shade, he was feverish. Sensing this, the Indians carried him under a great tree that marked the center of the village and brought water. He did not find the taste especially to his liking, for it seemed that the blue-green water was slightly tainted by minerals, although it was not the least bit salty.

For perhaps twenty minutes, Dunn lay under the huge cottonwood tree, the center of everyone's attention, including a great many tongue-lolling dogs of all shapes, colors, and sizes. The people chattered and seemed more than happy to spend the afternoon studying him. Dunn had no idea what was going to take place next, but he felt no anxiety, other than that his wounds might prove fatal or at least crippling. To occupy himself, he removed his diary from its tightly wrapped oilskin and took up his pencil. Why not give these people something more interesting to observe?

My Dear Miss Holloway: It is quite a miracle that I am alive, much less writing to you now. The Howland brothers and I left Major Powell and the others, fearing certain death on the impending cataracts. I didn't really want to leave the Major, but I felt that I must or the brothers would go off alone and stand no chance of surviving on the North Rim. What a fool I was! We were attacked by Indians and I was the only one of us to escape with my life. Somehow, I reached the bottom of the canyon and the other side of the river. I was rescued by friendly Indians and am now their guest in a most beautiful canyon. These people are farmers, not warriors. They are well fed and appear to be quite happy, numbering several hundred. I am wounded and battered but hope they can work another miracle and heal me, for I have never seen an Indian people that did not have great knowledge of wild plants and their medicinal benefits.

I wonder if I shall ever see your beautiful face again or if you will ever read these words. I have no idea if I shall ever be able to leave this canyon. I do not even know what lies beyond its towering, ragged and red rims. All I can do is try to remember your sweet face and our love and pray to God that we will yet be reunited. It appears

*that someone, perhaps the head chief, is approaching
so . . .*

"Well, I'll be damned!" a big, gray-bearded man bellowed
as he hobbled into view, lurching heavily on his crutch. "What
kind of pilgrim have we got washed up on heaven's shores!"

Dunn blinked a couple of times. What he saw approaching was a huge, rounded slab of a man dressed
in buckskins and moccasins very much like his own,
only in much better condition. The man wore a coonskin
cap and his meaty face was deeply tanned above his
gray whiskers and thickly matted chest hair. He wore a
silver and turquoise necklace and many rings on his
thick fingers in addition to an ornately beaded belt that
held a Green River knife. By that knife alone, Dunn
recognized a mountain man and explorer, probably one
who had come in search of beaver and stayed to grow
old and self-important among these peaceful Indians.

At the arrival of the old white man, the Indians came
closer to see what would happen next. Dunn pushed himself
erect. He was taller, but only because the old codger in buckskins was bent over that crutch and probably had shrunk with
age.

"Who the hell are you!" the old man demanded to know.

"William Dunn. I was attacked on the North Rim and almost
killed by the Kaibab Paiutes."

"Them's nasty devils all right. We've fought and beat 'em
a time or two, by gawd!"

"Who are *you?*"

"My name is Zack and I'm an old friend of these Havasupai
Indians. I expect they're related to some Indians off to the
west called the Hualapai that's been fighting soldiers. Or else
to the Hopi to the east."

"How did you find this place?"

"It sort of found me," Zack told him. "I'd been here once
lookin' for beaver, but there weren't none. Later, I got into a

bad fight with the Mojave Indians over near Fort Yuma. They cut an ankle tendon so I couldn't escape and tried like hell to make me their slave. Can you imagine?"

"No," Dunn said, "I cannot."

"Well, they did. But these Havasupai—who call themselves the 'people of the blue-green water' and have been warring with the Mojave for centuries—saved my rancid old bacon. I came to live with 'em. They decided that I was good medicine and let me stay."

"That's it?" Dunn asked with amazement.

"That's it. I've been here over twenty years. Married one of their women, but she died more'n ten years ago. Left me with a daughter."

Dunn heard the man's voice soften at the mention of his daughter, but then it hardened again when Zack added, ". . . and her damned grouchy old grandmother. A more contrary woman you've never seen, and I been saddled with her ever since Ouita died."

Dunn's world began to spin. "I'd better sit down."

"You feelin' poorly, huh?"

"Yeah," Dunn said, finding it hard to believe that the man would need to ask such a stupid question. The arrow was still sticking out of his arm.

"Well, lie back down on that litter and I'll have 'em carry you over to my wickiup. We'll see what we can do to patch you up."

"You must have a medicine man."

"I'm it," Zack declared. "There are a couple of us in this village, but the best one is up on the rim, and he won't come down until next spring. From the looks of you, Pilgrim, that'd be too late to save your hide."

Dunn supposed this was true. He sank to his knees and carefully rewrapped his journal before jamming it into his pouch.

"What the hell you writing, your last will and testament?" Zack wanted to know.

"A journal."

"A what?"

"I'll tell you later."

"I can't read it myself."

"It's personal anyway," Dunn breathed, feeling faint.

"Well then, never you mind. I just *won't* read the damned thing," Zack groused. The Indians pushed Dunn back down on the litter and carried him inside.

Zack's house had the shape of a plains Indian tepee, tall, with spiked poles wrapped in ratty animal skins. All the other wickiups were dome-shaped and covered with adobe packed over branches.

"I liked the Sioux way better," Zack explained, drawing his big hunting knife and raising it between them.

"What are you about to do?" Dunn asked.

"Cut open your breeches and take a look at that hip. Is it broken?"

"No, and don't you even think about cutting open my britches!"

"Well then, shuck the hell outa 'em and let me take a look. I can see that you've hurt your wrist and your nose. And there's nothing pretty about that arrow in your arm. But it's your hip I'm really worried about."

Dunn glanced through the open doorway toward the other members of the tribe who had followed and were now bent over, peering into Zack's tepee with great intentness. "How come you stayed with these people? Did you find gold down here?"

"Nope. I just like these people more'n I like our own. The Havasupai work when they have to, but they also know how to have fun."

"My name is Bill Dunn. What's your full name?"

"Zack, just like I told you. And I'm one of these people."

"Why?"

"Because I've earned their trust and respect. That's something I never had in no town nor city. Bill, do you like peyote?"

Dunn had heard bad things about the drug. "No."

"Too bad," Zack said, clucking his tongue with genuine regret. "You and me could have had some fine visions."

"My only vision is to get back to civilization."

"You're already in a civilization. A sight better than the one you been used to. Which brings me to the question—how did you wind up beached in the bottom of the canyon with an arrow in that arm?"

Dunn was not at all willing to admit publicly that he was a deserter and a coward. "I was a member of Major Powell's expedition that came all the way down the Colorado River on boats."

"Starting where?"

"The Green River."

"How many men and boats?"

"Four boats. Nine men. I got attacked by Indians while hunting up on the North Rim."

"So, how'd you escape the Paiutes?"

"Wasn't easy. I just outran them back down into the canyon."

"And what happened to all your friends?"

Dunn looked away. "They . . . they'd already gotten into the boats and lit out when the arrows started to fly."

"And they just left you!" Zack was clearly appalled.

Dunn hated the half-truth. "It was every man for himself."

"Jaysus," Zack whispered. "That's what I mean about white people. Indians wouldn't ever do that. But never mind. We need to dig that arrow out and make some good medicine. Otherwise, your arm will turn black as a beetle and you'll fever up and die."

"I won't let you cut off my arm."

"Don't worry. You'll either get well and keep your arm, or it will poison you to death. Fair enough?"

"Yes."

"Good. So let's get to diggin'."

When Dunn's leather shirt was removed, Zack tried but

could not pull out the Paiute arrowhead. "I better get some help."

"Who?"

"My daughter is up the canyon gathering wood with a few of the other women. They've pinned wilder men than you while I dug out Mojave arrows. But I can't do much about your nose."

"Never mind that. I was never handsome anyway."

"Were you beaten by the Paiutes before you escaped, or did you leap off the North Rim, bounce a couple of times, and generally rearrange your appearance?"

The old man's attempt at humor was wasted on Dunn, who replied, "It was the river. I had to swim for my life. Unfortunately, I was swept over a waterfall and down some bad rapids."

"I don't know how you ever made it across with the Colorado being so high and fast this summer."

"I got lucky when the rapids finally tossed me onto the beach like a dead fish."

Zack left and Dunn closed his eyes and dozed until the man returned with his daughter and a wrinkled old woman who had to be the grandmother. The two were slightly out of breath. Both carried large, conical woven baskets full of firewood.

"Josie," Zack said to his daughter, "this is Bill Dunn, and he needs our help."

Josie was in her teens and had large almond-shaped eyes. "Hello?" she said, glance shyly dropping away.

"She understands English?" Dunn asked, looking at Zack with surprise.

"Sure. Kids pick up things quick."

Josie was very pretty, and she had inherited her father's height. Her hair glistened with reddish highlights. Slender and graceful, she reminded Dunn of nothing so much as a young doe whose large, curious eyes mirrored a strong but gentle inner spirit.

"A real beauty, ain't she!" Zack exclaimed.

"Yes, she is."

The old woman began to cackle in her native tongue, and Zack breezed through another introduction. The woman smiled at Zack, and he saw that she was missing all her teeth. She looked very old and frail, yet her movements were as quick as those of a small bird, and her voice held an undeniable authority.

"Pleased to meet you," Dunn said to the ancient Indian.

"She's got a long name, but I call her Maud."

"Why?"

Zack grinned maliciously. "I met a Frenchman once who had a mother-in-law of the same name. He said Maud translated to mean something like 'battle-axe'—and that sure fits Maud!"

The old woman built a small fire while Zack sharpened his knife on a stone, then fanned its blade back and forth across the flames.

"Well, let's get this business over with," Zack grumbled, nodding toward his Josie and the old woman.

"Now wait a minute," Dunn objected, "I don't need anyone to hold me down."

"You might."

Dunn grabbed a stick which he intended to bite hard. "Let's get this done while you still have good light."

Zack wasted no time. Gripping the protruding and splintered arrow shaft, he cut into Dunn's bicep and then began to pry the arrowhead free, creating a fresh torrent of blood. Dunn bit hard on the stick, face rigid and pouring sweat. He didn't know how long it took the old mountain man to extract the arrowhead, but it seemed like forever.

"Got it!" Zack finally grunted in triumph. "Yep, it's Kaibab Paiute all right. I've dug out a few of these along with those of the Mojave."

Maud had a steaming, greenish poultice ready to apply to the wound. While she held it in place, Josie bandaged it with a strip of soft buckskin.

"The poultice will draw out the arrow's poison," Zack promised.

"It burns and it's causing me to bleed faster."

"Yep," Zack said, looking well satisfied with all the fresh blood. "The more you bleed, the less poison your body will have to fight off."

Josie sponged his brow; her touch was cool and compassionate. Dunn gazed into her eyes and whispered, "Thank you."

"You are welcome," she answered, her own gentle face moist with perspiration.

"Josie, get two or three flat sticks about as long as your finger's span and let's splint Bill's wrist."

"How bad is it?" Dunn asked.

"Not bad," Zack answered, "there's so much swelling that I can't tell if it's broken or not."

Dunn felt drained. He closed his eyes and let them splint his wrist. He was rolled onto his belly while Zack tugged down his britches a little and examined his hip.

"Is it broken?"

"No," the man said, grabbing Dunn's knee and pushing his leg up and down to measure its range of motion. "But it's sure black-and-blue. I saw one this bad once when a freighter got kicked by a big Missouri mule. He was lamed up for a month before he could hobble around. But you'll be walking soon enough, Bill. And you won't have to gimp around like me, either."

"Glad to hear that."

"Hungry?" Josie asked as the old woman left the tepee.

"No, just sleepy."

"Feed him anyway," Zack told his daughter. "He can sleep afterward. He's lost a lot of blood and needs to regain his strength."

Dunn was too weak to protest as he was rolled onto his back again. He dozed until Josie returned a short time later with food.

"You must eat," she insisted, then poked a wooden spoon full of beans at his battered face. "Eat."

Dunn did as the lovely half-breed girl ordered.

Eight

My Dear Miss Holloway: After not having written to you since shortly after my arrival in Havasu Canyon, I suppose that it is silly for me to take up pencil now and share my most private thoughts. I have, quite frankly, never been quite so content as in this hidden paradise. However, after this summer's harvest, I have decided that I must leave the Havasupai and return to the outside world. I do not want to become like my best friend Zack, who has shunned his past and his own kind.

My dear, there still burns in me a hunger to redeem myself in your father's eyes, even though I am quite sure that by now you are lost to another man. I have had my temptations from the young Indian girls, but have remained faithful to your shining memory. This is a good life among a good people, the best I have ever known. Zack thinks me crazy not to remain here, but I have suddenly and inexplicably become as restless as before. Because of this, I will soon be leaving these gentle people. In the event that I am killed by someone or something up on the South Rim during this next journey, I hope this journal is found. Your sweet name and address are written on the first page with a note requesting that this journal be forwarded to you for whatever value it may yet have. My guess is that you and everyone else assumes me dead, murdered by the Paiutes along with the Howland brothers.

Unless I can see you to explain in person, the world will never know the true and tragic circumstances that brought me to Havasu Canyon, a place that time mercifully has forgotten.

Your devoted admirer,
William Dunn

As he closed the pages of the journal and brushed its leather cover, Dunn recalled the circumstances that had brought him to the Havasupai. And he supposed that it was that shame that had kept him locked between these towering red rock walls, happy to live only for the day and not to think about tomorrow.

The Havasupai had accepted him just as freely as they had Zack nearly a quarter of a century before and as they had accepted a Spanish priest in an earlier time. Ashamed and isolated, Dunn had embraced the Havasupai way of life, which he had discovered was divided between this canyon and the South Rim.

Each fall, after the harvest, the Havasupai Indians dried their harvest of squash, beans, and corn on the roofs of their houses. Afterward, a stock of vital seeds for the next year's crop was hidden safely in rock and mud granaries built high up on the sides of their canyon so that it could not be lost in a flood or discovered by foraging animals. When this work was done and the cottonwood trees began to weep their yellow leaves, The People climbed out of Havasu to spend the autumn and winter on the rim, hunting and trading with their distant cousins and neighbors, the Hopi and the Hualapai.

During this cold season, they busily harvested piñon nuts and dug up the heart of the agave plant, which they roasted in stone-lined pits for several days before eating it with great relish. As the weather cooled, The People separated into small hunting families that stayed in close communication. Rabbits and mule deer were their favorite game animals, but the Havasupai were occasionally able to shoot or trap antelope and even Bighorn sheep. The Indians had learned to coat their flint arrowheads with a deadly paste of scorpion, centipede, red ant, and spider poisons. During the winters, Dunn had found that he enjoyed hunting with bow and arrow and actually had become quite respected for his skill with those native weapons.

In the spring, The People journeyed back down into their canyon and immediately set to work repairing their irrigation canals and readying their fields for the planting of corn, beans, gourds, sunflowers, and squash. Dunn judged that they had about two hundred acres of irrigated fields that yielded a bountiful crop from the dark red soil. The Havasupai used juniper sticks to dig seed holes. After the first kernel of corn was planted, another kernel was slowly chewed, then spit toward a pair of white marks on the canyon wall that symbolized the two ears of corn presented to their people by their ancestors. Prayers and offerings were given for a good harvest and the Havasupai were rarely disappointed. They worked very hard to irrigate and tend their precious crops which began maturing as early as June.

Shortly after the harvest, their friends, the Hopi from the east and the Walapai from the west, were invited by Chief Navajo into the canyon for a festival. This was the favorite time of the year and Dunn eagerly joined the Indian people in feasting and dancing. There also was much excited trading between the visitors and their hosts and the most sought after commodity were the Havasupai buckskins, prized above all others for their pale color and softness. The method that the Havasupai women used to tan such exceptional hides was a tribal secret, but Dunn had watched them long enough to know that the elements used were the animals' brains and the marrow of its spine. Mixing those two ingredients with the special blue waters of Havasu Creek gave the Havasupai buckskins their very special color and texture.

Now, the autumn harvest was almost completed once again. Dunn stood beside the blue-green water of Havasu Creek and watched as the people finished gathering the last of their beans and corn. Already, there were other tribes of Indians arriving, so that the beautiful canyon was filled with laughter.

Whenever Dunn thought about leaving The People, he recalled his foolish decision to desert the Powell Expedition. And then he would remember Seneca and Oramel Howland's terrible screams for help. In nightmarish detail, Dunn recalled how he had hidden in the rocks and then run for his worthless life—abandoning his friends as he had already abandoned the major's courageous expedition.

These sharp recollections filled him with such shame that he would flounder and sometimes even consider ending his life. Perhaps it would be better to disappear than one day to be discovered and have his story told and retold, perhaps until it reached Philadelphia. If Powell and others believed him dead at the hands of the Paiutes along with the Howland brothers, then there would be no shame to his father and his beloved Miss Holloway. But, if he were discovered alive, everyone would know he had again abandoned his responsibilities.

"Bill?"

He turned, knowing it was Josie. "Yes?"

"Are you sad again?"

He started to shake his head, but knew that she would see through the lie. "Yes, I am."

"Why are you so sad today while everyone is so happy with the harvest? Does it not bring you joy also? You worked hard beside us all summer. You should be happy, too."

"I am happy for the good harvest," he admitted. "But I miss my own people."

Clearly, Josie did not understand. "Listen," he said, wishing he could tell her the whole truth about what he had done, "I *am* happy for the good harvest and this celebration. But I need to go away very soon. This canyon is closing in on me."

"And you would never return?"

"I didn't say that."

A tear slid down Josie's cheek, reminding him again how much this young woman had come to love him despite his

best attempts to avoid a romantic entanglement that could end
only in heartbreak for Josie, as well as in anger and bitterness
for her protective father.

"What is there better for you out there?" she asked. "I
watched you writing something. Was it to that woman?"

There was so much pain in Josie's voice that he could not
bear to tell her the truth. "No," he lied. "I was just writing."

"But for what reason?"

"So that I could remember this place . . . and you."

She smiled, suddenly radiant. "Would you read your words
about me."

"Oh, come on," he hedged.

"Please. I wish that I could read, too. If you had time to
teach me, I would do that," she said, reaching for his journal
and opening it to the last entry.

Dunn stared at his words and then he pretended to read as
he made up what he thought would make Josie happy. "I have
enjoyed my time in Havasu," he began, "and have made many
friends among The People. Especially Zack and his lovely
daughter, Josie."

"You think me lovely!"

"Yes," he replied, pleased to be honest at least in this regard.
"Very lovely and very good."

Josie's eyes glistened and her fingers brushed his arm, then
came to rest on the page. "Tell me what else you wrote about
me, Bill."

"I . . . I said that you are a very hard worker and have a
very pretty smile and enjoy teasing and telling stories of your
people."

"That is true." She pointed across the canyon to a pair of
prominent rock sentinels, which Dunn knew were called
Wigleeva and were considered to be the Havasupai's guardian
spirits. "Did I tell you the story of how we came to believe
that they are our protectors?"

"No," he said, closing his journal, glad for a change of subject. "Tell me now."

"As you can see," Josie said, "the bigger one looks like a man carrying a child on his back."

"Yes, I can see that."

"And the second is the mother. Long ago, our people became too many for Havasu and so one group decided to leave and go to the east. One man, carrying his child with his wife following, was the saddest of all to leave. After they had climbed to the rim, they looked back for one last time. Their hearts—and then their bodies—were turned to stone. The people believe that, if those stone people ever fall down, it will be the end for us."

"Do you believe that?" Dunn asked.

"I don't know what to believe," she admitted. "My father does not believe those things, although he would not say so before the others. But . . . never mind."

Dunn leaned closer. "But what, Josie?"

"But I believe that, if *you* leave, *my* heart will become like a stone."

Dunn suddenly pulled back, upset by Josie's sincerity. "No, it won't."

"How would *you* know? You are like my father, all white man. You could not understand or ever believe."

Dunn changed the subject again. "Josie, I may not understand or believe in your legends, but at the same time, I don't think *you* can understand how *I* feel . . . or think."

"You have talked to my father about that other woman. Is she the reason you are leaving?"

"No," he said emphatically. "I've lost her and any chance I might have had to prove myself."

" 'Prove yourself'?" Josie frowned. "Explain that, please."

"It's hard to explain," Dunn told her. "You see, in our society, a man is expected to prove his worth."

"Why?"

Dunn ignored her question, pushing on and forming his own thoughts as he carefully chose his words. "Proving yourself is especially important when a man wants to take a wife. For

example, when a young man comes to *your* father wishing to
take you as his wife, isn't he expected to bring gifts and to
present himself well?"

"Yes," Josie replied, still looking puzzled. "But . . . but, if
he has no gifts, he can return again. Is it not this way with
other people?"

"No, it is not. If a man . . . or a woman . . . does something
so bad that he is judged unworthy . . . then he is . . . finished."

"You mean he has lost all honor?"

"Exactly. I know that other Indian people sometimes use
banishment as a form of punishment. Is that not the way of
your own people?"

"No," Josie answered, casting her eyes toward the canyon
walls. "Where could they go?"

"I have no idea," he replied. "I don't know where to go
now myself."

"That is easy! Stay with me and we will have many strong
children. It will be just like my mother and father, only I will
not die and leave you alone with Maud."

Despite himself, Dunn had to smile.

Josie reached out and took his hand. "We will be leaving
this canyon soon for another winter of hunting. We will have
a big harvest and plenty of rabbit skins so that we will be
warm against the cold."

"I would like to do that, but . . . I just don't know."

She squeezed his hand tightly. "If you stay another winter,
you would forget that other woman and think only of me."

Dunn was tempted. Josie was attractive, eager, and now of
marrying age. Dunn could hardly have ignored the longing,
admiring glances that other young men cast in her direction.
If he left Josie for even one cold season, she might marry
someone else, leaving him with even more regrets should he
decide to return and stay with the Havasupai.

"Bill?"

He pulled his attention back to her and saw the questioning

in her eyes. "Josie," he began, "I'm not exactly like your father. I'm different."

"You are sadder."

"Yes," he said, momentarily thrown off-balance. "Much sadder."

"It *is* that damned girl," Josie said with disapproval. "Again, please, what is her name?"

"Cynthia. Miss Cynthia Holloway."

Josie wrinkled her nose. "That is an *ugly* name."

Dunn was amused rather than offended by this jealous and childish response. "Josie," he promised, "I will never speak that name to you again. Miss Holloway lives only in my past. But I am a restless man and I need to leave your people."

"You will never return."

"I *will* return," he promised. "Maybe even to stay. But for whatever reason, I need to go away now."

"Maybe I will marry someone else if you go," she warned as more tears slid down her cheeks.

He placed his hands on her shoulders. "Perhaps you *should* marry someone else. There are many good men who want you for a wife."

Josie folded against his chest. "You are making a big mistake. A very big mistake!"

"I expect that I am," he told her. "But that's the pattern of my life. Anyway, I promise that I will be back."

"Maybe I go with you." She sidled up very close, so close he could feel her warmth. "I could make you very happy."

His mouth went dry with desire. The only thing Dunn knew was that, while he had lost Cynthia, he would always love her, and that was unfair to Josie.

"You know that is true, Bill."

"Yes," he said, easing her away. "I'm sure that you could, but I could never return the favor. Josie, you must find someone else who can love you in return."

Josie pulled away, scrubbing tears from her cheeks with the back of her hand. They sat in a strained silence until she finally said, "Tonight we dance the Circle Dance. Please dance with me."

"We will all dance together."

"But mostly you should dance with me," she insisted.

"Yes," he promised, watching Zack and a Hopi approach.

"I will see you tonight," Josie said as she hurried away.

"Bill," Zack said, limping over, "this is Chief Mestica of the Hopi and he speaks a little English. As you know, the Hopi and the Walapai have always been our friends."

Dunn bowed slightly to the chief, who was surprisingly young, not yet thirty. "You friend of One-arm who ride the water?" Mestica asked.

"Yes," Dunn answered, knowing at once that this man was speaking of Major Powell. "I was his friend."

"Why leave One-arm?"

"To hunt."

Mestica's black eyes flicked to Zack, who nodded. He returned his gaze to Dunn and said, "One-arm say three men killed by Paiute."

"You've actually *seen* Major Powell?"

Mestica nodded.

"Where?"

The chief pointed upriver. "He come to place where river is low below clear water."

Dunn searched his memory for such a place. "Is it above or below the marble canyons?"

Mestica shrugged, obviously not understanding.

"They're *shiny,*" Dunn explained, raising his hand and making a polishing motion toward the cliffs. "The rock glistens and is of many colors, but mostly red."

Mestica did not understand these words in English so Zack translated them until the chief spoke back in his own tongue to indicate that he had seen Powell and a new group of men encamped just above the marble canyons. The chief was describing a gentle landing with a good beach where the cliffs stood a little farther back from the big river.

"It must be just below what the major called Paria Creek," Dunn said, feeling a rush of excitement. "How many days' walk?"

Mestica understood the question and held up both hands with all ten fingers splayed.

"Ten days," Dunn whispered. "Any Paiutes?"

Mestica shook his head and pointed toward the distant North Rim. "Paiutes."

"How many men are with Powell this year?"

After Zack's translation, the Hopi chief indicated that there were at least six or seven and they had four boats.

"Zack, I'll be leaving tomorrow."

"To meet up with that Powell fella?"

"Yes."

"Well, why don't you just sit here and wait for 'em to float by?"

"Major Powell might not attempt passage all the way through the Grand Canyon again. He might do his studies from either the North or the South Rim."

"You should just stay with us since Powell and his men abandoned you to those murderin' Paiutes. Given that fact, why would you give a damn about seein' 'em?"

"The major is still my friend," Dunn said, hating his deception.

"Your friends got a real poor way of treating you," Zack said, furrowing his brow. "But never mind that now! Chief Mestica has traded me some of his special hooch for some hides. Let's get drunk and have a little farewell party."

Dunn figured he could use a drink after hearing about Powell bringing another expedition back to explore the Grand Canyon. His urge to see the fine man in the hope of trying to redeem himself suddenly became an obsession.

"I'll be leaving in the morning," he told Zack as they went to his hut and squatted down outside under the shade of a brush arbor.

"Then that's all the more reason to get good and drunk,"

Zack declared, uncovering a large crockery pot. Josie appeared from inside the hut and used a wooden dipper to fill their cups with the clear liquid.

"To your health and speedy return," Zack said, raising his cup to the setting sun.

"And to yours," Dunn said, touching cups and then tipping the liquor down his throat.

The experience was very much like swallowing molten rock. Dunn blanched and his eyes bugged. His face erupted with a cold and prickly sweat and he was glad that he was sitting down.

Zack was laughing and it was all that Dunn could do to choke, "What *is* that stuff!"

"Powerful medicine!" Zack cried, pouring them a second cup. "It's gonna make you feel about ten feet tall and stronger than a Missouri mule! Drink up, lad!"

Dunn felt a loud buzzing in his head, as if he had swallowed bees. The sunset flared, then grew so brilliant he closed his eyes. He had never felt quite so much affected by so little liquor before and he'd sampled some powerful drink. He drank another cup and the sky washed into crimson.

After that, he decided that he certainly was enjoying whatever he was drinking and that he would drink much more. Zack told mountain man stories until after dark and then the drums and music started. Josie lifted him to his feet and they danced the Circle Dance, holding hands and going around and around in dizzying circles. Zack laughed so hard his ribs ached and that seemed to amuse The People very much.

It was fun to make The People laugh and Dunn wished he could always be so funny. The firelight played tricks with their faces and he saw many things long forgotten. He remembered other fires from nights long ago when he was young and camping in the woods with friends. Now, he was dancing with Josie, who seemed as intoxicating as the liquor. The firelight turned her hair and skin to a beautiful copper. She reminded him of a mythological Greek goddess as she danced, her moist skin glistening in the firelight. When the music stopped, he pulled her out of the firelight and into the starlight. They ran toward the sound of the falling water, to the deep blue pool, and then waded into the water, hearts keeping time to the distant beat of drums.

Her flesh burned his flesh, as hot and intoxicating as Zack's liquor. He pulled her into the water and they steamed. She pulled him back to the shore and they made love as the starry heavens spun 'round and 'round. It should have been redemption, absolution, revelation, but, God forgive him, there was Miss Cynthia Holloway, circling around in his drug-fevered mind. Dunn clung to Josie, tighter and tighter, until she moaned and he lost himself in the woman and the star bursts of the Grand Canyon night.

"Wake up!"

Dunn groaned. He felt as if he had fallen off the rim of the Grand Canyon. His brain was on fire. The sun was high and, when he cocked one eye open, he saw Zack and many of The People standing around in a circle. He blinked, then realized he was naked and lying with Josie.

Dunn started. He tried to detach himself from the woman but her eyes flew open and she clasped him tightly.

"You have taken my daughter as your wife," Zack proclaimed, his thunderous voice echoing through the canyon. "It is good that you have decided to take this woman. She will make you a fine wife and bear you many handsome children."

Dunn groaned again. He rolled his head around to see all the people, who were smiling and looking very amused and happy with this arrangement.

It hurt his head to speak, but he spoke anyway. "What was *in* that liquor?"

"It was mescal," Zack said, his own eyes bloodshot, but his ruined old face triumphant. "It gives a man great things—vision, strength, passion, wisdom. I thought you needed some of each and . . . you did!"

"You tricked me."

"No!" Zack's expression hardened. "Mescal doesn't cause men to turn against their own natures! You did what you have been wanting to do for a long time. You took my daughter for your woman."

Dunn felt as if the top of his head was going to detonate. How could he possibly convince this pigheaded man that he was still haunted by the memory of his beloved Cynthia and that he never could love another. "Zack, last night was a mistake. I . . ."

Zack's hand dropped to the Green River knife he carried at his side. "You have torn the flower of this canyon away from me, Pilgrim! You had better take care what you say next."

Josie kissed Dunn's whiskery face and began to cry again. He was trapped. Wasn't it enough that he'd already ruined his own life? "Josie," he said, "I *have* to go!"

She didn't hesitate, even for an instant. "Then we will go together."

Dunn glanced up at Zack, anticipating a violent objection, but though the old coot's shoulders sagged in defeat, he dipped his chin in reluctant agreement. *So,* Dunn thought, *this is our fate—mine to take a wife whom I cannot love—hers, even worse, to take a man who is incapable of giving her love.*

"Zack, I want to talk to you alone," he said, struggling to his feet and staggering off a way.

"What the hell is it!" Zack demanded between clenched teeth.

Dunn wanted to make very sure that they understood each other. "I don't love your daughter, Zack. I never will."

"Why the hell not?"

"Because I can't forget Cynthia."

Zack actually groaned. His eyes turned wintry and then he said, "You told me that was finished."

"It is, but . . ."

"Then latch on to your only chance at happiness, you gawd-damn fool!" Zack's fingernails bit into his shoulders. "I don't know why Josie wants you and not someone else. She's as happy as I am among these people, but she's always had a curiosity about the white way. She thinks you're more exciting and interesting than all the others. I think you're just messed up in the mind."

"You're closer to the truth."

Zack released his grip and leaned so close that Dunn could taste his breath. "I don't care who's right or wrong, Bill. All I care about is that my daughter is happy. You *make* her happy or I'll kill you with my bare hands."

"She deserves more. Don't you see that?"

"Sure she does! But she wants you! It's that gawddamn simple, man!"

Dunn supposed that it was that simple. "All right," he heard himself say, "I'll make you this promise. I'll try to make her happy. I really will. I'll never raise a hand to her, and I'll treat her like a lady."

Zack opened his mouth to speak, then closed it. His blood-shot eyes were wet when he said, "Just try but, if it doesn't work out, my Josie will know when it's time to come on home . . . if we've still got a home."

"What does that mean?"

"I never told you much about this," Zack said, "but the soldiers killed off a lot of the Hualapai. Waged war on 'em and those that weren't slaughtered were driven off to some damned reservation a couple of hundred miles away on the Colorado River."

Dunn expelled a deep breath. "Why didn't you tell me this before?"

"What good would it have done?" Zack asked. "Chief Navajo and me both realize that we couldn't put up much of a fight against the United States Army. So we've kept the peace. The lucky part is that this canyon is so damned hard to get in and out of that it isn't likely that too many prospectors or ranchers would ever try to take it from The People."

"But what about up on the South Rim where we winter?"

Zack just shrugged. "I don't know," he said. "Maybe we'll have to fight for that land someday—but we'd lose and probably be killed off or rounded up and sent to a reservation just like the Hualapai."

Dunn was greatly troubled by this news. "Zack, why are you telling me this now?"

"I got my reasons," he said. "One of them being that I've felt right from the start that you might be willing to help us save our lands."

"Why, of course I would, but . . ."

"But you're running away from us," Zack interrupted.

Dunn turned away. "I'll be back before long," he finally said. "I'll be back to help these people in any way that I can."

"Your word on that?"

Dunn turned to see that his friend had extended his hand. Dunn didn't hesitate, and they shook on the pledge. "My word on it, Zack."

"That's good enough for me," the old mountain man said, looking happy again. "And, as for Josie, you'll never have to tell her if you don't want her around. She'll just know. Now, smile and act like you're the luckiest sonofabitch in the whole damned world."

Dunn squared his shoulders and forced a broad smile. Then, he trudged over to Josie and took her in his arms and kissed her mouth. It wasn't a hard thing to do. She was good and beautiful and maybe . . . in time . . . she could wash away memories of his beloved Cynthia.

Nine

It was just after daybreak and the canyon heat was already rising. Now that Dunn's brain and blood finally had been flushed of the mescal, it was time to leave so that the climb would not be so punishing as the temperatures soared.

"I want to talk to you alone before you go," Zack said, looking grim and pale. He had not stopped sipping mescal since learning of his daughter's impending departure.

Dunn accompanied the man a little way up the canyon. Zack found a flat rock and began to toss pebbles into Havasu Creek. They sat in silence for a good quarter of an hour before the old mountain man finally said in a dejected voice, "I shouldn't have given you that mescal. If I'd just left well enough alone, you'd be long gone and my daughter wouldn't be leavin'. I'm here to say that, if you want to go without her, you can."

"What would happen to Josie?" Dunn asked, surprised by this complete change in attitude.

"If you left her, there are still plenty who would take her for a wife."

"But she wouldn't be treated with as much respect," Dunn said tightly, because he knew this to be true.

Zack's big fists knotted. "Of course not. And you wouldn't ever be welcomed back. All of us would lose respect, but you the worst, for putting shame on my daughter."

Dunn stared across the water, his mind roiling like the current. "What do you *really* think I should do, Zack?"

"I'm hoping you'll leave by yourself. Josie is my world.

You know that." When Dunn said nothing, the trapper continued, "But it'd break her heart . . . and I ain't sure what it'd do to her spirit."

Dunn wasn't sure, either. Three days ago, he'd made the decision to.go find Powell and beg the man's forgiveness. Two days ago, he'd gone crazy with mescal and deflowered a young Indian maiden, then reluctantly accepted her as his wife. Now, he was being offered his freedom again.

"I'm afraid for her out in the world," Zack confessed. "Josie don't know the ways of the whites, though I've taught her English and tried to prepare her for the future. Even so, she don't realize they'll consider her a squaw and a half-breed. That she'll be looked down on by women and lusted after by men. That, if you ain't strong and willin' to lay down your life to protect her, she'll be destroyed."

Dunn realized that the man's fears were well founded.

"Are you strong and willin' enough to protect my daughter?"

"I haven't a gun or rifle. I have no money. I have nothing but my fists, my bow, and my arrows."

"I have a rifle and a gun. I've hid 'em all these years in a cave out of the weather but I've no ball nor powder, 'cause I used 'em up long ago. Rifle is a .52 caliber Sharps. Pistol is an old .36 caliber Navy Colt. They got better firearms now, but both shoot straight."

"I don't even know where I'm going after I find Major Powell," Dunn confessed. "Might go to Denver or on to California. I just don't know, Zack."

There was a long silence and then Zack said, "I got gold. Lots of gold that I've been tradin' for over the years. Figured the day might come when I'd need to buy weapons for The People so that they could at least put up a good fight against the United States Army, or the miners or the damned land-grabbin' cattlemen. I want to give you half of my gold. I'll keep trading for more."

"Oh, no," Dunn objected, "I'm not going to be paid for taking your daughter. A girl like her needs no dowry."

Zack's voice roughened. "I wouldn't be *payin'* you to take her! I'd be givin' you the gold to make things *easier* for my girl! But I'd be asking things in return."

Dunn waited and wondered how much gold the old man was talking about.

"I'd ask that you never leave my daughter to the white wolves. That you swear on your mother's grave you'll be willin' to fight and die for her. That you'll treat her kind and teach her to read and to write, and to live among your people like a lady."

Zack drew a deep breath, bloodshot eyes squinting and burning into Dunn who said, "Go on."

"That you'll give her children and . . . and that you'll bring her back to Havasu Canyon once or twice a year and not stray too far."

"Whoa," Dunn ordered. "Before we go any farther, there's something I have to tell you."

"Get it out," Zack growled, releasing his grip.

"It isn't easy to say this," Dunn hedged, "but the truth is that I lied to you about how I came to wash up half-dead beside the Colorado. What really happened is that I *deserted* Major Powell and his expedition. I led two inexperienced men up to the North Rim, heading for a Mormon settlement. Then, when the Paiutes attacked, I deserted those two men, too. I ran for my life like a coward."

"We dug a Paiute arrow out of your shoulder."

"That's right, but only because they finally caught up with me. I managed to kill a few in a rock slide but, if the major hadn't left me a boat, I'd be long dead."

"Nobody wants to die," Zack finally said. "Nobody right in the head. That weren't no battlefield up there, and you weren't in no army."

"I abandoned two inexperienced men. They were greener than pilgrims, Zack! I left them on the run."

"Against how many Indians?"

"I don't know. Fifteen, maybe."

"And what could you have done to save them?"

Dunn couldn't answer.

After a few moments, Zack cleared his throat. "Maybe you are a coward, maybe you aren't. I do know that you were smart to run. And this Powell fella? He's the jasper that stole our green squash, ain't he?"

"Yes, but . . ."

"So, he's a sorry thief and has no damn right to judge anyone."

"And that's how you really see all this?" Dunn couldn't believe what he was hearing.

"Yep. Now, are you takin' my girl, or are you leavin' Havasu Canyon alone? You heard the deal. You ain't goin' to take her back to the East, nor to Denver, California, or Santa Fe."

"What can I do for her in these parts?"

"With gold, guts, and guns, you damn sure ought to be able to find something to make yourself useful."

"I'm still going to find Major Powell."

"Then do it! But he ain't no priest in no confessional. And after you seen him, find a place within a couple of days' ride of Havasu to settle. All this South Rim country is still free for the taking. Won't be for long, though. There's army forts and settlements springin' up in this new Arizona Territory. It'll grow, and I want you and Josie to grow right along with it."

"Where's the nearest fort?"

"That'd be Fort Rock, only about a two or three days' walk to the southwest."

"I'm walking east to find the major."

"No matter because out that way you could go on to Fort Defiance. Be a lot closer, though, to double back down south and visit Fort Whipple or Fort Verde. Safer, too."

"What about crossing the Colorado River and traveling north?"

Zack wagged his chin back and forth. "You'd soon run into

them bloody Paiutes that murdered your friends or else the Mormon settlements at Kanab, St. George, and Cedar City. Take your pick."

"I've nothing against Mormons."

"Neither have I. There's a fellow named Jacob Hamblin. Nice fella, and I'd trust him with my life. But he's Mormon first and my friend second, if you follow my meaning."

"I do," Dunn said, for he had met a few Mormons and considered them very good people but clannish, probably because of all the persecution they'd endured back East before arriving in Deseret.

Zack skipped a rock across the water. "Well, Bill, what's your decision?"

Dunn stood and walked to the edge of Havasu Creek. He looked down toward the Havasupai village and he could hear the waterfalls thundering. He knew full well that he'd been quite happy during his long stay among the "people of the blue-green water" and that he really did want to come back. He also had taken a beautiful young wife. This cantankerous old mountain man was offering him an undisclosed but probably sizable amount of gold, and all that was being asked in return was that he use the gold to make a life for himself and sweet Josie somewhere within a hundred miles of this canyon paradise so that they did not lose contact with the Havasupai. Never mind that he probably never would love her with the passion he'd felt for Cynthia. Someone had once told him that there was never a love like a young man's first love. Perhaps that was true. But Cynthia Holloway was fantasy now, and Josie was his future.

"Well?" Zack demanded impatiently.

"All right," Dunn said. "You win."

"No, *you* win."

"You're right," Dunn conceded. "I'm a lucky man."

"Luckier than you realize."

There was something that Dunn needed to make clear. "I'm not doing it for your gold."

"If I thought you were, I wouldn't have offered it. Besides, your half won't come to twenty pounds."

"Pounds!" Dunn could hardly believe his ears.

"I been collectin' it a long, long time. And I do expect we'll be needing it someday to buy weapons. Who knows? Could be we can buy some peace and keep from losing this canyon." Zack winked. "Money talks."

Until now, Dunn had regarded Zack as a good man, but simple. Well, he might be simple, but the old coot was smart enough to prepare for the future. Perhaps he remembered how so many other Indian people had been annihilated or driven from their lands into exile on miserable government reservations.

"You ready to leave?" Zack asked.

"Yes," Dunn said, "but I don't know how to thank you. You saved my life, now you're giving me your daughter and a chance to make a future."

"One bullet could end it all," Zack warned. "And *never* tell anyone that I gave you the gold and that there's more hidden in this canyon."

"I swear I won't."

"If I were you, I'd forget about that one-armed squash thief and I'd look for some land to mine, log or ranch. Maybe all three."

"Is there any gold in this canyon . . . or in the Grand Canyon?"

"Not that I've been able to find," Zack told him. "What I've collected has come from trading with other Indians. The way I see it, the blessing of this canyon is that it's surrounded by nothing but sky and rock."

A short time later, Zack presented half his gold. He also gave Dunn his weapons and a last piece of advice. "First thing, you buy yourself enough ball and powder so that you can learn to become a dead shot."

"I will, and I'm already a crack rifle shot."

"Good! Then teach Josie how to shoot straight and quick.

This country is fillin' up with varmints, and I don't mean the four-legged kind. There's one other thing I want you to have."

"You've already given me more than enough."

"Here," Zack said, extending something wrapped in a fold of soft doeskin.

"What is it?"

"Call it what you want, but I believe it has strong medicine."

Dunn unwrapped a small twig figurine made in the likeness of a horse. He saw beauty in its simplicity. "Did *you* weave this?"

"It came from the ancient ones. It is my most special gift and I gave its mate to Josie years ago. This one belonged to her mother."

"I've never seen anything quite like it," Dunn marveled, holding the figurine up and examining it closely. Its creator had woven the perfect horse figure from a single split branch.

Dunn knew that he was holding something special.

"Are you sure?"

"Yep. I've always carried it with me on hunts and travels and felt protected. Besides, now that I've given this one away, I intend to poke around in some of the old Indian caves and find another or two."

"I will treasure this," Dunn promised, carefully rewrapping and placing it in his pack along with their skin water bags.

Josie came to him with their rabbit-skin blankets as well as his bow and arrows. Not wanting to drag things out and feeling the sun growing hotter by the moment, they said farewell to "the people of the blue-green water" and started following an ancient trail that led up the dry wash where Hualapai Canyon branched away from Havasu Canyon. As soon as they left the village and water, the air seemed to become heated, and they both began to perspire freely as they followed the wash deep between the high red rock walls. Where before there had been cottonwoods, wild grapes, willows, and heavy foliage, the pas-

sage now became very hot, dry, and seemingly lifeless. From
past experience, Dunn knew that the deeper you went into the
Grand Canyon or its side canyons, the hotter it became, especially farther from the water.

Hualapai Canyon was no exception. Very soon, they left the
smell and sound of the river. The plant life became such desert
plants as yucca, cactus, mesquite, and the agave—the hearts
of which The People so loved to dig up and roast.

Dunn estimated that it was about six miles from Supai to
where they had to navigate a very steep and dangerous trail
up to the South Rim. By the time they reached it, they had
consumed half their water and wanted to rest in the shade for
a few minutes.

"How are you doing?" he asked.

Josie's breathing was barely audible while he was already
puffing. "Better than you, my husband."

Dunn chuckled because it was certainly true. He had
climbed out at least a half dozen times, constantly amazed at
how easily the Havasupai hiked up this cliff while he labored.
What he wouldn't give for a horse or a mule this very moment—providing it was surefooted, because the trail became
quite narrow and dangerous.

Dunn let his eyes run back down the canyon toward Supai.
He knew that old Zack and Maud would be feeling very low
right now and missing Josie. Well, he'd bring her back for a
visit before long. And even though the heat was intensifying,
Dunn could not help but admire the harsh beauty of the terrain
they'd just hiked. As in the Grand Canyon, he saw layers of
limestone, sandstone, and shale, the softer shale forming a pale
terrace while the harder rock was usually darker and formed
a series of cliffs that steepled to the rims. Down in their canyon, the Havasupai called the stone cliffs "Red Wall" but up
here, where the geology was younger and paler, they called it
"White Cliffs." Dunn seemed to recall that Major Powell had
spoken of warm, shallow oceans forming the sandstone layers

but now they seemed to Dunn to resemble a stack of alternating corn and flour tortillas, some thick, some thin.

"Well," he said finally, "let's get this over with. Just don't run away from me, Josie."

"Never," she pledged, taking the lead, which suited him just fine.

Carrying the gold and their heavy packs and with the temperature approaching a hundred degrees before noon, they moved steadily but without hurry and stopped often to drink water. Even so, Dunn's buckskins were drenched with sweat as they hauled themselves up what would have been considered a terrifying trail by most white people.

"In the days when Maud was a girl," Josie called back, "there were places where thin ledges ended and you had to climb old ladders to reach the next ledge. But The People have made this a good, easy trail now."

"I take issue with that," Dunn said, puffing and resisting the compulsion to look down at the baking boulders which rested far, far below.

"Sure it's good," Josie told him with a quick smile. "You know that we can even ride our horses up and down this trail now. It is much better now that the old and the weak people can ride and not have to be carried."

Dunn had learned that these Indian people not only were in superb condition but also had absolutely no fear of heights. Each fall and spring, when The People relocated, he had seen children as young as five and six years old running and playing on these scary mountain paths as if they were frisky young mountain goats.

It took all morning to achieve the South Rim. When they finally stood together, tasting the hot, sage-scented wind sweeping across the Coconino Plateau, Josie took Dunn's hand and said, "It will be all right, my husband. We will make a good life up here together."

"I swear that we will. And we'll come back often to visit."

She believed him. He saw the trust in her eyes. Dunn had

no idea if Zack had told her about his cowardice, but he felt quite sure that the past did not matter to this girl. She loved and trusted him and had placed her life and fate in his hands. And rather than be troubled by this thought, it gave him confidence and determination. He pulled her close and kissed her mouth hard and she wound her arms around his neck. They stood like that, lost in time just like the canyon below.

And then they moved eastward along the rim. The empty weapons and the sacks of gold were cumbersome, but Dunn knew they were the foundation of their future. Maybe Powell would have ammunition to sell. If not, he would find someone else eager to trade ball and black powder for gold.

The first two nights, they made camp in familiar bush wickiups used by the Havasupai during the winter times. These shelters were always nestled among the piñon or in the lee of rocks where they were protected from the winter winds. They were filled with good memories but they reminded Dunn and his new wife that they had turned their backs on the Havasupai way of life for an unknown future.

It rained hard the first night. Josie was skillful in making a pallet for their bed and their fire was warm and cheery under the closely thatched roof.

"When we finally settle, I'm going to build you a cabin," he promised, "with a wooden floor and a big stove to cook on."

"What is a stove?"

He described it for her and she giggled. "Why so much trouble when I can cook on the ground?"

"It's just easier."

"I do not think so," she disagreed. "But I will try."

He held her close and they gazed into the fire, hearing the boom and thunder roll across the land. "Josie," he asked, "have you ever been among the whites?"

"No," she admitted, "but my father has told me much about them."

"None of it good, I'll wager."

When Josie did not respond, Dunn knew he had pegged it right. "We will not live in a town," he said. "I've lived away from them long enough not to want to do that again."

"I am glad. But what will you do and where will we go?"

"I'm not sure. Maybe we can do something for the major's new expedition. I do have a way with horses. I like them and have trained a few. Maybe we could mustang for a living."

"Mustang?"

"Catch and break wild horses to sell," he explained.

Josie did not seem very excited about this idea and, when he asked her why, she said, "I think wild things should be left wild."

"Then we could also buy sheep or cattle and raise them on this South Rim for selling to the army posts and to the Mormons. Hell, I don't know, Josie. Your father also suggested logging and mining, but I'm no prospector and can't tell the difference between real gold and fool's gold. And as for logging . . . well, there's mostly juniper and piñon pine in this country. There are some big trees on the North Rim, but I'm not sure if I'm willing to risk our lives up in that high Kaibab Paiute country."

"We could raise corn, squash, beans, and other things," she said. "I know how to do this."

Dunn was as cool to this suggestion as she'd been to his mustanging idea. "Darling," he said, "we'll just have to play it out and see what works. There's no money in beaver and there's no buffalo in these high deserts, so that rules out two other pursuits that I at least know something about. But don't worry, we'll do fine."

"I know that," she said, snuggling closer under their rabbit-skin blankets.

Dunn held her tight and they fell asleep together, the way it ought to be with a man and his wife. And that night, he was so tired that he didn't even dream of Cynthia.

When they awoke the next morning, the storm had blown past and the sun was shining. There was no longer any danger of being caught without water, for there were many full rock basins that would not evaporate for a good many days.

Dunn and Josie went hunting and, while he missed his first bow shot at a cottontail, her aim with a rock was truly a thing to behold. The rock struck the varmint and knocked it silly. Josie dispatched it with a second rock and they were soon gnawing on roasted rabbit. In addition to the rabbit and the food that they carried, Dunn had developed a taste for the roasted pine nuts that the Havasupai gathered each fall on this plateau to supplement their diets.

For the next few days, Dunn and Josie traveled steadily, never venturing far from the South Rim and usually walking near enough beside it to gaze into the vast canyon. At nearly every bend in the river, Dunn pointed out to his wife a site well remembered from his time with Powell, yet he marveled because everything appeared so very different from this lofty perspective. He was continually astonished at how, from an altitude of three thousand feet, formerly savage rapids and cataracts now took on the appearance of inconsequential patches of white water.

One day they chanced upon a small band of mule deer. Dunn's fingers itched to take aim with the Sharps rifle, but, lacking ball and powder, he nocked an arrow and spent the better part of an hour stalking the deer, only to watch it bound gracefully away.

Josie giggled. "You would starve out here without me. Or at least become very skinny."

"You're probably right," he admitted a little sheepishly. "But just wait until you see me in action with your father's old rifle."

Late one afternoon, their progress was stopped by an immense gorge that intersected the Grand Canyon. Josie looked up to her husband with questioning eyes.

"Have you ever seen this one before?" he asked.

"No."

"It's called the Little Colorado Gorge," Dunn explained.

"There's no way down here so we'll have to follow it eastward until we can find a crossing."

"Hopi and Navajo lands," she said, looking in that direction.

He nodded with understanding. "Well, my darlin', we might as well make camp right here. Maybe we'll find a crossing without having to walk too many miles out of our way. Don't want to wear you out and get your father or old Maud upset at me for mistreating my bride."

She favored him with a tolerant half smile that said plainer than words that she could easily outwalk and outclimb him.

That evening they built a roaring campfire overlooking the union of the two great canyons. Despite his best efforts, Dunn was seized by a fit of melancholy and nostalgia as he peered down at the exact spot where he and his fellow boatmen had enjoyed their campfire three years earlier. He recalled that Major Powell had decided to remain there for several days of rest and exploration. It nearly brought tears to Dunn's eyes to think how they had climbed up to inspect the Indian ruins and how he, Seneca, and Oramel had pressed on to the rim, where he'd managed to shoot an antelope. He remembered how incensed Oramel had been at his accidentally dropping the rifle and then heaving the carcass off the cliff so that it would not have to be carried down the treacherous path. Nothing had ever satisfied Oramel, but he hadn't deserved to be slaughtered by Paiutes.

Dunn and Josie followed the Little Colorado for two days before they finally located a crossing. Since it was late summer, the Little Colorado was nearly dry and they just waded across its languid current, straining its water and refilling their water bags before they climbed the north slope and angled back toward the South Rim. It was a long, mostly waterless detour, which left them both exhausted. By the time they reached the South Rim again, they were ready to make camp and rest for a day in the hope of finding good water and fresh meat.

As they made their camp, the sun floated low on the western

horizon. The Grand Canyon was dissolving into deep, purple shadows. It was then that Dunn happened to notice boats drifting down the Colorado River.

"No!" Dunn shouted in helpless frustration, bellowing at the top of his lungs. "Major Powell!"

But his voice was carried away by the hot, rising wind as Powell and his boats slowly disappeared around a bend.

Dunn groaned with frustration. He had missed the major, and the irony of it was that, had he remained in Havasu Canyon, he would have been present to greet this second expedition and offer them more green squash and other fresh vegetables from the Havasupai gardens. Afterward, he would have had a long, private talk with the major and cleared his conscience. Now, that opportunity was lost.

For a few moments, Dunn even considered retracing his steps, but he knew that it would be physically impossible to retrace their long and difficult Little Colorado Gorge detour, then overtake Powell's boats before they passed beyond Havasu Canyon. Besides, he would not abuse Josie in that way on the outside chance that Powell would remain a few extra days visiting her people.

Josie overtook him. "I am sorry," she said. "Do we go back now?"

"No," Dunn answered, heaving a deep sigh of regret. "The Hopi chief told me about a man named John Lee who has established a ferry crossing near the point where Powell has spent so much of the past year. Maybe Lee knows Major Powell's plans and can tell me where I can find him in the coming weeks. Most likely, he'll end up back in the Mormon settlements somewhere on the Virgin River."

"We could go there."

"I don't know," Dunn said. "The Paiutes would remember and kill me. They might kill you as well."

Josie said nothing, but he sensed that she was anxious, possibly even afraid for one of the first times in her young life.

"Don't worry," he told her before falling asleep, "I'm not going to put you in any danger."

"But I won't let you go on without me."

Dunn stroked her hair. "Let's just see what we find out when we meet this Mormon at his crossing. It's possible that the major is planning to return. If that's the case, we can make ourselves useful and wait."

"Is it so important to see this man?"

"Yes, it is."

They slept late that next morning and the sun was high when they made a little fire and Josie cooked their breakfast of piñon nuts and ground cornmeal. Perched above the huge union of two yawning canyons, they lingered until almost noon. The day was cooler, the sky a pale blue tablecloth decorated with cotton clouds. Dunn could see that the South Rim country to the east rose into an immense plateau, dense with desert pines. In the long, shimmering distances he could see great broken buttes, whose earthen colors promised to be as varied and vibrant as those exposed in the Grand Canyon by the river and the passing of centuries.

"This country is all new to you, isn't it?" he asked his wife as they walked through the day.

"Yes, this is Hopi, maybe Navajo, lands."

"Are the Navajo friends of the Havasupai?"

"Mostly friends. Sometimes in the cold season we steal their horses and sometimes they hunt on our lands."

Dunn was about to make a comment on that when a movement to the east caught his eye. He turned to catch a glimpse of horses. They were moving at a trot and, although several miles distant, he thought that the stallion was sorrel-colored and that he had about fifteen mares in his band.

"Navajo ponies?" he asked.

Josie shook her head. "Wild horses. Many wild horses in this country. Very hard to catch."

"I'll just bet they are," he said, "but I'd still like to give it a try."

She looked at him but said nothing.

Three days later, Dunn was successful in bringing down a fat buck just a few miles to the south of glistening Marble Canyon. He and Josie feasted well and smoked the roasted venison so that they could take as much of it with them as possible. The next afternoon, they pressed on again, Dunn anxious to meet Lee and learn everything he could about Major Powell's second expedition. What, Dunn kept asking himself, was that expedition's primary purpose? The Grand Canyon already had been explored and its visible archeological ruins inspected and noted on Powell's maps.

The more Dunn thought about it, the more he decided that Powell's second expedition probably would include trained scientists instead of rough adventurers like himself. They would be bent on collecting information to write up in academic and scientific publications. Dunn suspected they would be important fellows, but dry and colorless in comparison to the men of the first expedition, who had challenged a powerful and unknown river and then lived to tell the tale. Far better, Dunn thought, to have made history with a bolder breed of men.

"There's the crossing," he said, halting beside the rim to gaze down into the canyon.

They could see a huge ferryboat tied to shore but no cabin or sign of a homestead. "Well, Josie, I guess we might as well go down and see what we can find."

"It is deserted."

"Someone will return. This is said to be the only crossing in either direction for hundreds of miles."

Josie hesitated.

"Is something wrong?"

"Will there be women at that place?"

"I don't know." Dunn studied her. "Do you want there to be women?"

Josie shook her head.

"Why not?"

"Maybe you'll like one better."

Dunn pulled her close and held her tight. "My dear," he said, "you are beautiful and you are my wife. Don't worry."

"But maybe you will find a white lady to love here—one like Cynthia!"

Her words were arrows to his heart. Not trusting his voice, Dunn took her hand and they began to search for a way down to Lee's Ferry.

Ten

There was a long slanted shelf leading down to the Colorado River, and Dunn could see by the wagon tracks that it had been graded and used by emigrants. He expected that most of those who crossed here were Mormons sent by their church to homestead in the northeastern Arizona and northwestern New Mexico territories. As for the crossing itself, it was located just below a wide bend in the river where the current was slow and the water not more than ten or fifteen feet deep. By the time he and Josie reached the bank of the Colorado River, the sun had already slipped below the rim.

"I see the ferry and another boat, but I don't see a cabin," Dunn said. "I seem to recall that your father said it was located a half mile or so up the Paria River."

"I didn't know that he'd been here before."

"Maybe he hasn't," Dunn said. "Probably one of the Navajo told him."

"I have never been in a white man's house," Josie said, looking a bit apprehensive. "What is it like?"

"No two are the same," he told her. "Some are large with real wood floors, others are cabins no bigger than a small wickiup with dirt floors. Back East, there are great mansions two and three stories tall with winding staircases, but my father's house was just a little place at the edge of town."

"Did Cynthia live close by?"

"No," Dunn said with a frown. "She lived in a part of town where the houses were very big with a lot of rooms."

"Did you love any girls before Cynthia?"

"Just the usual boyhood crushes."

"What does that mean?"

"It means I took a liking to a few girls when I was young. But nothing serious. Shoot, Josie, there must have been a few boys that you liked when you were younger."

"None. The Havasu boys always teased me because I was tall and looked different."

"And what did your father do about that?"

"Nothing. He said if they made me angry, I should fight."

"Fight boys?"

Josie clenched both fists, displaying a web of pale scars crossing her knuckles. "My father showed me how."

Dunn didn't doubt her for one minute; Josie was a very strong young woman. She stood as tall as most Havasupai men and carried a lot more muscle than fat. Dunn could well imagine that she had been respected as a fist-swinging tomboy by the Indian children.

"I'll get a fire going and then let's feast on venison, squash, and beans. In the morning, we'll figure out how we're going to keep our provisions, as well as our gold and weapons, dry while crossing the river."

Before they went to bed, Dunn decided to bury half their gold for safekeeping. He and Josie chose a spot about fifty feet up the side of the canyon that was not likely ever to be washed away in a flood. They marked the spot with a big quartz rock.

"If anything bad should happen to me," he instructed his wife, "dig up this gold and take it back to your father. He'll know how to put it to use."

"Nothing will happen to you that does not happen to me."

Dunn wanted to tell her that no one ever knows his time to die. But that would have only upset Josie, so he made love to her instead and they fell asleep watching shooting stars streak over the huge canyon. They slept well that night beside the Colorado. The familiar sound of the river was a lullaby in

Dunn's ears and the high canyon walls shielded off the rising sun until midmorning. When he finally awoke, he ground the palms of his hands into his eyes and then saw Josie taking a bath.

"How's the water?"

"Feels good!"

Dunn glanced across the Colorado toward the beached ferry just to make sure that no one had arrived in the night. Then, he stripped off his pants and dived into the river. It was cool and refreshing.

"Hey!" he called, "I can swim across easy. I'll bring that boat back here and we can load up all of our things and I'll row you to the other side."

"Maybe I should swim with you," Josie said, looking anxious.

"It's all right," he assured her. "This crossing is as gentle as it looks. Be right back."

Dunn was a very good swimmer, which was one of the reasons he'd dared to join Powell's expedition. When he reached the other side, he wasted no time in dragging the boat into the water. Her name was the *Nellie Powell*.

The boat was about the same size and construction as the original *Emma Dean*, which Dunn had used to save his life from the Paiutes, then destroyed on the rocks at Separation Rapids. Now, when he took the oars, they seemed made for his hands. When he began to row, the familiar strain on his muscles reminded him of the hundreds of miles he'd pulled and portaged just three years before with the major. Dunn gritted his teeth and rowed hard, enjoying the exertion. He had no difficulty whatsoever in recrossing the Colorado.

"Let's load up," he said as soon as he beached the little vessel. "And whatever you do, hang on to our gold."

Josie did not place great importance on that treasure. "If we lose it in the river, there is always more."

Those words made Dunn realize the impossibility of trying to explain to his wife how gold brought out the very worst in white people. To most southwest Indians, gold was far less precious than the majority of pretty rocks or shells and certainly no more valuable than turquoise or silver.

When Josie was seated in the boat, Dunn pushed off, rowing hard for the opposite shore, amused by the anxious but excited expression on his wife's pretty face. Josie had never ridden in a boat before, and she was as thrilled as a child at Christmas.

"Whew! I'm out of shape for rowing," Dunn confessed when the boat finally reached the opposite shore, almost a hundred yards downriver. "Let's unload here and then we need to drag this boat back up to where I found her."

When the *Nellie Powell* was back in place, they took a few moments to inspect the huge flat-bottomed ferry. Josie was very impressed with its size. "I have never seen such a large floating thing!"

It was immense. Dunn judged it to be large enough to carry several wagons at the same time. He figured that the heavy logs needed to build such a vessel had to have been dragged down from the North Rim, and it was easy to imagine the considerable time, expense, and effort this must have required on John Lee's behalf. The ferry was also well constructed, and, since there was no cable strung across the water, Dunn supposed that it was propelled by the current itself and steered by its immense rudder. After a crossing, it would need to be dragged back upriver by a team of mules or horses, then floated back across to Lee's landing. And, because there was white water both above and below this gentle stretch of crossing, the passage would have to be done with great skill or all would be lost on the downriver rocks.

"There's the trail leading up Paria Creek," Dunn said to his wife as he started off. "I expect that's where we'll find the Lee family."

As they started up the creek, Dunn had a difficult time imagining why anyone would bring a family to this desolate place and attempt to homestead. Like the Grand Canyon itself, this canyon formed by Paria Creek was extremely inhospitable and forbidding. Never before had cliffs appeared more tortured, their pocked and scarred faces crudely raked and roweled by the ages. Paria Canyon soon narrowed to less than a quarter of a mile, locked between two-thousand-foot-high red rock cliffs already baking in the morning sun. Unlike Josie's Havasu, this canyon was fed only by a creek that meandered sluggishly through willows and a few other hardy trees.

Dunn began to perspire heavily as they followed the well-worn path up the canyon past the place where the Powell Expedition had turned back three years before. He recalled that one of their party, a fellow named Jack Sumner, had stopped, gazed disapprovingly up this canyon and announced that it was "desolate enough to suit a lovesick poet."

They'd all laughed and headed back down to the Colorado River, appreciating Sumner's apt description.

"Up there," Josie said, pointing ahead. Dunn was amazed to see the beginnings of a large fruit orchard, two log cabins, and several acres of irrigated farmland.

"Well, I'll be," he said. "Who would have thought that any-one would find such a place as this way out here?"

"I would have," Josie told him. "It's not so different from my own canyon."

"Yes," Dunn had to agree, "I expect that is so. I hope that they've got something cool to drink."

Josie fell a couple of steps behind as Dunn hailed the small, humble log cabins dwarfed by the ragged vermilion cliffs. A few moments passed and then a woman carrying an infant stepped outside, followed by two gangly boys who looked to be about ten or twelve years old and a pair of girls about seven or eight. They didn't look afraid of strangers, and the little girls actually called out and came running.

Josie visibly relaxed at the sight of the happy children and their family. The twin girls peered up at her a moment before one exclaimed, "My name is Rachel and this is my twin, Ana! What's your name?"

Josie knelt down so that she could address them at eye level. "My name is Josie Dunn and this is my husband, Bill."

The two girls curtsied and Ana, all smiles, blond hair, and freckles, said, "Pleased to meet you."

Their older brothers were named William and Ike. They were shy and a little formal, but Dunn recognized a calm strength and competency in them that belied their youth.

After introducing the boys, their mother said, "My name is Emma and this is my baby, Frances Dell. Welcome to our home here at Lonely Dell."

"Much obliged," Dunn said, introducing Josie. "We've come from Havasu Canyon where my wife's people live."

"My husband has told me of it," Emma said, unable to keep her eyes off Josie. "And it's always so nice to meet another woman out in this country. Those of us who can stand this country are few and far between."

"I saw your husband's ferry," Dunn said. "It's a fine piece of work."

"Thank you," Emma replied. "Wouldn't you like to come inside the cabin and rest? I've some cool water in the cellar and we'll have supper before long."

"We don't want to put you to any trouble," Dunn said.

"No trouble. I expect that Mr. Lee is around here someplace and will show up by suppertime. He doesn't generally miss a meal unless there's real trouble."

Emma led them inside her cabin, which was spotless. Its hard-packed dirt floor was swept, and there were bunks lining all the walls. Dunn could not imagine how a family could live in such tight confines, for the cabin's dimensions were not nearly as large as their ferry. Even so, the cramped little interior had a welcoming, orderly appearance, and they were invited to sit in two of the four handmade chairs at a long plank table.

"I hope you're hungry," Emma was saying as she poured them water. "The cow has run off again up the canyon, so all I can give you to drink is water, but . . ."

"Water is fine," Josie said, wide-eyed with curiosity as she gazed at every article and piece of furniture.

Emma bustled back to her stove, the baby in her arms sleeping peacefully. "What brings you to Lonely Dell?"

"We're just venturing about," Dunn told the woman as he realized it sounded vague and evasive.

"You should have been here last week," Emma said with a smile. "We had Major Powell's expedition camped less than a stone's throw from our cabin. He and his men stayed quite some time. They'd wintered in Kanab and are going down the river again."

"How is the major?" Dunn asked.

"Oh, he's fine!" Emma glanced over her shoulder. "Do you know him?"

Dunn took a deep breath, his eyes touching those of his wife before he answered, "Yes, we've met. He's a fine man."

"He is at that," Emma said. "Mr. Lee holds him in very high regard."

They talked until dinnertime, but John Lee did not appear. Emma didn't seem at all concerned and commented that he was "probably chasin' that darned cow or else working on the irrigation ditches."

As the afternoon wore on and the temperature climbed to well over a hundred, they moved outside, where they could sit and visit under the cottonwood trees. Emma was so glad to have visitors that she did most of the talking. She had a slight foreign accent and they learned that she, like hundreds of other Europeans, had been recruited by Mormon missionaries. Emma and a dear friend named Rachel had been converted to the Church of the Latter Day Saints and had jumped at the opportunity to come to America. For the promise to work on behalf of the Church for one year, they and over eight hundred other converts had been given free passage on the chartered sailing ship *Horizon* out of Liverpool, England. Arriving in the United States, they were then given free railroad tickets to St. Louis.

"But after that," Emma said, "we were all on our own. They pointed a thousand of us toward Deseret and gave us handcarts. But we started westward too late. We should have wintered in Iowa City, but we didn't and paid dearly for that mistake. I was with the Martin party and we lost over a hundred souls to the Lord and far more than that number lost toes, ears, noses, and fingers to the frostbite. But I was lucky and came through in good shape. I met Mr. Lee about a year later and we were married early in 1858."

"And how long have you been here?" Josie asked.

"We just came at the start of this year," Emma said. "Mr. Lee said that we could make a go of it here, but I had my doubts. As usual, though, my husband was right. It hasn't been easy building these cabins and planting an orchard and the fields, but we're going to prosper if we don't quit or something bad happens."

"Like what?"

Emma looked away quickly. "Only the Lord knows. Floods, rattlesnakes, accidents or Indians, the fever . . . or the treachery of our own kind. They can all take you quick."

Dunn glanced at Josie, but she did not look at him. Instead, she began to ask about the food and things more interesting to women. Dunn wandered up the creek, studying the fields and the lay of the land. He had lived long enough among his wife's people not to be fooled by the red soil and the aridness of the ground. The Havasupai also lived in a very deep canyon and they had proved that the soil would yield a bountiful harvest if irrigated and worked. So too, it seemed, would these few hard-won acres cleared and now planted by John Lee and his industrious family.

Dunn would have gone looking for the man, but it was too hot to go wandering about. He started to return to the Lee homestead when he noticed a woman. She was crouched down and working to dig out a fair-sized boulder with the aid of a heavy stick. Even though her dress was dirty and damp with perspiration, she was quite young and attractive. Her hair, long and with a reddish cast, fell almost to her waist. The woman was so intent on struggling to remove the boulder from the field that she did not notice him until he was only a few feet away. Looking up quickly, Dunn heard the sharp intake of her breath.

"I'm sorry," he said, "I didn't mean to startle you."

"Who are you?" she demanded, springing to her feet, hand still clutching the stout branch.

Dunn introduced himself, quite sure that this also was one of John Lee's wives. He ended up by saying, "I was kind of hoping to meet your husband, Mrs. Lee."

"I'm not one of them. My name is Kate Callahan."

"I apologize, I just thought . . ."

"You thought wrong."

"I did," he admitted. "Can I help you with that boulder?"

Kate had it in her mind to say no, but apparently changed it. "I guess so."

Dunn pulled out his hunting knife and dropped to his hands and knees. He hated to dull the blade in dirt, but he figured he could always sharpen it again, so he began to dig under the boulder until he could get a firm handhold.

"Maybe if you jam that digging stick under the other side, between us. . . ."

"All right."

Kate shoved the stick under the boulder and with a nod to signal that she was ready, they both put their backs into the effort. For the first five or six seconds, the rock didn't even budge, and Dunn figured it was a hopeless cause, but Kate showed no sign of giving up and pride wouldn't allow him to do so first, so he just kept grunting and straining. And, pretty soon, their efforts paid off because the rock moved, and then they really put the muscle to it until it popped out of the hole and rolled onto its back.

"Whew!" Kate said, sagging down to her own knees. "It would have taken me all day and then some to dig that one out."

"It's too big for either one of us to handle alone," he said, leaning back and trying to catch his breath. "But we did make a pretty fair team."

Kate gave him a funny look, and then she slapped the red dust from her hands and headed off without another word.

"Hey" he yelled, "where are you going?"

"To get a mule to drag that damned boulder out of the field, where else!" she called back to him as she disappeared into the willows.

Dunn climbed wearily to his feet. Kate Callahan was a fine-looking woman, but she sure didn't have Emma's sweet disposition. He couldn't help but wonder about her, though. She seemed so out of place here and so . . . well, angry and defiant. Not at all like Emma or the dutiful wife of a polygamist. Dunn thought maybe he ought to go after the woman and see if she needed any help catching up a mule, but he decided to hell with it. Kate hadn't even thanked him for his trouble or for dulling the finely honed blade of his Green River knife. So, feeling annoyed, he just headed back down Paria Canyon toward the Lee cabin. Kate could do the rock dragging with a mule whose hide was considerably thicker than his own.

John Lee and Kate showed up at the cabin just a little before sundown and dinnertime. Dunn watched them march across the field several arm lengths apart, and he didn't get the impression they were even speaking to one another. It didn't surprise him when he recalled how offended she'd been when he'd mistakenly called her Mrs. Lee. Dunn would liked to have asked Emma about Kate, for she was quite a mystery, but he knew better than to show any curiosity and risk seeming improper or causing Josie to be jealous. So, instead, he concentrated his attention on Mr. John Lee himself. He was a large, commanding figure in his late fifties or early sixties. His hair was mostly gray, and he sort of plodded along, but there was no mistaking his physical strength nor missing the determined jut of his jaw and those dark, piercing eyes.

"Welcome to Lonely Dell!" he called out in a hearty voice. "Welcome to my home."

"Thank you," Dunn replied, shaking the man's large, callused hand and then introducing himself and Josie to the Mormon homesteader as he explained that they had most recently come from Havasu Canyon.

"How did you come to get acquainted with the Havasupai?" Lee asked.

Dunn took a moment to clear his throat while he weighed his answer. Everyone assumed he was dead and, for the time being, maybe that was just as well. Besides, he wanted to surprise Major Powell and tender his own difficult explanation, rather than have the man learn the fate of his three deserters secondhand.

"I just sort of dropped in on the Havasupai," he said vaguely. "I found those people to be especially friendly and hospitable. They invited me to stay with them awhile. First thing I knew, I was there a couple of years. Josie and I just recently were married."

"Well, we wish you a long and happy union," Lee said, obviously meaning it. "But, to be honest, ma'am, you look more white than Indian."

Josie met his eye. "My father is a white trapper."

"Would his name be Zack?"

"That's right."

"Never had the pleasure of meeting him," Lee said, "but I've heard he's a colorful character with an appetite for Indian gold."

"That's quite a ferryboat you have there," Dunn said, changing the topic. "How come you built it so big?"

"To tell you the truth, I hadn't meant to make it half so large, but I got to working on it with a couple of my friends over at Kanab who needed to ferry a flock of sheep across the Colorado River. I expect that we'll have quite a bit of traffic at this crossing over the years and that's why we're settling in permanent."

"What kind of traffic?"

"My brothers of Zion," Lee said. "I take it you're not yet among the chosen?"

"Chosen for what?"

"Why," Lee said, "for the *real* Kingdom of God."

"No," Dunn replied, "I am not. But I hold nothing against you people or those of any religion . . . including those who believe in many gods and spirits, like the Havasupai."

"Are you just traveling through, or will you be returning to Havasu Canyon?"

"We are just poking around," Dunn told the man. "Actually, I was thinking about settling near the Grand Canyon of the Colorado."

"In this country, there are only Indians and people of my faith. No room for any others."

Dunn was thrown off-balance by Lee's words, which were certainly not meant to be encouraging. "Well," he said, looking at the man squarely, "I expected the Indians might be hostile."

Lee chose to overlook the remark. "We have had trouble with the Paiutes as well as the Navajo, but that seems to be under control for the time being."

"The North Rim Paiutes are said be very warlike."

"They can be," Lee agreed. "But we treat them fairly and we are more than willing to pay them a 'tribute' for the use of their timber and grazing lands."

"What kind of a tribute?"

"Usually sheep or cattle. Some horses. My flocks of sheep and a few head of cattle summer up in the Kaibab Paiute country. Other members of the Church also have worked hard to maintain a peaceful arrangement with the Paiutes and make good use of that excellent North Rim grazing and timber."

"I thought I heard somewhere that three of Powell's men died at the hands of those Paiutes."

Lee's brow furrowed. "I'm afraid that's the truth. I know it is because, while Powell was here, that was his sad discovery. However, the Indians he questioned said that they actually tried to *help* the three men, who were found dying of thirst. But once the three recovered, they became belligerent and there was a fight. A Paiute was killed and all three of the white men died."

Dunn clenched his teeth in order to remain silent.

"Is something wrong?" Kate Callahan asked.

"No," Dunn replied.

"It's just that . . . well, it must have been a terrible fight."

"Had to have been," Lee agreed. "From what I hear, two of the three deserters were brothers. The other was said to be quick-tempered and headstrong. Such a man, in a fit of rage or frustration, could very well precipitate a battle despite impossible odds. Wouldn't you agree?"

"I suppose."

Lee leaned in a little and pinned him with his dark, probing eyes. "Are you ready for the Kingdom of God? Are you of an open mind and heart?"

"You mean, toward becoming a Mormon?"

"Yes, because the Almighty Himself must have sent you and your wife here to learn the truth. And, as I said, all this canyon country belongs to the State of Deseret. That ferry of mine was paid for in part by my Church because we intend to colonize northern Arizona and New Mexico and bring to the Laminites the true word of the Lord."

"Well," Dunn said, choosing his words with care, "I expect that we won't be staying very long. We're just poking around."

"Are you in need of a job?"

"What kind of a job?"

"I require an honest and responsible person to tend my livestock."

"I'm no stockman, Mr. Lee."

"Are you a good rifleman?"

"I am."

"Fine! That's the most important thing. The grizzly and the wolves have been playing havoc with my flock. They killed most of the spring lambs, and I'm just trying to summer there without getting wiped out."

"Isn't there anyone protecting them?"

"I've hired a succession of stock tenders, but all of them are just farm boys trying to escape hard labor. They are good boys, but not equal to the job. They get homesick in a month or two and want to go back to Kanab, St. George, or Cedar City. But you're newlyweds, so it just occurred to me that you might even like the arrangement."

"I don't . . ."

"There's a fine mountain cabin at Jacob Lake you could use. It's plenty big enough for two and the country up there is cool and healthful. You'll find plenty of game and I'd pay you. . . ."

"No thanks," Dunn interrupted.

Lee jammed his hands into his bib overalls and hunched forward, looking intense. "Mr. Dunn, I'll be honest. I'm in a desperate fix. Sheep and cattle prices are terrible right now, but they'll be far better next spring. If you would tend and protect my livestock on the North Rim the rest of this summer and on the South Rim this winter, I would be willing to pay you very, very well when I sell them next year."

"How well?"

"Fifty dollars a month."

"No."

"All right, fifty a month and a quarter share of next spring's lamb and calf crop."

"Why don't you and your family go up there and tend them yourself, then bring them back this fall and graze them in this canyon?"

Lee shook his head, expression darkening. "I can't. You see, I've . . . I've got other projects that need my full attention."

"Sorry," Dunn said, meaning it, "but the answer is still no."

"Why not? You could more than double your wage if you can protect my interests."

"The Havasupai and the Paiutes aren't exactly on friendly terms, and I don't want to put my wife at risk."

"But she wouldn't be! As I explained earlier, we're at peace with the Paiutes. We've worked hard and always been at peace with them. They need us and our tribute as much as we need their grazing lands and timber."

"I understand, but still can't forget those three white men they killed."

"All that business has been accounted for. Those men were murdered by a renegade bunch from the north," Lee assured him. "And, if you don't believe me, you can ask Major Powell when he comes through this fall."

"He'll be coming back through the North Rim country?"

"Well," Lee said, "I *hope* that's the case. And, if he does, he knows of that cabin and will most assuredly spend at least one night there."

Dunn glanced at Josie to get her reaction to this news, but she wouldn't meet his eyes.

"Listen," Lee continued, "I swear that I wouldn't put you or your wife in danger. The Kaibab Paiutes often come to visit us right here at Lonely Dell. We consider them friends, and we treat them with respect. Now, won't you reconsider?"

Dunn wanted to say yes, but he couldn't quite bring himself to do that. The memory of what had happened to him and the Howland brothers was still too painful.

"I'll even accompany you to the cabin," Lee told him. "There's a boy there who is about to abandon his responsibilities and I *must* bring him a replacement. I'm at my wit's end."

"Then maybe you'll have to take his place."

"Like I said, I have other interests . . . wives and homesteads."

Dunn was surprised and it must have shown because Lee added, "This is too big a country for weaklings or men of limited vision. Those of our faith believe not only in the teachings of Brigham Young, but also in God and in ourselves. We have learned through years of persecution that God helps only those who help themselves. And I assure you, we *do* help ourselves."

"Well," Dunn said, "Josie and I are not of your faith. You know nothing about us."

"I disagree. Why? Because, you left the security of Havasu Canyon seeking opportunity. That tells me that you have courage and initiative. These are very rare qualities among nonbelievers who generally prefer sloth and strong spirits."

"I *like* strong spirits. Except for mescal."

"Think about my offer for a few days while you enjoy our hospitality," Lee urged. "Rest and refresh yourselves. We will have supper at six and certainly welcome your company."

"Thank you."

Kate Callahan smiled at him, green eyes flashing as she passed, carrying a very heavy sack of grain toward the cabin. Dunn automatically reached to tip his hat, then caught himself and blushed. Not sure of what else to do and suddenly feeling flustered, he snatched the bag from her hands saying, "That's too heavy for a lady."

"I'm strong. And anyway, how do you know that I'm a lady?"

The question was so surprising that Dunn was momentarily at a loss for words. But not Josie, who pushed in between them and, wrestling the sack of grain from Dunn's arms, raised her chin defiantly. "I'm strong, too!"

Kate arched her eyebrows in amusement, then turned back to the wagon for more goods, saying, "Then I guess we *all* are strong."

"Dammit, Josie!" Dunn swore, overtaking his wife and wrestling away the heavy sack. "What's got into you?"

"Nothing. What's the matter with *you!*"

Dunn saw some of the children watching them and he felt a rush of embarrassment. "Let's not quarrel in front of these people, all right?"

"Bill, you behave yourself!"

He had never known a jealous woman before. Cynthia certainly hadn't been the jealous type. But Josie was. Dunn turned on his heel and went to help unload the wagon. He passed Kate, who raised her eyebrows in question. It caused him to blush, and he looked away quickly to see Josie standing with feet planted apart, black eyes smoldering.

Dunn managed a weak smile, and then he hurried to help with the unloading.

That evening, they had a wonderful dinner, which Dunn enjoyed immensely. John Lee spoke with pride and affection of his other farms, but this isolated Colorado River crossing was his obvious favorite.

"Think about it," he said after dinner. "This is the only safe Colorado River crossing for hundreds of miles in either direction. There are going to be a lot of people fording the river here, in need of my ferry and services. I'm going to charge three dollars a wagon and two bits a head for livestock. Four bits each for horses."

Dunn thought the prices exorbitant. "And you really think they'll pay that much?"

"Of course! Right now, the river is as low as it gets because we had an extremely mild winter. Most years, even this late in the season, you can't ford the river without my ferry. What I've got here will become far more valuable than any gold mine."

Dunn found that hard to believe but saw no point in arguing.

"I owe this to my friend," Lee continued. "Jacob Hamblin and his Paiute Indian guide, Naraguts, discovered this crossing more than ten years ago and recognized its strategic importance in terms of commerce."

After their fine dinner, Lee invited him outside and they walked down to the Colorado to watch the big river roll. "There is," Lee reflected, "such peace here in this deep red canyon."

Dunn glanced sideways at him, catching an unexpected and undisguised sadness in Lee's voice. It was hard to imagine that this strong, forceful man had suffered persecution because of his religion, but this was likely the case.

"Then I take it you don't miss humanity."

"No," Lee said, "but Emma does. I settled here to make a new life, to give the Hopi and the Paiutes the gift of our faith and to provide a service and prosper and grow in all ways. I am very happy here and I think Emma and the children already have accepted their lot."

"And Kate Callahan?" Dunn asked. He waited for an explanation, but none was forthcoming. Instead, Lee abruptly changed the subject. "Have you thought more of my offer?"

"No," Dunn admitted. "I enjoyed the company of your family and the excellent dinner too much to think about the days to come."

Lee turned to him. "I watched you with your Havasu bride. You seem content."

"Content?" Dunn shrugged, for he had never thought of himself as either contented or discontented.

"I could help you find truth, happiness, and prosperity."

"But only if I join your church, right?"

Instead of taking offense, Lee smiled with tolerance. "You're very direct. I like that in a man. So I'll be equally direct. Protect my livestock until I can market them next spring and I promise that you'll find yourself a much wealthier man. By then, we will have gotten to know each other far better and we can talk about the other thing at that time."

"You're saying that I'll be under no pressure to share your beliefs or join your church?"

"That's right. We're talking business. We'll speak of larger things as time goes by. So what do you say?"

Dunn was inclined to say yes. It was true that he had gold, but he had no knowledge of how to put it to good use. Also, he could not help but like and admire this pioneering family.

"I'll speak to my wife tonight and give you an answer tomorrow."

"Good! If you agree, we'll be leaving as soon as possible for the cabin and my livestock. Every day we delay is costing me money."

Dunn understood. A short time later, after expressing their thanks for the excellent meal and company, he and Josie excused themselves and walked down to the riverside and made their bed.

"What are you going to do?" Josie asked him pointedly.

"I don't know," Dunn said, tossing pebbles into the river. "Josie, he's made me a very good offer."

"We already have gold."

"That's true, but this man has something more important than gold—he has vision. I can learn from him."

"About his religion?"

"That, too."

"And what of the Paiutes?"

"John says that the ones who attacked me and the Howland brothers were renegades from up north. He thinks that we were the ones at fault for the killings, but I'm the only one on the face of the earth who knows the truth."

"Will you tell this truth to your major?"

"You bet I will!"

"So, you want to take this man's job and live on the North Rim."

It wasn't a question, and Dunn realized he'd already made his decision. "I guess I do," he admitted, "but I won't go unless you agree."

"I will never leave you," Josie said, rolling over and pressing close to his side.

"Then it's settled," Dunn said, feeling excitement starting to build. "And I'll tell John that we'll accept his offer but that I'll need ammunition for my weapons."

"I want my own rifle."

Dunn wrapped his arms around Josie and kissed her lips.

"I think that can be arranged," he whispered, remembering and forgiving her jealous outburst toward Kate Callahan as they began to make love.

Eleven

John Lee, Dunn, and Josie departed Lonely Dell on horseback two mornings later and led three pack mules carrying ammunition and supplies. Dunn was pleased to be back in the saddle. As a boy, he'd owned horses and had soon discovered he possessed a special talent for working with them. Josie enjoyed horses but had not ridden much. Horses had never been a very important part of the lives of the "people of the blue-green water," except to pack food and household goods in and out of Havasu Canyon. Havasupai hunters preferred to stalk their game on foot, and the few horses that Dunn had seen in the canyon were domesticated mustangs, descendants of tough little horses that had escaped the Spaniards centuries earlier and then flourished in the American Southwest.

Once caught and trained, the animals had become like pets although they were expected to forage for themselves during the summer and to scavenge for their own winter feed on the South Rim. Dunn had ridden them and even demonstrated to the Havasupai a few tricks about breaking and properly training the animals, but the Indians had not been interested. To The People, horses were just beasts of burden and, in desperate times, a source of meat.

It had taken Dunn quite some time to understand this attitude toward horses because he had always thought them very special creatures. They were, he believed, the most beautiful of all animals, even the mustangs who lacked conformation and good breeding. Wild horses were often jug-headed, with crooked legs and other undesirable physical characteristics. But, while they lacked refinement, Dunn very much admired their endurance, hardiness, and ability to survive on little forage. His greatest objection to the mustang was its diminutive size; he preferred a larger riding animal. At over six feet tall, Dunn felt as if he was close to dragging his heels.

To Dunn's way of thinking, a perfect match would be to crossbreed the hardy little mustangs with Thoroughbreds. He figured such a union would produce a saddle horse possessing the mustang's endurance and ruggedness with a Thoroughbred's speed and superior size. Such a crossbred would prove to be an extremely good stock horse. And, as they rode eastward, every time that Dunn saw a band of mustangs, he envisioned that perfect match.

The country they entered after leaving the Colorado River was at first quite inhospitable, a heat-punished series of stepladder ridges dotted with scrubby piñon and juniper pine. Deeply eroded arroyos and canyons clogged with sage and heavy brush bled off the higher plateau. The vistas, however, were spectacular and once, after stopping to let their horses blow, Lee pointed toward the east and said, "They call that the Painted Desert. It's Hopi and Navajo country."

As far as the eye could see, there was a palette of desert colors, predominately reds and ochers, a vista of sand broken by crested buttes and high, tabletop mesas. Way off in the distance, Dunn could see a dark and ragged slash in the earth marking the Grand Canyon.

"How high is the North Rim?" Dunn asked.

"I'd estimate it averages seven or eight thousand feet. These piñon and juniper will soon give way to spruce and ponderosa pine, some over a hundred feet tall. A lot of my friends just call the entire plateau Buckskin Mountain because it is so thick with mule deer. They'll be migrating down to the lower grasslands in a few weeks."

"Is that a fact."

"That's right. From June to October, this country is a paradise, but winters are cold and the snow really flies. There are a lot of wild mustangs in this country and, like the deer, they trail on down toward the canyon when the snows begin to get deep."

"What about your cattle and sheep?"

"You and Josie will need to drive them out of the higher country in early October. You can usually winter up at the cabin, which you'll enjoy because it rests beside a big pond. Actually, we've named it Jacob Lake after my friend."

"And how deep does the snow get there?"

"It doesn't usually get more than five or six feet. But, if it's an especially bad winter, you'll need to drive both the cattle and the sheep down to my crossing, and we'll ferry them over to the South Rim country."

Because of the difficult terrain and constant climbing, they stopped early to make camp. A balmy desert wind pushed up from the east but, to the northwest, the silhouette of a tall pine forest stood out sharply against a crimson sunset.

They were up early and back in the saddle just after sunrise. Lee had grown quiet and Dunn could see that the man was worried about what he would find when he located his sheep and cattle.

"How long has it been since you visited your last stockman?" Dunn asked.

"About two months. Joseph promised that he'd stick it out until I found a replacement."

"Has he had any trouble with the Paiutes?" Josie asked.

"None at all. He's got orders to give them one steer and one sheep a month."

"Is that about what the other members of your church also pay in tribute?" Dunn asked.

"Some pay more, some less. Depends on how many head they run on the Indians' traditional hunting lands. Sheep and cattle compete for grass with the deer, elk, mustangs, and other wild animals. The Indians are plenty aware of that fact, and they expect just compensation."

"I see."

"The Kaibab Plateau is fine ranching country, except for the winters."

"Which animals do better, sheep or cattle?"

"Hard to say. Sheep can thrive on the lower desert land and do well enough on its grasses and brush. Sheep forage better in the high country, cattle in the mountain meadows. But, looking at it from both sides, I think it's a wash. The only real difference is that the predators take a lot bigger toll on sheep and lambs than they do on the cattle and horses. Our leader and prophet, Brigham Young, strongly recommends that his missionary families do not rely entirely on cattle, or sheep, or even farming but instead on all three. That way, if prices or sickness devastates one means of your family's livelihood, you have others to sustain you through difficult times."

They rode all morning and finally topped the immense plateau in the early afternoon. The air was much cooler and carried the sweet mix of pines and spruce that Dunn recalled having reveled in when he and the Howland brothers had finally crawled out of the Grand Canyon. They began to cross low mountain meadows, sometimes marshy and ringed by the white-barked aspen. In such places, the grass was belly deep to their horses. These meadows were awash with colorful wildflowers, most of which Dunn could identify, thanks to Major Powell and his lectures. They were riding across one such meadow when they heard the gobble of wild turkeys.

Lee carried a shotgun, but all Dunn had was Zack's big-bore rifle. Even so, he wrapped his reins around his saddlehorn and lifted the heavy weapon to his shoulder.

"You ready?" Lee asked, lifting his shotgun.

"I am," Dunn replied. "Josie, gallop up ahead and flush those turkeys out of the grass, then move out of our line of fire."

She put her heels to her mare and the animal jumped forward and went racing across the meadow, sending five turkeys skyward.

"Take your pick!" Lee shouted.

Dunn chose the largest. He wasn't too keen on killing it with a .52 caliber rifle ball, but he tracked the bird until it was well above Josie and then he fired. Seventy yards away, the huge gobbler's labored flight was halted abruptly, as if it had smashed into an invisible wall. A shower of feathers erupted as its body spun crazily back to earth. Lee fired his shotgun a moment later and a second bird plummeted into the meadow.

"Nice shooting," Lee said with admiration.

"Not so bad yourself."

"Perhaps, but I was firing a ten-gauge shotgun that puts up quite a pattern. But with a single ball, well, that was as good a shooting as I've seen in a long, long time."

Dunn appreciated the compliment. He had surprised himself, since he hadn't fired a shot in over three years and had never tested Zack's rifle. But the old man had sworn that his Sharps shot straight and he hadn't exaggerated.

They collected the birds and continued across the plateau, which looked very much like the country that Dunn and the Howland brothers had made the tragic mistake of entering. They saw plenty of mule deer and, once, a mountain lion, which Dunn, at Lee's insistence, took a wild shot at but missed.

"He was out of range," Lee said. "I shouldn't have asked you to bother. But it wasn't a complete waste of ammunition because that cat probably has taken a few of my stock, and I want him to know that he'd better beware."

"So we're close?"

"Yes," Lee said, "we could come upon Joseph and my livestock at any time now. Naturally, he has to keep them moving from meadow to meadow, so he might be just beyond the next bunch of trees, or still another twenty miles away. But we should find them soon enough."

"Did the young man have dogs?" Josie asked.

"Certainly," Lee replied. "Two out of the same litter as the pair you saw back at Lonely Dell. They're big and strong, but no match for wolves or cougars."

"Look!" Josie exclaimed. "A band of mustangs."

"I try to shoot them," Lee said, voice turning bitter. "They're multiplying too fast."

"It's a big country."

"Not as big as you'd think," Lee said, scowling with disapproval. "You see that blue-roan stallion?"

"Yes." The stallion had about twenty mares, a particularly large band. He was a magnificent animal, larger than most of the mustang stallions that Dunn had seen in this country. And now, with head weaving back and forth like the rattles of a snake, he trumpeted a challenge, then reared, pawing the air.

"Damn his hide," Lee swore. "I'll bet half of those mares belonged to me at one time. He's a clever thief. His sire was a draft animal that escaped a friend's corral over in Kanab, that's why he's so big. His dam was probably a common mustang, but you can see that he inherited the best of both parents."

"I can," Dunn said, shielding his eyes and clucking his tongue with admiration.

"Come on," Lee urged, "let's see if we can get close enough for you to shoot him with that big old hunting rifle."

Josie started to protest, but Dunn reached out and touched her hand. "We're in the livestock business now. We've got to protect our interests."

"No!"

"It's all right," Lee said. "There are plenty of his offspring to take his place in the years to come. But maybe they won't be such accomplished thieves."

Josie didn't accept that explanation, but she held her tongue.

"I've never gotten this close," Lee said after they'd cautiously advanced until they were within range of the big Sharps. "I can't believe our luck! He must be feeling especially bad today."

"He doesn't realize the range of this rifle," Dunn said, dismounting and then laying the big weapon across the top of his saddle. He took careful aim for Lee's benefit, but just before he fired, booted his horse sharply in the ankle, causing it to jump. The rifle fired and Dunn's shot was off the mark.

"Dammit!" Lee swore, then apologized to Josie as the stallion and his mustangs charged into the trees.

Josie had seen Dunn kick his saddle horse and it must have been hard for her not to smile, but she managed.

"You keep an eye out for that one," Lee ordered. "I expect you'll get him before the aspen turn, and I'll be very grateful."

"Grateful enough to give me a bonus?"

Lee stopped frowning. "Sure, he said, "but you'll have to cut me a patch of his hide for proof."

Josie and Dunn exchanged private glances, both knowing that the stallion had nothing to fear.

They rode on and on, always higher, and, while they saw plenty of dried sheep and cattle droppings, they saw nothing fresh. Finally, at dusk, they made camp in a stand of aromatic spruce and roasted one of the turkeys.

"We'll find Joseph in the morning," Lee vowed.

Dunn nodded, but he could tell that his new employer was far more worried than he cared to admit. And, were it not likely to cause Lee even more anxiety, Dunn would have asked him if it was possible that the Mormon boy had been murdered by the Paiutes. Tribute or not, Dunn had already decided that he would never completely trust them.

Early the next morning they were back in the saddle. Lee had told them that there were very few streams on this plateau besides two that ran in the bottoms of feeder canyons draining spring runoff into the Grand Canyon. There were, however, a great many marshy meadows, ponds and even a few small, alpine lakes which teemed with native trout.

"Major Powell told me that this plateau is mostly limestone and that it absorbs melting snow and falling rain like a sponge," Lee told them. "He says that it is probably riddled with underground caverns and subterranean passages, some of which open into the sides of the North Rim, creating spring waterfalls."

"Did he see many grizzly?" Dunn asked.

Lee was riding in the front, and he didn't turn as he answered. "A few, but mostly black bears. I lose most of my stock to mountain lions and wolves. Because of that, I'll give you a dollar a pelt for every one of them you kill and fifty cents each for horsehides—half price for bear cubs, wolf pups, cougar kittens, colts, and fillies. If you chance across an adult grizzly and kill it, I'll pay you twenty dollars for its pelt. So you've got plenty of incentive to keep busy shooting up here. That's why we're packing in so much extra ammunition."

Dunn was riding in single file behind Josie, and he watched her twist around and frown with disapproval. He knew that she accepted hunting as a means to survival, but Lee's proposition was an entirely different matter. Dunn figured he wasn't going to get nearly as much of a bonus as Lee expected . . . unless he wanted to lose Josie's respect.

"That's a cow up ahead!" Lee shouted, kicking his horse into a trot.

Dunn could see the cow—or what was left of her. She had been slaughtered and devoured right down to the bone. There were more dead cattle in this clearing.

"Dammit!" Lee cried, leaping from his saddle and striding over to the brittle hide stuck to whitening bones. Lee used the toe of his boot to turn the hide over, then squatted and thumbed back his hat. "She carries my brand, all right. Dunn?"

"Yeah?"

"Check the others carcasses for my Rocking J brand. I expect they're all my cattle, but I have to be sure."

Dunn gave his reins to Josie and began his inspection. It didn't take long. "They're all yours, John."

"How many in this clearing?"

"Ten, maybe fifteen."

"I'm afraid that we're going to find a lot more like these,"

Lee said, suddenly looking old. "I just hope to God young Joseph hasn't been killed or badly injured."

"You mean by Indians?"

"No!" Lee lowered his voice. "As I said, there are a lot of black bear in these parts and they can be dangerous, especially mothers with cubs. Cougars have been known to jump men, and there are a few grizzly left."

"Is that what you expect killed these cattle?"

Lee shrugged. "Grizzly will slaughter an entire herd just for sport but so will a pack of wolves. I expect I may have lost my sheep as well."

"What about the dogs?" Josie asked anxiously.

"They wouldn't leave the sheep unprotected unless they'd also been slaughtered," Lee grimly reported, climbing back onto his horse. "But it's Joseph that has me most worried. I can stand the loss of cattle and sheep, but that young man . . ."

Lee was so overwhelmed by emotion that he couldn't finish. Dunn mounted his horse and grabbed the lead rope to their pack animals. "Hang on," he told his wife, " 'cause we're about to travel a lot faster."

Lee was a good rider and had the best horse. He didn't look back as he went hunting for Joseph and whatever remained of his livestock. As the long morning passed, they discovered a trail and followed it to some more dead cattle. They found another trail, only to discover the same grisly remains. Dunn thought that the cattle had been pulled down by wolves since many of them appeared to have been hamstrung. Also, bears have a tendency to bury their kill and come back to it later but these cattle had simply been slaughtered and then left for the scavengers.

It was late in the afternoon when they finally burst over a rocky ridge. Lee sawed on his reins so violently that his horse almost squatted, then began to fight its curb bit.

"Whoa!" Lee shouted, jumping from his saddle.

When Dunn and Josie overtook the Mormon, it was easy to see why he'd pulled up so abruptly. They were on the lip of one of the canyons that fed into the Grand Canyon. Down below, there were sheep, perhaps a hundred. A dog spotted the men first and began to bark, voice echoing hollowly up and down the side canyon. A moment later, a young man crawled out from under a makeshift canopy of brush. Even at a great distance, it was clear that he was thin and weak and needed a fork-branch crutch to push himself erect.

"Joseph!" Lee shouted.

The boy managed to wave. The dog, recognizing Lee's voice, barked with excitement, then came tearing up the slope. The sheep started to bleat in bewilderment, turning this way and that as if trying to decide which way to run.

"Find a way down with our horses!" Lee shouted, tearing down the precipitous grade, falling, sliding and then jumping up and racing on. The dog jumped at him, knocking Lee flat and then licking his face, tail wagging furiously. Lee pushed it away and hurried to the canyon's floor to embrace Joseph.

Dunn expelled a deep breath and collected their horses. Turning to Josie, he said, "I guess we'd better scout a way down and find out what happened."

"I do not see a trail."

"There has to be one," Dunn said, "or the boy and those sheep wouldn't be alive."

They turned north and started to follow the big side canyon, searching for a way to reach its floor and the little stream that had kept the boy and the sheep alive. They rode nearly five miles before they discovered the place where Joseph and his dogs had led the flock down. The trail was clear but so steep that Dunn and Josie dismounted and led their animals down, not trusting their footing.

It took several difficult hours to reach the Mormon farm boy and what remained of Lee's flock. And, all the while, Dunn was expecting bad news. In that respect, at least, he wasn't disappointed.

"It was the wolves that struck first," Lee said bitterly. "And after the first couple of nights, the scent of blood and death drew in mountain lion and a grizzly. Joseph says that my dogs fought both and one was killed. He used up all his ammunition. The cattle scattered so bad he had to leave them to fend for themselves while he and this dog fled down into this canyon and tried to hide what remained of my flock."

"Didn't he even have a horse?"

"It broke its hobbles and ran away when the grizzly attacked. Joseph broke his ankle running after it."

Josie went over to the boy, who was lying on a dirty blanket. He appeared to be no more than fifteen or sixteen years old and it was obvious that he had really suffered. He had lost his hat so that his face was sunburned. His clothes were ripped by brush and he was covered with cuts and scratches. He was very thin and shaky but still in possession of all his mental faculties.

"Ma'am," he said, when she knelt at his side, "I'm a stinkin' mess. I'll mend, though. But I got a broken ankle. Anything you can do about that?"

Josie examined the ankle. It was large and swollen. Fortunately, bone had not broken flesh, so she knew that Joseph would eventually recover, although he might never walk again without limping in pain.

"What can we do?" Dunn asked his wife, for he knew that Zack had taught her a thing or two about Indian medicine and healing.

"A splint and cold water. Maybe I can find some good medicine."

"A poultice then," Dunn said, eyeing the ankle closely. "Joseph, can you wiggle your toes?"

"Not without almost passing out because it hurts so bad," Joseph said through clenched teeth. "I'm sorry, dang it! I just . . ."

"You did all that you could, Joseph. Don't give it another thought," Lee said, patting the young man on the shoulder. "I'm proud of you for saving these sheep and yourself."

A tear slid down Joseph's burned cheek and Dunn was suddenly proud of both these Mormons. Lee wasn't blaming the boy nor was he as concerned with his huge losses as he was for Joseph's welfare. Josie looked relieved and impressed. She scouted the canyon and soon returned with leaves and berries, then got a fire started and made a poultice.

"It won't be as strong as I could make for him in Havasu Canyon," she said. "But I think it will help."

It did help. They had a long, fitful night, but the swelling and discoloration in Joseph's ankle were greatly reduced the next morning.

"We need to get him out of this canyon and back to Kanab as soon as possible," Lee announced. "I figure it's about seventy miles to the northwest. We could make it in four days at the outside, if Joseph can stand up to the pain."

"I can stand up to it, sir."

"What about the flock?" Dunn asked. "We can't expect them to match that pace."

"You're right," Lee agreed, scrubbing his eyes with his knuckles. "Any ideas?"

Dunn had given the matter some thought. "Josie and I will get what's left of your flock out of this canyon even if we have to lash them in our saddles and carry them to the top. After that, we can herd them to that cabin you talked about at Jacob Lake."

"Then you'll need the dog."

"Yes. And I think there's a fair chance that we might pick up some of your cattle and more of your sheep on the way."

"Don't count on it, especially finding more sheep," Lee told him. "There are just too many predators up here for them to survive very long."

"Sometimes they will hide," Dunn said. "As we pass, they'll hear the bleating and maybe come to join up with the rest."

"Can't hurt to hope, I guess," Lee offered, "and maybe I can bring back a few men to collect what cattle of mine we can scare up. If Major Powell is still in Kanab, he might even offer to help."

"I'd sure like to see him."

"We'll see. But help or no help, I'll meet you at the Jacob Lake cabin in a few weeks—a month at the outside."

"All right," Dunn agreed. "I suggest we each take three horses, two for riding, one for packing supplies."

"Makes sense."

With that decided, they fed themselves on the second turkey and then Josie removed the hot poultices that she had kept applying all night and splinted poor Joseph's ankle.

"Sure looks a lot better," the farm boy said, mustering a tight smile. "I don't know what medicine you used, but it worked."

"Havasupai medicine," she told him. "You are a brave man."

Joseph blushed and quickly looked aside. Soon, they had him in the saddle, and Lee was leading the three horses up and out of the canyon.

"Let's just hope they aren't jumped by a cougar or attacked by another grizzly," Dunn worried aloud. "All John has is that shotgun and a pistol."

"Maybe I should give him the rifle he loaned me."

"No," Dunn decided, "we're the ones who are going to have to fight off the predators."

Josie understood. She went over to the dog. It was skin and bones and pretty chewed up, with blood matted in its long black-and-white coat. She gently hugged the animal, and it whimpered softly, then licked her arm.

"Did Mr. Lee tell his name?"

"No, but Joseph did. His name is Pepper. The one they lost was called Salt."

"Pepper," she said, stroking the animal's head. "You are a *good* dog!"

Pepper whined and flapped his tail up and down. Despite his mauled appearance, he actually seemed to smile. Dunn figured the animal weighed about eighty pounds and was no match for a cougar, grizzly, or wolf, but more than big enough to fend off coyotes or bobcats.

"Let's see if we can drive the flock up that trail," he said after Lee and Joseph were gone and the sun was well above the rim.

"And, if we can't?"

"Then we're out of a job."

Twelve

Without their valiant sheepdog, Pepper, the entire flock would have died huddled in the bottom of that canyon. Despite the animal's injuries and their own confusion and lack of experience, Pepper was tireless in driving the sheep up onto the plateau. Dunn and Josie discovered many ewes, lambs, and wethers that had been mauled or were too weak to scale the canyon's sides. In every case, they were forced either to abandon or haul these distressed animals to safety, lashed across their saddles. It was a long, long day, but they managed to get every reasonably healthy member of the flock out by sundown.

"Now what?" Josie asked, staring warily into the gathering dusk.

"Now we build a huge bonfire," Dunn said as the exhausted sheep began to bed down for the night, "and we keep a vigil for predators. If they come, we fight them off."

"I don't see how," Josie fretted. "Pepper isn't in any shape to challenge wolves or even coyotes, much less a bear."

"There's a nearly full moon," Dunn said. "My feeling is that, if we can just reach Jacob Lake cabin, which Lee told me was only about twenty miles northeast of here, we can get things under control."

"And what if we can't?" Josie asked. "What if things are just as bad when we get there?"

"Then we'll push this flock off the Kaibab Plateau and on down to the Colorado River at Lonely Dell, where there is plenty of graze. I just hope we can find some of Mr. Lee's scattered horses and cattle."

Pepper drew the flock together, then positioned himself beside them while Dunn and Josie worked, dragging timber into the clearing. Somewhere out in the gathering darkness, they both heard the scream of a mountain lion.

"We'd better keep our rifles handy," Dunn said as he started the fire and fed it tinder until the flames began to lick hungrily at the mound of deadfall.

In a short time, the fire was roaring. The flock was nervous, but first one, then others, began to bed down for the night. While Josie started a second cooking fire, Dunn picketed the horses. The horses were nervous and had not exhibited any interest in grazing.

"I expect that there's a bear or lion waiting just outside the firelight," Dunn said when Pepper began to rumble deep in his throat. "And these sheep are half-terrified and plenty spooked after the nightmare they've already survived."

"I don't know what else we can do for them," Josie fretted.

"We can kill whatever it is that wants to feed on lamb or mutton again tonight. Josie, do you see that big pine tree just over yonder?"

"Yes."

"I'm going to give you a boost up to its lower limb. I want you to take a length of rope and tie yourself in place, then . . ."

"I'm not going to do that! What if you were attacked by a mountain lion or grizzly? Or even a pack of wolves!"

"That's not likely to happen," he told her, hoping to sound confident. "Animals have an instinctive distrust of man. They'll go after our flock, not me. What you could do up in the tree is give me more warning and have a clearer line of fire."

Josie didn't like the suggestion, but she finally agreed. They finished their evening meal, and, just as the stars were beginning to appear, Dunn escorted her to the tree and cupped his hands.

"Put your foot in my hands and get ready to grab that limb when I hoist you overhead."

"I don't like any of this," she said. "My father wouldn't like it, either."

"I know, but he'd like you down here even less. Here we go!" he grunted, giving her a strong upward boost. Josie grabbed the stout lower limb of the pine and hauled herself into position. The trunk of the tree was so thick that the best she could do was to loop the rope around her waist and then around the next higher limb.

"If I doze off and fall, I'm going to hang myself," she muttered as he handed her a rifle.

"Then don't fall," he suggested, throwing more wood on the bonfire until he could see his wife very clearly. She was perhaps fifteen feet above the ground, plenty high enough to be safe from a grizzly or lion, even if he were killed.

Out in the clearing, Pepper whined softly and Dunn heard the distant howl of a timber wolf. It was mournful and eerie and caused the hairs along the back of his neck to stand up on end. *Maybe,* he thought, *we should have kept moving through the night toward whatever protection could be found at Jacob Lake.* But it was too late for second-guessing now. At the sound of the wolf, many of the sheep had clambered to their feet, heads jerking this way and that as if they could not decide which way to stampede. Pepper began to circle the flock. Dunn couldn't always see the dog, but he could hear its growling.

"Something is working in close and preparing to attack," he said to Josie. "Be ready."

She didn't reply, but Dunn heard bark scrape and knew that she was working herself into a good firing position.

Suddenly, Pepper roared, charging the edge of the trees. Dunn heard a terrible hissing and snarling. "Pepper!" he shouted.

But it was too late; the cat had attacked the dog and was probably driving it backward, although it was impossible to tell for sure in the dark. Dunn threw his rifle to his shoulder and heard the two animals fighting. Then, Pepper yelped. Knowing that the dog was going to be killed and that he could not protect the flock without a dog, Dunn fired over the pair.

The lion screeched and jumped back. Josie's rifle barked and the cat vanished into a thick stand of aspen.

Pepper was down. Josie jumped from the tree and landed running. The sheep, now on their feet and milling in panic, scattered as Josie ran to the dog. Dunn finished reloading and went to join them, fully expecting to discover that the sheepdog had been fatally mauled.

"He's still alive," Josie said.

"Here," Dunn said, shoving the heavy rifle at her and scooping Pepper up in his arms. "Let's get him over to the camp and see how bad it is."

Pepper whimpered softly. He had fresh blood on his flanks where the claws of the lion had ripped a nasty gash. One side of his face was bleeding but, otherwise, he didn't seem to have suffered any fatal injuries.

"I'll take care of him," Josie said. "You see if you can do anything to calm down the flock."

Dunn reloaded both their rifles then hurried back out to the flock. Sheep weren't exactly a mystery to him, but neither was he experienced at handling them, especially under such desperate circumstances.

"Easy, easy," he began to croon as he went around and around the flock, rifle up and ready to fire. "Easy, sheep."

The sheep didn't look a bit easy so Dunn, for want of a better idea, began to sing them "Silent Night, Holy Night." Sure, it was still summer, and he was singing a Christmas carol, but the words were familiar and soothing. Dunn had a good voice too, deep and pleasing. Cynthia had loved to hear him sing. Once, he'd even thought about taking guitar lessons so that he could really serenade his first love. But he hadn't, and now the idea seemed vain and foolish.

Each time Dunn circled the agitated flock and came back

around to the bonfire, he pitched on another big hunk of wood, sending a billowing shower of embers skyward into the limbs of the taller trees. No matter. He was not worried about starting a forest fire because the ground was damp and grass too full of moisture. The flames grew so high that Dunn could see the entire flock, standing tense and bleating with fear. Dunn could also see Josie tending Pepper. The dog was on its feet again, which was comforting. Dunn didn't believe there would be any more mountain lions coming, and probably not any wolves either, for they would have scented the dead animals left behind in the side canyon and be feasting well for the next several nights. He did worry about bears, especially grizzly, who were so ferocious that they feared nothing, not even man.

But nothing more came their way during that long, anxious night. In the morning, they broke camp and continued to Jacob Lake, with Pepper driving the flock. Across those miles, Dunn saw no sign of cattle, nor did any more sheep join up with their flock. John Lee had taken a huge financial loss.

Jacob Lake was little more than a shallow pond, but it was picturesque and surrounded by a large meadow ringed with aspen, pine, and spruce. The cabin exceeded Dunn's expectations, and he was relieved to see that it also included a small shed and two large, well-built corrals where they could pen all of their stock at night, making it far easier to ward off predators. Even without Pepper's help, they managed to drive the sheep into the corrals, which had not been used all year and were knee high in meadow grass.

"Let's water the horses and turn them in with the sheep and they'll be fine until tomorrow," Dunn said, feeling the lack of sleep.

The cabin had heavy shutters and a solid door to keep out bears. There were tins of canned food inside as well as dried fruit. It was roughly furnished with a few chairs and beds, but Dunn could see craftsmanship in the timbering and knew that a person could winter in warmth and comfort. Josie got a fire going on a little cast-iron stove and they dug into their provisions to throw together a meal.

"Tomorrow I'll shoot a mule deer," Dunn promised after they were finished and had walked outside to check out their surroundings.

"Do you expect more trouble tonight?"

"Maybe. Wouldn't hurt to build another fire between this cabin and the corrals and then tend to it."

"We've got to sleep sometime," she told him.

"I'll sleep tomorrow," he said, unable to stifle a big yawn. "If trouble comes, it'll most likely come in the night."

Josie took his hand. "Why don't you sleep for a while right now, and I'll wake you when I can't stay up any longer."

Dunn felt he ought to argue, but he was out on his feet. Josie had gotten some sleep last night after Pepper's fight. The pair of them had slept side by side until dawn. So Dunn guessed he had better get some sleep of his own before he collapsed. Either that, or he'd become so bleary-eyed that he wouldn't be able to defend the flock or his wife.

"First, I'll help you get a bonfire started in the yard," he told her, spying a fallen pine that was in a state of advanced decay.

Dunn was so exhausted that every movement was an effort, but he forced himself to haul wood until daylight gave out, and then he allowed himself some badly needed rest. He collapsed on one of the blankets that they'd found in the cabin and, the next thing he knew, the sun was peeking over the tallest pines and the meadow was sparkling with dewy diamonds.

"You slept like a baby," Josie told him.

He knuckled his eyes and gazed around. "I guess I did at that. You must be half-dead after sitting up all night."

"I fell asleep beside you," she admitted. "I woke up only a little while ago."

Dunn climbed to his feet. After all the previous day's exertions, he was stiff but much clearer-headed thanks to a good night's sleep.

"What are we going to do now?" Josie asked, turning toward the corrals full of bleating sheep.

"They need to be watered and fed," Dunn said. "I expect we ought to keep at least one of the horses saddled and bridled, just in case."

"In case of what?"

Dunn realized he was still worrying about the Paiutes as much as any predators. He didn't want to admit that, so he just said, "In case we need them in a hurry."

She raised her eyebrows in question, but he ignored her and looked away, pretending to be preoccupied with other thoughts. "I'll saddle one and tie it beside the cabin. The other two can wear hobbles so they can graze with the sheep."

"I think we ought to keep *two* horses saddled and bridled," Josie argued. "The third can always be hobbled and grazing. That way, if renegade Paiutes came, we'd *both* have a chance of escaping."

They tied a pair of horses to aspen near the cabin door, then hobbled and turned the third horse out to graze. When Dunn opened the corral gate to let the sheep out, they didn't seem to want to move. They only bleated and stared at him with deep-seated suspicion.

"What else can I do for you?" he asked, planting a foot on the lower rail of their corral.

The sheep had something on their minds, but Dunn couldn't figure it out, so he sent Pepper into the corral. As he'd expected, the presence of the growling dog got the sheep moving. In fact, they almost ran Dunn over in their haste to escape from Pepper.

Pepper was limping and in pain, but he was all business when it came to the flock. Head low and moving fast, he made a quick circle around the meadow, then chose a place and sat down, eyes riveted on the sheep. After a tense ten minutes, the flock decided that they could graze on the fresh meadow grass.

Dunn kept watch, too. He had his rifle and it was powerful enough to stop a grizzly or any other wild thing that came searching for an easy meal.

"How are they?" Josie asked, coming up and sitting down beside him on a fallen aspen. Dunn noted with approval that she not only carried her own rifle but also the six-shot pistol that she had gotten on loan from John Lee.

Dunn slipped his arm around Josie's waist and pulled her close. "I could enjoy being in the sheep business with you, darling. The way I see things, we've got plenty of food, a good cabin, plenty of time to relax, and I couldn't ask for more beautiful country . . . or company."

Josie flushed with pleasure. "I hope it's a long time before John Lee returns from Kanab."

"So do I."

The next thing Dunn knew, they were slipping off the log and rolling playfully about in the sweet-smelling meadow grass. Dunn really hadn't been thinking about making love but, with Josie squirming and giggling in his arms, and with the warm sun shining brightly through the forest trees, it seemed like the natural thing to do.

Afterward, she held him tight and said, "What would you like more, a boy or a girl?"

He sat up fast. "Are you with child?"

"I think so."

"Holy Moses!" Dunn gulped. "You can tell *that* fast?"

"No, stupid," she said, throwing her head back and laughing at the sky. "Of course not. It happened awhile ago. Maybe as far back as the night you rowed me across the Colorado."

"Are you sure?"

"I am changing inside. What do you think?"

He took a deep breath. "Well, Josie," he began, "I just haven't hardly had time to get used to the idea yet. But I will, and I don't care if it is a boy or a girl."

"I want a girl. You should want a boy."

He threw his hands up and let them fall. Josie couldn't help but find him amusing. And while she'd hoped he would be extremely happy, she knew that he really had been caught by surprise. Maybe, she thought, she should have waited awhile and let him come to realize it as she filled with their child.

"I'm very happy," he told her. "I expect that, if the child is a boy, he will be tall, dumb, and ugly like me or, if it's a girl, smart and pretty like you."

"You say that but you know you're smart and handsome."

Dunn fell back into the grass, reaching for her. "Whatever you say," he told her as their lips met again.

In the following days and weeks that passed, they slept outside and kept a good fire going to ward off predators. One night they were visited by a grizzly. After hearing it growling and rattling the corral poles, Dunn ran out and fired at the beast's silhouette. He must have struck it with a ball because the animal roared and went lumbering off, with Pepper snapping and growling from a safe and respectful distance. The next morning, Dunn found a trail of blood and, that afternoon, he saw circling buzzards several miles away and knew he'd killed the bear.

Autumn arrived, wearing a mantle of rainbow colors. Crimson and gold leaves curled on their branches, then took flight, swirling and dancing with the wind. Every few days, Dunn and Josie relocated the flock to a new meadow and they both took satisfaction in watching the playful lambs grow.

"We don't really know much about what we are doing," Dunn said one blustery afternoon, "but I suspect that John Lee will approve when he finally returns."

Josie was about to say something when Pepper began to bark. They looked up and saw nine Indians standing at the edge of the forest, watching. Dunn felt a shiver pass through his body. "They're Kaibab Paiutes," he told his wife as he tightened his grip on his rifle and tried to recognize some of the Indians who had killed the Howland brothers. But everything had happened so fast that terrible dawn that he'd never really had a good look at any of their faces. He just prayed that, if any of these were the same murdering Indians, they did not recognize him either.

Josie looked up at him, asking herself the same silent question.

"I don't think this is the same bunch," Dunn whispered. "But I could be wrong. If we're lucky, they're just here to collect their 'tribute.' "

"And if we're not lucky?"

"They'll want everything," he said, not wishing to elaborate.

The Indians were dressed in a curious mixture of rabbit skins, buckskins, and white man's clothing. Some wore boots, others moccasins. All were armed, most with bows and arrows, but a few had old muskets and Indian trade rifles.

The Paiutes raised their right hands, palm out in greeting. Dunn did the same, whispering, "Josie, I want you to mount up and stand ready to run in case of trouble."

"I'd never leave you!"

"All right then, get *both* horses ready," he said, "and take them around behind the cabin. If they have bad intentions or one of them remembers me from three years ago, we'll have to run because there are too many to fight."

Josie untied the saddle horses and quickly led them around behind the cabin. Dunn kept his eyes on the Paiutes and his hands on his rifle. Lee's assurances notwithstanding, he figured he would never trust Paiutes after the North Rim killings.

These Paiutes were in no hurry. They ignored Pepper's commotion and studied the flock, pointing out, Dunn supposed, the merits of this sheep and that. When at last they came around the flock toward the cabin, Dunn forced a smile and tried to look pleased by their unexpected company.

"Hello," he said, nodding respectfully.

The Indians studied him for several minutes before one

started to go around him toward the cabin but Dunn shifted sideways, blocking his path. "Do you want sheep to eat?"

The Indian was short and powerful. He wore a blank expression as he studied Dunn from head to toe. Dunn felt his flesh begin to crawl. This man seemed to recognize him. He stepped back and spoke to his companion, once gesturing to the west and making angry signs. Dunn was sure that the end was near and he lifted his rifle a few inches, finger caressing the trigger. At least, he thought, if a fight started, Josie and their unborn child might still escape.

But one of the older Paiutes kept shaking his head and they began to argue. Dunn waited, feet planted solidly and sweat trickling down his spine until the leader's arguments won out and the man finally turned to Dunn and surprised him by saying, "No cattle?"

"No cattle," Dunn breathed.

The Indian made a face to express his extreme displeasure. Dunn shrugged, hoping to indicate that the matter was entirely beyond his control.

The Paiute's spokesman turned to his companions and they began arguing again. Dunn couldn't understand a word of what they were talking about but supposed there was some disagreement among them concerning the number of sheep they would demand and whether he was the one who had escaped the North Rim three years before after killing several of their warriors. After what seemed an eternity, the Paiute's spokesman grunted, "Where cattle and John Lee?"

"Cattle dead. John Lee is in Kanab. Here soon."

The Indian understood him perfectly and relayed the message to his friends, which created another round of negotiations. Finally, the spokesman turned around and held up both hands, with all ten of his fingers splayed. "This many sheep."

"No," Dunn said, shaking his head vigorously and holding up two fingers.

The Indians reacted with shock and outrage. Dunn shrugged with indifference although his palms leaked sweat and his heart raced. The Indians didn't appear to notice. Their discussion continued for nearly an hour before they began to negotiate again. After what seemed an eternity, the Paiutes and Dunn agreed that the Indians could choose any four sheep.

They slaughtered one big ram and hurriedly butchered it within sight of the flock. They burned meat and gorged on it half-raw, enjoying themselves very much while Dunn and Josie kept a nervous watch from their cabin and corrals. The next morning, however, the Paiutes and their three unfortunate sheep were gone and an uneasy watchfulness returned to Jacob Lake.

"I still don't feel very safe," Dunn said that afternoon. "I think one of them recognized me."

"We'll just hope you're wrong," Josie said. "Anyway, they easily could have slipped into the corrals and gotten a few more head last night before departing, but they didn't."

"Pepper would have had something to say if they'd tried."

Josie had her own reservations. The Indians had watched her closely and Josie had felt their palpable dislike for her. They did not know if she was part Navajo, Hopi, or some other Indian people, but they knew she was not Paiute and, therefore, not to be trusted.

Several days later, John Lee arrived, accompanied by a tall, gawky man in his mid-forties. He was balding, wore a pair of wire-rimmed spectacles on a string around his thin, sunburned neck, and his coat was stuffed with a ruler, writing pads, pencils, and some bleached bones. He had great bushy eyebrows and sideburns, sunken cheeks, and an owlish expression, as if he were either very wise or frozen in a constant state of wonder and amazement. His smile was fleeting, but his eyes were warm and of the palest shade of blue.

"I am most pleased to meet you," the man said, his huge, bony hand reeling out at the end of an enormously long arm. "And I hope that I pose no great inconvenience."

"This is Dr. Walter Sutherland," Lee said. "Professor Sutherland is an archeologist who, like Major Powell, has a keen interest in geology. The professor was chosen by the academy of science to work with Major Powell but missed him by only a few days."

"It was all my fault," Sutherland admitted, shrugging his wide rack of shoulders. "I tarried too long in Wyoming, digging for . . . well, never mind that. I'm afraid I've really botched things up and have no one to blame but myself."

The man looked so repentant that Dunn found himself making excuses. "Well, Dr. Sutherland . . ."

"Walt," the scientist corrected. "First names, please."

"All right. This is my wife, Josie."

Sutherland had been trying to keep his eyes off Josie right from the start, but now he blushed like a schoolboy when Josie extended her hand and they were introduced. All the professor could do was shift his feet nervously and whisper, "Pleased to make your acquaintance."

"What happened to Major Powell?" Dunn asked, trying to hide his own disappointment.

"He'd already left Kanab for Salt Lake City and then he was going back to Washington to present his new survey reports," Sutherland explained. "It was terrible of me to miss him that way."

"Didn't he know you were coming?"

"I sent a telegram to Green River with instructions that it be forwarded as soon as possible to either Lonely Dell or Kanab. But the message was lost somehow, and Major Powell had no idea I was being sent."

Dunn could see that the archeologist was even more disappointed than he to have missed Powell.

"Dr. Sutherland wishes to remain in this canyon country and do as much work as possible. I have offered to help him and suggested that he might even wish to stay here at the cabin a few days in order to search for relics."

"I've already found a few interesting bones!" the professor exclaimed, reaching for the ones in his pockets.

"It's your cabin," Dunn said, not interested in old bones. "I'm sure that the four of us will get along just fine."

"I have to return immediately to Lonely Dell and take care of my family."

"But . . ."

"Please," Lee said, cutting off his protest, "something has come up. I must see my family at once."

"Trouble?"

Lee shook his head but now that Dunn really looked at the man, he could see that the Mormon had dark circles under his eyes and appeared upset and anxious. Dunn figured he must have had a very difficult time getting young Joseph to Kanab and then on to a doctor.

"What's left of my flock," Lee was saying, "looks very healthy."

"We've lost only a few to sickness," Dunn said, "not a one to the predators. The Indians took four the day before yesterday."

"Yes," Lee said, "I know. We met them and I had no choice but to eat raw mutton."

"How is the young man?" Josie asked.

"Joseph is recovering," Lee assured them. "He's on his way to Salt Lake City to see a doctor, but indications are that the ankle is healing nicely. Josie, he is in your debt."

"I was glad to help."

"Now," Lee said, "let's settle in for the night and then I've got to get an early start."

"What are we supposed to do with the flock after you leave?" Dunn asked.

"Keep up the good work. The Paiutes are all predicting a bad winter, so I've decided that you should bring the sheep down to the Colorado River in a few weeks. We can winter them there and not risk heavy winter losses."

"Are you still planning to sell them next spring?"

"Yes, definitely." Lee shook his head and he suddenly looked quite old. "I'm finished with livestock other than what

I need for my own family. It's a highly risky business in this wild country, and I'll not take the responsibility for another young sheepherder almost getting killed."

"Perhaps I will buy them," Dunn said, voicing what he had expressed only a few days earlier to Josie.

Lee was quite surprised. "You?"

"That's right." Dunn could tell that this man assumed him to be almost penniless. He was not offended, but neither was he about to reveal that he was anything but poor, thanks to Zack's generosity and his Havasupai gold.

"Well," Lee mused. "If you were in a position to buy the flock, I should be happy to sell them to you."

"At what price?"

Lee turned and measured his flock. "What is the exact count?"

"One hundred and twenty-four. Two-thirds of them are ewes, but some are too old to breed and had no lambs last spring. There are fifteen rams and the rest are wethers and spring lambs."

"They are well bred and in good condition."

"Thanks to us," Dunn said, smiling at Josie, "and to Pepper, who would have to be included in their sale."

"Let me sleep on it and give you a figure in the morning," Lee finally decided. "And you have cash?"

"Even better," Dunn told the Mormon. "I have gold."

"Then I'm sure that we can come up with some agreement."

"Yes," Dunn said, expecting that Lee was going to want to dicker every bit as much as the Paiutes. "And while you're figuring, I'm going to want to use this North Rim country for summer pasture."

"I'm afraid that it's not mine to offer."

"I know that," Dunn said. "It belongs to the Kaibab Paiutes. But you can still inform everyone—including your own people—that I have your *permission* to summer my flock on this North Rim plateau. Otherwise, I've got a flock and no place to fatten them next summer."

"I can't give you permission to use this North Rim under any circumstances," Lee said. "It is claimed."

"In what way?"

Lee's voice took on an edge. "I think that I might as well be candid. This country is simply spoken for by the members of my church. However, a nonbeliever might find peace and prosperity over on the South Rim."

"Excuse me," Sutherland said, looking very uncomfortable with the way this conversation was going. "I'll just have a look around."

Dunn waited until the man was out of hearing, then he turned to Lee and said, "We both know that the South Rim is far more arid with less grass than this higher country."

"Yes, but much safer and with far milder winters," Lee explained. "It's excellent sheep or cattle country, and it's still ripe for the taking. Even telling you that much could get me into more trouble than I am in already."

Dunn didn't understand, but he did believe. Something was very wrong with Mr. Lee. He was obviously caught in some difficulty which he could not speak of and that troubled Dunn as much as it piqued his curiosity.

"All right," Dunn said, "then I'll take your sheep over to the South Rim. It's closer to Josie's people anyway."

Lee did not attempt to hide his relief. "That's a very, very wise decision. As I said, the winters up here are terrible and the Paiutes can be unpredictable. You would do well to use my ferry to get this flock across the Colorado and then move them to the far rim."

And not antagonize your church leaders, Dunn thought to himself.

"Fine," Dunn said. "I'll pay you a fair price. Josie and I are expecting a child and we have to prepare for the future."

Lee managed a smile. "Congratulations to you both," he offered.

"Thank you," Dunn said, not liking himself for what he said

next. "And any agreement we reach will, of course, be in writing."

"Of course. Just bring the flock to Lonely Dell and then we'll come to final terms."

"All right," Dunn agreed. "We'll leave tomorrow. But what about Professor Sutherland?"

Lee glanced over at the scientist, who had gone off on the pretext of exploration. "I'd forgotten about him momentarily. Could you possibly remain here just a few more days? The grass is still good, and it's too early for snow. It will take you only three or four days to drive them down to the river."

Dunn didn't mind, and he knew that Josie wouldn't either. Besides, it would give him a chance to learn a few things from the professor, maybe even about Major Powell's accomplishments in the past three years.

"Very well."

"I'll give you a good price," Lee promised. "But first I need to talk to Emma and get some things settled at home."

"Of course."

Lee marched off, leaving Dunn wondering why the man was so agitated. Perhaps, Dunn thought, their former shepherd boy was in far worse condition than John Lee cared to admit.

Thirteen

John Lee was up before dawn and Dunn was waiting to say good-bye and receive instructions concerning the welfare of the flock. The two men stood in the semidarkness and watched a thin, silvery thread of sunlight begin to seep into the eastern horizon, revealing storm clouds. Dunn was sure that rain was coming this day; he could hear the distant rumble of thunder. Beside him, Lee stood with his hands stuffed deep in his coat pockets, wearing a sad and pensive expression.

"What is wrong?" Dunn finally asked. "Is there something you're not telling us about the health of your young shepherd?"

"No," Lee said, "Joseph will be just fine."

"Then have I said or done something to offend you?"

"Heavens, no!" Lee exclaimed. "You and Josie have done just fine. You saved the flock and I'll take that into account when I sell them to you."

"Then what is troubling you?"

"It's that obvious, huh?"

"Yes."

Lee inhaled deeply of the pine-scented forest. "I love this high North Rim country. The winters here are difficult and my wives and children would dislike the cold and snow, but I may soon relocate up here to this cabin. Perhaps I'll go into logging."

"But you talked with such optimism about the ferry crossing and the role that it would play in the growth of northern Arizona."

"Why can't a man change his mind?"

"He can, but how would you begin to log this country? Who would buy this timber and wouldn't it cost a fortune to harvest and haul to St. George or even Kanab?"

"Yes," Lee quietly admitted, "it would."

"Then why abandon the crossing?"

When Lee did not answer, Dunn continued, "I've listened well to you and learned a great many things about business and commerce which ought to help me to make my own mark in this canyon country. To be honest, you changing course in mid-stream seems entirely out of character."

Lee managed a thin smile. " 'Out of character,' you say? Well, I may not possess the kind of character that you imagine."

Dunn's confusion intensified. This was a very, very different man from the one who had greeted him at Lonely Dell and whose kind hospitality had been so freely given.

Lee cleared his throat. "Bill," he began, "since the flock is a very mixed lot and a number of the ewes are too old for breeding, I'll sell the adults to you for a flat one dollar a head. You can have the lambs for fifty cents."

Dunn wasn't up on prices, but he was quite certain that the Mormon elder's price was extremely fair. Dunn figured he could buy the entire flock and still keep most of his gold for other investments.

"Well?" Lee asked.

"That would be acceptable."

"Good! I'll have a signed bill of sale waiting at Lonely Dell. If I'm absent when you bring the flock down, you can make your final count and pay my eldest wife Emma in gold."

"Fine," Dunn said, "but where would you be?"

Lee started to speak, then seemed to change his mind. "Good-bye, Bill. I know nothing about your past, but that doesn't matter. You're an honorable man and everyone has a skeleton or two hiding in his closet."

"Are you in trouble?" Dunn blurted, impulsively reaching out to stop the Mormon from walking away.

"Nothing to concern yourself with," Lee said, removing Dunn's hand and then going to saddle his horse.

Without even looking back to wave or say good-bye, Lee swung into the saddle and disappeared into the forest. Something was very wrong, Dunn knew, and he wished he could help because he genuinely liked and admired John Lee. Perhaps some difficulty or conflict had arisen in Kanab between Lee and his church. What other possible explanation could there be for his dramatic change in outlook?

Dunn walked out to the corrals, with Pepper limping along behind. Together they circled the pens, searching for bear, lion, or wolf tracks but did not find any. The sound of thunder was louder now and the flock was on its feet, anxiously milling about in the corral. Dunn briefly considered hurrying after Lee to ask if it would be better to keep the flock penned until the storm passed, but it would be difficult to overtake him. Dunn decided to leave the flock in the pen. Autumn mountain storms rarely lasted more than a day or two. The last thing Dunn needed was to endanger the flock or have them scattered over mountain and meadow by thunder and lightning.

"Looks like we could get quite a drenching," a voice said from behind him.

Dunn turned to see Dr. Sutherland standing a few feet away. The man was smoking a pipe, and now, as he cupped a match, his pale blue eyes squinted behind his thick spectacles.

"Yes," Dunn said. "I think so."

"It's a shame that Mr. Lee had to leave us so soon."

"He's got a long ride back, and it's definitely going to storm."

Sutherland puffed in silence for a moment, then commented, "I am afraid that Mr. Lee might have a number of storms to face."

Dunn regarded the archeologist warily. "What does that mean?"

"I probably shouldn't say anything."

"You already have. Let's hear the rest of it."

Sutherland expelled a deep breath. "Well," he said quietly, "I fear that our friend is in very serious trouble with his church and the authorities."

"What makes you think so?"

"When I was in Kanab, I could see that everyone was quite upset, but none so much as Mr. Lee. I am an outsider, and I had no wish to hear gossip, but I couldn't help but notice that Lee was in serious difficulty. I offered my condolences, but that seemed to upset him even more. I'd like to help in some way, but I couldn't help overhearing Mr. Lee's name associated with the federal authorities."

"We both know that our friend John Lee is a fine, honorable man," Dunn said. "So why don't we go back inside, have some breakfast, and you can tell me the purpose of Major Powell's second Colorado expedition."

Sutherland nodded in agreement. He knocked ashes from the bowl of his pipe and asked, "Are you familiar with Major Powell's first trip down the Colorado River?"

Dunn chose his words carefully. "I've heard about it, yes. His journals have been widely published and read. Why did he undertake a second expedition?"

Before Professor Sutherland could reply, a tremendous clap of thunder shook the earth, and Dunn felt the first cold slap of rain. The professor glanced anxiously at the sky and then hurried toward the cabin, with Dunn following right behind. Only Pepper, their saddle horses, and the flock remained as the wind strengthened before the onrushing storm.

A pelting rain soon began to lash the Kaibab Plateau. Dunn wished that he had barns to protect the sheep, but he figured they'd just have to tough things out. There wasn't much they could do but sit and visit, so Dunn and Josie fed the stove until it glowed and banged with heat, then sat back to talk with their new guest.

"I met Major Powell two years ago," Sutherland began when they were seated at the table. "His extraordinary account of his journey made him a highly popular and energetic speaker—and one I still envy. I would give anything to possess his charm, courage, and skill as a speaker."

"It took some courage to come out here by yourself," Dunn pointed out.

"Thank you," Sutherland said, blushing a little. "But despite Major Powell's great success on the Colorado, there were a few jealous academics who felt that his scientific observations and mathematical calculations were questionable."

"Questionable?"

"Yes!" Sutherland exclaimed with genuine outrage. "Can you imagine! And these were exactly the type of scholarly do-nothings who had never left the sanctuary of their ivory towers. Never gone out into the field and risked anything, much less their lives. Oh, they made me angry, I tell you!"

Dunn had not suspected that Walter Sutherland possessed such passion, but here it was, a well-hidden facet of the archeologist's character that Dunn both liked and respected.

"Tell me something, Dr . . ."

"Walt. Remember?"

"All right, Walt. Am I correct in assuming that these jealous and petty attacks on Major Powell incensed and challenged you to come out here on your own?"

The professor nodded. "Yes," he said quietly. "While listening to those mean-spirited critics, I realized that I had never really risked anything either. I realized, too, that while I admired and wanted to defend Major Powell and his findings, something deep inside me also wanted to criticize and diminish the major's courageous undertaking. It was then that I knew I *had* to come out here and try to make my own mark. That it was necessary before . . ."

Dunn leaned closer. "Before what?"

"Before time and the last of my small personal courage was gone and I became old, tenured, and complacent. Before the best I could do was find fault with the doers. Before I was just like the yapping hounds who wanted to diminish Major Powell."

"I see."

"I argued in word and in writing that, whatever shortcomings there might be in his findings had to be excused given the circumstances. After all, he and his boatmen almost starved or drowned and the major lost several of his journals at Separation Rapids. But," Sutherland continued, "all turned out well. Powell's critics were in the minority and we managed properly to shame them. And soon, he received a well-deserved government subsidy to mount a second Colorado River expedition. This one was to include scientists such as myself and be far better executed than the first trip with its rough, uneducated frontiersmen."

"Had they not been rough and ready, they would have given up the expedition long before reaching the Grand Canyon," Dunn said.

"My dear friend, I certainly do not mean to disparage anyone. Most certainly not those brave members of that first historic expedition. I just meant to point out that the *scientific* aspects were a bit incomplete. However, anyone would agree that Major Powell's 1869 expedition ranks as one of the greatest feats in the annals of American history."

"What was so 'incomplete'?"

"To begin with," Sutherland began, puffing on the pipe, "even I had to admit that a few of the major's readings were questionable, especially those taken in the last, most difficult stages of the expedition, when they were all weak from hunger and their lives very much in jeopardy. But the main focus of scientific contention was that Major Powell's evolutionary theories created a veritable firestorm of controversy regarding the formation of Grand Canyon and its dates of origin, measured, of course, in millions of years."

Dunn was about to defend Powell's theories, which he remembered so well, when Josie brought him a plate of breakfast, kissed his cheek, and said, "Isn't it nice to have company?"

Her warning was clear. Dunn forced himself to relax and allow the professor to talk without argument or further questions.

"This second expedition," Sutherland continued, "was well funded and organized. You see, because of the extreme hardships faced earlier, the second voyage was to have supply points along the rim and the river. With the help of a fine man named Jacob Hamblin and a Kaibab Paiute chieftain named Chuar, Major Powell explored this rim country and established supply points so that there would not be another episode of near-starvation among his crew members."

"Good idea," Dunn said, recalling the acute hunger and distress he and his companions had experienced in the last few weeks of their harrowing river journey. "Where did the second expedition begin?"

"At Green River, Wyoming, just like the previous one," Sutherland replied. "The major's party included a geologist, a photographer, an artist, a mathematician, and a surveyor, as well as a cook and a geographer to do professional map work. But there was no archeologist, which was why I came to join him. Three specially designed and improved oak boats were used along with a pine boat. The party made it as far as Lee's Ferry, where they spent some time before going on to winter in Kanab."

"I see."

"Unfortunately, last winter was very hard in the Rockies and the Colorado River was extremely high this spring. That made it necessary for Major Powell and his second expedition to abandon the Colorado River at Kanab Creek. Their main fear was being capsized and drowned at Separation Rapids."

Sutherland tamped his pipe thoughtfully. "I can't say that I blame the major for not boating all the way through the Grand

Canyon again. After all, he had already lost three men who abandoned the expedition. They died while attempting to reach Kanab."

Dunn forced himself to concentrate on his breakfast and to sound casual when he asked, "Any more details concerning that sad episode?"

"You mean of the deserters?"

Dunn swallowed hard. "Yes."

"The Indians say that the whites provoked a confrontation and were killed in a fight."

"Why would three desperate men 'provoke' a fight with the Paiutes?" Dunn demanded.

"I have absolutely no idea," Sutherland confessed. "Quite frankly, I suspect that the Indians murdered them and then decided to concoct a story to protect themselves against retribution."

"Now *that* makes sense."

"It doesn't really matter anyway," Sutherland replied. "The three deserters met a tragic end up here on this very plateau, and there is little hope that their remains will ever be found."

"Why? I thought you were good at finding bones."

Sutherland smiled with amusement. "I hope to find some at least a few centuries older. Major Powell's journals indicate that he and his first party visited no less than eight archeological sites inside the Grand Canyon.

"Not only did they discover ruins, but also priceless artifacts—pottery, arrowheads, grinding stones, even a few woven baskets that might be thousands of years old!" Sutherland's pale eyes gleamed. "Would you care to hear my theory?"

"Uh . . . sure, Walt."

"From what Major Powell has described, as well as from what I've thoroughly researched and read about the earliest Spanish explorers, this canyon country might be the cradle of human history!"

"Are you serious?"

"Of course I am!" Sutherland cried. "I have even gone to

Spain and read the oldest recorded accounts of exploration of this country, the first on record being that of the Coronado Expedition. Much later, there is a fascinating account written by an old Spanish missionary named Francisco Tomas Garces, who descended into a paradise called Havasu Canyon and lived with those Indians. Fr. Garces himself says that he saw evidence that those people were from a very ancient civilization."

Dunn tried not to reveal his sharp interest. "Did the old padre describe this 'evidence'?"

"No," Sutherland admitted. "But a padre would not lie! I'm sure that I can find the same evidence he saw one hundred years ago. I've only to find this canyon."

"My wife is from that canyon."

"She is!" Sutherland's eyes bulged with astonishment and excitement.

"I lived there myself."

"Good Lord!" Sutherland cried. "Then maybe I can persuade you to take me there."

Dunn shrugged. "Maybe."

"It might be the center of at least the North American human civilization," Sutherland gushed. "Why? Because of the Grand Canyon itself!"

"I still don't follow your reasoning, Professor."

"All right," the man said, "you've seen the Grand Canyon at Lonely Dell and I've spent hours reading and hearing descriptions of it. I've even studied Powell's drawings until I think I could identify many of its major landmarks, usually spires, pinnacles, and airy fortresses of stone. What do you suppose sculpted and created those amazing, detached monuments of stone, some separated from both the North and the South Rim by thousands of feet?"

Dunn knew the answer because of the major's many impromptu geology lessons. "Erosion. The spires and pinnacles were once a part of the main rim, but erosion cut them away from the rims. It continues to shape and diminish them with each passing day."

"Precisely!" Sutherland agreed. "And what are the major forces of erosion?"

"Wind, rain, snow, ice freezing and thawing in every tiny crevice. But mostly the great river itself."

"Excellent! How did you become so learned in geology?"

"I . . ."

But the professor wasn't listening. Caught up in his own excitement, his mind was running and finding its voice. "But erosion is highly variable, very selective. It seeks weakness, shuns hardness and strength. And that is why, where you see pinnacles and spires, it is because they are protected by a very hard caprock. But even caprock, given enough time, must weaken and disintegrate. And as erosion takes place, we see the pages of history turned back until the time of creation. And on each page, or in each layer of rock exposed by the ravages of time, we can find evidence of living things. Human civilizations on top, then the time of prehistoric animals that roamed and ruled the earth, then the simple shells and sea fossils, and finally, the most basic forms of life."

Sutherland's words had trailed down to a whisper. "There was an Ice Age. Did you know that?"

Powell had spoken of it, but Dunn chose to shake his head.

"Well, there was," Sutherland mused, his eyes lost in the distant past. "And, in the depths of the Grand Canyon, the temperature is many degrees hotter than on either rim. And so, if you were a very, very ancient people trying to survive a time of ice and cold, wouldn't *you* descend into the bowels of the earth and seek the warmth."

"Yes," Dunn said, "I would."

"And so, too, would the first North Americans, and the animals they hunted and the plants those animals consumed." Sutherland's pale eyes burned. "Don't you see the truth of my theory? The inescapable logic of my hypothesis?"

"I do," Dunn said, meaning it. "I sure do."

Professor Sutherland bounced to his feet and began to pace back and forth, unable to contain his excitement. "It is my ambition to date not only the ruins already found by Major Powell, but to discover new ruins and to date the creation of the entire *canyon!*"

Unnoticed, Josie had entered the cabin to hear the last of the professor's theory. Now, she hurried to find and show off her little split-twig figurine.

"How old do you think this might be?" she asked, presenting it in the palm of her hand.

"My Lord," he cried, "where did you discover this treasure!"

"My father found it in Havasu Canyon where my people live and farm every summer," she told the archeologist. "He also gave one to my husband."

Sutherland's gaze lifted to Dunn. "You have one of these and you didn't even mention it to me?"

"I would have," he said. "Would you like to see it and compare them?"

"More than anything in the *world!*"

Dunn produced his own split-twig animal figure. Sutherland reverently placed the twins side by side on the table and reached for his pack. In a moment, he had a magnifying glass to his eye and was studying the two artifacts with great intensity. He kept clucking his tongue against the roof of his mouth and making excited little chirruping sounds in his throat, like a bird in the mating season.

"Well," Josie finally asked.

"Please describe everything around the site where these treasures were discovered," Sutherland whispered, unable to pull his attention from the figurines.

"I can't, because my father found them in a cave."

"Was there anything else in the cave?"

"I don't know."

"Was the cave up high on the side of a cliff, or down low

in the canyon?" Sutherland asked, picking one of the figurines up and turning it this way and that under his magnifying glass.

Josie shrugged. "I don't know that, either."

"I *must* visit that cave," Sutherland whispered, finally looking up at Josie and Dunn. "I am not familiar with this type of work, but I am sure it will cause a sensation back East. Would you be willing to sell either or both of these. . . ."

"No," Josie said. "Not at any price."

Sutherland slumped with disappointment. "I understand, and that is fine. We can probably locate more, but these are perfect works of art and antiquity. I would estimate that they are several thousand years old. They are exactly the kind of evidence I need to advance my scientific theories. Where is this canyon?"

"As you well know from your research," Dunn said, "it is on the South Rim, below Kanab Creek but above Separation Rapids."

"And how," Sutherland said in a voice that fell to a whisper, "would *you* know that?"

Dunn's heart skipped, and he created his own trap. "What do you mean, Dr. Sutherland?"

"I mean that the location of Separation Rapids is known only by those who have seen Powell's diaries and maps or heard his stirring lectures."

Dunn formed his words with great care. "Mr. Lee told me all about Major Powell and the tragic story of those three men. From his descriptions, it was easy enough to figure the location of Separation Rapids as well as Kanab Creek. And, of course, having lived among the Havasupai Indians for several years, I'm very well acquainted with the South Rim."

"Of course you are," Sutherland said, "and I must visit Havasu Canyon as soon as possible."

He gently stroked the two figures. "These are truly remarkable. Has anyone photographed them yet?"

"No."

"Do you mind if I take measurements and make some sketches?"

"Of course not," Josie said, glancing over at Dunn, who also nodded his consent.

While they watched, Sutherland got out a pad of paper and several pencils and a protractor, which also served as a ruler. "Josie, did your father ever mention seeing any pictographs?"

"What are those?"

"Pictures drawn by the ancient ones on cave walls. Often, they are simple drawings of hunters and animals, the favorite colors being blacks and reds."

"No," Josie said, "I don't think he did. I certainly never saw any and I'm sure that he would have shown them to me if they were in Havasu Canyon."

"They are there," Sutherland assured her. "For we know that every civilization is compelled to leave visual records. Do your oldest people have any idea how long your tribe has lived in Havasu Canyon?"

"Untold generations."

"I hope to provide that answer with a little more precision," Sutherland told her. "What is surprising is that Major Powell never spoke of visiting Havasu Canyon during his 1869 expedition."

"He never came up Havasu Creek to our village but instead stole our green squash from the lower fields."

Sutherland clapped his hands with delight. "So, those were *your* squash! Actually, when Major Powell addressed our academy of scientists in Washington, D.C., he rather sheepishly recounted that experience and got a wonderful belly laugh from the audience."

"We did not think it so amusing."

"No," Sutherland said, smile fading, "I'm sure that you did not."

He held the two figurines up before him, adjusting his spectacles and peering at them closely. "This pair was definitely made by two different men. At first glance, they appear to be identical, but the weaving is dissimilar and even the twig itself appears to be a slightly different kind of wood. And this is *very* interesting!"

"What?" Dunn asked.

"Look here," Sutherland told them. "Can you see what was once a spear but which has been broken away?"

Dunn squinted. "Do you mean that little dot of wood?"

"Exactly! Notice that only *one* of these figurines had a shaft driven through its chest, which represents a ritualistic killing."

Dunn and Josie leaned closer. Sure enough, one of the figurines had been speared through the heart.

"But why one and not the other?" Josie asked.

Sutherland expelled a deep breath. "I suppose because your ancestors knew that it spelled doom if they killed *all* the game in this country. But that's only a hasty theory."

Dunn heard thunder and, stepping over to the door, he whistled for Pepper to come inside, but the dog would not leave his flock, even though they were safely corralled.

"I'm going outside to rescue Pepper, even if I have to carry him in here," Dunn announced. "He's thin and not healed yet from his last fight. We can't afford to lose him."

"I agree," Josie said, reaching for her rabbit-skin coat. "I'll help you."

"I don't need help," Dunn told her firmly.

"I don't want *you* to get sick."

As soon as Dunn had left, Sutherland carefully placed the split twig figurines on the table, saying, "Your husband is certainly a fine and intelligent man. Exactly how long did he live with your people?"

"Many seasons."

"Where did he come from?"

"Back East."

"He seems *very* interested in Major Powell."

"He is," Josie admitted. "But you should ask him these questions."

Sutherland didn't look up but instead found a pad and pencil and began to sketch the figurines.

The storm broke late that night and passed over the Grand Canyon, moving south. Because Dr. Sutherland was so eager to see the canyon, they decided to leave at once and trail the flock south to the rim, then double back to the northeast and follow it all the way to the Lee's Ferry crossing.

Josie was feeling a little morning sickness and was looking forward to seeking comfort and advice from Emma Lee, though she would have preferred that her first child be born among her own people in Havasu Canyon. The main complication, of course, was that they intended to buy this flock of sheep when they reached Lonely Dell.

As they started southward, it became apparent that their guest preferred to do his scientific thinking out loud. Sitting on his horse or walking through the heavy forests behind the flock, Dr. Sutherland would discuss his theories and observations on geology and archeology as if to a colleague, often breaking into an animated and passionate argument. The poor man carried on these conversations for hours while the white-tailed Kaibab squirrels chattered back at him from their overhead perches.

Pepper was a blessing. The dog just seemed to know instinctively where he was supposed to drive the flock, and they made good progress. Finally, they pushed out of the forest and there it was—the yawning, spectacular Grand Canyon, with its layers of rock and the glitter of the Colorado River flowing like a silver thread far, far below. At first sight of this natural wonder, Sutherland froze in his tracks and threw his arms toward Heaven.

Dunn and Josie left their flock and hurried over to join the awed professor, who had tears in his eyes. They all stood poised on the rim, feeling the hot wind sweeping up from the depths of the canyon. To the east, Dunn actually could see the great union between the big and the Little Colorado rivers. A pair of golden eagles, dwarfed by space to the size of sparrows, soared effortlessly over immense stone cathedrals.

Sutherland sighed with contentment. "My friends, I listened to the eloquence of Major Powell as he expounded on the beauty of this canyon, and I've dreamed of seeing it, but this geological wonder mocks description and all but God's own infinite imagination."

Dunn agreed. It had been weeks since he'd seen the Grand Canyon, and he'd already forgotten the majesty of its size and varied colors. And what Sutherland would soon discover was that the canyon's appearance was ever-changing. As afternoon shadows deepened, the reds would become increasingly darker, taking on the color of wine, while the features of the rock would soften, gradually losing focus. Straight across the ten-mile chasm was an excellent view of the South Rim. And, at this place, it looked to be of the same elevation, but Dunn knew that to be untrue; it was actually much lower. Even ten miles away, it was clear that there were very few trees along the South Rim, which was a big contrast to the forests now surrounding them. And beyond, perhaps a hundred miles away, Dunn could see familiar snow-clad peaks, probably created by centuries-old volcanoes.

"What is it," Sutherland breathed, "that drives us in a desperately futile attempt to describe what we are seeing? How can we possibly tell anyone how all this looks? Even Major Powell's beautiful words and descriptions now seem pitifully inadequate. Do you . . ."

"What?" Dunn asked as the man struggled for words.

"Do you feel like that canyon is inhabited by gods and goblins, by Vikings and trolls and ships and moles?"

"No," he said, grinning.

"Everywhere I look I see monolithic figures from the past, moving and changing, burdened only by the stretch of eternity. I watch proud titans who lean triumphant over vanquished stone soldiers, once betrayed by the weakness of their fiber and substance."

Dunn glanced at his wife. Josie took his hand, and they walked away, leaving the scientist to his wild and secret imaginings.

"What are you thinking?" Josie finally asked when they were alone.

"I was thinking of what he said. Of how I never could talk or write like that."

"He sounded crazy to me."

Dunn chuckled. "Oh, he isn't crazy. He's just . . . different. I like him a lot. He is very complicated. Something is driving him and I think he's been broken. That's why he's come out here to find himself."

"In the Grand Canyon?"

"Maybe. And while he was talking, I was thinking that my life really didn't have much meaning before I left Green River with the Powell Expedition."

"What about Cynthia?"

"She's just a memory."

"One that brings sadness and pain?"

"No, because I no longer have any desire to go back East and change my life. Today, everything centers around you and the life I hope to make for our children."

"As a shepherd?"

"I've learned from Mr. Lee that it is best not to put all your trust in a single enterprise. I'd like to build our flock, but I'd also like to catch wild horses, raise cattle, and perhaps even mine for gold."

"I'd like to have our child in Havasu Canyon. I want my father and the Havasupai women nearby."

When he said nothing, she added, "It's very important."

"All right," he said. "Then we'll just have to work it out that way. But I can't leave our flock unprotected up on the South Rim."

"Someone in the village would watch over them for a

while," she told him. "And then, when I am stronger, I could come up and stay with you as always."

Dunn nodded. It would work out. For all of them, including Professor Sutherland. They just had to have faith and not give up trying—and not leave one another. *Yes,* he thought, squeezing Josie's hand as his mind ran back three years to that morning at Separation Rapids, *the most important thing of all is that we hold on tight and* always *stick together.*

Fourteen

Josie was feeling poorly. Dunn knew that she was having difficulty sleeping, and he wished she could rest instead of being constantly on the move. With the help of Pepper, and even Dr. Sutherland, he pushed the flock hard up the North Rim and finally onto the trail down into the Colorado River canyon itself. He approached Lee's Ferry late one afternoon with a bawling flock, a footsore dog, and an exhausted wife.

Dunn had galloped the last few miles to Lee's cabin to alert the Mormon family of their arrival and his wife's condition.

"She's probably just got the usual morning sickness," Emma Lee said, "but don't you worry, Kate and I will make her comfortable."

The woman's calm, reassuring manner put Dunn's worries to rest. "I didn't expect this severe stomach sickness, and I doubt that my wife did either, Mrs. Lee. As I'm sure you could tell, Josie is very strong and . . ."

"Physical strength has nothing to do with childbearing," Emma interrupted. "Some women have it easy, some very hard. There is no way to predict. But don't worry, your young wife will get plenty of rest and attention in our home."

"Thank you." Dunn looked around. "Where is your husband?"

"He's just off someplace again," Emma said, hurrying to the creek with an empty pail.

"Will Mr. Lee return soon?"

But the woman didn't hear him and Dunn was left to himself.

"Yes, he will—if he can."

Dunn pivoted to see Kate Callahan standing just outside the little cabin. He had been so anxious about Josie that he hadn't even been aware of the woman's presence.

"Miss Callahan," he muttered, for lack of anything better to say.

There was an awkward silence before Kate said, "I'm very sorry about Josie not feeling well. She probably just needs lots of rest."

"I expect you are right. Will Mr. Lee return this evening?"

"No."

Before Dunn could ask her anything more, Kate turned and walked away. After a moment, Dunn followed her toward the family's orchard of young pear, apricot, peach, and plum trees.

"Will you tell me what is going on here?" Dunn asked when he overtook the young woman. "I was supposed to meet Mr. Lee here so he could sell me the flock."

"Are you sure you want to do that?"

"Yes. We've even arrived at a price."

"Then, congratulations," she said, without a smile or a trace of sincerity.

"Thank you."

"Do you have any idea what is *really* going on?" Kate asked.

"No, I don't," Dunn admitted. "Are you going to tell me?"

"It's not my place. But this family is in big trouble. Maybe you can even help."

"How?"

"You could take Mr. Lee and your sick wife back to Havasu Canyon and hide him." She turned her face up toward the eastern cliffs and her eyes searched the rim. "He's hiding somewhere up there right now."

"From what?"

"Ask him."

Dunn detested guessing games. "I already asked Mr. Lee that question up at Jacob Lake when he arrived looking so upset. I didn't get an answer, and I didn't get one from his wife, either. Is *anyone* going to tell me what the hell is going on?"

Kate's voice took on an edge. "My suggestion is that you keep asking these people until you get a satisfactory answer."

"And what if they *never* give me one!"

"Then find one of his other wives and ask her!"

Dunn was caught off-balance, though Lee had once admitted to being a bigamist. "Kate," he said, "I just wish you'd tell me what is going on."

"If I did that," she told him, "I'd get myself in even more trouble. It's for *them* to tell you, not me. But I will say this— you'd better stop worrying about John Lee and start worrying more about your wife."

With that, Kate turned to leave, but Dunn wasn't about to let her go without trying to find some answers. "Listen," he said, catching up with her, "as long as I'm supposed to keep asking everyone questions, let me ask *you* one."

"What?"

"What is someone like you doing in this desolate place? And exactly what kind of trouble are *you* in?"

"What makes you think I'm not just here for a family visit?"

"You don't fit in here at all."

"And neither do you," Kate snapped, leaving him in a huff.

The following afternoon, Dunn spotted John Lee riding down Paria Canyon toward Lonely Dell. Dunn had been listening to the professor theorize on the ebb and flow of all civilizations. According to Walt Sutherland, archeology suggested that weaker civilizations were always driven onto poorer lands, or else assimilated into the stronger civilizations. These stronger civilizations were always seeking better and larger hunting territories.

"It can't be proved exactly," Sutherland was saying, "but most archeologists and anthropologists theorize that what happened on this North American continent—in terms of cultural warfare—was quite similar to that which took place in other parts of the world. And by that, I mean that the history of mankind—on *every* continent—has always been one of conquest and defeat, interspersed with brief periods of tranquillity. Sad but true, the natural state of man is to be at war."

Dunn took his eyes off the approaching rider, frowning at Walt. "And that's the conclusion you reach based on all your years of education and study?"

"Yes. As far back as recorded history and even beyond, the evidence all suggests an endless cycle of warring civilizations."

"Well, because I have lived with the Havasupai, I respectfully disagree," Dunn said, watching Lee cross the creek and guide his horse around the edge of his irrigated fields.

"You have every right to disagree, and I'd be the first to admit that there are exceptions to every rule. In some cases, tribes and civilizations have been driven into surroundings so isolated or inhospitable that they serve as an effective buffer from their enemies. Examples might be your Havasupai, or isolated peoples in Polynesia or Alaska or in the sub-Saharan deserts. But these are always unique cases and generally result where a weaker people have taken refuge in an undiscovered or undesirable environment."

Dunn needed time to think about that.

"You wait and see," Sutherland promised. "Once in Havasu Canyon, I believe I can point out and logically explain why the Havasupai enjoyed a long period of uncontested peace. And, unless I am badly mistaken, it will be because Havasu Canyon is too small or undesirable to attract enemies."

"That's ridiculous. Havasu Canyon is an oasis . . . a hidden paradise."

"If that were so, then stronger or fiercer people would have seized it long ago. The same applies to the entire Grand Canyon. I theorize that its inhabitants were always driven here as a last resort. My research leaves no doubt that the Spaniards, in their zeal to convert the Hopi and Navajo to Christianity, drove many of them into hiding, perhaps in this very canyon."

"You're saying they didn't come of their own free will?"

"Hardly. People are aggressive, but territorial. They never leave their own lands and go to others, but instead attempt to *expand* their territory."

"Professor, in my humble view, you have a very bleak view of human nature and of the history of civilizations."

"On the contrary! I make no moral judgments. Conquest is a natural occurrence. War and encroachment beget societal and cultural evolution."

Dunn was in no mood to listen to this depressing theory. He was far more interested in meeting Lee and trying to get to the bottom of the Mormon settler's mysterious difficulties.

"Good to see you," Lee said, dismounting to extend his hand.

Dunn was shocked at John Lee's haggard appearance. The man had dropped twenty pounds and aged as many years just since they'd parted at Jacob Lake. Dunn could not help but blurt, "John, you look like you've ridden to hell and back. What is wrong!"

"Wrong?" Lee began to lead his weary horse toward the corrals. "What do you mean?"

Dunn grabbed Lee's arm and pulled him up short. "I want an answer."

"Let go of me. My troubles are none of your concern."

"I thought we were friends."

"You worked for me. Remember?"

Dunn took a deep breath. "Unless I get some answers, I'm not going to buy your sheep."

"We also have an agreement," Lee said after a long pause. "If you choose to break that agreement, so be it."

"Listen, I just want to help. I understand that you might like to visit Havasu Canyon. Perhaps even winter there."

Lee froze, then finally said, "Who told you that?"

"I'd rather not say. My wife wants to go to see her people. Professor Sutherland is chomping at the bit to come along. Why don't you join us? You'd find it restful."

"I imagine that's true. But what about the flock?"

Dunn had already put considerable thought to the matter. "We could winter them along the South Rim just above Havasu Canyon. There's plenty of graze in that country, but first we'd have to figure out a way to cross the Little Colorado Gorge."

"I know a way, but it would take us into the Navajo land and add a week of travel. I have a better idea. Why don't I winter them right here in Paria Canyon? It would be much easier for everyone, including the sheep. You'll have your hands full taking care of your wife and new baby. Then, in the spring, I'll trail them over to Havasu and have the chance to meet your new child."

"Are you sure that would be all right?" Dunn asked, unable to hide his relief.

"Of course! Consider it done."

"I'll be glad to pay you for the extra time and trouble."

"Now *that* would be appreciated," Lee told him.

"Would the Navajo object?"

"I'm sure we could buy passage with a few head of sheep. I've always wanted to see Havasu Canyon. I hear that it's especially beautiful in the spring. By the way, have you paid Emma yet?"

"No."

"Do so now and I'll write you a bill of sale."

"Why the hurry?"

Lee's eyes flicked nervously upward toward the rims of Paria Canyon, and Dunn saw the hunted look in the man's eyes before he said, "I just think it would be in everyone's best interest to do that right now."

"All right. But Josie is unwell and needs to rest a few more days. As soon as she's stronger, we'll leave for Havasu."

"With the professor?"

"Yes," Dunn said, sensing that Lee did not want the scientist to remain at Lonely Dell under any circumstances.

Josie wanted to leave at once, but the weather turned cold. Everyone insisted that she keep to her bed at least a week to regain her strength before the long trip up the South Rim to Havasu Canyon. Dunn found it enjoyable to watch his wife interact with Lee's household. She enjoyed children and fit right into the boisterous but well-behaved family, laughing and playing with the children and having a fine time talking to Emma and Kate about everything that sparked her lively curiosity.

Professor Sutherland was also eager to reach Havasu Canyon, but very much enjoyed spending evenings with the educated and well-read Lee, both expounding their disparate theories of religion and evolution. Quite often Lee and the professor would get into heated discussions, and then Dunn would head in search of peace and quiet. Josie, whose people believed in many gods who inhabited all things on earth, disliked these loud and seemingly endless debates.

"Do white men always argue about their gods in such angry ways?" she asked her husband one night as they stood on the banks of the Colorado listening to the river song.

"Not always. But those two men have strong personalities and opinions. Besides, I have the impression that they enjoy the arguments and intellectual fights."

"But why?"

"I don't know," Dunn confessed. "They just do."

"I am glad that we are leaving tomorrow to see my father and my people again."

"Who said we were leaving tomorrow?"

"Can't we?"

"I suppose that would be all right, if you are feeling well in the morning."

Josie kissed him. "I will be."

"Good," he said. "Then we had better go inside and announce our plans. Dr. Sutherland will be pleased."

Sutherland *was* pleased and, early the next morning, they saddled the horses and located a pack mule, then said good-bye to everyone.

"You take care of yourself," Dunn said to John Lee.

"I'll try. And I expect that you ought to get a good spring lamb crop," Lee said, following them toward the river with his family in tow. "Maybe I should have waited to sell the flock to you then."

Dunn appreciated the attempt at humor. "You've got my gold, I've got the bill of sale. You're working for *me* now, remember?"

That caused Lee to chuckle. And as they neared the banks of the Colorado River, Dunn hoped that whatever kind of trouble John Lee was in would pass by the time they met again above Havasu Canyon. He wanted to help Lee, but both of them knew their first obligation was to their wives. That being understood, there was nothing to do but part and hope that they would meet again under happier circumstances—he with a son or a daughter, John Lee with a trouble-free heart.

"Let's go!" Sutherland called.

"If you run across any Navajo," Lee said, "tell them you are my friend and you'll be well treated. Also, you have rifles and pistols, just in case you should run into scalpers or outlaws."

"I appreciate that," Dunn said, mounting his horse and striking out for the river.

"Are you sure you don't want me to ferry you across?" Lee called.

"No! The river is low now, and it would be too much trouble!"

So they swam their horses across and climbed the broken red hills on the other side until they were back on the tabletop. Then, they turned south, looking toward a much anticipated visit with the happy "people of the blue-green water."

* * *

Two weeks later, they had a joyous reunion with the Havasupai, who had already migrated out of the canyon onto the South Rim and were preparing for winter. When Zack saw his daughter was swelling with a child, he burst into song and Maud clapped her hands together and cackled with glee.

"Why, damned if I ain't finally going to be a grandpa!" Zack kept yelling, pounding Dunn on the back.

Dunn introduced Dr. Sutherland, and the archeologist wasted no time mentioning his desire to discover more of the figurines and to learn the circumstances and locations where Zack had found the earlier pair.

"Well, now," Zack said, eyes narrowing, "I expect that information is pretty valuable."

"It would be if more figurines are found."

"Why, of course. There's plenty more!"

"Then, where are they?"

Zack scowled. "What do you mean?"

"I mean that you'd have taken them all, wouldn't you?"

"Not necessarily."

"I think you certainly would have. And, anyway, your daughter already told me that you hadn't been able to locate any more."

Zack threw Josie an exasperated look, then returned his attention to the professor. "I guess you're going to need a lot of guiding around in the canyon to find the caves and the diggin's, huh?"

"I could use someone trustworthy and familiar with the terrain."

"I expect that I'm your man." Zack swept his buckskin-clad arm full circle. "I know *all* this country. Yes sir, there's not a scorpion or even an ant that I haven't stepped or pissed on once or twice!"

"Then can we descend into the canyon and begin to explore?"

"Sure! But after we have a little feasting in celebration of Josie's return!"

The celebration lasted four days and might have gone even longer except that an ice storm blew in from the north and the temperatures plummeted at night to well below freezing.

"I don't understand why the Havasupai choose to winter up here when it's so much warmer down in Havasu Canyon," Sutherland said, rubbing his hands briskly over Zack's fire.

"It's because there's no hunting down there," Zack explained, "nothing to add to the crops we growed last summer. Besides, sometimes you can get a big flash flood down in the canyon after a storm like this."

"But why couldn't we at least live in a warm cave up on the side of the canyon?"

Zack leaned forward across the fire. "Listen, Professor. In the first place, caves ain't warm in the wintertime. All you have to do is wake a hibernatin' bear to find that out. And, in the second place, these people have been wintering up here on the South Rim so they could hunt and collect pine nuts to go with whatever we could grow down in the canyon during the summer. So now you want to come in and *change* everything on account of you don't like this storm?"

"It just doesn't make any sense to me," Sutherland said, teeth chattering. "I mean, we are freezing up here when we could be much warmer down on the canyon floor."

Dunn said, "Professor, when this storm passes, I'll take you down in the canyon to look for those figurines and show you the ruins."

"Thank you!"

"I will go with you," Josie told them.

"I think you'd better stay up here," Dunn said. "You've had a difficult time of it and you need rest. Besides, I won't stay more than a couple of weeks. I'll return long before our child is due."

"I'm coming," she insisted.

Zack glowered at Dunn, challenging him to lay down the law to his daughter. Out of stubbornness, or spite, Dunn just nodded to Josie and said, "All right. I want you along."

"Damn foolishness!" Zack groused.

The weather cleared that night and Dunn, Josie, and Sutherland headed down the steep, difficult trail into Havasu Canyon the next morning. The footing was slick and the trail had washed out in many places, making the descent extremely difficult for the horses, so difficult that they were often forced to dismount and lead the animals over the most treacherous stretches of the trail. It took them the entire day to reach the deserted village and its resting fields.

"So this is it," the archeologist said, studying the now quiet canyon. "I expect that it doesn't look much different from when Padre Francisco Tomas Garces came here in 1776."

"I heard Chief Navajo speak of a priest coming here long ago," Dunn said. "But, as you know, he is very old and he could not remember any details. Was he the first white man to see this country?"

"Oh, no," Sutherland replied. "The very first was a small expedition of Spaniards who arrived in 1540 with the Coronado expedition, which was seeking the Seven Lost Cities of Gold. But they had big problems and Coronado sent a detachment under Garcia Lopez de Cardenas. It was Cardenas and his suffering soldiers who were the first white people to record seeing the Grand Canyon."

"What were their impressions?"

"They regarded the Grand Canyon as nothing but an obstacle in their path. Major Cardenas sent three young soldiers down into the canyon in a desperate attempt to find a way across or, at least, to bring up water."

"Did they?"

"I'm afraid not," Sutherland answered. "But the three gallant soldiers considered it a miracle of God that they were able to return to the South Rim with their lives. A few years later, they each wrote a vivid account of that experience. They were widely read in Spain."

"Did they reach the bottom of this canyon?"

"No. Cardenas arrived on the South Rim somewhere to the

east of Havasu Canyon; no one knows exactly where because his description is very vague. Father Garces, a true missionary, was the very first to visit Havasu, and made many expeditions into the Southwest. I have read copies of his journals and know that, when he arrived here, the trail down from the rim was far more dangerous than it is today. At one point, the padre said that he actually had to use a rickety old ladder to descend a particularly bad place."

"Was he well treated?"

"Yes," Sutherland replied. "The Havasupai were just as hospitable a century ago as they are now. Father Garces wrote that this canyon was so deep it was not fully bathed by the sun until ten o'clock in the morning. He also marveled at the same intricate and highly developed irrigation systems that we now see watering the Havasupai fields. The Havasupai prevailed upon Father Garces to stay as long as he wished. He rested and feasted for five days and then, much refreshed, traveled to the Hopi pueblos. It was Father Garces who first called the Grand Canyon by its current name, as well as consistently referring to the 'Rio Colorado.' He wrote that, as far as he could determine, Havasu Canyon was the only occupied Indian village left in the entire Grand Canyon."

"It isn't exactly *in* the Grand Canyon," Dunn kept pointing out. "Havasu is a side canyon."

"Oh, yes, but the village really is in the Grand Canyon," Sutherland insisted.

"Do you know whatever happened to Father Garces?"

"He was martyred by the Indians five years later," Sutherland replied. Quickly changing the subject, he forced a smile and said, "And so, where are the nearest ruins?"

"We'll have time to show you in the days to come," Dunn promised. "They're around."

"I'm sure they are," the professor said, eyes bright with anticipation. "This canyon really is a paradise."

"Funny you should admit that."

Sutherland gave him a strange look. "Why?"

"Because," Dunn said, "if it's such a paradise, then it's desirable and—according to your theory—all desirable places are claimed by conquest. But as far back as any of the 'people of the blue-green water' can remember, there never has been an invasion or a war here."

"Probably there has been," Sutherland snorted. "In fact, my guess is that these people no doubt conquered an even weaker tribe. It would likely have happened many centuries ago; therefore, it's not the least bit surprising that no one would have any record or memory of the conflict."

Dunn glanced at Josie who just shrugged her shoulders as if to tell him that Sutherland was not the kind to alter his theories, no matter what future facts might be revealed.

That night, they made camp in the deserted village. The air was warm and the heavens bright with glittering stars.

"It is good to be back here again," Dunn said.

Josie was very pregnant, still lovely but quite thin. Dunn again wondered if he should have insisted that his wife stay up on the rim. *Well,* he thought, *we will do all the work and she can rest down here where it is warmer. In a week or two, the professor will tire of this canyon and we can leave with or without any newly discovered split-twig figurines.*

This decision made, his mind was at peace.

Fifteen

Dunn had chosen to winter in Havasu Canyon because it would be easier on Josie down in its warm, protected depths. Less than a month after their arrival in the largely deserted Supai village, Zack and grandmother Maud had come to join them. Since there were no crops in the fields, the short, crisp winter days were leisurely. To pass the time, Dunn and his father-in-law either accompanied Professor Sutherland on his archeological digs or enjoyed target practice with the ammunition Dunn had bought from the Mormons at Lonely Dell.

"Haven't lost my eye," Zack boasted to Dunn one blustery winter afternoon as they were target shooting against the canyon's wall. "And you're not a half-bad shot either."

Dunn was actually the superior marksman, but he concealed that fact by occasionally missing on purpose.

Up until the last month of her pregnancy, Josie had accompanied them on many of the professor's archeological explorations. Sutherland's enthusiasm was contagious and unflagging, even though they had failed to discover any more of the ancient split-twig figurines. But they did find a few minor prehistoric sites. One was a rock-rimmed hole at which Dunn wouldn't have given a second glance but which an excited Sutherland termed a "kiva." The professor explained that a kiva was believed to have had great spiritual significance for the earliest Grand Canyon dwellers. It was also easy to find arrowheads and, in the caves, very old shards of pottery and delicate wisps of reed baskets. But most interesting of all were the professor's own random musings and the day-by-day evolution of his archeological theories.

"To understand the history of man in North America," Sutherland began, as he spoke to Josie and Dunn one afternoon after spending hours digging, "you both need to know that most archeologists hold the view that the earliest humans on this continent migrated across the Bering Sea from Siberia at the close of the Ice Age.

"Now, you may well ask—given the comparative lushness of California and the East Coast or, for that matter, almost anywhere else on this continent—*why* early man would choose to come to such an inhospitable place as this canyon country in the heart of the great Southwest."

Dunn glanced sideways at his wife, struggling to keep from grinning. Both he and Josie knew full well that the professor loved to pose and then answer his own questions.

"The reason the earliest humans migrated to *this* harsh canyon country is because it has undergone a profound climatic and ecological transformation," Sutherland told them, waving his hand about. "Don't forget, in early prehistoric times, it was once covered by a vast inland sea. We know this is true because we can easily identify ancient sea fossils in many layers of the Grand Canyon lime and sandstone formed millions of years ago. Also, just a few hundred miles to the east, there are vast petrified forests where there is no forest today."

"What are 'petrified forests'?" Josie asked.

"Trees turned to stone."

Josie's eyes widened in disbelief but the professor didn't notice as he continued to theorize. "I believe that, as these inland bodies of water slowly evaporated, tropical forests flourished, and with them came dinosaurs. In time, the land dried and the tropical forests were replaced by the types of vegetation we see around us now and that, in turn, this new vegetation attracted different species of animals. My guess is that there became fewer and smaller carnivores and larger and more numerous grazing beasts. These new herbivores became the staple diet of hunter man."

"Did buffalo once roam in this country as they did in the Great Plains?" Dunn asked.

"I'm sure they did," Sutherland replied, "although that remains to be proved."

"Were Havasu and the Grand Canyon already formed?" Dunn asked.

"Most definitely! And, by the time the first humans arrived, the canyons were already so very old that they wouldn't have appeared that much different than they do today. For centuries after the Ice Age, the entire Southwest must have been a hunter's paradise. However, like the Garden of Eden and any paradise visited by man, it was eventually lost."

"We ruined all this, too?"

"No, no! The weather underwent a drastic change. This country became much drier and hotter, so that all that was left were a very few rivers, creeks, and springs. Everything else just dried up, leaving this southern plateau hotter than the top of a stove."

"And what happened to those very first people?" Josie asked, leaning forward with intense interest.

"I'm certain that they worked extremely hard to adapt—just as humans around the world do today. I theorize that, as water and game became more difficult to find, those people turned primarily to agriculture, as your people have, Josie. Perhaps they survived that way for many centuries."

"Are my people their descendants?"

"I think so. We call those first people the Anasazi. I believe they were forced to abandon the Grand Canyon and migrate eastward in search of better farmland. I think they are the ancestors of today's Hopi and Zuni Indians. For the next several centuries, they flourished, but, as they became more and more successful, their own population pressure forced them back here, and they became the Havasupai and Hualapai."

Josie frowned. "I think we were The People first, and long before the Hopi and Navajo. Will you be able to tell us this for sure before you leave our canyon?"

"Thank heavens, no!" Sutherland exclaimed.

"What do you mean?" Dunn asked. "Why *wouldn't* you want to know?"

"I sincerely believe that—without a very large element of mystery—science quickly loses its greatest appeal."

Dunn frowned. "I still don't understand."

"Let me put it this way," Sutherland began. "I'm trying to explain that I very much appreciate the fact that I will never fully know the answers to your questions and neither will any future generation of scientists. This is extremely fortunate. Otherwise, if any one of us learned everything, what would be the point of continued exploration and discovery? Why would any future generation of middle-aged archeologists like myself feel entirely reinvigorated like a first year graduate student on his first field trip?"

"I don't know," Dunn said, beginning to grasp the man's point.

Sutherland stopped chipping at the rock between his feet as his pale blue eyes surveyed a ridge. Dunn could almost read the scientist's thoughts, for he had often witnessed that same intensely focused look in Major Powell's eyes as he surveyed a promising new area of geological interest.

"Don't misunderstand me," Sutherland said before he set off to investigate the ridge. "I really do want to know *all* the answers. How could anyone with an active mind and fair degree of curiosity *not* want to know? But I never will. That just goes to show you that it is only in our *quest* that we find true joy."

After the professor had left them, Dunn looked to Josie and said, "Have you ever seen or heard anything like him?"

"No. Have you?"

"Yep. Major Powell. But, half the time, I didn't understand him either."

* * *

In the spring, Josie delivered a healthy baby boy. It was a great occasion and, when Zack brought out the dreaded mescal, Dunn threw caution to the winds and began to make toasts. That night, they danced around the campfire and serenaded the moon, which seemed to throb with a strange inner light. The next morning, Zack and Dunn crawled heavily to their feet under the reproachful eyes of the women and staggered into the Havasupai sweat lodge, where they remained until all the mescal was baked from their pores.

"What are you going to name your son?" Zack asked.

"I don't know. That'll be Josie's choice. She did all the work."

"Seems fair then," Zack grumped. "But she mentioned last week that, if it was a boy, she wanted to name him Kit."

Dunn was not overly fond of the name. "Why?"

"Because she grew up hearing so many tall tales about my old friend, Kit Carson."

"You actually knew him?"

"Sure did! Kit and I went to the mountain man rendezvous back in 1835 on the Green River, a stretch of water that you know something about."

"I sure do."

"Well, Kit got hisself into a fight with Shunar, a big, mean French trapper, and whipped him down to a nubbin. About that time, Kit had an Arapaho wife . . . or maybe it was a Cheyenne . . . I don't recollect. But she was the prettiest thing you ever saw. Someone called her a 'damned squaw' and the next thing that fella knew, he was swallowin' his own teeth. Kit was generally peaceful, though. He took a bath every week, even in winter. And when Kit Carson made a promise, it was something that you knew he'd keep."

Zack sighed. "You know, I've been in Havasu Canyon so long that I lost track of Kit. Would you know what happened to him?"

"I'm afraid that he passed away several years ago over in southern Colorado."

Zack's eyes teared, and it was a time before he could ask, "Of natural causes?"

"I think so."

"I always figured old Kit would get hisself et by a bear or scalped by an Indian. He was as fearless as a wolverine and smart as a fox, though I always did question what he saw in that damned publicity hound, John C. Fremont. Why, Kit let that peacock get all the explorin' credit while he did all the work! Hellfire, Fremont couldn't have found his way out of a corner without Kit Carson takin' his lily white hand."

Dunn chuckled. Zack was not subtle. "I'm going to go take another peek at my new son."

Josie and the infant were resting in her grandmother's hut while Maud tended the cooking fire. When Dunn squatted down beside his wife and son, he explained his feelings about the name.

"I never expected us to name our first boy after me," Dunn admitted, "but I'd appreciate you not naming him Kit. Chris or Christopher is fine, but a 'kit' is a damned kitten or cougar cub."

"All right, then, Christopher," she agreed, peeling back the blanket to regard their new baby. "Isn't he strong and handsome."

"Sure is!"

Actually, Dunn thought poor Christopher was wrinkled, ugly and about the most pathetic-looking thing imaginable. Dunn found it impossible to believe he had looked so poorly once himself, but he sure wasn't going to mention that to his wife.

"Here," Josie said, *"you* should hold him, too."

"Oh, that's all right."

"Come on," she insisted.

Dunn steeled himself and took the child. Feeling his cold, rough hands, Christopher opened his eyes and stared at Dunn's whiskery face. Then, his little body shook, his face turned scarlet, he squeezed his eyes shut and howled as if he were being murdered.

"Here," Dunn said, anxiously returning the baby to his wife, "he likes you a whole lot better."

Josie put the baby's face to her breast. Seconds later, Christopher was greedily suckling, and his color had returned to normal.

"He'll get used to you," Josie promised.

"I hope so. The professor told me that he will be ready to leave Havasu Canyon before too long, and that he wants to explore along this South Rim. I should go with him and help John Lee drive our flock over here. I'm kind of worried about him and his family."

"If you wait just a little longer, I'll come with you," Josie told him.

"You should stay and rest through the summer in Havasu Canyon."

"Please don't leave until I'm strong enough to go with you. It won't be long."

"All right," he agreed. "But I just thought you might like to spend this summer with your people and then . . ."

"Our place is with you."

Dunn was touched. "I guess it is. And I've decided that the best place to start a ranch is on this South Rim instead of the North. That way, we won't have the hard winters and we can be near your father, grandmother, and all the Havasupai people. There is some fine grazing land up on top."

"It's The People's traditional hunting land," Josie reminded her husband.

"Oh, I know that, so we'll use your father's gold to make sure that someone else doesn't have a chance to buy it up."

Dunn's mind was churning. "One thing I learned from Mr. Lee is that, to make a success in this hard country, a man has to be willing to do a *bunch* of different things. That way, if one goes sour, the others can keep him propped up. So, we'll raise sheep *and* cattle as well as try to do some mustanging.

There are a lot of wild horses on this range and there are two separate U.S. Army posts within two hundred miles of this canyon. They always need horses and there's no reason I shouldn't be helping to supply them."

"You have big plans."

"Most as big as the Grand Canyon! Of course, I may not pull all of 'em off, but I mean to try. Now that I got a family, I'm going to work hard to give you and Chris the very best."

"We'd be happy living right here if you were happy, too."

"I know that. But I just wouldn't be happy. I mean, it's a fine way of life, farming in the summer with your people and then hunting up on the South Rim all winter. I don't think I've ever been so content, but . . ."

"But what?"

"I've got a burr in my side that says that I can do a lot more. I don't want to grow old wishin' that I had done more with my life. Besides, ranching and mustanging sure sounds a lot more fun than watering and weeding an old Havasupai squash or cornfield."

"Then we'll be ranchers and mustangers," Josie said happily. "And we'll have this fine son to help us when we grow older."

"And I hope many, many more children," he answered, giving his wife a tender kiss.

That spring they had a week of hard, drenching storms which came without warning and furiously pounded Havasu Canyon with rain and even hail. Rolling cannonades of thunder dislodged giant boulders from the cliffs and hurled them at the canyon floor, wiping out everything in their paths. Searing bolts of lightning speared the trembling pines up on both rims, causing them to explode like Chinese rockets.

These violent thunderstorms usually spent their fury in less than an hour but were so intense that Havasu Canyon would quickly be inundated by thousands of gushing waterfalls plummeting off its high rims. Havasupai fields became shallow lakes and formerly dry arroyos boiled with angry red water. Even Havasu Creek turned mean, knocking over willows and trees while escaping its banks and threatening to wash out the entire Supai village. At such times, The People grabbed their food and belongings, their children and their dogs, and hurried to higher, safer ground.

"It's easy to see," Dr. Sutherland commented after one such savage storm as they huddled in a cave about fifty feet above the sodden canyon floor, "how these canyons were formed. Why, I'll bet that Havasu Creek is carrying tons of silt and gravel down to the Colorado River each passing minute. Nothing man will ever create will equal nature's power."

"I'm glad I'm not rafting on the Colorado right now," Dunn said.

"It has probably risen fifty feet in less than twenty minutes." The professor pointed a finger up to the opposite rim of Havasu Canyon. "Look up at the cliffs! With all that water pouring down, you can actually see their geological features changing. If you ask me, the power of these thunderstorms really defies the human imagination."

The storms passed and, because of the foresight of The People, who had carefully stored the next year's seed crop in high and dry caves, nothing important was lost. Besides, everyone in Supai realized that these storms were mostly a blessing because the heavy rains prepared The People's fields for an easy and early planting. A few days after the bad drenchings, Sutherland found a stone axe that had been washed to the surface. He excavated the site for weeks, hoping to find what he called a "dig," then surprised everyone by announcing that he fully intended to depart Havasu on his own.

"I've covered nearly every inch of this canyon and as far up and down the Colorado River as I can reach," Sutherland told them. "I really want to see more of the South Rim, where

I fully expect to find some ancient villages. I'm prepared to do so alone."

"I don't think that would be such a good idea," Dunn said. "You could be badly hurt."

"I've been badly hurt before."

"All right, killed."

Sutherland nodded. "Thanks for your concern. But I am prepared to take any and all risks. Why? Because, all my life, I've taken the safe and comfortable road. It's time to take whatever risks are necessary for my profession. Just as you are about to do when you leave this hidden sanctuary."

"But you don't *know* this country," Dunn gently argued. "It won't tolerate even little mistakes. It's unforgiving. Professor, I . . ."

But the archeologist just smiled. "Listen, Bill. You've become a very dear friend. And one of the things I most admire about you is that you've never tried to run anyone else's life. So please don't start attempting to make my decisions now. All right?"

Dunn forced himself to nod and say no more, but in his heart he vowed that he would keep a close and protective eye on the professor. Otherwise, he probably wouldn't even make it through the searing dog days of summer.

As they prepared to depart from Havasu Canyon, Dunn still wasn't comfortable with the idea of his wife and baby leaving, but Josie was adamant that they not be separated. Besides, there was the matter of John Lee and his mysterious difficulties with his own Mormon people in Kanab and maybe even in Salt Lake City. Despite Lee's repeated rebuffs, Dunn was anxious to see if he could help the man. Finally, there was the matter of his flock. It was almost lambing season, and Dunn especially wanted to be with the sheep at that critical time of year.

"We are ready to leave," Josie announced one cool and windy morning. "I'm strong enough now and so is Christopher. Dr. Sutherland is ready, too."

Dunn caught their three saddle horses. The animals were uncooperative, which was not surprising since they hadn't been ridden during the winter. There simply was no need for them down in the canyon. Dunn's tall bay gelding didn't want to be saddled after its long winter vacation.

"That big horse is going to toss you clear outa this canyon!" Zack crowed, obviously hoping his prophecy would come to pass.

Seeing the mischief in the gelding's rolling eyes, Dunn led the spunky horse into Havasu Creek before he mounted. As expected, the gelding tried to buck him off but just couldn't do much damage given the water and the sandy river bottom footing. The big bay horse crow-hopped and snorted and made quite a fuss, but even a child could have ridden it to a standstill.

Zack snorted with derision. "Some cowboy you are!"

"No sense in showing off or giving a horse an even break," Dunn yelled back as the gelding humped its spine a few last times.

"Could you have stuck him on solid ground?"

"Yep. But why risk getting pitched?"

"Smart," Zack allowed. "And, the truth be known, you sit a horse even better than me. You've got a knack with 'em and that's for certain."

Dunn forced the already-weary gelding up and down Havasu Creek for a quarter of an hour before being satisfied that the animal had achieved a more peaceable frame of mind. Then, he rode out of the creek and dismounted. He spent a few minutes scratching the gelding behind both ears to show that there were no hard feelings, and then he unsaddled and turned the horse into the corral.

Dunn was grinning when he turned to his father-in-law and said, "It felt real good to sit a horse again. There is just something about being in the saddle that makes a man feel that everything is right with the world."

"Damn right there is!" Zack enthusiastically agreed. "Why,

that's *exactly* what I used to tell Josie's mother before our nightly wrestle . . . but she didn't always understand."

The old badger burst into gales of laughter and Dunn could only shake his head. The man was incorrigible, and there was nothing to do but to snake the kinks out of the other two horses.

The next morning, they bid an emotional farewell to Zack, a weeping Maud, and the other Havasupai before leaving Supai village. Several hours later, they began to pick their way up the steep switchbacks leading to the South Rim. They were just getting to the halfway point when the sky suddenly darkened and they heard the all too familiar and ominous rattle of approaching thunder.

"Dammit!" Dunn swore, reining in his horse and twisting around in his saddle to address the others. "Maybe we'd better go back to Supai and try again tomorrow! I don't think we can make it to the top before this storm hits us!"

But both his wife and the professor overrode that suggestion. "We'll be at the top in less than an hour, and we can get into a wickiup," Josie said. "Let's go on!"

Dunn was as eager as anyone to achieve the rim and strike out for Lee's Ferry, but he wasn't a bit eager to risk the health of his wife and his infant son.

"Hurry!" Josie urged.

"All right, but don't either of you blame me if we get a good drenching."

"It'll feel good," Sutherland shouted from the rear as they continued up the narrow and precipitous trail.

Dunn shifted his weight forward over his horse's withers and urged the puffing gelding up the steep, narrow trail. They made steady progress, and each time he looked back, Josie's smile told him that everything was fine. Little Christopher Carson Dunn was secured in a traditional Indian cradle board strapped to Josie's back. A flap of soft buckskin shielded his head from the sun and, now, the first hard, pelting drops of rain.

"Damn!" Dunn said, glancing back over his shoulder at Josie and farther back, with his head bowed, the professor. "Yahh! Come on, horse!"

His bay gelding was trying, but it was badly out of shape after spending the entire winter free to graze in Havasu Canyon. To make matters even worse, the trail was soon gullied with running water and the footing became increasingly treacherous. Dunn's anxiety soared. He kept glancing back at Josie. Suddenly, a stupendous clap of thunder shook the canyon, and then a bolt of lightning lanced into the rock wall just a few dozen feet overhead, showering them with dirt and pebbles.

Dunn's gelding spun completely around in a fit of mindless terror and attempted to bolt back down the trail. It was all that he could do to keep it under control, and his blood turned to ice when he saw that Josie and her mare were gone. They'd just disappeared!

Dunn threw himself from his gelding and the panicked animal went racing back down the trail, almost knocking Professor Sutherland's horse over the side. The professor spilled heavily onto the trail as both animals galloped away, heading for the safety of the canyon floor.

"Josie!" he shouted, lunging to the edge of the trail and leaning out into the driving rain to stare downward. "Josie!"

Dunn was nearly insane. Jumping to his feet, he raced past the stunned professor and down the steep, switchbacking trail. It began to hail so violently that he felt as if he were being riddled by buckshot. The red rock turned slick with the ice and he kept falling, his momentum almost sending him over the edge. It seemed to take forever to reach Josie and the mare on the switchback directly below.

Dunn threw himself at his wife, who was lying facedown, covered with mud. Nearby, her mare was barely alive, thrashing and groaning.

"No!" he bellowed when he saw that Josie's neck was broken and her eyes stared at him in death.

The baby coughed and then began to wail. Dunn tore away the buckskin flap and Christopher, with the rain driving into his tiny face, howled. Dunn bent forward over Josie to protect her broken body and that of their son from the storm. Close by, Josie's mare began to shake and wave its hooves like broken wings until its entire body convulsed, then stilled.

Dunn was lost in his grief. He rocked back and forth over his dead wife and his wailing son. Later, he felt a hand on his shoulder and heard Dr. Sutherland's urgency in his ear.

"Bill! We've got to get off this cliff before the trail washes out and we're trapped up here!"

Dunn realized this was true, but he could not bring himself to release Josie. Understanding this, the battered and shaken professor gently pulled Dunn to his feet, then bent and unfastened the cradle board from Josie's back.

Sutherland shouted into the wind, "Her body must have cushioned Christopher's fall and saved his life."

Dunn nodded, stupid with grief.

"Help strap him onto my back," Sutherland yelled. "I'll carry the baby down. You carry Josie!"

And that's the way they got back down into Havasu Canyon, with Dunn, staggering, slipping, and sometimes falling with the beautiful but broken Josie in his arms and the professor wearing the Havasupai cradle board.

The People met them out in the storm because they had been alerted by the empty-saddled horses racing into their village. When Zack and Maud saw Josie covered with mud and her head hanging crookedly, they knew that she was dead and collapsed, wailing with grief.

Professor Sutherland would not hand Christopher over to anyone but insisted on carrying the infant back into the Havasupai village. Only when he was under the protection of Maud's wickiup did he succumb to the true depths of his own heartache.

* * *

They cremated Josie in Havasu Canyon, adhering to the old Indian traditions. Dunn did not trust himself to the opiate of the mescal, but Zack soaked his brain in it until he entered a kinder world. Maud handled the grief better than any of them by devoting herself entirely to little Christopher, holding and rocking and singing to him every waking hour of those long, sorrowful days of mourning. Fortunately, there were several other women nursing babies in Supai, so Josie's boy did not go hungry.

Professor Sutherland went off and busied himself with excavating a promising site for artifacts, but there was no joy in his efforts, and he soon gave it up to wander about on the canyon floor like a spirit in search of a soul.

Late in May, all The People came down to farm in the canyon and Dunn, knowing that he had to do something or go crazy, joined the spring planting and repairing of the complex Havasupai system of irrigation. He worked from sunrise to sunset and ate very little. When the planting was done, he preferred to climb halfway up the rim to grieve at the place where Josie died.

"It is best that we depart Havasu now," Professor Sutherland told him one moonlit evening. "You need to get away from here for a while. There is too much to remind you of Josie. And besides, you have to get on with your life, and so do I."

The archeologist waited for a reply, but when none was forthcoming he said, "I have spoken to Zack and Maud. They will raise Christopher until you are settled and ready to care for your son."

Dunn accepted this decision without comment. He knew only that Sutherland was right—he *had* to get away because everything in the canyon reminded him of Josie. He could not even notice a beautiful flower without the crushing pain of remembering how he had given her one. Or watch children playing under the waterfalls and recall how he and Josie had played in the water like children after working hard all morning in the Havasupai fields. Compared to this desolation, the slaughter of the Howland brothers had been nothing.

"Come on," Sutherland gently urged, "we'll catch up a pair of horses and *lead* them out of this canyon. We'll ride to Lee's Ferry and see what we can do to help that man and take possession of your flock."

"I care nothing about that flock anymore."

"You have a son," the archeologist reminded him. "Christopher is going to want a promising future and it's up to us both to give him one."

Dunn reached into his pocket and held out Josie's split-twig figurine. "Here," he said, "she always said that you ought to have it."

The professor's hand snaked out, but then retracted to his pocket. "I . . . I can't."

"Why!"

"It's too much."

"Take it!"

Sutherland swallowed hard, but he took the remarkable Anasazi prize. "Thank you *very* much!"

"I'm ready to leave now," Dunn announced as he went to catch up their horses.

Sixteen

When she saw the dozen or so mounted Indians, Kate Callahan was glad she had a gun and a rifle and knew how to use both. The Indians reined their ponies to a standstill, blocking the progress of her bleating flock of woolies. Upset and confused, Pepper ran forward, barking and growling. When one of the warriors fitted his bowstring with an arrow, Kate whipped her horse forward and shouted, "No! Pepper, back!"

Kate had taught Pepper hand and voice commands so that he would become a good working sheepdog. He was fiercely protective.

Her response to save the dog was so unexpected that the hunter returned his arrow to his quiver as Pepper wheeled about and then began to circle and tighten up the milling flock. Now that her faithful dog was no longer in danger of being shot, Kate slowed her horse. She was wearing a six-shot percussion pistol, but a rifle seemed more intimidating, so she kept it cradled in her hands and tried to look brave. Kate suspected that these horsemen were Navajo, who were usually friendly, but there were a few renegade bands that wouldn't hesitate to murder her and steal the flock.

Kate was afraid they would smell her fear and so she reined in her sorrel about twenty yards in front of them and lifted her hand in a gesture of peace. She did not recognize a single one of the horsemen and kept her rifle pointed in their direction. When the Indians did not respond to her greeting, Kate lowered her hand and rode even closer, knowing that Indians refuse to shout. If these were Navajo or Hopi rather than far-ranging Paiutes, they would know some Spanish and English.

"Hello," she said, hoping that they did not hear the distinct tremor in her voice. "Navajo?"

One nodded as they urged their ponies even closer. These were stocky, bare-legged, and proud men. Their silver and turquoise jewelry contrasted sharply with their dark skin. Some of them wore headbands, all wore breechclouts and fringed leggings.

"Navajo land," one of the riders said gravely as he made a circling gesture with his free hand.

"Yes," Kate agreed.

She knew this, but had hoped to avoid the Navajo during this crossing at the Little Colorado River.

The Indian's eyes swept over her like a hot desert wind. "Good rifle. Good horse. Many sheep. Bad dog."

Kate had watched John and Emma Lee dicker down at their ferry crossing often enough to realize that these Navajo would expect a stiff toll for grazing sheep across their land. Emma had tried to prevent her from leaving with the flock, warning her that this very thing might happen—or worse. But Kate hadn't listened, and John wasn't going to be around anymore to stop her.

"Five sheep," she told them, holding up the splayed fingers of her left hand.

The Navajo understood and made sour faces, as if they'd bitten into a lemon. Then, their spokesman raised both his hands, opening and closing them four times.

"No," Kate said in a determined voice. "Forty sheep are too many."

"Navajo take good rifle and good horse. Take *all* sheep! Kill bad dog and eat, too!"

It was as much of a threat as the Navajo would make, and Kate knew that it was no bluff. Her first instinct was to give the Indians forty sheep and attempt to reach the rim above Havasu Canyon without further payments. She did not need to remind herself that this flock did not belong to her and that she was under no obligation to William Dunn. None whatsoever. But Kate had often heard John Lee remark that Indians viewed conceding to a bad bargain too quickly or easily to be a definite indication of weakness. Weakness, Lee had said, spawned contempt and contempt invariably resulted in exploitation. The last thing Kate wished was ever to be exploited again—she would rather die.

"No!" the leader said in an angry, guttural voice as he reached back over his shoulder and drew an arrow, eyes burning into Kate.

Kate's reins slipped from her hand and she unholstered the old six-shot Navy Colt that Emma had given her. The walnut handle of the pistol was broken, but it fired, and Kate knew that she could kill at least two, maybe even three, of the Navajo before they put their first arrow into her chest.

For almost a minute, all that could be heard was the bleating of the sheep and Pepper's panting as the dog moved around and around the flock, keeping them tightly bunched. Then, slowly, the Indian raised both hands, opening and closing them twice.

Kate made herself wait as if she were considering a very difficult decision. Her face feeling as tight as dried mud, she finally nodded in agreement. "Twenty sheep."

The Navajo jabbed a forefinger at Pepper. Kate's elation died and she gripped her pistol even tighter. No matter what, she would not allow Pepper to be killed and eaten.

"No." To emphasize her point, she dismounted, ground-tied her sorrel, and went over to the dog, who whined anxiously. Dropping to one knee, Kate scooped the dog up in her arms and carried him to her saddle. As a puppy and even as a young dog in training, she'd often squeezed Pepper between herself and the pommel. Kate had not done so for quite some time, and it was all she could do to hoist the full-grown animal into the saddle and keep the sorrel from shying away in fear. To his credit and intelligence, Pepper didn't squirm or attempt to leap from her arms. He climbed onto the empty saddle as if he'd done it every day and crouched there, whining softly until she remounted and found her stirrups.

The Indians thought a dog sitting on a horse in front of the woman was highly amusing. They smiled, then began to laugh, dissipating the tension. Pepper didn't understand and growled, but Kate reached under his neck and stroked his rumblings into silence. Had she been John Lee and had her hands been free, Kate might have attempted to cut out the flock's culls and weaklings for these high-handed Indians. Instead, she sat quietly holding her dog while the Navajo drove their horses into the flock and cut out twenty of the best sheep, all of them fat and in their prime breeding years. They had their hands full trying to keep them from rejoining the main flock, and when one large and noisy ewe proved to be particularly difficult to hold, the Navajo drove an arrow through her body, then began butchering the ewe even before she stopped thrashing.

"Let's go, Pepper," Kate ordered.

The dog leapt from the saddle. Being trained to separate the flock was something that Pepper knew and understood. Rams and lambs, for example, were often cut away from the ewes and wethers to be doctored or castrated. Pepper quickly had the majority of the flock hurrying westward while the Navajo began to gather wood for a roasting fire.

Kate never looked back. She crossed the Little Colorado River Gorge and pushed the flock up the other side and kept them moving well past sunset. Two days later, while following the South Rim again, she ran into Bill Dunn and the professor on their way back to Lonely Dell.

When the two men saw her, they galloped forward, and Pepper would have raced out ahead to defend his flock if Kate hadn't ordered him back. A few minutes later, however, the dog recognized the familiar faces and actually put on a rare display of tail wagging to let them know he was happy to see old friends.

Kate had anticipated a warm and enthusiastic greeting, but Dunn and the scientist drew in their horses looking somber and upset.

"Miss Callahan, what in bloody blue blazes are you doing way out here alone!" Dunn demanded, his eyes searching the eastern horizon, probably for John Lee.

Kate had to struggle to curb her own anger. She'd expected gratitude and now this man was yelling at her as though she were a truant child.

"I came to deliver your flock."

"Where's Mr. Lee!"

Kate could not trust herself to speak to Dunn, so she addressed the professor. "You're looking very fit and rested, Dr. Sutherland. It appears that Havasu Canyon agreed with you."

"It did," Sutherland said somberly. "Until only a few weeks ago."

Kate blinked. "What happened?"

Sutherland looked to his companion. "Bill, why don't you just tell her about Josie and get it over with?"

Dunn nodded but was unable to meet Kate's eyes when he whispered, "There was an accident and Josie was killed."

Kate bowed her head. "I'm sorry. For her, and for . . ."

"The boy is alive and well, thank God," Dunn said, heaving a deep sigh. "He's being cared for in Havasu Canyon."

Kate didn't understand. "You mean that you just left him?"

"What else could I do!" Dunn snapped. "Christopher doesn't know me from Adam! I need to get this flock and . . ."

His voice broke and a long moment passed until Dunn collected himself to say, "I'm sorry, Kate. I had no right to raise my voice at you. I ought to be grateful, but you took a foolish risk in bringing this flock out here alone."

"It worked out," Kate said. "But right now, these sheep need water and I was told that there was a spring just a few miles ahead and a good bed ground with plenty of feed."

"You were well informed. We camped there last night,"

Sutherland said. "Wouldn't mind camping there again to-night."

"Then that's what I think we should do," Kate said, looking at Dunn for agreement.

Instead, he asked, "Why did you come all this way out here alone?"

"I'm not alone," she corrected. "I have Pepper, my good mare, and the sheep."

"You know what I mean," Dunn said, not smiling at her attempt to sidestep the issue.

"I'll explain after we get to the spring and the bed ground. I've pushed your flock hard since leaving Lee's Ferry. We've come over a hundred miles, and some of the lambs are strug-gling."

"Sure," Dunn said. "Look, Kate, I'm sorry."

"You already apologized," she reminded him. "And under the circumstances, you're more than forgiven. Josie was a fine woman."

Dunn swallowed hard and reined his horse toward the flock. After he was gone, the archeologist explained, "Bill is taking his wife's death very hard. We *had* to get out of that canyon because the memories were just too painful."

"How did it happen?"

"We got caught in a storm coming out of Havasu Canyon. A bolt of lightning spooked our horses. I was thrown to the ground but Josie's mount spun, lost its footing, and fell over the side. Josie had their son strapped in an Indian cradle board. Somehow, that poor woman managed to land facedown and save her son from being crushed to death."

"Bill looks awful. What's going to happen to him now?"

"He's strong and will eventually recover. Having a son to work for and think about will be the very best kind of medi-cine. Our friend already feels a healthy responsibility for the child."

Sutherland drew out a handkerchief and wiped sweat from

his face. "On the other hand, Bill might just ride away and never be seen or heard from again."

"Yes," Kate agreed. "I sense that he's run away from something before. There's always been a sadness or guilt hidden in him, even when he brought Josie to Lonely Dell."

"Kate, if the man takes ahold here and builds for his future and that of his boy, he'll recover. But if he runs away from this pain, I'm afraid that he may never find himself again."

Kate suspected that Sutherland was correct. "Come on," she said, "let's get to camp. I'm afraid that what I've got to say isn't going to raise anyone's spirits."

With that, Kate rode off to help Pepper move the flock toward the spring somewhere just ahead.

It was dark and the stars were beginning to appear as they sat huddled around a campfire less than a mile from the South Rim of the Grand Canyon. Kate had already learned all the details of Josie's tragic death, and now the two men were waiting to find out why in the world John Lee had allowed her to push the flock of sheep over to the South Rim.

"John Lee isn't coming back to Lonely Dell," Kate told them. "A warrant for his arrest has been issued by the federal authorities. When found, he will be tried in Beaver, Utah."

"For what?" Dunn asked.

Kate glanced at the professor, then back across the fire at Dunn. "Have you ever heard of the Mountain Meadows Massacre?"

"No."

"What about you, Professor?"

"I'm afraid that I have, but I thought that it was all just rumors. . . ."

"No," Kate said, her voice turning cold. "It really happened. I was there. My parents were among the murdered. I was spared because I was just a small child."

"What are you talking about?" Dunn asked, his voice dropping to a whisper.

It was an effort to speak. "It's not something I really *can* talk about, Bill," Kate said. "At least, not without tears."

"Would you like me to tell him?" Sutherland asked, looking very worried.

Kate nodded.

"Bill, the Mountain Meadows Massacre occurred when a wagon train of California-bound emigrants were ambushed in a valley called Mountain Meadow in southwestern Utah by Mormons and Indians. More than a hundred men and women, mostly from Arkansas, were massacred. Not one adult was spared."

"But why!" Dunn exclaimed, looking from one to the other.

Kate's hands knotted and she said, "It's not easy to explain or even to understand, much less forgive. After the massacre, I was raised by the Mormons. During those years, they told me again and again how their people had always been persecuted for their beliefs, especially for polygamy. They were driven out of Missouri, then later suffered the same fate in Illinois, where their leader, Joseph Smith, and his brother were murdered by a lynch mob. Brigham Young, their present day leader and head of their church, had no choice but to bring them to the West—to Deseret. But here they were despised because of their practice of polygamy. Did you know, for example, that John Lee has had nineteen wives?"

Dunn's jaw dropped before he said, "Kate, are you sure he's had *that* many?"

"Of course I am. He intended for me to become the twentieth, but I refused."

"Where are all of them now?"

"Most of them left him after Mountain Meadows, but those who remained loyal are living on small homesteads which Mr. Lee regularly visits. He is, as you might have noticed, especially fond of Emma and Lonely Dell. He has fathered many, many fine children by all of his wives."

Dunn considered this astonishing news for a moment, then looked at Kate saying, "I'm sorry about your own parents. I can hardly believe such a terrible thing could have taken place."

"Believe me, it *did,"* Kate said. "But you have to know a little of the background. You see, when my parents' wagon train entered the state of Deseret, relations between the Mormons and the United States government were strained very nearly to the point of war. In fact, President Buchanan actually had sent soldiers here to put down what he believed to be a rebellion. Tensions were at the breaking point and everyone expected the worst. A rumor started that our wagon train was harboring federal spies and ammunition. To make matters even worse, the local Paiutes were furious because earlier emigrants had cleaned out most of the game from their traditional hunting grounds and had cut down piñon pine nut trees, the major source of their winter food. Those Indians were facing a winter of starvation and demanded revenge. They attacked my parents' wagon train but were repelled. Then, they threatened to attack the Mormon settlements if those people did not help them wipe out the intruders!"

Kate had to stop. Tears were brimming from her eyes and streaming down her cheeks. She angrily scrubbed them away with her sleeve. "I won't go into the terrible details. Under a flag of truce and the leadership of our own John Lee, the Mormons talked my father and the other emigrants into surrendering their weapons, swearing that they would be protected. Instead, the entire wagon train was massacred and plundered. I was one of eighteen young children spared."

Before Dunn or the professor could say anything, Kate jumped up and rushed off to be alone.

Dunn started to rise and go after her, but the professor shook his head. "My friend, I suspect that she has never confided that tragedy to anyone else. I think that you ought to leave her alone right now. Kate is a very strong person, and she's not going to throw herself off the rim of the Grand Canyon, if that's what you're worried about."

"The thought never entered my mind. But . . . but what was she doing, living at Lonely Dell with the ringleader of those murderers?"

Dunn shook his head. "I just can't believe that a man like John Lee would be involved in such a horrible crime. He's too good, too wise and . . ."

"Maybe," Sutherland interrupted, "Mr. Lee will be exonerated."

"From what Kate said, that doesn't sound likely."

"I can't help you with any answers," Sutherland told him. "Even if it's true that the Mormons feared attack by the Indians and the United States Army, and that particular wagon train really was filled with ammunition and federal spies . . . well, it still doesn't excuse what occurred at Mountain Meadows."

Dunn agreed. He kept glancing anxiously toward the rim. "Are you sure Kate will be all right?"

"Yes," Sutherland replied, "I have the feeling that we are dealing with a very remarkable young woman."

"I wonder why she ever came to Lonely Dell . . . unless it was to . . . naw," Dunn said, shaking his head.

"Were you going to say that she must have come intending to murder John Lee?"

"I'm ashamed to say that I was."

"Don't be ashamed," Sutherland told him, "because I was wondering the very same thing. Given the terrible circumstances of her childhood, what other reason would Kate have to seek him out?"

"I don't know and I suspect that I had better not ask."

"Me, neither," Sutherland said, firing up his pipe and turning his attention to the early evening stars.

They remained at the spring for a week, none of them sure what to say about Kate's revelation or what to do next. Fortunately, the graze was excellent and the springwater sweet. Finally, however, Kate announced that she was returning to Lonely Dell.

"Why?" Dunn asked.

"Now that her husband has been arrested, Emma could probably use my help."

"She has strong sons and daughters."

"Well," Kate said, looking away, "the truth is that I can't think of anywhere else to go. I've no family left back in Arkansas, they were all part of that wagon train. Anyway, what about you and Professor Sutherland?"

"He wants to stay on the South Rim and hunt for ancient ruins."

"He would never survive in this country alone."

"I know," Dunn said, a trace of exasperation in his voice, "and I've tried to convince him of that, but he refuses to listen."

"I'll talk to him."

"It won't help. He has strong reasons for being out here, reasons that are driving him like a pair of Spanish spurs."

For the first time in a good long time, Kate smiled. "Isn't it amazing how we all have our secret and sorrowful mysteries? You, me, *and* the professor?"

Dunn started to object but caught himself in time.

"So," Kate said, breaking an awkward silence, "will you or the professor make the next confession?"

Dunn thought about his own dark secret and said nothing.

"All right then," Kate said, "can I at least ask what you intend to do with this flock?"

"I have no idea." Dunn frowned. "Josie and I had planned to start a ranch and do some mustanging. Two months ago, I had big plans, but now . . . well, now I just don't know."

"It's none of my business," Kate said, "but, if for no reason other than to maintain your sanity, you ought to go ahead with your plans."

"I may," he said, "for Christopher."

"I'd love to visit Havasu Canyon someday. Is it as beautiful as its legend? And is the water a special blue?"

"Yes, very beautiful and very special."

"This may sound odd, but I discovered that Lonely Dell has its own beauty," Kate said, knowing it took time to appreciate Paria Canyon, the Vermilion Cliffs, and the incredibly beautiful sunrises and sunsets that turned the Colorado into a river of fire. "Emma and I agree that, when we first arrived, we thought it was . . . terrible. But it grows on you after a while."

"I can't imagine you staying there very long," Dunn told her. "I don't know why, but I can't."

"Will you stay close and protect Dr. Sutherland?"

"As close as I can and still start a ranch," Dunn said. "But I'll have to be gone at times."

"And who will care for your flock?"

"I don't know," he admitted. "Perhaps the Havasupai. I hadn't thought that far ahead."

"You should," she told him. "You *have* to, if you're going to succeed out here."

"Did Major Powell ever come through the crossing this winter?"

"No. He's returned to Washington." Kate saw the obvious disappointment. "Is he the only one who can hear *your* confession?"

"As a matter of fact, he is."

"Too bad," she replied, walking away in preparation for leaving.

That evening, Sutherland said, "Kate shouldn't be allowed to go back by herself. What if she meets the Navajo again, and this time they insist on her horse or rifle?"

"I've been asking myself the very same question, Professor. But what can either of us do? We can't force her to stay here and, anyway, there's no reason for it."

"She knows sheep and Pepper is devoted to her," the professor said. "Why don't you hire her?"

"Me?" Dunn couldn't believe he had heard correctly.

"That's right."

"Why, I couldn't do that!"

"Give me one good reason why not? I know that you have plenty of gold. You can afford to pay her."

"And be *responsible* for her!"

"Have you always been so afraid of responsibility?"

"Yes, dammit! And I should have taken responsibility on that trail out of Havasu Canyon and not let you and Josie override my concerns. I should have insisted that we turn back until the weather cleared."

"So, you're filled with guilt despite the fact that your wife and I both voted to push on. Or have you conveniently forgotten that fact because you enjoy feeling overwhelmed with remorse?"

"Stick to archeology, Professor! You're way off track."

"Am I?" Sutherland shrugged his broad shoulders. "Some people collect guilt the way I collect bones. It makes them feel better."

"You're talking crazy," Dunn said, then spun on his heel and marched away.

Dunn was still trying to figure out what he should do about Kate the next morning when she saddled her horse and then called Pepper over to say good-bye. Watching the pair, Dunn was again reminded of how devoted Pepper was to the young woman.

"I'd give Pepper back to you," Dunn said, "but we both know how badly I need him to protect the flock."

"Of course." Kate stood up. "You'd better take ahold of Pepper's collar until I'm out of sight. I'm afraid he'll want to follow me."

Dunn came over and extended his hand. "I can't thank you enough and I wish you a quick and safe journey back to Lee's Ferry."

She managed a smile, hugged Dr. Sutherland, and mounted her horse. Without a good-bye, Kate galloped off but did not go a mile before she heard Pepper's frantic barking and swiveled around in the saddle to see the dog making a beeline after her.

Kate reined in her horse and turned around. Pepper was barking and wagging his tail.

"No!" she scolded. "You *have* to go back!"

But the dog didn't understand. She had never been able to teach Pepper how to stop offering her his complete loyalty and devotion. Feeling bad for making the dog confused and unhappy, she rode back to the sheep camp.

"You're going to have to tie him up," she told the two men. "And keep him tied until tomorrow."

"I'll use a heavy rope," Dunn said. "I'm very sorry about this."

"So am I."

When the dog was tied, Kate galloped away. She put two fast miles between herself and the camp before she glanced back. Pepper wasn't coming, but she could still hear his faint barking and it almost broke her heart.

That night, Kate made a cold camp down in the Little Colorado Gorge, hidden in a stand of willow trees where she was unlikely to be seen by the Navajo. She listened to the river gurgle and to the rustlings of night animals. She kept both her firearms close to her side and drifted off to sleep when the moon finally floated over the rim as round and golden as a Mormon melon.

At dawn, she was suddenly awakened by Pepper licking her face and yipping with joy. A short piece of rope attached to his collar had been chewed apart.

"Pepper!" she cried, hugging the squirming dog tightly. "What are we going to do now? Dunn and that flock can't make it without you."

Pepper didn't seem to care. He kept yipping and licking her face. Kate fed him some jerked lamb and watched the sun float over the eastern rim of the Little Colorado. After a while, she knew that she really didn't have any choice but to take Pepper back and remain with William Dunn and his new flock.

Seventeen

"Kate, I can't help feeling that you shouldn't stay with us," Dunn said, voicing a growing concern as he and Kate stood beside the Grand Canyon.

"What you really mean is that it doesn't *look* right," Kate responded. "But don't worry about my reputation. I know how to take care of myself."

"I'm sure you do."

"I was raised on a farm," Kate told him, "where I learned about horses, sheep, and cattle almost as soon as I was walking. Later, while growing up on a Mormon ranch, I found out even more about livestock. I trained John Lee's sheepdogs and worked right alongside that family at lambing and shearing times—including this spring when you didn't show up and John wasn't around to help."

"There's no questioning your knowledge of livestock," Dunn tried to say, "but . . ."

"And I know this country far better than either of you men. Maybe I can even help keep you from making a few disastrous mistakes and losing the flock."

Dunn suspected this was true, and he already regretted getting Kate riled. Trying once more to mend fences, he said, "I didn't mean that I was worried that you couldn't hold your own out here. I am worried about . . ."

"We're back to my reputation, aren't we?"

His embarrassed silence told that she had correctly guessed his concerns. "Listen, both of you. To begin with, my reputation is already shot among the Mormons, and no one else knows or cares about me anymore. All I expect is that you pay me a fair wage and that we keep things strictly business. Agreed?"

"Fine," Dunn said, feeling bruised by her abruptness. He had tried to protect Kate from slander and, in return, she'd stomped on his objections as it they were the babblings of a naive child. "I'm glad we have a clear understanding. Now, what do you consider to be a fair wage?"

"Fifty dollars a month for me *and* Pepper."

Dunn decided it would be unwise to inform this woman that, when he'd bought the flock, the dog was supposed to be part of the deal. Besides, it was clear that Pepper's deepest loyalty was to Kate. "Agreed."

"Then it's settled," Sutherland announced. "If we were in a city, I'd take you both out for dinner and we'd celebrate with champagne. I have a feeling that this is an historic beginning."

Dunn wasn't sure if the professor was being sarcastic or not. "Walt, this is no big deal. After all, I've only a few hundred mangy sheep without even a home range."

"Then that should be your first priority," the professor said. "Kate, where can our friend go to file legal title to northern Arizona ranchland?"

"The nearest territorial land office is in a town called Prescott. It's maybe a hundred miles to the south."

"What does it cost an acre?" Dunn asked.

"If it's like Utah, some is free for homesteading but much of it is going to cost you money."

"I have gold," Dunn said, glad that he and Josie had dug up the rest of it before leaving Lee's Ferry. "I'd prefer to ranch along the Coconino Plateau. I'd like to have my range close to the winter hunting lands of the Havasupai."

"This is all good cattle, sheep, and wild horse country," Kate told him. "In fact, I saw three bands of mustangs just yesterday."

"I've also spotted a few. I was wondering if I could trap and sell them to the army as cavalry mounts."

"Do you know anything about mustanging?"

"No. Do you?"

"I'm afraid not," Kate had to admit. "But we can learn by trial and error. Better yet, you could hire experienced mustangers to teach us their tricks."

"I expect that would be the best way," Dunn agreed. "Maybe I could hire a couple of top-notch vaqueros."

Sutherland had lost interest in the conversation and had dismounted. Now he was squatting on his heels, absently pecking away at the earth with his sharp rock hammer. He looked up and said, "If you two have everything settled, then I guess this is where we part company. I'm going to backtrack along the rim. One of the Havasupai told me where I could find a half-buried Anasazi ruin. He said it was hidden in a thick stand of piñon and juniper pine and very easy to miss."

"Professor," Dunn said, "be reasonable. You can't stay out here all alone!"

"Sure I can."

"You'd starve!"

"Before I could get a harvest, I might at that," Sutherland conceded. "I guess I'll have to ask for the loan of a rifle so I can shoot a few antelope until I can become skilled at setting rabbit traps and learning what native plants and insects are edible."

"You tried shooting in Havasu Canyon. You're a terrible shot. Remember?"

"Then I'm afraid I'll need quite a lot of ammunition."

"What about water?" Kate asked.

"The Havasupai told me there is a little spring near these ancient ruins. A spring that never goes completely dry."

Sutherland dug into his pockets. In addition to the usual assortment of small bones, he dragged out a few dozen corn, squash, and bean seeds. "I didn't spend all winter in Havasu Canyon and not learn something about farming and irrigation.

It's still early enough in the season to plant and reap a fall harvest."

Dunn sighed. He wasn't getting through at all. "Professor, you just won't listen to reason, will you?"

"Not *your* reason," he replied. "So please let's discontinue this discussion. You see, I know exactly what I'm doing and the magnitude of the personal risks involved. I'm happy with my decision."

"All right," Dunn said, "but as soon as we locate a ranch site, we'll be back to pay a social call."

"You'll be checking up on me, is that it?"

"Yes," Kate said, "we will."

He inspected a rock, decided it held no mystery, and placed it back in its original position. Putting his hammer back into his saddlebags and slapping the dust from his hands, Sutherland remounted his horse. "I wish you both wouldn't worry so much about me. I have come to realize, just lately, that I've spent my whole life preparing for this scientific adventure. I have learned everything ever written about the way the Anasazi once flourished. I mean to recreate their ancient ways of hunting and farming, except that I will have the enormous advantage of owning superior vegetable seeds, a saddle horse, matches, and a modern rifle."

"But Dr. Sutherland, you're *not* Anasazi," Dunn said. "I don't mean to be unkind or give insult, but you're a middle-aged scientist who hasn't known suffering or hardship."

"Then it's high time that I did!" Sutherland's eyes grew distant as he gazed out over the canyon, watching cloud shadows play across the North Rim walls. "You see, it was not until I spent this past winter in Havasu that I realized I have a deep yearning to live very simply. I *have* to do this in order to better understand how the Anasazi thought and adapted to this harsh country. I want to experience their struggles, failures and triumphs and I want to know them in a deeply personal way. I couldn't do that at the university, and I couldn't do that living on your ranch in a cabin. Can't you understand?"

"But even the Anasazi failed and were forced to leave the rim country," Dunn reminded the scientist. "At least, that's what you told me."

"As I might also fail," Sutherland admitted. "But I'll be wiser and stronger."

"Not if failure results in your death! Professor, we're not dealing with some theoretical situation you can analyze or read about in a textbook. This country is . . ."

He raised his hand. "Beautiful, yet very cruel and unforgiving. I know all that, Bill. But I'm willing to take the risk. And, if I get sick or think that I am losing my mind, I will either come to visit you or saddle my horse and ride back to Havasu Canyon."

Dunn pulled his own rifle from its boot. He gave it to the professor, along with a full box of cartridges he had packed in his saddlebags. "Then good-bye, Dr. Sutherland. Kate or I will ride over and check on you every few weeks."

"Only if you would enjoy doing so. When you go to Prescott, could you bring me back some pipe tobacco, coffee, and flour?"

"Of course."

"I can't pay you right now, but . . ."

"You can pay me later."

"Thank you," Sutherland said, deciding that he had better leave while he still held his resolve.

It took Professor Sutherland a few days to locate the ruins. He would have missed them if it had not been for the sharply contrasting swath of green grass and all the animal tracks leading to a spring-fed stream that trickled only a few hundred yards before quietly seeping over the edge of the South Rim. After stopping to water his horse and allow the hungry animal to graze, Sutherland noticed that the full length of the meandering stream was defined by a series of rock dams. The dams had been trampled by animals or partially washed away, but their basic outlines were still visible to the trained eye. Sutherland immediately recognized them as the work of the Anasazi—a word derived from the Navajo which meant "ancient ones" or "enemy ancestors." Those people had arrived in this area soon after the birth of Christ and had left many prominent cliff dwellings, including those in Marble Canyon which Powell had described. Even the most exhaustive literature search had turned up very little information about the Anasazis' origin or their canyon country existence. The big mystery was why they had abandoned their great cliff dwellings. Some believed that they had either been annihilated by enemies or that a prolonged drought had forced them to emigrate to the Southwest, perhaps to become the Pueblo peoples. Sutherland, being a strong advocate of the theory of cultural evolution generated by constant warfare and conquest, hoped to find evidence supporting his thesis among the Anasazi ruins.

He believed such evidence would consist of mass graves whose skeletons bore the marks of the violence of war. Crushed skulls, broken bones, spearpoints and arrowheads buried in bone, war axes and signs of mutilation or even cannibalism would strongly support his hypothesis.

On the other hand, evidence of a prolonged drought would be far more difficult to detect and to defend in the scientific community. Such evidence might be found only in the tree rings of preserved timbers used in Anasazi shelters, perhaps also in tools or in the stunting of bones, which could indicate slow starvation and extreme water deprivation. Professor Sutherland hoped that, if he could discover and document the tree rings on the logs used by the Anasazi during their habitation, he would be on solid scientific ground.

On his first glorious day of discovery, he spent all morning crawling around on his hands and knees studying the terraced Anasazi gardens. Hours passed like minutes. The sun grew very hot and his unattended horse slowly shuffled off into the pines, searching for shade.

Yes, Sutherland thought with growing excitement, each terrace along this little waterway was once carefully shaped, and was *still* bowl-shaped despite the ravages of passing centuries. Grazing animals, the benefactors of Anasazi ingenuity, now enjoyed the broken dams because, hundreds of years later, they encouraged the profusion of tender spring grass. The professor shivered with excitement. And look! See how many of the heavy base rocks forming each dam still fit together so nicely!

It was all quite perfect, he decided. And it was a luxury to close his eyes now and visualize the ancient ones tending the terraces, using stone implements to dig the holes for planting and then carefully placing each precious seed in the moist earth.

Of course, he thought, *once the first green shoots of corn or squash appeared, the Anasazi must have kept a constant vigil along this stretch of oasis. If not, deer or rabbits would quickly have gobbled up the new plants and there would have been no harvest.*

The archeologist was grinning as he followed the succession of broken dams right down to the very rim of the Grand Canyon. If he were those people trying to survive in this arid land, would he allow even a drop of precious water to be lost over the rim?

No, of course not! Sutherland then noticed a water-filled stone catch basin suspended just below the rim. It was about the size of a washtub and had definitely been chipped out of the rock by human hands. Had the Anasazi lowered pottery or watertight baskets into the basin for water, or had they even climbed down and bathed there while dangling a thousand feet up in the sky?

Sutherland laughed out loud at the vision of taking a bath surrounded by space. Yet, he was quite sure that the Anasazi had not been afraid of falling to their deaths. And the big washbasin could have been reached. Even now, as he edged out over the rim, toes digging for purchase, he saw faint footholds chopped out of solid rock. Sutherland had to fight off the desire to climb over the rim and see if these ancient cuts would support his own weight.

At that moment, he happened to raise his head and gaze out across the vast expanse of open air and see a condor soaring effortlessly on the rising thermal winds. This was not the first time he had seen these huge birds on the wing. Caught in a rare moment of indecision, Sutherland teetered at the very rim of the canyon, one leg dangling, bare toes wiggling toward the stone cuts.

He very much wished to examine the catch basin, even to bathe in it like the Anasazi. On the other hand, if he really were thinking like an Anasazi, wouldn't the sudden appearance of a condor be associated with death and thus considered a warning not to climb over this rim?

The professor decided not to climb over the edge. Instead, he went to find the half-buried ruins described by the Havasupai. That's when he stumbled across his horse, dozing in the shade. The animal had stepped on and broken one of its leather reins.

I should be more careful and must remember to unsaddle and then hobble this animal. And maybe I should also remove that rifle from its saddle boot and hide it out of the weather. This horse is going to be a bother, especially in the winter when the grass is dead and he has nothing to eat. Poor horse. Has no idea he might have to sacrifice himself in the name of science.

Sutherland hurriedly unbridled, unsaddled, and hobbled the gelding, then gave no more thought to it as he resumed his explorations. He soon discovered the Anasazi ruins. At first glance, the slight depressions in the earth and the little eroding adobe mounds no bigger than anthills seemed insignificant. Most would have dismissed them without guessing that they were all that was left of a small but flourishing village.

Sutherland closed his eyes, believing that, if he were in a proper state of mental receptiveness, the Indian spirits would aid him in his discoveries. But now, as he stood frozen between two slight depressions that he suspected were the remains of kivas or underground houses, he could hear nothing but a wren chirruping in the bush.

After several moments of listening for the ancients to speak and tell him where he should begin his explorations, Sutherland realized he was not yet in a proper state of communion with the spirits. That would come later. He was not a superstitious man, and he held no stock in voodoo or black magic, but he did believe in spirits. There were too many accounts of them over the centuries to be discounted. Sutherland was sure that spirits were benign, except those who haunted their murderers.

The professor sat down in one of the round depressions and drew his bony knees up to rest his chin. The vulture was now circling overhead and Sutherland realized that the bird had decided that he was a potential meal. He waved and shouted and the vulture veered off and sailed out over the canyon. Sutherland grinned. He would prevail here no matter how many months or years it took to reconstruct and then write a series of academic papers, perhaps even a classic text, on this, his life's crowning achievement. He would show everyone that he *did* possess the talent and the courage to make the necessary sacrifices to achieve lofty scientific stature.

He would show them *all,* by jingo.

Twenty miles to the south, Dunn twisted around in his saddle and gazed back toward the Grand Canyon. The distance was so great that he couldn't see anything but for the slightly raised and darker North Rim.

"You're thinking about our professor, aren't you," Kate said. "I've been worrying about him, too."

"I don't know how I'm going to feel if he comes to a bad end. I've been imagining all the unfortunate things that could happen to him on the rim. Accidentally tumbling into the Grand Canyon isn't even the worst of them."

"I think Walter is far more competent than he appears. Mr. Lee told me Walter has a very good sense of direction."

"I'm not worried about him getting lost. I'm worried about him being killed by renegade Indians or outlaws."

Dunn rose in his stirrups. "Look there, Kate! Mustangs!"

The mustangs probably had been watching them for quite some time from a high, rocky bench to the southeast. They were about a half mile away. There were some colts with their mothers, and the sight of them brought a smile to Kate's lips.

"Bill, have you been thinking how we might catch them?"

"Zack and I used to talk about mustanging. I learned that the Hualapai have had some success catching wild horses by driving them into box canyons or into deep arroyos."

"Sounds like a good idea," Kate responded, "but how do they know which canyons and arroyos to block?"

"Apparently, the trick is to spend time watching the band's daily movements. Horses are territorial, and they'll have a definite eating and drinking routine. There aren't many good springs in this country. I'm sure we'll have no trouble figuring out their drinking habits."

"After we catch them, are you prepared to risk your neck to break them for the army?"

"I am," Dunn told her. "But I'll not be foolish or take unnecessary punishment. I always try to buck broncs out in a river or in deep sand. And I'll do it without breaking their spirits."

"That sounds good to me," Kate agreed. "I know that there's a time for spurs and quirts, but I'd prefer to use them as little as possible. Spanish spurs are cruel, and I've seen horses with their flanks raw and bloody as meat. You can bet that I didn't let that pass without offering a good piece of my mind."

"You're quite a scrapper."

"I've been fighting all my life for one thing or another," she admitted. "Usually, I get what I'm after."

* * *

They selected a headquarters that same afternoon. It offered a good spring, which fed a big grove of cottonwoods, as well as a large grassy valley surrounded by miles and miles of open grazing land.

"This would be ideal!" Kate exclaimed. "The ranch house could go up on that low rise so it would overlook the valley. We could build corrals and divert that stream so that it would irrigate the entire valley."

"Yes," he agreed, twisting around in his saddle. "I'd judge we're about thirty miles southeast of Havasu Canyon. I think Zack would approve and agree that we're far enough away so that we'll not be intruding on the Havasupai's winter hunting grounds."

They tasted the water. It was clear, sweet, and cool. Dunn couldn't help but wonder if it bled into the earth and was the main source that fed Havasu Creek. If so, that would be a very favorable sign. He knelt and scooped up a handful of earth. The place already felt like home.

"Kate," he vowed, "I'm going to sink my talons into this big, empty land and make it into a fine ranch."

Kate breathed in deeply of the grass and the sage. She decided that she preferred this open land to the close, hot Paria Canyon that John Lee had chosen. "This is just a big, lonesome place; it's nothing at all like Emma's Lonely Dell."

"Maybe we ought to call it the Lonesome Valley Ranch," Dunn said. "What do you think?"

"That's as good a name as any," she told him as she went to share the news with Pepper.

Eighteen

If it hadn't been for the sharp and painful memory of losing Josie, Dunn would have been a contented man as he and Kate began to construct a cabin and pole corrals for the livestock. It was hard work, and they did not have the proper tools. Dunn was wondering how they were ever going to complete the cabin when he and Kate discovered three frightened Hualapai Indians cowering under the cottonwood trees, two of them wounded.

"What happened?" Dunn asked after he and Kate had finally convinced the Hualapai that they were out of danger.

Using sign language and broken English, the fugitives explained that their people had been force-marched to a reservation called Topaz on the lower Colorado River. Those who refused had been hunted down and either captured or shot. Many who had made the cruel, hundred-mile crossing of the pitiless desert to Topaz had died.

"All Hualapai either dead or very sick," one of the gaunt Indians told them. "We run far away from that bad place."

Kate went for her medicine while Dunn promised, "Don't worry, you'll be safe here at Lonesome Valley Ranch."

With plenty of good food and Kate's nursing, the three Indians quickly recovered and stayed on to help build the ranch. Dunn was grateful, for he had not been sure how he and Kate would have managed to lift and place the upper logs that comprised the walls of their new cabin and barn, then use lighter timbers to build a good roof. Like the "people of the blue-green water," these Hualapai were hard workers and eager to learn.

After a month, Dunn tried to pay them in gold dust, but they requested a fat ewe and her lamb instead. Then, they led both animals back to their old villages west of Havasu Canyon to share the bounty with their starving people. Three more young men had returned with them.

"I can't pay you all what you're worth," Dunn had explained to the six Indians, "but I'll pay you three sheep a month and do my best to keep anyone from ever forcing you back onto that reservation at Topaz."

The Hualapai were very grateful and quickly accepted Dunn's offer of food and protection.

Near the end of summer when their cabin, a barn, bunkhouse, and pole corrals were up and receiving the finishing touches, Zack arrived unexpectedly from Havasu Canyon with Christopher strapped to his back in a cradle board.

"Maud died and so I didn't see any reason to stay," he told them. "That old woman's heart was broken; she never got over losing Josie."

"None of us have," Dunn said. "I'm sorry to hear about Maud, although I know how hard she was to be around."

"Oh," Zack said with a shrug, "we had our daily differences, but we also had sort of an unspoken agreement."

"And what was that?"

"She had to be the boss." Zack managed a thin smile. "I'll bet that old lady is already telling her Great Spirit how to run things in the happy hunting ground."

"How did you know where to look for us?" Dunn asked, eager to lift the soft buckskin cover and admire his son.

"Well," Zack said, "first I struck out along the rim and ran into the professor! He's having himself quite a time and diggin' like a badger. He said to say hello and told me about where to find you."

"Look at this big kid! He's growing so fast!" Dunn exclaimed as he peeled the buckskin aside and stared at his son, who was gazing at him with big brown eyes. Dunn lifted him free and Christopher gurgled happily.

"Would you just look at him!" Dunn said, turning and showing the baby off to Kate.

"He's a *very* handsome boy."

"That he is."

"Who *are* you?" Zack asked, looking from Dunn to Kate and back again.

"This is Miss Kate Callahan," Dunn said, feeling his cheeks warming. "She was a friend of John and Emma Lee, but now she's working for me."

"Working?"

"That's right," Kate said, looking Zack right in the eye. "Bill hired me and my sheepdog. To be honest, he's still not much of a sheepman and might have lost about half of his flock without me and Pepper."

"Well, then," Zack said, glancing at the dog, "I'm glad you both hired on!"

Next, Zack turned to study the six Hualapai. He must have recognized at least some of them because they began to talk in the Hualapai tongue. Dunn guessed that the Indians were telling Zack about their ordeal with the soldiers and about the hellish Topaz Reservation.

"Damn!" Zack swore when the Indians were finished. "I knew that the Hualapai were having a hell of a time with the United States Army, but I didn't know they were being hunted and shot down like wolves!"

He turned to Dunn. "We should pay a visit to that Topaz Reservation and give the army billy-by-gawd hell!"

"I can't," Dunn told his father-in-law. "I'm trying to build a ranch. Besides, I have to get to Prescott and file for legal title to this valley and as much of the surrounding grazing land as I can afford."

Zack scowled. "You ain't done that yet?"

"No. We've been far too busy trying to get buildings and corrals up before winter."

"Well, you better get movin'! How you going to feel if

some jasper comes along and claims all of this because he paid off some government fella first?"

"I'd feel pretty bad."

"Of course you would!" The old man lowered his voice. "Could be, I'll ride along."

"Maybe you ought to stay up here with Kate and Christopher."

"I got more gold," Zack said, gesturing toward a heavy buckskin bag. "What do you say?"

Dunn figured he'd have been a fool to decline the offer. "All right."

Zack clapped his hands together. "Can I use Kate's horse?"

"Yes," Kate said, "but she'd better come back sound."

"Thank you, Miss!"

That evening, Dunn left Zack and the others and strolled out to their big corral. It was an exceptionally clear night, brilliant with stars. The jutting silhouettes of the San Francisco peaks were bathed in soft moonlight and Dunn enjoyed listening to the yip-yipping serenade of coyotes. Pepper came over to share his company. The dog growled low in its throat and Dunn reached down to scratch behind his ears saying, "They're a long way off tonight, Pepper, so stop fretting."

Kate appeared to join them. "Is this a male only gathering?"

"Nope," Dunn said. "Glad you came to join us."

"Are you excited about going to Prescott with Zack tomorrow?"

"I guess that I am."

"How long has it actually been since you have visited a town?"

"A long time," Dunn confessed. "I expect that I'm going to feel out of place. I'm also worried about you and Christopher."

"Don't be. The Indians would protect us with their lives."

"Is there anything I can bring you back from Prescott?"

"Now that you've asked, I'd like a couple of new dresses. Mine are almost in tatters. Also, some ribbons and a pair of new shoes." Kate reached into her pocket. "Actually, I've a list and some money for . . ."

"I'll pay for everything out of all the wages that I still owe you."

Kate took a step closer. "Just be careful, Bill. Maybe both you and Zack have forgotten how cruel and conniving some men can be."

"I'll keep that thought in mind," he said, folding up her list and putting it in his shirt pocket.

"And you should buy some new clothes for yourself," Kate urged. "A nice new Stetson, three or four pairs of Levi's and shirts and things. Your moccasins are worn-out and you need a couple of pairs of boots, a high-heeled pair for riding, one with lower heels and thicker leather for ground work. Oh, and buy us some warm winter coats."

Dunn looked down at the stiff buckskins he was wearing. "Nothing wrong with these, Kate."

"And buy some soap," she said, ignoring his remark. "I've put it on my list—you should put it on yours as well. And a tin bathtub and some towels, pots, pans and eating utensils, a stove and plenty of food. Don't forget coffee and . . ."

"Whoa!" he protested. "Good Lord, Kate! Zack and I are going to Prescott to buy *land,* not someone's entire general store so they can retire."

"Medicines. Bill, we need bandages and medicine for ourselves, the Indians, and our livestock. And salt and some things to cook with and some candles. Maybe we can even get some glass next spring for windows and I'll sew curtains."

Dunn reached out and gently but firmly placed his hand over her mouth. "Kate," he said, "this is going to be a *fast* trip. Just buy the land, pick up a few supplies, and then hurry back as fast as we can."

She pulled his hand away. "No need for that. If you've got to ride that far, make the most of it. That's the way John Lee thought. What you'll have to do is buy a buckboard and an honest team of mules or horses. Just a pair will do for now.

And we'll need tools—nails, hammers, saws, and those kinds of things."

"Kate, buying this ranchland comes first."

"Why, of course, it does! But once that's done, don't be a piker! Buy what we'll need for the winter and next spring. And for heaven's sake, don't forget to buy plenty of rope."

"Why?"

"For catching wild horses this winter. Remember? And we'll also need hobbles, halters, and . . ."

"All right! All right!" Dunn threw up his hands with exasperation. "Kate, we'll buy a wagon to carry everything. Now, what can I buy for Christopher?"

"I'd look for clothes and shoes. He'll be walking before you know it. And we need warm blankets for everyone," Kate added. "It gets very cold out here in the wintertime."

"How would you know?"

"The desert is *always* cold in the winter."

Dunn knew she was right. "It sounds to me like I'm going to need more than a buckboard."

"A sturdy Conestoga wagon would probably do it—if you can find one at a good price. To pull it, you'd need at least four oxen. As long as we're talking about buying livestock, a pig and a cow would be nice. Christopher needs fresh milk."

"You're making my head ache," Dunn told her as they walked back to the cabin.

"I should go along and make sure you buy everything we'll need," she told him, "but I don't dare leave the flock."

"Kate, I couldn't do this without you," Dunn confessed. "And if . . ."

She rose up on her toes and gave him a peck on the cheek, then hurried away.

"Now what did you do that for?" he muttered as Pepper began to growl again.

At dawn the next morning, Dunn lifted Christopher from his blankets and took the baby outside to show him the kind of sunrise he could never see from deep inside Havasu Canyon.

The boy waved his little arms as the sun floated off the eastern horizon to bathe the Coconino Plateau. The moment shared with his son gave Dunn such joy that he felt his throat ache with gratitude. If only Josie was still with them, he could never have asked for anything more.

"Chris, I know that Lonesome Valley Ranch doesn't impress you a bit right now," Dunn whispered hoarsely, "but someday it will look like a fine place—one of the biggest and most successful in the entire Arizona Territory. And you're going to help me build it right into the next century. There will be no more quitting or running away. I promise you this time I'll stand and fight to the death, no matter what the odds. And we'll fight for our friends the Havasupai and the Hualapai, too. That's what your mother would have wanted and expected of us, and that's the way it always will be."

It was as much of a speech as Dunn had ever made to anyone in his life, but Christopher wasn't in the least bit interested as he gazed up at the Arizona sunrise and gurgled with pleasure.

"Breakfast is ready!" Kate called.

That morning, everyone ate in silence. Dunn laid out plenty of work for the Hualapai Indians. Kate would do the cooking and most of the sheep tending.

"It's about a hundred miles to Prescott," Zack reckoned out loud. "And I believe that it is still the territorial capital of Arizona."

"You're not sure?"

"No. They might have moved her on down to Tucson."

Capital or not, Dunn was determined to file for the rights to this fine valley and as much of the surrounding grazing land as he could afford. Not being a man who liked good-byes, he went to saddle and bridle his sorrel gelding.

"Here's a sack of food," Kate said, tying it around his saddlehorn. "Zack says that Prescott is a hard two-day ride. You are taking your six-gun along with the Winchester, aren't you?"

"Got it right here," he said, patting a bedroll tied behind his cantle.

"When you get to Prescott, you need to keep yourself well armed," Kate said. "There may be . . ."

"I'll do it," he promised. "And stop worrying. Zack and I look so rough and ornery that we'll scare off any hardcases, along with all the respectable women and children."

Kate forced a smile. "We'll look for you to return in about a week or ten days."

"That should be enough time."

Pepper followed them about a mile south, then stopped and barked a few times before trotting back to the flock. Dunn looked over at his father-in-law and smiled. Zack was feeling his oats. He showed his yellow teeth and booted his mount into a gallop. Dunn gave his sorrel its head, but the spunky gelding tried to drop its head and buck. Dunn barely managed to keep from getting pitched. Dragging the sorrel's head up, he gave it a hard lashing across the rump with his rawhide reins. The sorrel grunted, laid its ears back tight, and went racing after Zack and the mare.

The trail to Prescott was longer than Dunn had expected and all uphill. Finally they entered a high valley surrounded on three sides by pine-covered mountains. Pulling his horse up to catch its wind after a tough climb, Dunn said, "I never expected anything this big. Why, there must be a couple of thousand people living in Prescott."

"Yep," Zack agreed, frowning. "They're just crawlin' all over each other like ants. I'm already sick of the sight."

"And there are mines everywhere," Dunn said, pointing to the surrounding mountains that were dotted with tailings. "And what's the name of that big fort just northeast of town?"

"It's called Fort Whipple."

"Why do they need a fort?"

"Apaches," Zack spit with obvious distaste. "They are the

meanest, toughest Indians ever born. Apaches have hunted and raided through this country for a long, long time, and I doubt they're happy about all these white folks coming here to settle."

"Nothing lasts forever."

They rode into town and found a livery to board their horses. It wasn't much of a livery, but Dunn noted that the stalls were clean and the horses well fed.

"How much is your board?"

"A dollar a day," the liveryman said, not batting an eye.

"Jaysus!" Zack exploded. "That's awful!"

The liveryman, short and wearing faded bib overalls, no shoes and a Mexican sombrero, just shrugged his narrow shoulders. "There's a couple other liveries in town, but none of them any cheaper. Hay and grain have to be freighted up from around Ehrenberg. That costs aplenty."

"Where's Ehrenberg? Clear over in California?"

"Nope, just a couple hundred miles across a desert to the Colorado River."

"Can you point us to a good, clean hotel or boardinghouse?" Zack asked. "Someplace where we aren't likely to be robbed and that will feed us decent food."

"Try Fort Misery."

Dunn wasn't sure that they'd heard correctly. "Fort Misery?"

"It's far and away the best boardinghouse in Prescott. It's owned by Señora Ramos, but everyone calls her 'Virgin Mary' because she's so kindhearted."

"Is she . . . ?" Zack asked, grinning like a loon.

"Is she what?" the liveryman asked.

"A virgin?"

"Well, I expect not," the man said as he led their weary horses toward the stalls. "The 'Virgin Mary' has a bunch of kids."

"Keep that bag of gold hidden under your blanket," Dunn warned before they left the barn and headed toward Fort Misery. "I don't want to advertise that we're almost rich."

"Well," Zack said, as he slowed and craned his neck into a crowded saloon called Quartz Rock, "at the prices around here, I'd say that there must already be gold and silver aplenty in Prescott."

Dunn agreed, especially when the Virgin Mary, a large, happy woman with a baby at her immense breast, charged them an outrageous $25.00 a night—in advance. She also informed them that she was a good cook and that her boarders were expected to behave like gentlemen.

"Breakfast is at seven and don't be late for any of the meals or you'll go hungry."

"Not at your prices," Dunn said.

"For breakfast, I cook you venison and chili, biscuits and coffee. For dinner, you get roast venison, chili, corn bread, and goat's milk. For supper you get rabbit stew, chili, tortillas, apple pie, and coffee."

The Virgin Mary winked. "You boys live here long enough, I make you both very fat!"

"And very broke," Zack snorted.

"I think you need a bath and some whiskey," she told them. "I send up at no extra charge."

That made Dunn think better of the Virgin Mary and her boardinghouse. Besides, the food that night was good and the beds were soft and without lice. The next day, bathed but still shaggy and dressed in their buckskins, they visited the central plaza, the popular meeting place of miners, freighters, businessmen, soldiers, and Indians.

Mostly, folks in Prescott talked and argued about the weather, politics, and mining. Dunn overheard that the biggest mines, ones like the Congress and the Crown King, were doing so well that they were even willing to take a chance and hire drunks off the streets. There were also land promoters waving maps and deeds, as well as vendors hawking everything from Indian jewelry to fresh vegetables and city lots.

Dunn had a time keeping Zack out of the many saloons along Montezuma Street. One particularly determined fellow, whose nose had been bitten off in a barroom brawl, managed to get past Dunn and peddle a bottle of whiskey called Old Tangleleg to Zack for a gold nugget worth twenty dollars.

"You drink that and you'll probably go blind," Dunn warned as they entered the territorial land office and stated their business intentions.

The public land manager, Mr. Gilbert, was more than happy to deed over 25,600 acres of sagebrush in exchange for Zack's heavy bag of gold.

"Here's the map. Let's just shade in your ranch location and I'll have the papers drawn up and notarized. A copy for you, a copy for us, and that's all there is to it."

"But how do we know the exact boundaries without a survey?" Dunn asked.

"We don't," Gilbert said, not looking the least bit concerned. "The legal description of your ranch will be based on latitude and longitude. We'll have to start at one recognizable geographic point on our government map—you pick and describe it in the deed—and I'll figure out the boundaries of your Lonesome Valley Ranch and plot them on the map."

"How big is 25,600 acres, Mr. Gilbert? Until now, I've never owned any land, so that figure doesn't mean anything to me."

"Well," the man said as he began scribbling numbers, "there are 640 acres per square mile, which is equal to one section. You are buying forty sections, which will cover exactly forty square miles. In country like that—even if you dig wells and do some irrigation—it will still require a lot of acres to support a cow and her calf."

"So how many head can I run?"

Gilbert finished his computations. "I'm afraid you can handle only about twelve or thirteen hundred cows and their calves—so your ranch isn't really all that big by Arizona standards."

"Forty square miles sounds like a pretty big hunk of land to me," Dunn argued. "How many sheep would my forty sections support?"

"I'm no rancher," Gilbert assured him, "but I've often heard it said that you can run five sheep for every cow and calf, so that would mean you could support almost five thousand sheep. But those are very rough estimates. And, like I warned you, Mr. Dunn, without any year-round source of reliable water . . ."

"We have a spring," Dunn said, pinpointing his Lonesome Valley on the map. The valley is pretty grassy."

Gilbert leaned closer. "Humph," he said, "looks like they forgot to mark in that spring. If I'd have known that, I'd have charged you more per acre. You see, I only charged you Arizona Territory's 'desert rate' because I thought you were buying dry land."

"It's just a trickle of spring runoff," Zack said quickly. "It ain't no year-round spring, that's for sure. Dries up by June and everything green is gone by July."

Gilbert studied their faces. "May I ask how are you going to water your stock?"

Dunn said, "We're hoping that the water table is high enough in a couple of places so that we can dig a few good wells."

"And if you can't?"

"Well, everything in life is a gamble, isn't it?"

"This is a big one," Gilbert said, patting the bag of gold. "But that's your business, not mine. At any rate, I suppose the desert rate per acre is still fair. As you can tell from looking at the maps, I have sold other ranches to the north, although none so near the Grand Canyon."

"What if I want to buy more land?"

"Bring more gold or cash," Gilbert said happily. "I can honestly say that there isn't going to be any land rush soon that far to the north. Not unless gold or silver is discovered. If that should happen, you couldn't afford to buy more property unless you were King Solomon himself."

While Zack wandered outside to sit in the sun and sip on his whiskey, Dunn picked the landmark point for the north-

eastern boundary of his ranch. He chose a well-defined promontory not more than fifteen miles from the rim of the Grand
Canyon. It took less than an hour for Mr. Gilbert to draw up
the documents and have them notarized.

"Nice doing business with you," Dunn said.

"Make a success out of it and come back to buy more ranchland," Gilbert told him. "Arizona is long on land but short on
cash, although that probably will change."

"Why? Because of more gold and silver discoveries?"

"That, and settlers. Did you know that there are land promoters selling Prescott property back in Boston and New York,
as well as half a dozen other Eastern cities?"

"No. Why would anyone leave the East to settle out here?"

"Lots of reasons. No humidity. Relatively mild winters.
Cheap town lots and the chance to strike it rich in the surrounding hills. Those Easterners think the Wild West is America's land of opportunity. We've also been getting some
tourists."

"Here?"

"That's right. I've had several people ask to see the Grand
Canyon. This fellow, Major John Wesley Powell, has created
some real tourist interest. But most people quickly change their
plans and stay close to town when they discover how far it is
to the Grand Canyon and the poor condition of the trail going
there."

"Who knows," Dunn said, "maybe someday they'll run a
stagecoach right up to the rim."

"Sure!" the man laughed. "And then a railroad so they can
build a big hotel and sell ice cream!"

Dunn chuckled, but he secretly wondered if someday there
would be a good living to be made off Grand Canyon tourists.
As he folded his deed and slipped it into his pocket, he said,
"Can I rest assured that this land title will also be recorded
in the territorial capital down in Tucson?"

"You can," Gilbert promised. "But I'd bet good money that,

by the time you want to buy more land, *Prescott* will be the territorial capital again."

"That would be handier," Dunn told the land official as he went out the door.

Given the exorbitant local prices, Dunn was unable to buy everything on Kate Callahan's list. He did get a pretty good deal on an old freight wagon, harness, and two mules named Sue and Sally. He also bought a pair of squealing piglets packed in a flimsy wooden crate and spent far too much money on a milk cow and a couple of laying hens. High on his priority list were Kate's new ribbons and dresses. He bought her three new outfits and a half-dozen ribbons for her hair. Then, using a piece of cloth on which she'd traced the size of her foot, Dunn bought Kate two pairs of shoes. Well satisfied, he then outfitted himself with stiff blue Levi's, red flannel shirts which were light but not nearly as long-wearing or comfortable as his dirty old buckskins, a new Stetson that cost eight dollars, and two pairs of boots.

Zack bought a new pistol and a Winchester repeating rifle, along with several boxes of ammunition, but he chose to squander the rest of his gold on saloon whiskey and women. Dunn had to carry the drunken old badger outside and pitch him into their waiting wagon.

"How much gold do you have left?" Dunn asked the old man who was lying in the back of the wagon half-drunk and singing bawdy songs.

"Spent it all. Every last ounce! What's the use of keepin' it?" Zack demanded. "Ain't nothin' to spend it on in Havasu Canyon!"

"What about all that talk you gave me about needing the gold someday to defend the Havasupai and their way of life from the white man?"

"Hell," Zack muttered, "after what happened to the Hualapai, there's damn little hope of keeping the whites from taking over Havasu Canyon!"

"You're probably right," Dunn said as he drove along,

deeply troubled by the thought of prospectors or settlers pushing their way into Havasu Canyon and enslaving the Havasupai.

"Hold up the wagon!" Zack cried after they'd put Prescott far behind. "I gotta get out before I get sick all over the supplies!"

Dunn reined the mules in and set the brake. They had tied their saddle horses and the cow behind their supply wagon, and it took a little doing to get Zack to his feet.

"You shouldn't drink that Old Tangleleg and whatever else kind of whiskey you can buy off the street," Dunn told the man as he led him off to one side. "Some of that stuff can make you go blind!"

Zack wasn't paying any attention as he vomited again and again while Dunn clutched his britches to keep him from toppling over. "You finally finished?"

"Yeah. Could use some more whiskey."

Dunn went back to the wagon for a canteen. But first, he uncorked the three bottles of Old Tangleleg and let them drain empty.

"Here," he said, uncapping the canteen. "Pour some into the palm of your hand and wash your mouth out before you use that canteen. That way, you won't foul our drinking water."

"You sound like a man that's done this before," Zack wheezed, doing as he was ordered.

Dunn helped Zack back to their wagon. "You're going to sit up with me. If you go back and lie down, you'll just get sick again."

"You're a bossy bastard when you get a good man down, ain't you!"

Dunn couldn't suppress a smile. "We'll make an early camp so you can get your head clear. Tomorrow morning, though, we'll leave before dawn. I want to be back to the ranch by tomorrow night."

"What's the big hurry? Them women and the Hualapai are going to take care of things better than we could."

"You're probably right."

"I *know* that I'm right," the old man said, hanging his head between his knees and grunting every time the wagon took a hard jolt.

They did get an early start the next morning, and if it hadn't been for the milk cow, they'd have made very good time. But the cow, its udder flopping under its belly and getting scratched by the sage and brush, became miserable and balky. There was no road, not even a pair of rutted tracks to follow. Instead, they made their own trail, roughly following the tracks they had made coming down from Lonesome Valley Ranch. Zack, suffering from a hangover but showing good color again, was as quiet as the land they crossed.

"In a few more miles," Dunn told him, "we will be on our ranch."

"*Your* ranch," Zack corrected. "I want no part of playing nursemaid to a bunch of stinking sheep."

"I figure to run cows and horses, too."

"Early next spring, I'm going back to Havasu Canyon," Zack vowed. "I mean to work in the fields, hear the Indian women sing, remember better days."

"I wish I had known your wife. Josie told me many things about her mother, but it's not the same as knowing someone."

"She was beautiful," Zack whispered, his eyes blurring with tears. "And wise and gentle. Josie had all the best of her mother and none of the worst of me."

"I think your daughter had many of your good qualities," Dunn said.

"Like what?"

Dunn didn't have time to answer because a volley of shots broke the high desert stillness.

Zack whipped around and grabbed his new Winchester. "Whoever is shooting is damned close. Just over that hill yonder!"

Before Dunn could stop him, Zack jumped down from the wagon and ran back to Kate's mare. Not taking the time to saddle or even bridle it, he used the mare's lead rope to fashion an Indian hackamore and hauled himself onto the animal's back, yelling, "You stay here with our outfit, Pilgrim! I'll be right back!"

Dunn drew in the mules and set the brake. He ran back to his horse and began to saddle it fast, continually glancing over his shoulder and hearing more shots as well as shouting.

When the sorrel was saddled and bridled, Dunn hesitated a moment. He didn't want to leave the wagon, the two agitated and screeching piglets, and Christopher's new milk cow. But when he heard another volley of rifle fire, Dunn knew he couldn't stay behind.

Mounting the sorrel, Dunn gave it a hard kick so that the horse knew this was no time to be bucking and messing around. The gelding lit out after Zack and the mare, who had left a faint rooster tail of dust.

When Dunn flew over the hill, he saw two scalp hunters standing over Zack, lying all twisted up in a heap. One of the men was holding his bloodied side and was bent over in pain. Kate's mare was still running, now no more than a speck on the western horizon.

The scalp hunters saw Dunn and jumped for cover, firing their rifles. The sorrel gelding took a bullet in the chest and Dunn felt its legs break at the knees like matchsticks. He kicked free of his stirrups and catapulted over the tumbling horse.

Dunn flattened on the ground. He jammed his rifle forward and began to return fire. His third slug knocked the already-wounded man over like an empty milk can. Dunn ducked while the other man shot the sagebrush to pieces over his head. Dunn's heart was racing as he tried to gather his wits.

He waited almost a minute before he dared raise his head. The scalp hunter was making a hard run for his horse. Dunn planted his left elbow firmly in the dust and began to fire. He was shaky and missed twice before he bowled the scalp hunter over with a leg shot just as the man reached his tethered horse.

The animal tried to break free as its owner crawled forward, reaching for the tied reins. Dunn took careful aim and shot him in the back. The horse broke loose and ran off a little way, blowing loudly through its distended nostrils.

Dunn swayed to his feet and knocked the dust from his new clothes. He levered a fresh shell into his rifle just in case one of the two men was playing 'possum. But they weren't, and neither was Zack.

Dunn sank to his knees and rolled the old man over. Zack had been shot three times and must have died very quickly. He looked at peace, except for his still-bloodshot eyes.

"Dammit, old man," Dunn choked, "why couldn't you just wait for me? Maybe, if you had . . ."

Dunn shook his head. Zack had been miserable since losing his only daughter. He'd died well—perhaps just the way he would have liked.

Dunn heard whimpering. He stood up and followed the sound until he located a Hualapai man, his wife, and their little boy hiding in the sage. The man had been shot and the woman looked scared to death.

"It's all right," he assured them, making sign and using gestures to show that he was a friend. "Don't run away again. I'll be right back with my wagon and something to bandage that bullet hole. Then we'll get you help."

The man understood enough English to follow Dunn's meaning. "No Topaz?"

"No Topaz. Lonesome Valley Ranch."

The two Indians exchanged glances and relaxed.

Dunn rode one of the scalp hunter's horses back over the hill to his wagon. When he returned, he first piled Zack, then the other bodies in the wagon, wedging them in between boxes, tools, and sacks of supplies. He used a tarp to cover them and then helped the Hualapai family onto the wagon seat.

"How old is the baby?" he asked, pointing to the woman's cradle board as he bandaged the man's deep flesh wound to stop the bleeding.

She didn't understand and Dunn was in too much of a hurry
to elaborate. After gathering all the horses and adding them
to his own bunch of tethered animals, Dunn climbed back into
the seat beside the Indians. The man had to be in considerable
pain but his chin was up and he was composed.

"I have a son . . ." Dunn told them as he drove back over
the hill and angled north through the sage. "His name is Christopher and he's about your baby's age. Maybe my kid and your
kid will grow up to be fast friends."

The Hualapai didn't say anything, and Dunn guessed that
he couldn't very well blame them.

Nineteen

Kate Callahan stood apart from the gathering of spectators and the tense firing squad. A stiff March wind cut at her face and she could not stop the tears as she watched John Lee sitting atop a trunk, saying farewell to his sons and a few loyal friends. John was not afraid. Sometimes, he would glance over at her and just stare, but Kate read no malice or hatred in his expression. In fact, the worry that had deeply lined his face after being a fugitive these many years was now absent and he looked at peace.

"It is time," the federal marshal announced, consulting his pocket watch. "You Lee boys ride your horses off like I ordered. Git!"

William and a half dozen other young Lee men and boys hugged their father one last time and whispered their tearful farewells. Kate couldn't bear to watch, but she heard the creak of their saddle leather as they mounted and rode off.

"John Lee, have you any last words to say?" the marshal shouted so that all could hear as he stepped forward with the black executioner's hood.

John Lee climbed up to stand upon his closed coffin. He regarded every anxious face, then turned to Kate and finally, to his sons, who had reined their horses around. When he spoke, his voice was loud and unwavering.

"This is wrong!" he bellowed. "I killed no one that day. Not one! Lesser men who *did* kill are attempting to absolve their guilt and shame with my blood. But I am ready to die. I trust in God, and I have no fear. For me, death holds no terror."

And with those words, he bowed his head and the hood was placed over it. Kate could not bear to watch anymore. She turned away and began to hurry toward her own horse.

"Ready! Aim! Fire!"

She didn't hear the sound of the bullets striking John Lee or his body when it crashed to the earth.

"Kate!"

Her name had the strident tenor of a profanity. She pivoted to the voice as she untied her reins. She had never seen the Mormon elder before, and she reminded herself that she would never see him again. He towered menacingly over her, fists clenched at his sides. His eyes burned with hatred. "Are you *finally* satisfied?"

She raised her chin. "I brought a man to justice. Yes, I am satisfied."

"They would never have caught John if it hadn't been for you pretending to be a family friend. You tricked and betrayed that poor family!"

Kate climbed into her saddle. None of these friends of John Lee would ever forgive or understand but she wanted them to know that she had also paid a very dear price. "Because of John Lee and the rest of you, I have never known the love of my own family. Never felt my mother's arms around me when I was growing up or had the support of my father and brothers. Because of you all, I am *still* alone."

"Someday you will answer for this travesty in hell!"

Kate picked up her reins. "I've already been there and back," she told him in a wooden voice. "John is arriving there now and I'm sure he'll be saving a place for you and the other Mountain Meadows murderers."

"Don't come back!" the man screeched as she rode away. "Don't you *ever* come back, you Jezebel!"

Kate whipped her horse into a gallop and let the cold cutting wind chill her tears.

* * *

It was almost sundown when Dunn galloped into his ranch yard after another trip to Prescott. Professor Sutherland appeared from inside the ranch house with little Christopher toddling along behind.

"Well, hello there," Dunn called with surprise. "Whatever got you away from your excavation?"

"I'm watching Christopher."

Dunn didn't understand. He glanced around. "Where's Kate?"

"She rode off to a place called Mountain Meadows."

Dunn blinked with surprise. "That's clear up in Utah. Why would she . . . ?"

"They were executing John Lee," the professor grimly interrupted. "She said that she just *had* to be there."

Dunn badly needed a moment to collect himself. He walked over to scoop up Christopher saying, "I'm afraid that Daddy's going to have to leave again."

"Can I go with you?" the child asked.

"Maybe next time. Professor, how long has Kate been gone?"

"About a week."

"Then I'd best be riding for Lee's Ferry Crossing. I'll find and bring her back even if I have to ride all the way up to Salt Lake City."

"If I can borrow a horse, I'd like to go with you," Sutherland announced. "You and Kate are my best friends, and I won't be able to concentrate on my work until I know that Kate is safe."

Dunn was doubtful that Sutherland was up to such a long, difficult ride. They might get lucky and meet Kate over the next hill or at least before the crossing of the Little Colorado . . . but they might have to ride all the way up into the Utah Territory to find her.

"Professor, it'll be a hard trip."

"If I can't keep up with you, I'll return to my excavation, providing you agree to stop by on the way back."

"Fair enough," Dunn relented. "We'll leave tomorrow morning at first light."

"What about Christopher?"

"I'll ask one of the Indian women to look after him while we're away."

That evening, Dunn spent as much time as he could with his son, reading him stories and telling him all about Prescott. And when the boy fell asleep, Dunn put him to bed and went to work lining out a month's worth of work. He'd decided to put Mi-ta in charge of things during his absence. It was an easy choice because Mi-ta was a strong, dignified Hualapai in his mid-twenties who spoke good English and was extremely conscientious about his ranch duties.

Two years earlier, the poor fellow had been run down and captured by hunters, who had whipped him bloody before he'd managed to escape. Only a few months before that, Mi-ta's wife and daughter had died of the ague on the Topaz Reservation. The man was a survivor. Dunn decided that this was an ideal time to put Mi-ta to the test. If the Hualapai managed to keep harmony among the Indians and protect the ranch and its livestock, Dunn figured that he would promote Mi-ta.

After dinner and when the lights were out, Dunn continued to fret over Kate. Why it had been so important for her to be present at John Lee's execution. Perhaps, with Lee's death, a lot of things in Kate's troubled background would surface and help to draw them close. Dunn hoped so. There was something standing between Kate and him and he was sure it had everything to do with John Lee and the infamous Mountain Meadows Massacre.

Dunn was awake long before sunrise. He fried thick lamb chops and boiled potatoes for himself and the professor. They enjoyed a large breakfast and Mi-ta soon had a pair of their best mustangs saddled.

"Mi-ta will be in charge of everything on the ranch," Dunn

announced just before mounting his horse. To make sure that this was understood by everyone, he handed the Indian his extra Winchester rifle. "If trouble comes, Mi-ta will decide what to do until my return."

Dunn mounted his horse. "Ready?" he asked the professor.

"I hope so."

"Then let's ride."

Dunn set a fast pace for Lee's Ferry and they reached the rim of the Little Colorado Gorge long after sunset. He was worn down by too much hard riding but the professor showed little interest in sleep. Instead, the scientist went off to sit and stare into the deep, twisting gorge. Dunn went over to join the man he now considered his very best friend.

"Walt, how you holding up?" he asked.

"I'm going to be sore, but I'll survive."

"I'm grateful to have you along," Dunn said as the stars began to appear. "Were you thinking about exploring this canyon for more Anasazi ruins?"

"As a matter of fact, I was," Sutherland admitted. "You know, if this gorge was located anyplace *except* near the Grand Canyon, it would be considered an absolute geological phenomena."

"I suppose so," Dunn absently agreed.

The following day, they rode their weary ponies over a hump of granite and then followed a steep wagon road down to the Colorado River. Years ago, this difficult track was named Lee's Backbone. Many a Mormon wagon had stalled on its slope attempting to exit the deep canyon and reach new settlements in northern Arizona and New Mexico.

"Would you look at that," Dunn said, pointing across the river toward a rectangular rock fortress. "I wonder why they built a fortress here, of all places?"

"Maybe they've had some Indian troubles," Sutherland replied. "Hey, look!"

Dunn turned to see a man, two women, and a cluster of children appear from inside the fortress to wave at them in greeting.

Dunn waved back, then motioned to indicate that they needed a ferry ride across. Within minutes, the pair were bringing the large, flat-bottomed ferry across. When it beached, Dunn attempted to lead his mustang onto the ferry but the animal balked.

"You'll probably have to blindfold 'em," the ferryman suggested. "Most people do."

"Thanks."

Blindfolded, their mustangs became docile as they were led onto the ferry.

"Hang on!" the ferryman shouted as he gripped the twelve-foot-long tiller. He was short but very powerful and threw all his weight and muscle into his work. The huge ferry slowly eased into the current and sluggishly plowed its way across the river.

It was always an exciting trip, and Dunn knew full well that several lives had been lost during mishaps. The professor's eyes were as round as silver dollars until they were safely on the other side and the ferry was dragged up on the beach and secured.

"My name is Warren Johnson," the bearded man said, shaking their hands with a heavily callused paw. "I'm running the ferry now, and that is my family yonder."

"Fine, big family," Sutherland said, waving at the children, who waved back but did not approach.

"The Lord has blessed me with two healthy wives and many strong children," Johnson agreed. "It'll cost you each a dollar for the crossing and we'll feed you good for ten cents each. I've got grain and grass hay for those mustangs and . . ."

"Is Mrs. Lee still living at Lonely Dell?" Dunn interrupted.

"She is. Husband was killed, if you didn't know."

"We knew," Dunn said. "Is there another lady with Mrs. Lee?"

"Yeah, if you mean that traitorous *woman* named Kate."

Dunn said nothing more but paid Johnson for their crossing.

"My wives are real good cooks," the ferryman said, dogging their heels up the Paria River. "And we've got supplies for sale."

"Thanks anyway," Dunn said, "but we'll take our food and rest at Lonely Dell."

"I don't know why Mrs. Lee doesn't sell out to me and move along," Johnson complained as they remounted. "Ain't nothing left for her here. She ought to just leave after what happened to her husband."

A short way up the trail they met Daniel Lee, Emma's oldest son, carrying a fishing pole and burlap sack. After a brief greeting, Dunn said, "How is your family?"

"Tolerable."

"Is Miss Callahan here?"

The lanky teenager scowled. "Yeah, but I don't know what for. I sure ain't talking to her. She betrayed my father. Made out like she was our friend and then told the authorities just when and how to catch Pa."

"We're sorry about Mr. Lee."

"He never killed none of those wagon train people! The only thing is, Brigham Young needed someone important to blame. Someone who wouldn't buckle and tell everyone what *really* happened. So they shot my father down like a rabid dog."

"How is your mother handling it?"

The boy squared his bony shoulders and visibly calmed himself before saying, "Ma is real, real strong."

"I never doubted that for a second," Dunn replied as he and Sutherland continued up Paria Canyon. Dunn kept following the nearly overflowing Paria, wondering what kind of reception they would receive at Lonely Dell.

They saw both Emma and Kate bent over and busily hoeing in the cornfields. The two women wore large straw hats to protect themselves against the sun and their blouses were dark with dust and perspiration. They were so busy that they didn't even notice their visitors and Dunn admired their industry, especially given the intense canyon heat at least one hundred degrees and climbing. Dunn noticed an acre of vegetable gardens and how a fine peach orchard was in full bloom. Since his last visit, two more buildings had been constructed and the little homestead was looking both permanent and prosperous.

"Why hello there, Bill!" Frank French called as he emerged from down by the creek. Frank was the prospector who had always shared John Lee's unwavering conviction that there was a fortune in gold and silver resting somewhere in Paria Canyon.

The man was coated with fresh mud and badly winded. Instead of a pick he held a shovel and was hustling to prevent a network of irrigation canals from being washed away. The canals were all running full and Frank was desperately trying to keep up with overflows and washouts as he irrigated the orchard, the vegetable garden and the cornfields.

"Professor, let's give the poor fellow a hand," Dunn said, as they dismounted and tied their horses, then grabbed extra shovels.

"Thank you!" Frank said a short time later when the danger was past. "The trouble is that this Paria River never runs with the same flow. In springtime, it washes out. Late in the summer, around August, the flow almost stops and it's hard to get enough irrigation water. But then, along comes a big cloudburst up on the rim and suddenly it's full and washing out everything again. I tell you, it keeps a fella jumpin'!"

"I can see that you've really been working to improve the irrigation," Sutherland told the weary prospector. "There's been a lot of improvements since we were here years ago."

"We've all been working like beavers," Frank said, obviously pleased by the compliment. "Mrs. Lee and her kids took the death of Mr. Lee real, real hard. I expected that poor woman to quit Lonely Dell the minute she got the news of her husband's execution, but she ain't. Matter of fact, Emma is working harder than ever, maybe to keep her mind off her sorrow."

"And what about Miss Callahan?" Dunn asked.

"She ain't been here long, but she's been a real comfort. 'Course, William and some of the older children hold Kate to blame, but Emma knows better'n that. She's a forgiving woman."

"I'm glad," Dunn said as he untied his horse and led it around the cornfield to join Kate and Emma. "Ladies," he shouted, "could you use some help?"

He had startled them. Kate laid down her hoe, straightened her back and hurried forward to meet them.

"It's good to see you! Bill, I'm sorry that I left so suddenly. But I'm really needed here at Lonely Dell and . . . what happened to Christopher?"

"He's back at the ranch in good company," Dunn answered.

"How is Emma?"

"She's doing much better," Kate said, glancing back at Emma who had gone to greet the professor. "She's resigned to whatever happens next."

"We met Mr. Johnson down at the ferry. Is Emma going to stay here?"

"Her people will buy her out sooner or later," Kate explained. "Since cash is short, I expect she'll have to take payment in sheep or cattle. But there have already been a few Mormon settlers visiting from Kanab with the idea of buying her out. She says her church intends to buy the fort and the ferry and put Mr. Johnson in charge. I hope to heaven they'll be fair."

"They ought to be after the way things have turned out for this family," Dunn said. "But why did you feel the need to come here?"

Instead of answering immediately, Kate led him down to the river. She knelt and began to wash her bare arms and then to cool her face. "I suppose I came because of guilt. When I lived here before, I was filled with hatred and revenge. It was like a poison in my blood. After a few months, I knew that I had to stop plotting and scheming revenge. That's about the time that you and Josie arrived. When you returned from the Kaibab, I waited until the next spring and decided to get away by bringing Pepper and your flock down to the South Rim."

"Did John know what you were doing?"

"Not at first. He figured it out quickly, though. And that's why, when I asked him if I could deliver the flock, he agreed despite the elements of danger. After that, when Pepper left your flock and followed me to the South Rim, I just decided that it was a sign that I should stay and help you build the ranch. It was only to be for a little while, but then Christopher arrived and you needed even more help, so . . . well, I just kept on staying."

"I couldn't have done it without you," he told her. "But that still doesn't fully explain why you came back here."

"When I heard that John was captured and sentenced, I simply *had* to come. I think I might even have needed to see John fall apart and beg for mercy. To show cowardice and weakness, but he didn't. Instead, he was calm and forgiving right up until the last instant."

"That doesn't surprise me in the least," Dunn said. "John Lee was too strong a man to fall apart."

"Yes," Kate said, "he was."

Dunn glanced back over his shoulder. Sutherland was leading their weary saddle horses back to the Lee cabin. "Kate," he said, cupping his hand in the clear stream and taking a drink, "forgive me for asking this, but did you fall in love with John Lee?"

Kate allowed herself a smile. "No," she said, "John was old enough to be my father. Emma's as well. He was strong, intelligent, and admirable. I suppose that I *did* grow to both love and hate him, but I never could sort out my true feelings. That probably doesn't make sense."

"Not to me," he admitted.

Kate laid her hand on his arm. "You have to understand

that I knew, as a little girl, what had happened to my family and that entire wagon train. I felt shame, guilt for being alive, hatred, every strong emotion you can imagine. I used to plot how I'd kill John Lee and the other leaders of that massacre. I thought I might even go crazy and kill myself someday. It took years before I trusted myself to hold a gun or a rifle."

"We all live in our own secret prisons," Dunn said.

"I *know* your secret," Kate said. "A member of Powell's second expedition passed through here recently and told me about a 'William Dunn and the Howland brothers' murdered by the Kaibab Paiutes up on the North Rim. Obviously, you escaped."

Dunn felt a great relief that Kate finally knew his darkest secret. He was surprised to find that he even wanted to talk about it. "There isn't much to tell. The brothers and I had been quarreling. Things were not going well, so I went off by myself to rest beside the North Rim. I fell asleep and awoke at dawn to hear screams as Oramel and Seneca were being attacked by the Paiute Indians. I had my chance to fight and die bravely beside them, but . . . but instead I *ran* to save my life."

"It was the only thing you could do. What point would there have been in throwing your own life away?"

"I've reminded myself of that for years, but it still troubles me. I ran all the way back down into the Grand Canyon with the Paiutes close on my heels. When I reached the top of Separation Rapids, I jumped into a waiting boat. Moments later, I struck a rock and was thrown into the river. I washed up on the opposite shore and the Havasupai saved my life. You've heard the rest."

Kate took his hands. "So, we've finally learned each other's deepest, most shameful secrets."

"Most of them, anyway."

Kate raised her eyebrows. "You have more?"

"I didn't love Josie," he admitted. "Not when I married her. I was in love with another woman."

"Do you still love her?"

"Once in a great while, I still write to Cynthia Holloway, even now. I know that's crazy, because I can't even remember her face. The funny thing is that, as the years pass she looks more and more like . . . well, never mind."

"What?"

"The Cynthia Holloway of my dreams has become *you*, Kate. Does that make any sense?"

"Yes, I'm happy to say."

"I think it means I'm in love with you."

"I think it does too," she whispered, so happy that she wanted to scream or take wing like the hummingbirds who swarmed here in the spring.

"Kate, we've been working side by side at the ranch for years now. You've become Christopher's mother. We're a family. I think we ought to be married."

She pulled her hands away and retreated. "Oh, Bill, I'm sorry, but I just can't!"

"Why not?"

Kate's head rocked forward and she clenched her hands to her breasts. Dunn thought he heard a low sob. "Kate?"

"I am *married."*

"Married!"

"Yes," she choked, raising her head. "To someone I pray you'll never meet."

Dunn's world shattered into a million pieces. "But whoever he is, you can't love him!"

Kate sat down on the riverbank and stared at the water. Dunn sat beside her, his mind whirling in turmoil. "Tell me about him. Please?"

"All right," she said. "His name is Monty Ford and he is locked up in a Colorado prison for attempted murder committed during a failed bank robbery. It wasn't his first. He was once one of the most feared and successful bounty hunters in Montana, Wyoming, and Colorado. But trapping or killing outlaws didn't pay enough so he turned to bank robbing. I had no idea of that when I met him, and he was extremely charming. Later, after I knew what he was and the terrible things he had done, I agreed to testify against him, but I couldn't because I was legally his wife. He swore to find and kill me no matter how long it took or how far I ran. And, since I couldn't testify as to his murders, he received less than a lifetime sentence and is expected to be paroled in a few more years."

Dunn's fists knotted by his sides. "But he'd *never* find you at our ranch! And, even if he did, we'd protect you."

"You wouldn't stand a chance against Monty. He's a professional gunfighter, back shooter, and ambusher. He knows ways to hunt and kill men that you can't even imagine. He is cruel and would enjoy killing your son while you watch, then torturing me, and finally killing you. He'd want to do it very slow."

Dunn saw her terror and did not doubt for a moment the likelihood of her terrible predictions. "Kate, how could you marry someone like that?"

"I was very young, naive, and confused. Monty was the exact opposite of everything a good and upstanding member of the Church of the Latter Day Saints was supposed to be and, at the time, that was all important. Monty drank, fought, and cursed. He was big, wild, and devilishly handsome. He rode into Deseret thumbing his nose at the whole Mormon kingdom and I'd never seen anything like him in my life. He smoked and swaggered and no one dared oppose him."

Kate sighed. "I know this sounds terrible, but I wanted to hurt the Mormons who had tried to raise me in their faith. I eloped with Monty thinking I could straighten him out and make him a good wife, but, after I spent two years of hiding while he rode the outlaw trail, he was finally caught and sent to prison."

"Then we'll change our names," Dunn decided out loud.

"No," Kate said, "even that wouldn't work. Monty knows my true past and once, I even wrote him all about John and Emma Lee and my own sick plans for revenge at Lonely Dell.

He wrote back suggesting I poison the whole family and watch them die slowly."

Dunn groaned.

"Monty will ride straight here to Lonely Dell. If Emma refuses to tell him where I've gone, he'll slaughter her family and burn this homestead to the ground."

"But she'll be gone by then! Frank French said that she wasn't staying. That the Mormons are ready to buy her out."

"So how difficult would it be to track Emma down?" Kate demanded. "Or us? How many people have made the crossing down at Lee's Ferry these past years that would remember either one of us and tell Monty where we've gone?"

"Dammit, I'm not afraid of him! I'm not running away, either."

"You still don't understand," she said, as patient as if speaking to a child. "Monty is *evil*. He would track us to the end of the earth. He's not like *anyone* that you've ever known. Not only would your life be in danger, he might even decide to kill Christopher!"

Tears filled Kate's eyes. *"That's* why I can't stay with you and Christopher putting both your lives in danger. Can't you imagine what it would be like always wondering when Monty suddenly would appear?"

"Then I'll go to that Colorado prison," Dunn said. "I'll strike a deal. If he'll leave us alone . . ."

"No! He'll *kill* you no matter what you say or do. He hates whatever he can't have for his own pleasure!"

Dunn picked up a rock and savagely hurled it into the river. "Then there's only one answer—I need to kill him first."

"How?"

"I don't know," he admitted, "but we've got a couple of years to figure it out. Until then, will you marry me?"

"It wouldn't be legal."

Dunn didn't give a damn. He reached into his pocket and brought out the silver and turquoise ring he'd commissioned a Prescott silversmith to adorn with a large, sparkling diamond.

"Kate, I want you to wear this," he said, slipping it on her finger. "Legal or not, we belong to each other and Lonesome Valley Ranch is *our* home. It belongs to us and to Christopher and to the Indians who have worked for us these past years. We're one big family now. I won't let *anyone* take that away."

She managed to nod. "All right—lovers. Best friends. Ranching partners. But only on the condition that you let *me* decide how to stop Monty. It has to be that way because you have no idea how my husband's sick mind works."

"All right," Dunn reluctantly agreed. "May I at least ask if you have any ideas how to take care of him?"

"Only that we could ambush Monty as he walks out the prison gate."

"Bad idea," he said, not sure if Kate was being serious or not.

"We'll figure out something," she promised. "But for now, I can't wait to see Christopher and the professor again."

"Can I tell them we're engaged? They'll see that ring and want to know."

"Yes," Kate said, holding her hand out to him so that the diamond sparkled, "let's announce to them that, God willing, we *are* going to marry someday."

Twenty

Professor Sutherland's crowning moment of glory had finally arrived. For many happy years, he had lived the life of a real archeologist on the South Rim of the Grand Canyon. And now, he was about to be lionized for his exhaustive pioneering work on the ancient Anasazi.

Everything was perfect. The room was filled to capacity with the most prominent members of the American Archeological Society while blue smoke curled capriciously around the elegant Italian crystal chandeliers. This was, everyone said, the gathering's best attended lecture.

"Gentlemen," Dr. Charles Milford, the current president of the society called from the podium, "if you would please take your seats, we will begin this session on time, which will allow us ample opportunity for questions."

Seated up on the dias, Professor Walter Sutherland squirmed in his chair, a box of carefully packed South Rim artifacts resting on his knobby knees. Sutherland knew his pulse was racing. He felt slightly nauseated from all the smoke and blamed that on the fact that he had given up his pipes for lack of tobacco these past years on the South Rim. He wiped his sweaty palms on his pant legs.

Get ahold of yourself, man! This is your hour of glory, your time to bask in the sun. It is professional vindication! These stuffed shirts are here because you have done something they envy.

But try as he would, Sutherland could not generate any joy.

Instead, he was nearly paralyzed by fear. What if this collection of prominent archeologists asked questions he had not anticipated and made him look like a loon?

Sutherland felt sure that his pulse was well over a hundred beats per minute. He removed his wire-rimmed spectacles and peered down at his notes, which swam like minnows before his myopic eyes. He wiped perspiration from his face and replaced his spectacles, but his notes were still illegible. To make matters worse, he was trembling so violently that the ancient split-twig figurine in the box on his knees danced with his collection of fossils and bones.

"Dr. Walter Sutherland," Professor Milford was saying, "has already been introduced, so I'll make my comments very brief. Suffice to say that I have known Walter for at least ten years and assure you that his scientific observations and theories on early North America are extremely . . . intriguing. Walter just returned from a bold and courageous exploration of the Grand Canyon in search of answers that will certainly advance our knowledge of early North American man."

The speaker cleared his throat and favored Sutherland with what he probably thought was a reassuring smile. "I have had the singular privilege of discussing his discoveries with Dr. Sutherland and, while the conclusions he draws are certainly open to honest scientific debate, they ought to at least be considered."

Sutherland smiled at the tepid applause.

Dr. Milford turned and extended his hand. "Professor, you have the floor."

He carried his box of treasures over to a gleaming walnut table that stood beside the podium. Trying to still his shaking hands, Sutherland removed his precious artifacts and carefully arranged them in a predetermined order. First the Anasazi bones, next the grinding stones, then flint arrowheads and spearpoints as well as several cracked pieces of decorated pottery. To these, he added a few animal bones scored by stone knifes and charred by Anasazi campfires, three two-inch cross cuts of a support beam found buried deep in their ruins and finally, his notes, sketches of the dig, and the extraordinary split-twig figurine. It was this last artifact which Sutherland knew would attract intense interest from his colleagues.

At last, Sutherland pulled his eyes from the comforting sight which represented his crowning achievement. The room was hushed with expectancy and, because he had learned to become a lover of silence, it was quite difficult to shatter the stillness.

"Good evening," Sutherland finally announced in a voice that he did not recognize. "I come to you from a place and a time that can hardly be measured in miles or millennia. I come to you from a time soon after the first human beings crossed over from Asia and migrated down the latitudes of North America—to settle and flourish in and around the Grand Canyon."

Sutherland gripped the sides of the podium. "How do I know that the Grand Canyon was the cradle of North American civilization? I know it because I have explored almost every foot of its rims and plumbed its depths. I have also conducted my excavations with the unprejudiced wonder of a child who might first gaze upon the universe without any *pre-conceived* ideas as to its creation.

"On this table, I give you *proof* that the Anasazi are the true ancestors of all the indigenous peoples of North, Central, and South America. I invite you to examine these artifacts, after my talk which clearly prove that Western civilization, as we know it, first existed with the people of the Grand Canyon about eleven thousand years ago. These ancient peoples chanced upon a country that was verdant—even tropical—but which, over the next eight thousand years, became arid and inhospitable as the tropics shifted south changing the climate of the Grand Canyon into the inhospitable state that we find today."

A hand shot up, then others. Sutherland knew that this was improper. Questions were supposed to be held until *after* the presentation. But now there were dozens of hands frantically waving. Sutherland attempted to ignore them because he could not afford to be sidetracked.

He gripped the podium even more tightly and lowered his eyes to his notes. "These are questions foremost in the minds of those in our profession who have read and studied Major Powell's official report entitled, The Exploration of the Colorado River of the West with its many illustrations by Thomas Moran, as well as the many scientific papers published by the Smithsonian Institution's Bureau of American Ethnology: *When* did the first people arrive there? *How* did they exist? And, *when and why* did they finally abandon that area, probably to resettle more to the southeast and become the Indians we presently know as the Pueblos?"

"Professor Sutherland," a heavyset professor from Harvard shouted as he rose to his feet, "how can you prove that the first Americans arrived in the canyon country eleven thousand years ago when we understand that you have nothing in your possession that could possibly be older than four thousand years?"

Remain composed. Do not show irritation at this blatant disregard for academic etiquette.

"Professor Bernard, I assure you that I have made detailed sketches that prove the Anasazi were in the Grand Canyon at least eleven thousand years ago. These sketches, which I will show you later, replicate the ancient drawings of those first Grand Canyon hunters. The art is consistent with the style found in European caves dating back to those prehistoric times. Please believe me when I tell you that I have faithfully reproduced these extraordinary pictographs which prove without a doubt that these first North Americans hunted mastodons and possessed a degree of spirituality that . . ."

"Mastodons! That's ridiculous!" Bernard bellowed. "Have you found any of *their* bones!"

Sutherland mopped his face. "No, but along the rim of the canyon and near the ruins which I have been excavating, there are fossils and shells that predate even that period. I have found them lying *among them* the first evidence of North American man."

"That's happenstance! It proves nothing!"

"May I *please* continue?" Sutherland drew himself up to his full and considerable height. His eyes burned from the cigar smoke and his head ached fiercely but he had worked far too long and hard to be crucified by these arm-chair scientists.

"From the tree rings that I have excavated from deep in the ruins left by those people, I estimate that a hunting culture existed in the Grand Canyon country for at least eleven thousand years. After the Ice Age when that part of America began to dry, the great mastodons and other animals began to starve as the tropical forests withered and died in a protracted drought. Man, being intelligent, was able to adopt a partial agrarian diet and learn to farm. And in this way, by *combining* farming and hunting, they were able to remain in and around the Grand Canyon until about 1100 A.D."

"Have you found evidence of farming!" another in the audience demanded.

Sutherland seized the question aggressively. "Yes! I most certainly have!"

He then began to describe the little dams and the hanging water basin that led him into his winter living in Havasu Canyon. "The Havasupai are a living example of a culture that has continued to use both farming and hunting to ensure their existence. Like the ancient ones, the Havasupai migrate between the baking depths of the Grand Canyon, where they exist as farmers, to the rim country, where they become hunters and the harvesters of piñon nuts."

A flurry of hands shot up and a lively debate ensued in the audience, causing Sutherland to skip his drawings and reach for his split-twig figurine.

"This," he shouted, "was given to me by a friend! It was found in a high cave in the side of Havasu Canyon and was undoubtedly a fetish to bring hunters good luck. Another split-twig figurine I saw was very similar but had an arrow symbolically thrust through its body cavity. When you compare it to the petroglyphs and the very well preserved pictographs drawn on cave walls in and around the Grand Canyon, it is clear that these people believed in spirits . . . or gods. They would call upon these spirits for help in almost every aspect of their lives. I believe they offered daily prayers and rituals imploring the spirits and thanking them for their every need."

"Does that mean," Dr. Milford asked, "that *you* can translate their exact meanings from the pictures and symbols?"

"Not their *exact* meaning," Sutherland confessed. "But I have spent so much time searching and examining their ruins that I have begun to achieve an intuitive understanding of . . ."

" 'Intuitive'?" the president raised his eyebrows. "We do not substitute intuition for hard data and evidence, Dr. Sutherland. I'm sure that you know that."

"Of course I do!" Sutherland heard the skepticism and the rumblings of dissent, but he knew he had no choice but to defend his use of the term and to at least make an honest attempt to teach them what he had found to be true, however much it ran in the face of science.

"Gentlemen," he began, "this is difficult to explain and at least as difficult to understand but I have found that, when you *live* in a primitive fashion—as the ancient ones did—and you *detach* yourself from modern civilization and learn to really *listen* to the wind and read messages in the smoke of your campfire, then and only then can you hope to commune with the ancient spirits who alone have the answers which all of us seek. In short, gentlemen, I am a scientist but I also believe that there are many unexplained phenomena that we cannot afford to ignore. And beside the Grand Canyon, one *cannot* ignore the ancient spirits!"

Sutherland closed his eyes and struggled to summon back his beloved canyon country, if only for an instant. He yearned for the sharp, spicy tang of rain-dampened sage in his nostrils and to feel again the grainy texture of the timeless red canyon earth which had become ingrained not only in his flesh but even into the very marrow of his bones. But the vision would not come. He struggled in vain for words to express how it felt on the rare moments when he had attained a true communion with the ancient Indian spirits.

"Friends and colleagues," he finally said, opening his eyes again, "please believe me when I say that I discovered truths about those ancient peoples best when I sat in their kivas, held their sacred bones, and studied their works, especially at sunrise and sundown when the Grand Canyon sky pearls pink and . . ."

"Enough of this nonsense!" a member of the audience bellowed. "Professor, have you suffered sunstroke and completely lost your senses!"

Sutherland felt as if his chest were exploding. He became so dizzy that he swayed on his feet, gripping the podium like a life buoy.

"Walter! Walter, are you all right!"

"Yes," he said, as he clung to the podium and then allowed himself to be helped back to his chair.

"Gentlemen!" Dr. Milford shouted, "this lecture has come to its end. It is obvious that Dr. Sutherland has suffered great physical hardship in the name of science. And, if for no other reason than that, we owe him our gratitude and a round of applause!"

The room applauded, but not enthusiastically. Sutherland lurched to his feet and managed to get to the table where he scooped up his hard won treasures. He could feel people crowding around him but, with the familiar rocks, sticks, and bones resting hard in his hands, he also felt the power of the ancients giving him strength and comfort. With their help, he detached himself from the present and allowed himself to become lost in a better time.

Am I saddened by all of this? Have I lost faith or interest in what seemed most important to me before? Professional recognition? Adulation? Respect? And, if so, what will replace those things?

That night, as he made his lonely way to the train station, he again reminded himself that he had lost nothing, only gained. This evening's disastrous lecture had simply proved what he had begun to suspect—that he did not belong in his own time or among his own people anymore. Instead, he now belonged to a time and a place that could not be measured by miles or millennia. He could not bear to face anyone, not even his friends at Lonesome Valley Ranch. Not yet; not for a good long while.

He would lose himself somewhere deep in the great American Southwest. Travel in search of more ruins and never stop accumulating even more convincing evidence of his revolutionary thesis. Yes, that was what he would do. But inevitably, when the pain was bearable, and the bitter taste of humiliation not so sharp on his tongue, he would return to the Grand Canyon and to his only real friends.

Many years later, gaunt and weathered from his long travels but grinning with anticipation, Sutherland came to visit his friends in Lonesome Valley. It was a cool day and he felt good and even strong as he stopped to survey the expanded log cabin, three large barns, the bunkhouse, and the corrals. He noted that Dunn had bought himself a windmill, which was pumping water into a large reservoir to irrigate the new hay fields.

Now this really looked like a prosperous northern Arizona ranch. Sutherland knew that Dunn had used his profits from the sheep business to buy more grazing land and several thousand Longhorn cattle.

Sound carried far in this country and he could hear the grunts of a bucking horse and the shouts of men. He focused on the contest taking place in a big corral and saw men perched on the top rail watching someone buck out a steel gray bronc.

Even a half mile away, he could hear the sharp crack of the whip, the hard, hollow thud of hooves on beaten earth. Which would win this struggle, man or beast? The answer came a moment later when an Indian was thrown over the bronc's head to land heavily on his back. The rail emptied and the dumped rider was dragged to safety. Moments later, the Indian was on his feet and Sutherland heard laughter.

He sighed with relief and a tired smile played across his cracked lips. It was good to be back among these people again. He should never have spoken to those scientists about his new awareness of Indian spirituality. How could they possibly have understood having never left their libraries, lecture halls and comfortable offices? Having never heard spirit voices moving on a high, lonesome wind, or felt almost as if you were sanctified by the daily ritual of Southwestern sunrises and sunsets, or been mesmerized for days without end, blessed as a cloud touched by rainbows and lost in the majesty of the mighty Grand Canyon?

How could they?

Sutherland held no anger and no regrets. After his disastrous Eastern visit, he had excavated fossils in Colorado, then reveled in small discoveries in both Old and New Mexico. But always, it had been the Grand Canyon which had called until he could no longer ignore her voice.

Several months earlier, he had returned to his South Rim excavations still embracing his solitude as if it were a lover. His mind was clear of all worries and ambitions and he had happily lost himself in the important work of excavating ruins and exploring new caves and archeological sites. He had found ways down to the Colorado that had not been used for centuries. And one day, he had even had the rare and very special privilege of witnessing the tremendous spectacle of tons of rock suddenly breaking free of the rim to cascade down onto the Tonto, then roll and rumble on down that great slanting plateau to make another glorious leap toward the river far, far below.

Last month Dunn, Kate and Christopher had discovered him and broken his solitude. They'd soon brought their Hualapai friends to build him a snug winter cabin with a real glass window overlooking the Grand Canyon. Sutherland was beyond being grateful.

Now, the professor shifted the bulky canvas pack on his back and strode the rest of the way down into the valley, passing a couple of milk cows and a pen of grunting pigs.

"Professor!" Christopher shouted, running out to greet him with a big smile on his face.

He gave the slender but rugged youth a hug. "You're growing so fast!"

"I'm learning to break wild horses, too!"

"Is your father or mother at home?"

"No, they're out riding."

"Then we'll just have to wait for them," Sutherland announced as he sat down on the porch and settled back to enjoy the sunset and wait for his friends.

Dunn and Kate arrived less than an hour later. After dinner, Sutherland followed Dunn outside where they could better enjoy the evening. The stars were ablaze and both men were quiet for a good long while until Dunn said, "We haven't had any time to really talk, but I was wondering about your trip back East. And you were gone for so many years. We were beginning to think that . . ."

"That I'd never return?"

"Something like that."

"I'll never leave again," Sutherland told him. "And, as for the trip back East, it was . . . interesting. I had the chance to meet and spend some time with Major Powell's protégé, a very amiable geologist named Clarence Edward Dutton of the new United States Geological Survey which Major Powell created and now directs."

"Really?"

"Yes. I also studied Major Powell's highly acclaimed report, The Exploration of the Colorado River of the West which was the culmination of his observations taken during both journeys down the Colorado."

"I would very much have enjoyed reading that."

"I have a copy at the cabin. It is beautifully illustrated by a wonderful artist named Thomas Moran. He's a genius and his masterful sketches and paintings of the Grand Canyon are creating a tremendous amount of interest and excitement back East. Thanks to Mr. Moran, I expect that the Grand Canyon may one day become quite a tourist attraction, despite its geographic isolation.

"One of the highlights of my trip was to see Moran's greatest work, *The Grand Chasm of the Colorado*. I was almost reduced to tears by its brilliance and beauty. We both know that the Grand Canyon defies all description—but Moran comes as close as any human could to capturing its essence. Congress bought that work of art for the amazing sum of $10,000 and it draws immense crowds. I had a United States senator tell me that Moran's masterpiece and his remarkable sketches were doing even more to raise public awareness of the Grand Canyon than Major Powell's writings and speaking engagements."

"Does the major's report tell you anything new?"

"Most certainly! As you know, neither I nor Major Powell are trained geologists, but Mr. Dutton and most true geologists are in agreement that the primary causes of the canyon widening are running water, wind, and the expanding roots of plants growing in rock crevasses. Also, given that we get hard winters even along this South Rim, it is clear that the constancy of expanding and contracting freezing and thawing water is a major contributor to the widening of the canyon."

"Did you tell him about our intense summer cloudbursts?"

"I did! Mr. Dutton had little knowledge of their incredible ferocity on this South Rim, but when I explained how great sheets of water cascaded over the rim after a summer downpour, he agreed that they would also play a major role in rim erosion. His own excellent geological report theorizes that the canyon has already begun to widen much faster than it deepens. He predicts that millions of years from now the Grand Canyon will become the 'Grand Valley.' A valley not only hundreds of miles long, but also hundreds of miles wide."

"How fascinating. And how about your own talk? Did it go well?"

"Not as well as I had hoped," Sutherland confessed with considerable hesitation. "My theories were challenged and my data were discounted, just as they discounted Major Powell's earliest Grand Canyon contributions. I had expected to be feted and lionized, but instead, I was attacked."

"How could they do that? You had a split-twig figurine, fossils, tools, drawings. I saw it all and . . ."

"I couldn't authenticate the dates of creation," Sutherland explained. "My hypothesis that earliest North American man settled in this region wasn't strong enough to ward off the skeptics."

"But . . ."

"And they ridiculed my awareness of Indian spirits. I should have anticipated their skepticism and realized that I sounded very unscientific. I know one thing for sure—I'll never return to the East and subject myself to that kind of ridicule and abuse. I'll stay out here and keep working and someday, someone more pleasing in appearance and more scientifically acceptable will present my discoveries and theories to the academic world."

"But they'll be *your* findings and thoughts."

"Yes, but it is the accumulation of knowledge and understanding that is to be cherished and valued, not momentary professional accolades, money, or public acclaim. Truly, I'm glad that I have at least figured that much out."

Sutherland looked closely at him. "We all have secret illusions that drive us to do one thing or another. But when we finally see reality, it can be mind liberating. Remember, Bill, you once clung to the mere illusion of a young woman whose heart you came West to win. But then, you met Josie."

"And look what happened," Dunn said, unable to conceal his sadness. "If I had not met her, Josie would have married one of her own people and still be alive."

"Is that how you really see your marriage and years spent together? As just a fatal set of circumstances? A cruel act of fate?"

"No," Dunn admitted. "There's Christopher, of course. And Josie and I were very happy."

"You'll be happy again with Kate."

"I intend to marry her."

"Excellent!" Sutherland exclaimed with obvious delight.

The man looked so pleased, that Dunn really did not have the heart to tell him about the threat of Monty Ford and so they sat in contented silence hoping to see a shooting star.

Twenty-one

One warm spring afternoon, Dunn returned from Prescott with three new men the likes of which his Indians had never seen before. These new men were vaqueros and their names were Señor Armando Vaca Ortiz and his two handsome sons, Juan and Lucio. The Mexican horsemen rode tall black geldings with bowed necks and Spanish fire in their dark eyes.

Dunn's Hualapai and Havasupai Indians could not stop staring at the vaqueros and their extraordinary horses. Instead of the old, scarred saddle that Dunn had worn down in places to its rawhide-wrapped tree, the vaqueros owned beautifully tooled and carved saddles topped by thick saddlehorns. Their silver bits and big-roweled Spanish spurs gleamed, and their braided bridles and reins were works of art. Dunn quickly introduced the vaqueros, who then wheeled their horses around and went to make their own camp near the river.

"There's good news," he told his Indians, "I've just returned from Fort Whipple where I was lucky enough to win a contract to supply the army with fifty head of horses. That's why I decided that we needed some real professionals. Those vaqueros are experts who have caught wild horses on both sides of the Rio Grande. I've agreed to let them take first pick of the mustangs and then every fourth animal right down to the colts and fillies. They plan to drive them down to Mexico, where they have a horse ranch just below the border."

Those Hualapai and Havasupai who understood English translated to their friends. Dunn unloosened the cinch of his own mustang, a powerful little blue roan that he'd managed to catch with a foot trap two years earlier along with a half dozen other mustangs they'd caught and broken to ride. The blue roan had been just a feisty colt then and wild as the wind but now was an exceptionally good saddle horse, one of the toughest and smartest Dunn had ever ridden.

He dragged off his saddle and sweat-soaked blanket, while continuing to describe his trip. "After Captain Benson saw the quality of our Arizona mustangs, he promised he'd buy fifty head broke to the saddle. He wants only first-rate cavalry mounts and I told him that's what we would deliver. He said, if I delivered as promised, he was sure that I could also help supply mustangs to nearby Fort Verde and at Fort Mojave on the lower Colorado River."

Dunn removed his hat and sleeved his damp forehead. "Another thing that impressed the captain was how well these mustangs can maintain themselves on so little native graze and feed. I told him that they were natural born foragers and that he could cut way back on army bought hay and grain and they'd stay in good working condition.

"I also made it very clear to Captain Benson that mustangs will save him a lot of expense and trouble because their feet are as hard as diamonds so they won't need to be shod every four to six weeks. It took some convincing to make him believe that we'd covered over a hundred miles in two days and our horses still looked fresh. These mustangs were their own best advertisement. The captain was smart enough to realize that, in this rough country, stamina, and toughness are more important than size and speed."

"How will they find these horses?" Mi-ta asked.

Dunn smiled for that was a very good question. "These vaqueros *know* the thinking of horses," he explained. "I have given them several weeks to learn where they will be easiest to catch."

Mi-ta and the others nodded with understanding. Dunn turned his horse over to one of the Indians and hurried toward the house to find Kate and Christopher and also tell them of his good news.

"Señor Dunn," Armando Ortiz said several weeks later as he squatted on his heels and used a sharp stick to begin a drawing that would cover almost fifty thousand acres of rangeland on the Coconino Plateau. "This is what my sons and I learn."

With a surprising memory for landscape details, Armando quickly sketched in the contour of the Grand Canyon, then the approximate boundaries of the Lonesome Valley Ranch and finally, every South Rim peak, watering hole and prominent landmark within seventy-five miles.

"Here we are, Señor," he said, drawing a small "x" to mark the headquarters of the Lonesome Valley Ranch. "And way out here is Warm Springs and here are all the other places where the wild ones must water."

Dunn had been so busy building his ranch herds that he'd never taken the time to map out the really isolated watering holes. He did know where the important, year-round sources of water were located because they were vitally important to his own livestock.

"Are you sure there is a spring in this place?" he asked, pointing to one of Armando's most westerly marks. "I've never seen or heard of it."

"I have," Mi-ta interrupted with excitement. "Our ancestors have always used that water, even in times of drought. Long ago, I think Spaniards discovered and named it El Caballo, maybe because it attracts so many wild horses."

Dunn studied the drawing, wishing that he'd asked Ortiz to put it on paper instead of sketching it in his ranch yard where it would soon be scratched away by their noisy flock of hens.

"Señor Ortiz," Dunn said, "what is your plan?"

The pointed tips of Armando's long salt-and-pepper mustache twitched and he jabbed the stick into the dirt. "With the help of your men, we will build a corral at Warm Springs. It will be a good trap because it will allow us to drive the mustangs down a steep, curving shelf of rock where they will be caught before they realize it."

"Is that where we begin the roundup?"

"No," Armando said, shaking his head. "We ride two days to El Caballo and wait there for the mustangs to come in to drink."

Dunn knew that mustangers often let thirsty mustangs drink their fill before chasing them out into open country, where they could be caught because their bellies were so full of water.

"Señor Dunn," Armando said. "We do *not* let them drink. We begin their long thirst, a thirst that they will come to believe can be quenched only at Warm Springs."

"What if they scatter in all directions?"

"The wild ones will not leave their home range," Juan said. "And when they find they cannot drink in other places, they must go to Warm Springs, where the trap waits. Eh?"

"Will some choose to die of thirst rather than be caught?" Christopher asked.

"Oh, sí! My father has seen this with his own eyes."

Everyone looked to Armando, who dropped his stick and began to roll a smoke. "This is true," he admitted. "Long ago, when my father ran horses in the Tularosa Mountains of New Mexico, I remember one band led by a black stallion we named El Diablo. All one summer, my father and I tried very hard to catch this animal, but he was very fast and very smart. One day, we found El Diablo grazing alone on a peninsula which we knew to be surrounded by quicksand."

Armando lit his cigarillo and his eyes lost their focus as his mind carried him into the past. He spoke in a low monotone, all the more riveting because it held no emotion.

"El Diablo was trapped. We shook out our reatas, knowing that we both could not miss. We rode toward the stallion and I remember El Diablo began to snort and paw the earth. I had never seen such hatred in the eyes of an animal, not even in a Spanish fighting bull. I looked at my father to see if he was afraid, and I think he was.

"When we got close and began to swing our reatas, El Diablo charged. Somehow, we both managed to make good throws and my father shouted that the stallion would at last be ours—but he was wrong."

"Why?" Christopher whispered.

"Because El Diablo ran as far as he could into the quicksand, trying to drag us in with him! My father, who had only a thirty-foot reata that day, had to jump from his horse in order to save his life. My horse broke his hind leg fighting to stay on solid ground."

"Then you lost all three horses?" Kate asked.

"Sí. But we were very lucky. El Diablo had decided that we *all* should die."

"At least," Kate said, "we won't have to worry about that kind of a sad ending up in this South Rim country."

"What about the Grand Canyon?" Dunn asked. "Would such a stallion leap from its rim rather than be caught?"

The smoke coiled from the vaquero's nostril and he dipped his head. "Sí."

"Then we had better keep them well south of it," Dunn said, looking to his men and explaining what he wanted done.

"Getting back to your plan, Señor Ortiz, what about the fillies and the colts? They will be the first to drop from exhaustion."

"And the first also to be saved with the water we carry," Armando assured him.

"Then you'll need mules or burros with water barrels?"

"Yes, with plenty of food and supplies."

Armando drew a few more small marks on his already-cluttered map. "The mules must be hidden in these places so that the wild ones do not see them. When they are very thirsty, they will have no choice but to go to our trap at Warm Springs."

Dunn looked at the Indians, then at his son, and finally to Kate. "Well, what do you think?"

"It ought to work," Kate said, not looking too happy. "Señor, how many days can mustangs last without water?"

"Three, maybe four days."

"We don't want to kill any."

The three vaqueros exchanged glances but said nothing.

"What?" Kate prompted.

"Some will die," Armando explained. "It cannot be helped. Some will break their hearts, their wind, and their legs. The army wants only the strong. This way we know which are not."

"No," Kate said firmly. "We're not going to kill off the weak and the old by running them to death."

"I agree," Dunn said. "We must do our best to allow the weaker animals to escape back to the watering holes we've left behind."

"This would be very difficult. The strong lead the weak, not the other way around, Señor."

Armando pushed himself erect and walked off toward the corrals with his sons as they sought to discuss the matter in private.

"I won't allow horses to be run to death," Kate repeated.

"I know, but we don't stand a chance of catching more than a few good mustangs without their help. And, if I fail to meet this first Fort Whipple contract, we'll never get another."

Armando and his sons reached an agreement and returned.

"We will do this alone," Armando announced to everyone. "You have my word that no wild ones will die."

Dunn and Kate tried to get the vaqueros to tell them what they had in mind, but they would say nothing. Instead, they only asked for supplies and pack mules, along with three kegs of water and buckets.

"I'm going with you," Dunn informed them.

He and Armando looked deeply into each other's eyes and the Mexican finally nodded in agreement.

"Christopher and I are coming, too," Kate added.

Dunn figured that was only fitting. They had as much at stake in this ranch as he did, and they deserved to come along. He turned to Mi-ta "You're in charge," he said.

"Are you sure you have a good plan?" Dunn asked Armando. "I don't pretend to know as much as you about mustangs, but I'm sure we'll have only one chance to drive them into our trap. If we fail . . ."

"We will *not* fail," Armando interrupted. "We leave tomorrow morning—and we cannot bring any mares."

"Why?" Kate asked.

Armando looked at Dunn as if to say that he was not the one to explain.

Kate's cheeks turned pink. "Never mind," she said. "I can guess."

When they arrived at El Caballo several days later, the vaqueros chose a hiding place downwind of the springs and muzzled their horses. Dunn was amazed at the size of the springs, which rested in a valley low enough to hide the tops of big cottonwood and willow trees. The valley was empty, but Armando assured him that the mustangs would appear to drink at dusk. "Their stallion is a sorrel, and we will first see him over there, to the east."

"How many mares in his band?" Kate asked.

"Many," Armando said.

"What are we going to do?" Christopher asked.

"I will show you," Juan replied as he edged back from the crown of the hill.

Just as the golden orb of sun began to dip into the horizon, a handsome sorrel stallion led his band of mares, colts, and fillies down to El Caballo to drink. He strutted like a king, the picture of nobility. With head held high, ears flicking back and forth and nostrils widely flared to catch any warning scent, the sorrel escorted his band to the water.

"He's so beautiful," Kate said in a low voice. "It would be a shame to . . ."

"Ssshhh!" Dunn whispered as one of the stallion's ears cocked in their direction.

They froze. After a minute, the stallion drank and his band followed his example. Soon, colts and fillies became frisky in the welcome coolness of early evening.

Juan Ortiz appeared on his tall black horse, leading his pack mule. The stallion's head came up suddenly. It reared, ears flattened against its head, then began to drive the band of wild horses away from El Caballo Springs into the open rangeland. Juan rode his horse to the spring and let both it and the pack mule drink their fill. Then, he set off after the mustangs.

"I don't understand," Dunn confessed. "What can one man do chasing so many mustangs?"

"He does *not* chase them," Armando explained. "He only follows—and follows."

"Why?"

"Because that is the best way," Armando said, coming to his own feet. He removed his sombrero and waved it in a big circle over his head.

Though the light was dying, Dunn saw the glitter of Juan's silver bit and spurs before the vaquero evaporated like smoke in the dusk.

They returned to their horses and rode them down to El Caballo Springs, where they made their camp. As soon as they had settled in for the night, Dunn said, "I don't understand this way you catch mustangs, Señor Ortiz."

"It is like this," the old man tried to explain. "In this country, all living things must share the water. If we remain in this place for a few days, another band will pass through and then another after that. Lucio will follow the next and then I go after him. Comprende, Señor Dunn?"

"What are Kate and I supposed to do?"

"Do you remember the little creek to the south?" Armando asked.

"The one nearest the San Francisco peaks?"

"That is the one. You go to that place and wait for your

own band of mustangs. It will not be so long. You see, at this spring and each of the others, we will tie a little ribbon on a stick. Wild horses will see the ribbon and pass on, even if they are very, very thirsty. They must come to you."

"And then what?" Kate asked.

"You must always stay in their sight. When they come upon a spring, let them drink a little so that the young ones do not die. Do not run them, just follow and they will keep moving until there is only one place left to drink."

"Warm Springs."

"Si!"

"How long might this take?" Kate asked.

"A week, two weeks. No longer. But remember, very little water, not much grass, and very little sleep."

"Then we all suffer," Dunn said, looking to Kate and Christopher.

"You do not have to do anything," Armando replied with an indifferent shrug of his shoulders. "We can catch enough wild ones for everyone."

"I'd prefer that we all did this together, Señor."

The Mexican frowned. "It will be very hard."

"As you know, life is hard."

In the days that followed, Armando told them many things about trapping the wild ones.

"I have seen terrible things. Along the border with Old Mexico, my sons and I are called mesteneros, which is the Spanish word for mustanger. I remember when my father and many of the mesteneros rode up from San Miguel into the Casa Amarilla country to trap mares for our Spanish stallions. Using strong relay horses, we chased a very large manada—what you call a band—for three days, until they were almost ready to die. Finally, we let them stop at a river to drink until their bellies were as round as gourds. After that, the mares were too heavy to run. They surrendered without a fight."

"What about their colts?" Kate asked.

"We kept only the strongest. I was very young and did not understand when the old mesteneros cut one knee of every mare so that the joint water flowed and the mares could never run again."

Kate paled. Several minutes passed before she could ask, "Does this cruelty still exist?"

"Sí. And I have even seen the nostrils of mustangs sewn up with rawhide so that they only could breathe enough to walk. Even worse than this, deep in Mexico, I once saw . . ."

"Por favor, Señor!" Kate exclaimed. "No more of this talk. How will we drive *our* mustangs to Lonesome Valley Ranch?"

"There are better ways," Armando assured her. "But I cannot say which is best until it is time to move the wild ones from the big trap at Warm Springs."

The next few days passed slowly while they waited for another band of mustangs to appear at El Caballo. If Armando was concerned about his sons, he hid it well and enjoyed long siestas.

"I have a feeling that sleep is going to become very scarce a few days from now," Dunn told Kate and his son one warm afternoon as the mustanger dozed peacefully in the shade of a big juniper.

A few hours later, a small band of mustangs approached the springs. Armando was awakened but, when he saw there were fewer than a dozen, he shook his head and resumed his nap. The mustangs left and it was another two days before a larger band appeared just at sundown. Dunn counted twenty-two mares and nine colts, but it was the stallion that captured a man's eye. He was a liver chestnut with a blaze down his face and three white stockings. Standing at least sixteen hands tall, he was magnificent.

"Muy caballo!" Armando exclaimed, emitting a low whistle of admiration. "This one *I* want!"

"You can have him if you can catch and break him," Dunn said, knowing a stallion of this size and strength had tasted too many years of freedom ever to be completely trustworthy. Such a powerful animal could end a man's life with one savage kick or strike.

Armando seemed almost youthful now as he hurriedly saddled and rushed to pack their water and supplies. It was all that the rest of them could do to leave the springs at the same time. The mestenero galloped ahead and the stallion whirled and began to drive his mares eastward, tails and manes streaming in the wind.

"Look at that man ride!" Dunn exclaimed as he took the lead rope to the pack mule and prepared to follow.

Everyone watched as the vaquero charged after the mustangs, whooping and yipping as he slowly faded into a huge cloud of dust. Dunn had never seen a finer, more graceful pair than Armando and his horse, each more perfect together than apart.

"Will I ever learn to ride like that?" Christopher asked.

"I don't know that it can be taught," Dunn answered. "But watch everything these vaqueros do and learn their ways. You will never see finer horsemen."

"Father, have you noticed how they whisper into their horses' ears?"

"No."

"I have. They do it only when they believe no one is watching. I think their horses *listen.*"

Dunn glanced aside at Kate to see if she was smiling. She was not. Turning back to Christopher, he said, "The next chance you get, ask one of them what they are saying. That would be good to know."

They had ridden all night and well into the next day, always keeping the large band of mustangs in sight. The weather had grown hot and the horses were starting to suffer when they finally reached Antelope Springs. Armando allowed the chestnut to water his band for a few anxious minutes. Then, whooping and waving, he charged down and scattered the band into the hills. Dunn watched Armando dismount and allow his own horse a good drink, then the Mexican waved for them to come and join him.

"It is going well," Armando informed them when they dismounted to water their mule and horses. "You rest here tonight, and I will be back in two days."

"How can you be sure?"

"The stallion has run west and there is no water in that direction. He is thinking that he can trick me and circle back around, maybe get a big lead and give himself and his band plenty of time to drink."

Armando chuckled. "But he will find *you* waiting here."

"Maybe we should allow them another drink," Christopher said.

"No," Armando told him. "If they drink again so soon, they will not start for Warm Springs, and we will never catch them. Comprende?"

Christopher yawned and dipped his chin.

"Good," Armando said. "You rest until I drive the wild ones back. When they come, chase them away."

"Toward Warm Springs?"

"They will have no other place to go."

Armando found a sack of grain, loosened his cinch, and fed his black horse, then let it graze for an hour while he took a quick siesta. Without another word, he then retightened his cinch, allowed his horse to drink again, and began to follow the liver chestnut and his band.

When the mustangs finally did return, Dunn could see that they were suffering from lack of water as they struggled forward, heads down and senses dulled with a raging thirst. Even the once-proud stallion seemed lifeless and indifferent to everything except the prospect of water.

"I don't like this," Kate said.

"It is nearing the end," Dunn said as he noticed that about a dozen yearlings and foals had fallen behind the main band and were coming straight for the springs on wobbly legs.

"These are ours now!" Armando called. "When they enter the water to drink, we will rope them!"

"And then what?" Dunn quietly asked.

"I will show you."

Armando took a packet of tough rawhide straps from his saddlebags, each about a yard long and notched with a deep "V" at one end. Dismounted, he singled out a handsome yearling colt and roped it by the forelegs, making a beautiful cast that he called the mangana and which caught the yearling's front legs.

"Hold him down!" Armando shouted.

All three of them piled on the yearling. Armando dismounted and came over to tie one of the rawhide straps to the colt's front ankle. "When he gets up and tries to run," he explained, "his back feet will step on this and he will take a hard fall. A few times of that and we could not *make* him run."

"Couldn't he also break his neck?" Kate asked with concern.

"Sometimes."

Before Kate could voice an objection, the vaquero remounted. The young mustangs were so exhausted that they were easy to rope in order to attach the rawhide strips. After only a few halfhearted attempts to run, the colts gave up any hope of escape.

Dunn and Christopher also went to work. Very soon, they had their hands full, catching, throwing, and holding the colts and fillies while struggling to attach the rawhide straps. After getting bitten and kicked a few times, they decided that Armando Ortiz knew what he was doing.

Twenty-two

The mustanging had happened exactly according to Señor Ortiz's plan. Juan's band was the first to rush into the carefully concealed trap at Warm Springs. After drinking their fill, they were roped and one front leg tied to their chests. Hobbled in this way, they had been driven slowly back to the ranch and penned in the corrals.

A week later, Lucio surprised everyone by bringing in *two* bands of mustangs. He explained that the leader of the second band had attempted to steal mares from the bunch Lucio had already been following. The two stallions had fought while Lucio stole their mares. The fighting stallions, battered and bloodied, had been left behind. With a good deal of chuckling, Lucio described the pitiful combatants who had followed him and their lost mares nearly to Warm Springs before turning about and limping off in search of other mares.

Señor Armando Ortiz, with help from Dunn, Kate, and Christopher, had trailed the largest band, led by the chestnut, back to Warm Springs, where he skillfully pushed the mustangs into their horse trap. When Armando announced his intention to make the chestnut stallion his first pick, both his sons strongly objected.

"If you do this, you must geld him first," Lucio warned. "For he is an outlaw."

"No," Armando told his youngest son. "It would ruin his spirit."

"But he has *too much* spirit!" Juan protested.

Armando prevailed. After he had picked out their share of the roundup, he began to work with the stallion each day. Because it was so strong and such a fighter, it was isolated in a stout breaking corral with a seven-foot-high circular wall.

For three days, the stallion would not eat and drank very little, but Armando stayed near and kept talking to the animal. No one knew what the old man said, for his words had meaning only to the chestnut. By the end of the week, Armando had worked a miracle. He was able to touch, then even halter the beautiful chestnut stallion.

Christopher stayed very close to Armando, watching and listening as the old mestenero talked to the stallion to rid him of his fears.

"He doesn't say anything in Spanish," Christopher explained one evening as he and his father sat and watched the vaquero ride the stallion around and around, his voice a constant murmur of encouragement. "But he doesn't speak in English either."

"Maybe," Dunn said, "he talks to it in Apache or some other Indian language."

"No," Christopher said, looking perplexed. "Señor Ortiz told me he has made up his own language and that his sons have *their* own language and that I have to make up my own. He says it doesn't matter what is said, only *how* it is spoken. And that it is spoken with great feeling."

"Did you tell this to Kate?"

"Yep. She said it was that way with men and women, too." The boy frowned. "I didn't understand her either."

When Christopher told Juan and Lucio what their father and then Kate had said about "great feeling," the two handsome young vaqueros laughed and then went back to the corrals and continued gentling and riding the mares.

Dunn marveled at their ability with mustangs. It wasn't that they had any tricks or methods that were unusual. Rather, the Ortiz men explained to him that it was important to move slowly around wild horses and also to talk to them in a calm voice. And, unlike bronc busters, they preferred to break their horses without a struggle. They would do this by first blindfolding and then tying up a foreleg as they got the mare accustomed to the saddle. They spent considerably more time easing their weight into and out of the stirrup—perhaps as many as fifty times before eventually swinging lightly into the saddle.

Sometimes the mares tried to buck on three legs but they fell and, after a while, their suspended foreleg was untied and they began to learn something about neck reining. Juan and Lucio worked in the breaking corrals from sunup until sundown and Dunn was amazed at what they were able to accomplish in their quiet, unhurried fashion.

One of the things that was most evident about the vaqueros was their artistry with the braided rawhide reatas. In their hands, the fifty-foot reatas became an extension of their bodies. During the time that they worked with the mustangs at the ranch headquarters, Dunn never saw them miss a cast. They had the ability to rope one mare out of a dozen milling horses without even whirling their loops overhead a few times before their throw. One moment they would be slouched in front of a group of nervous mares and the next, their reatas would be flying over the horses' heads to land softly on the chosen mare.

"They never fight the horses," Dunn told Kate one evening. "Bronc busters jump on a wild horse with a quirt and a pair of spurs and fight to win. These vaqueros win by persistence and relentless persuasion. They can be tough, but they prefer an easier way of taming a horse, and I'm convinced that their horses are going to be far better mounts. I have a feeling that Captain Benson is going to be very, very happy with these mares when we get them to Fort Whipple."

"Have you thought about offering Señor Ortiz and his sons a permanent job?"

"Sure, but I couldn't afford to pay them what they can earn

on their own. Also, in less than a year, they'll capture all the mustangs worth breaking in this South Rim country."

"What about cattle?" Kate asked. "We've doubled our herd and our range. Maybe they would be willing to work mostly with cattle."

"I'll speak to them about it," Dunn said, "but their family has a horse ranch down in New Mexico. I've heard them speak of it many times, and I know they are eager to return and to sell their share of the mustangs. Lucio and Juan both have girlfriends in Old Mexico as well as in Silver City."

"Well, then," Kate said, "I guess it would be pointless to offer them year-round work."

"I'm afraid so. The best we can do is to watch and learn. I'm hoping they'll return next year for another roundup. I've been thinking about all the horses that are running wild in the North Rim country."

"And all the Kaibab Indians," Kate warned.

"Yeah, them, too." Dunn sighed. "You know something? I haven't had any more dreams about the Howland brothers. In fact, a few days ago, I even wrote a little about that Paiute attack."

"I saw you writing in your journal. I'd like to read it sometime."

He thought about all the intimate words he'd written to Cynthia Holloway. "I don't think you'd find it very interesting," he said before excusing himself and going back to work.

That evening, just as the Ortiz men were riding off to their camp beside the stream, Professor Sutherland arrived in a state of high excitement.

"I have something to show you!" he exclaimed, placing a bulging burlap sack on their kitchen table. "Turn up the lamp!"

Christopher and Kate crowded around and Dunn watched the professor closely, realizing for the first time that their archeologist friend had aged a great deal since they'd first met at Lonely Dell. He was thinner. His hair and beard were now entirely white, long and tangled, giving him a decidedly wild and unkempt appearance. His pants were worn out at the knees, his shirt torn and faded, his skin burned to the color of coffee by constant exposure to the merciless Arizona sun. A stranger might think Professor Sutherland very frail, but Dunn knew that the man had the heart of a lion and a remarkable constitution fueled by an undying passion for archeology. Even so, Dunn could not help but wonder how many more years the scientist could endure his lonely existence on the beautiful but inhospitable rim of the Grand Canyon.

"What I am about to show you," Sutherland was saying, "is so remarkable that you ought to sit down."

Wide-eyed with anticipation, Kate and Christopher plopped down in chairs, but Dunn figured he could take it standing. He could see from the sack's bulge that this was no mere grinding stone or handsome Anasazi bowl.

"You found the entire skeleton of an ancient one," he guessed out loud.

"No! Something much, *much* more interesting."

"Thank God," Kate whispered.

The professor lovingly stroked the sack. "What I have found answers a very old question—namely, exactly where, in 1540, did Garcia Lopez de Cardenas and his small party of thirsty soldiers actually attempt to reach the Colorado River?"

"You found their *weapons!*" Christopher squealed.

"And some armor." Sutherland emptied the sack of a tarnished Spanish helmet, a coat of mail, and a short, wicked-looking Spanish dagger that was in remarkably good condition. It had held its sharp edge through the long centuries. In addition, there were four hammered buckles of various sizes that looked to be made of pewter.

"Can you believe my good fortune!" Sutherland exclaimed.

"How did you ever find this?"

"I took a few days off from my dig and went for a long hike along the rim. Just as I was about to turn around and return to my cabin, I noticed a trail leading off the rim at a very steep angle. At first, I thought it must be only a game trail, but then I could see that someone long ago had built a few rock steps in the most treacherous places. I had to edge my way down a dangerous chute of rock, but again discovered a few footholds and handholds beaten into the rock, so I *knew* that others had descended there, centuries ago. When I reached the bottom of the highest cliffs to the first plateau below the red limestone cap, I found this evidence of the Cardenas expedition!"

Dunn reached out and ran his hands over the rusty old Spanish armor and the sharp blade of the impressive, two-edged fighting dagger. "How did you ever bring these relics out?"

"It wasn't easy, I'll tell you," the professor admitted. "It took a couple of trips. But once I had it all up on the rim, I began to dig and poke around and I discovered the exact site of the Spaniards' old camp. It's not twenty miles from this cabin. Not seven miles from my *own* cabin! And just think! This helmet was worn by one of the three brave soldiers who tried to reach the river and get water!"

Sutherland's enthusiasm was contagious, especially when he began to tell them once again the daring story of how the three legendary Spanish soldiers, Captain Pablo de Melgosa, Juan Galeras, and a third man whose name had been forgotten had gallantly attempted to reach the Colorado River.

"Oh," he said, "I have had great fun trying to decide which of those three wore this helmet. I like to imagine that it was Juan Galeras and that the dagger belonged to the one whose name has been lost in time. I am quite sure that the coat of mail belonged to Captain Melgosa. And now, would you like to try it on, Christopher?"

They dressed Christopher in the armor of a sixteenth century soldier. Dunn would have given a hundred head of horses to have a picture of his son with both fists clutching the fighting sword and grinning through the face of the rusty and dented Spanish helmet.

"Can I find Tucson and show him how I look?" Christopher shouted.

"Of course," Sutherland said, "but be careful with the dagger. It's not a toy."

When he was gone, the professor said, "I wish that I could make those things a present to Christopher, but I'm afraid that they belong in a museum. Either the Smithsonian or in Spain. But I would like to give Christopher one of the Spanish buckles. It doesn't look like much, but they are actually priceless."

"He'll be very pleased," Dunn said. "Any idea what the buckles were used for?"

"Probably for belts, harnesses, or shoulder straps to hold water, packs, or even arms," Sutherland postulated. "Oh, and I've planted my Indian corn again exactly as the Anasazi did. I'll have a big crop this year and expect all of you, including the Havasupai and Hualapai, to come visit in mid-September for a big corn harvest festival."

"You know we wouldn't miss it," Kate said, fingering the buckles. "I'd love to have one of these myself. Any chance that you'll discover more?"

"Here, take this one," Sutherland said. "And I probably will find others. There is little question that I've found Cardenas's exact 1540 campsite. Sand and brush have buried it, but I'm sure it's only a few inches under the surface. I suspect that much of the evidence left by the Spaniards was carried off by the Indians either as curiosities or useful implements. It will take a few weeks to fully unearth the site. I'll probably find more buckles, little things, but no more prizes like the dagger and armor."

"I suppose," Kate said, "these pieces will cause quite a stir among your Eastern colleagues."

"Yes," Sutherland said with a pronounced lack of enthusiasm. "I should definitely write a paper for the archeological society, but I've been procrastinating for weeks now. However, it is my scientific duty and it shall be done. Perhaps I will sit down this very evening and write Dr. Milford a long and detailed letter outlining this discovery and asking how he would suggest the matter be handled. Would you mind delivering a letter to Prescott for forwarding to him?"

"Not at all," Dunn said.

"Thank you," Sutherland replied, rummaging around in his pack. "I seem to have forgotten my writing materials. Could I use yours?"

"Of course."

Three weeks later, Dunn posted Sutherland's letter at Fort Whipple while a very pleased Captain Benson took possession of fifty new saddle horses at thirty dollars each.

"I'll take another bunch like this next spring," the supply officer promised as they watched his cavalrymen exercise their new and well-behaved mares on the parade ground. "And I strongly advise you to take whatever you have left over to Fort Verde, which is just a long day's ride to the east. I'm sure they'll buy every last one of your mustangs. I'll even write you a letter of introduction."

"That would be much appreciated," Dunn said. "How about some beef for your hungry troopers this fall?"

"How many head could you deliver?"

"Five hundred head of Longhorns."

But Benson shook his head. "I could use no more than a hundred to carry us through the winter."

"I'd be happy to supply them."

"All right," Benson said, "the going price is ten dollars a head, maybe a little higher if they are prime."

"My cattle are in excellent condition," Dunn replied. "I've also got sheep to sell."

"I'll take fifty at three dollars a head," Benson decided after a moment of consideration. "Soldiers prefer beef, but you might try to sell your sheep to the Indians. For some reason, they seem to prefer mutton."

"I'll deliver fifty wethers along with a hundred head of fat cattle in October," Dunn promised, trying to hide his disappointment at the unexpectedly low sheep prices. "But for now, I'll wait outside for your letter of introduction and my mustang money, half of which I'm going to use to buy more ranchland."

"More snakes and sagebrush you mean, don't you?" the officer said with a wink. "Mr. Dunn, why don't you buy a ranch down here around Prescott, where there is plenty of water and grass?"

"There's plenty of water and grass up on the Coconino, if you know where to find it," Dunn told the army officer. "When I deliver my cattle and sheep this fall, you'll have your proof of how well livestock do up in my South Rim country. But thanks for your concern and for the business."

"My pleasure. I'll get that money and letter ready now. It won't take long."

Dunn returned to join Christopher and the vaqueros. "Señor Ortiz," he said, "Captain Benson would like to have bought a few of your mares. And he especially liked your new stallion."

"This one will never be for sale," Armando said, scratching the stallion's neck.

"After Christopher and I visit the land office and buy more land, including El Caballo Springs, we're headed for Fort Verde. Care to ride along?"

"No, Señor Dunn," Armando said, speaking for all of them. "It is time for us to go home again. You ride east, we ride south."

"Will you come back next spring?"

"Why?" Lucio asked with a half smile. "Now that we have shown you everything we know, you and Christopher can do it for yourselves."

Christopher blushed with pride.

Armando mounted the stallion and looked down at Christopher. "You have a special way with horses and have learned much about the wild ones. Take care of your father, and we will return next spring, and *then* maybe I will tell you my secret words."

"Señor Ortiz, you have no secret words," Christopher said, "you have something much better—a gift with horses."

"And so do you!"

"Here," Juan said, extending a rawhide reata. "My father and brother want you to have this."

Christopher hesitated. He had watched these men braid such a reata and knew the great skill and patience it required.

"Go ahead, muchacho!" Juan encouraged. "Besides, it is not quite so long as ours."

"It was broken by a stallion," Armando explained. "We have fixed it like new so you can practice the throws, eh?"

"I will practice every day!"

"You *must,* since your father could not rope even an old milk cow!" Lucio said, bursting into laughter. "Anyway, we expect you to be able to throw the mangana next spring and many other throws as well, eh?"

"I'll sure try," the boy told them as the vaqueros wheeled their mounts and rode out of Fort Whipple, leading their mustang mares.

"Adios!" Dunn called, realizing that the mesteneros loved freedom as much as the wild ones they hunted.

The quartermaster at Fort Verde took every one of Dunn's remaining mustang mares and gave him a written contract for a fall delivery of both sheep and cattle.

"Next time," the sergeant said, "you bring your mustangs to us *first.* We'll pay you two dollars a head more than Captain Benson."

"You can do that?"

"Why not?" the quartermaster asked. "We've got a rivalry going, and damned if we want their picked-over horses. But you do what you think best."

"Thanks, and I'll hold back a few of my best horses next

time," he promised before pocketing the money and the delivery contract and then joining Christopher.

"I'm sorry you had to wait so long while I attended to business," Dunn apologized to the boy. "I hope you found something to occupy your time."

"I sure did," Christopher told him. "Those four men over there are real nice. They were looking at our mustangs and wanting to know everything about them."

Dunn glanced over just in time to see the four gallop out of the fort. He had only a quick look, but his strong impression was that they were all extremely rough and dirty-looking fellows. Dunn knew it was unfair to make judgments based on appearance, but these men definitely were not the types that he wanted Christopher to be associating with. It was not to say that he did not admire his son's openness and trusting nature. Living out in the rim country with so few strangers, Christopher had never been exposed to liars, cheats, or worse. The boy still thought you could trust and accept all men at face value.

"Where are they from?" Dunn asked.

"They been just about everywhere, and now they're looking for ranch work. They even asked if we had any work at our ranch, but I told 'em I was afraid not and that we only hired Indians and vaqueros."

"Good answer," Dunn said, tousling his son's hair.

"And I told them all about the professor and his cabin on the South Rim. How he found Cardenas's Spanish armor along with bones, arrowheads, and Anasazi pottery. They didn't even know that the Spaniards once explored all this canyon country and they never even heard of the ancient Anasazi! I told 'em all about those people, but they were more interested in the Spanish soldiers."

After he was paid and had received his letter of introduction, Dunn stuffed the mustang money into his saddlebags, still thinking about the four men as they prepared to leave Fort Verde.

"You know, son, it's not always a good idea to tell strangers too much about yourself or your friends."

"Well, what else was I to talk about?"

"I don't know, but loose talk sometimes has a way of causing problems. So, in the future, I'd appreciate it if you just sort of listened more and talked less."

"All right," Christopher said, looking confused as they tightened their cinches and prepared to ride south.

Flagstaff had all the makings of a boomtown. Both Dunn and Christopher took an immediate liking to the bustling settlement nestled high under the snowcapped San Francisco Mountains, whose three most prominent peaks speared the clouds.

"I never expected to see so much going on here," Dunn said as they rode down through the center of town.

Everywhere they looked, buildings were in some phase of hasty construction, being made either of logs from the surrounding ponderosa pine forests or from an equally unlimited supply of red Coconino sandstone. The central street through town was muddied from a recent downpour, and the air was filled with the pounding of hammers and the rasp of saws as men swarmed over the buildings like worker ants.

Dunn could see why the town was so attractive. The valley soil appeared dark and rich enough for farming or growing hay, while the surrounding ponderosa forests ran as far as the eye could see under a deep velvet blue sky.

"It's handsome, isn't it," Christopher said, "but I like our open country better."

"You do?" Dunn was surprised.

"Yep. I feel sort of pinched in with all these trees. Don't see how a fella could enjoy a sunrise or a sunset lost between these pines."

Dunn chuckled and nodded his head in agreement, but he sure appreciated the cool, ponderosa pine-scented air.

"Look at that flagpole!" Christopher exclaimed.

Dunn followed the boy's eyes to take in a huge American flag waving from the top of a shaved sixty- or seventy-foot pine tree. The flag was snapping proudly in the breeze.

"Well," Dunn said, "at least now we know why this place was named Flagstaff."

They reined their horses in at a café, tied them to a hitching post, and went inside to enjoy a big meal of steak and potatoes. Dunn liked watching Christopher take in the novelty of a town almost as much as he enjoyed his excellent dinner. And when they were served huge slabs of apple pie for dessert, he had to grin when Christopher exclaimed, "We should do this a *lot* more often, Dad! Kate ought to come, too!"

"We'll ask her along this fall when we deliver our cattle and sheep," he promised, thinking it might be a fine idea for Kate to see new faces and things. On their ride up the main street, Dunn had already counted eight women in Flagstaff.

But then, he got to worrying. What if Kate visited and enjoyed the company of these women and the conveniences of a town so much that she did not want to return to Lonesome Valley? Kate had lived in cities before and perhaps the sight of so much social activity would stir forgotten longings, make her realize what a sacrifice she was making by being the only white woman living on the whole South Rim.

When he paid his bill, Dunn asked, "Why is there so much activity in Flagstaff?"

The owner, a short man wearing a dirty white apron, replied, "Things are looking up smartly because the railroad is coming and the Arizona Colonization Company keeps promoting this town."

"The what?"

"The land promoters! They're sending us people from Boston and them other big cities with promises that the San Francisco Mountains are made of almost solid gold."

"And those people believe that?" Christopher asked.

"Kid, some actually do. Some of those fools stay but most

go home within a few months. But I tell you, when the Atlantic and Pacific Railroad arrives, it'll really put Flagstaff on the map! Then you just watch and see what happens to our city lot prices!"

Dunn found it hard to believe that a town as small as Flagstaff could attract a railroad. "They're actually coming? Or is that just a rumor being spread by those land promoters?"

"Oh, no," the man interrupted, "they *are* coming. Contracts have been signed. Railroad survey crews have already crossed the New Mexico border. The word in these parts is that the government gave the Atlantic and Pacific Railroad more than three million acres of free land to build and operate a line all the way from Albuquerque to the Pacific Ocean. And our own Flagstaff is going to be sitting right smack-dab in the middle of 'er!"

"Three *million* acres?"

"That's right. They're getting alternating twenty-mile sections along both sides of the line. They'll log 'em bare and then auction 'em off to the emigrants. It's all pure profit."

"Why would our government give away such valuable land?"

"Because it *ain't* valuable without a railroad. Flagstaff's future would be flatter than a stomped horned toad!"

"I see."

"Maybe you ought to buy some land in these parts yourself, Mister."

"Can't," Dunn replied. "I'm already land poor."

"Where did you buy?"

"My son and I are partners in a ranch due north of here. Covers a lot of the land between the San Francisco Mountains and the South Rim."

"Jesus," the owner commiserated, "what a cryin' shame! That rim country is way too far from the railroad and everything. It'll never be worth much."

And with that, he took Dunn's money and hurried back into his kitchen.

Dunn couldn't help but feel low as he and Christopher prepared to leave Flagstaff for their Lonesome Valley Ranch.

"Maybe he's wrong, Father."

"I don't think so," Dunn said. "But the thing of it is, I didn't have any money to start with. All the ranch seed money came from your grandfather. Zack wanted to help me and his daughter, and he wanted us to stay close to Havasu Canyon so we could look out for our Havasupai friends. There was no way any of us could have predicted that a railroad would come to the south of us in our lifetimes."

"I still *like* our country better than this," Christopher said. "And we do have our good Indian friends, the mustangs, and the professor. We'd have had none of that if we'd bought land in Prescott or Flagstaff."

"You're right," Dunn agreed, already feeling better. "And I'm buying more rangeland every year. Christopher, do you know that we now hold legal title to almost a hundred thousand acres?"

"That's a lot of 'snakes and sagebrush,' " Christopher said with a grin.

"Yes," Dunn said, grateful to his son for reminding him of their blessings, "it is. Now, what's going on up there at the north edge of town?"

"I don't know," Christopher said, "but it sure looks interesting."

It *was* interesting. An Illinois salesman had erected a very peculiar kind of corral made of wire. Dunn had never seen anything like it. A big crowd had gathered around, and the salesman was standing on a tree stump. When he tried but failed to get everyone to stop talking and listen, he drew a derringer from his coat and fired it straight up into the sky. That caused everyone to shut up.

"Gentlemen and ladies," the salesman yelled. "This is the historic, unforgettable moment we have all been waiting to see. And, as you will recall, when I arrived in your fair town last week, I pledged that my company's new *barbed wire* was as light as air but as strong as steel. I swore to you that it would contain and even pacify a dozen of the wildest Texas Longhorn cattle that ever set foot in the Arizona Territory. Make 'em moo like old milk cows!"

The crowd laughed, and some even snickered, but the salesman didn't let that faze him at all. "And I also told you that our *revolutionary barbed wire* is cheap, won't sag in the heat nor stretch and break during a hard winter's freeze."

The salesman, a handsome and well-dressed man in his midthirties, paused for breath. "Well, ladies and gentlemen, it's as hot as it gets in Flagstaff and you all can see that this wire hasn't sagged—it wouldn't even sag in Death Valley, California. The only thing is, I can't prove that it won't snap in a freeze . . . we'll have to wait until December to do that, but it surely won't because our *barbed wire* was tested on farms in Illinois where the temperature stays far below zero for weeks at a time!

"Now then, how strong is *barbed wire?* Really?"

"It sure looks flimsy to me," Dunn said to Christopher as they sat their horses at the edge of the crowd. "It sure wouldn't hold any of our cimmarones."

"I'll bet it wouldn't even hold a strong ram," Christopher replied.

"And now, ladies and gentlemen, bring on the Longhorns and let's put my company's *barbed wire* to the ultimate test!"

The salesman's voice was drowned out by the sound of Longhorn cattle bawling as they were driven into the barbed wire corral by four bullwhip-swinging cowboys. What happened next was shocking and entirely beyond belief. The cowboys drove the bawling Longhorns straight into the wire. They struck it and then reared back, bawling like babies with blood coursing down their muzzles, necks, chests, and front legs.

"Drive 'em!" the salesman screamed. "Whip 'em!"

And the cowboys did. Again and again, they stampeded the huge Longhorns into the wire but the cattle only fell back, reeling and even bloodier, until they preferred a furious whipping to the cutting wire.

"Any doubters left?" the salesman from Illinois crowed.

There were none. No one wanted to see the Longhorns cut completely to ribbons.

"I got six thousand feet of barbed wire on hundred-foot spools and I'm going to sell it all today for a dime a running foot. Who wants never to worry about *anyone* illegally using his land again, be it a vegetable garden, a pasture, or your entire ranch? Who wants to fence it forever!"

"Father?" Christopher asked.

"There's no need for any of that on the Coconino Plateau. Besides, do you know how many feet of wire it would take to fence in a hundred thousand acres?"

"A lot."

"An entire trainload," Dunn told his son as he turned his eyes from the bleeding, defeated cattle and quickly rode away.

Nine miles north of Flagstaff, Dunn and Christopher came upon another highly unusual sight. A work crew was building an immense log cabin about seventy-five feet long and enclosing it with a stockade consisting of railroad ties set solidly on end.

"Howdy," Dunn called to one of the workman, "what kind of an army fort is this?"

"Ain't no *army* fort, Mister. This here is called Moroni after our Church's special angel, Moroni."

"I see. But why are you building it so far north of the town?"

"We just work for Brother John W. Young," the Mormon replied. "That's him standing over there. You got questions, he's got the answers."

"Thanks." Dunn rode over to meet Brother Young. "Hello there! What's going on here?"

"This is Moroni," Brother Young answered. "It will be our

protector, just as it always has been and always will be. My father is Brigham Young. I'm sure you've heard of him."

"I certainly have. What are you building here for?"

Young was a barrel-chested man, strong and intelligent-looking, with the presence of a born leader. "I've a contract with the new railroad to supply them with fifty thousand railroad ties. This is going to be a lumber camp and I won't have my brothers worried about attack by Navajo or Apache."

"A lumber camp?"

"That's right. Are you one of us?"

"I'm afraid not," Dunn said. "We own a cattle and sheep ranch up north along the South Rim."

New respect entered the Mormon's blue eyes. "And exactly how big would your ranch be?"

"Started off with forty sections of land but now we've title to just over a hundred thousand acres."

"How many head of cattle and sheep do you own?"

Dunn thought that the questions were a little forward but since he'd started off by asking a question of his own, he answered, "I own maybe six hundred head of Longhorns, all branded. And perhaps a thousand head of sheep."

"You don't know for certain?" the son of Brigham Young asked with an arched eyebrow.

"That's close enough for me."

"Would you be interested in selling out—for cash?"

"You want to *buy* my South Rim land and livestock?"

"Yes," John Young said, folding his arms across his thick chest. "Provided, of course, that the price is fair."

"Cattle are bringing fifteen dollars a head, but sheep only three."

"I'll pay that."

"And we've made a lot of improvements," Dunn added.

"All the better. I'll be happy to make you a very wealthy man."

Dunn scratched his jaw, thinking how odd it was that only a few hours ago he'd been feeling low for not buying land in

Flagstaff and now this man was offering to buy him out at a big profit.

"Why do you want it?" Christopher blurted. "Ain't nothing much between here and the Grand Canyon but snakes and sage."

"Well," Young answered carefully, "our people have done rather well with that kind of country up in Deseret. The thing of it is, the Atlantic and Pacific Railroad is about to put a lot of money into our pockets and land is a good long-term investment."

"We'll think on it," Dunn promised.

"Don't think too long," Young warned. "As you're probably well aware, Arizona land is cheap and there's still plenty of it in these parts—from the government land office—or from individuals like yourself smart enough to take a *reasonable* profit."

Dunn guessed that was true enough, but he also knew that Mormons were sharp businessmen who never bought anything unless they were guaranteed an excellent return.

After riding on, Christopher suddenly blurted, "Why does he want *our* ranch?"

"I think it's because Mr. Young figures both livestock and land prices will both go up fast after the railroad arrives."

"I hope you don't decide to sell out to him," Christopher said, looking worried.

"We'll see," Dunn replied, wondering how Kate Callahan would react to this surprising offer.

Twenty-three

The rains fell heavily in northern Arizona during the early months of summer. The open rangeland of the Coconino Plateau was ablaze with Indian paintbrush, phlox, lupine, golden aster, and an occasional prickly pear cactus with its delicate flowers. The Lonesome Valley Ranch livestock fattened rapidly on a banquet of succulent grama, wild wheat, blue and rye grasses. Dunn and Kate had a banner calf and lamb crop.

"I've never seen the range so beautiful," Kate said one afternoon as they rode out to gather cattle. "And who said that this South Rim country was a desert?"

"Beats me," Dunn replied, admiring the way the sun and the breeze played with her hair. "Kate?"

"Yes?"

"Why don't we just say the hell with it and get married after making our delivery to Fort Whipple this fall?"

His abrupt question caught her completely by surprise. "Now why," she exclaimed, "right out of the blue, did you ask such a silly question? You know that I'm still married."

"To an outlaw rotting in a Colorado prison," he told her. "If we can find a judge in Prescott, I expect we could get sworn statements and an immediate annulment."

"Bill, I'm sorry, but I just can't. And please don't bring it up again."

"Why not?"

Kate gave him a wintry smile. "We've discussed this already, and you know my reasons."

"I've heard them, sure! But every time I start thinking about them, your reasons make no sense. I mean, what if Monty is released and you never hear from him again? Does that mean you'll never be free?"

"I don't know," she finally answered. "But I know that I'll not put your life in jeopardy."

He had to struggle to keep from raising his voice. "Why don't you just let *me* decide how much risk I'm willing to take?"

"Let's not talk about this anymore," Kate said, lifting her reins. "At least we both agree not to sell this ranch to John Young."

"Kate, I'm not sure I can be happy as nothing more than partners and friends."

"Do you want your ring back?"

Dunn was almost angry enough to say yes, but he loved Kate, so he spurred his roan mustang into a gallop and headed out to gather their Longhorn cattle.

Their roundup took a full month, which was ridiculous considering that the country was open, except for the few places where it was thick with forests of piñon and juniper pine. But neither the Havasupai nor the Hualapai were skilled with cattle, so the roundup was far slower and more difficult than it would have been with a crew of veteran cowboys. Dunn really didn't care. The Indians were getting better all the time, and they'd learned a good deal from the vaqueros. Sometimes, they got so frustrated that they would leap off their ponies and dash after the Longhorns, shouting and waving their arms or chucking rocks.

Dunn vigorously objected to this practice because the cattle were big, quick, and half-wild. They had no fear of a man on a horse and even less of an angry Indian afoot. Dunn had to issue orders that everyone was to stay mounted, even if that meant losing wild cattle.

By the end of August, when they finally did get their cattle penned at the ranch, Dunn and Christopher were the only two who could rope the bawling Longhorns for branding and doctoring. Christopher was already a good roper because of his constant practicing with the Mexican reata, and Dunn was steadily improving. But two ropers weren't enough to handle so many cattle and, even when they did manage to get an unbranded calf or yearling stretched out, the Indians had to worry about dodging angry cows. When Mi-ta was almost gored by a rangy old brindle upset by the treatment of her calf, Dunn became very concerned.

"Next year I'm going to have to hire some real cowboys," he told Kate one afternoon when three hours of work had resulted in only eight calves castrated, earmarked, and branded. "Our Hualapai and Havasupai friends could learn from them and eventually take this work over again but, for now . . ."

"No, please," Christopher begged, his face covered with dust and sweat. "I'll start giving them roping lessons."

"With what?" Dunn asked. "That reata of yours is already nearly worn out."

"Then we should buy some grass ropes in Prescott or Flagstaff," Christopher said, coiling the reata and preparing to rope another calf. "Mi-ta and the others can practice all winter and be good ropers by next spring."

"I could use some winter practice myself," Dunn admitted. "All right, we'll buy up all the lariats and see if we can improve by next roundup."

Two days later, however, the four hardcases they'd seen at Fort Verde appeared at the ranch asking for jobs. If anything, they looked leaner and meaner than ever.

"We're doing all right," Dunn told the strangers.

"Don't look like it to me," the largest, a big fellow missing his left ear and riding a gray horse, drawled. "We was watchin' as we rode in and them Injuns of yours don't know squat about cattle."

"They're learning."

"From who?" another one of the four challenged. "You ain't no cow boss, that's for damned sure!"

"You're right," Dunn said, feeling a knot of anger well up in his stomach. "I'm not. But I *do* ramrod this ranch and all the land around it and I'm the one who hires and fires. Sorry, gents, but I'm not hiring."

The four exchanged disgusted glances. The youngest one was barely out of his teens. He looked over at Christopher saying, "Your old man is kind of thickheaded. Why, we could rope, castrate, and brand that whole pen of cattle in one damned day!"

Christopher coiled his reata before he replied, "You heard my father. He said we're doing just fine."

"I guess I judged you wrong over at Fort Verde, kid. Back then, you seemed halfway smart. Did the sun boil your brains this summer?"

This remark brought a chorus of guffaws from the other three and raised the hackles on Dunn's neck.

"Enough!" Dunn snapped. "You men are welcome to water your horses before you ride off this ranch."

The four glared insolently, ready and even eager for a confrontation. Dunn was unarmed while they wore sidearms and had Winchesters in easy reach. Dunn could hear his heart pounding.

"Well," the big one drawled, "if you're too damned dumb to give us a job working cattle, then I guess we'll have to go mustanging ourselves."

"That's fine as long as you don't do it on our land," Dunn said. "You'll see pine posts with tobacco cans nailed to 'em to mark our ranch boundaries."

"A post is a real small thing. Can't expect us to worry about hunting up your boundary markers."

"Big Jim is right," one of the others said with a sneer. "Big country like this'll just swallow up some piddlin' boundary post."

"Stay off our deeded ranchland," Dunn warned. "You'll see stock tanks at every watering hole. They belong to this ranch."

"I expect they'll serve real well for target practice," the one who had been silent now joked as his hand slipped closer to his gun.

A river of sweat made Dunn's eyes sting and his vision blur. He wondered just how ridiculous he looked standing unarmed in front of these four renegades who probably were on the run for cattle thieving, or worse. "You've been warned," he managed to say in a voice that didn't sound very convincing.

The big man jerked his handgun out of its holster and, without seeming to aim, fired at Dunn. Twenty yards behind him, a rooster that had been scratching about in the ranch yard was suddenly and violently decapitated. Wings beating frantically against the dust, the dying bird began to race around in circles.

"Goddamn you!" Dunn shouted.

Kate dashed into their cabin and emerged a moment later with a rifle clenched in her fists. She skidded to a halt, jammed the Winchester to her shoulder and aimed at the big man on the gray horse.

"You and your friends ride out of here right now!" she cried.

But the man with the smoking gun just grinned as he studied her like a hawk would a field mouse. Finally, he holstered his gun, tipped his dirty hat, and drawled, "Afternoon, ma'am. Hope you aren't upset over that rooster. But I had me a sudden strong feeling you might enjoy chicken for supper tonight. I'm afraid we can't stay to enjoy it with just you. Maybe next time."

Without waiting for an answer, all four wheeled their horses around and galloped off while the headless rooster tottered about ever more slowly until it tipped over like a kid's top.

That very hour, Dunn took to wearing a Colt on his hip and keeping a rifle in arm's reach. Christopher was allowed more ammunition for target practice and even Tucson was encouraged to blast away at tin cans. The boys were sent to hunt sage hens in the coolness of the early mornings and evenings.

"What will you do if those men return?" Kate asked.

"I don't know," Dunn replied. "I can't open fire on them just for riding into our ranch yard."

"But neither can you allow them to ride up close! They'd kill you and the rest of us and never give it a second thought."

"Some of the Indians can handle rifles, Kate. And they're all good with bows and arrows."

Her eyebrows shot up. "Bows and arrows? Do you really expect them to defend us and our ranch and lives with bows and arrows against men like that?"

"No," Dunn admitted, "I don't. So I guess that I'll be spending some of this fall's livestock money on rifles and ammunition as well as lariats."

"I'm afraid you must," Kate said, remembering how her husband had acted when he used his gun to kill or intimidate others. "And food and blankets. I'd better draw up another shopping list."

"Kate," he replied, "it might be a whole lot simpler if I just go into Prescott and buy us our *own* general store and haul it here on a couple of big freight wagons."

"That might be a good idea," she said, ignoring his attempt at humor. She placed her hands on her hips. "And while we're on the subject, it's almost mid-September and we need to ride over and visit the professor. He'll be offended if we don't bring everyone to his annual corn festival."

Two weeks later, everyone who could be spared headed for the South Rim to visit the professor and to share in his fall corn harvest. Over the years, it had become a tradition enjoyed by everyone at Lonesome Valley Ranch. To supplement the professor's delicious roasted corn, squash, and native greens, Dunn supplied mutton, beef, venison, and even a small keg of whiskey.

It was late afternoon when they finally topped a low rise and could view the distant Grand Canyon capped by a long dark bar that was formed by the distant and higher North Rim. Dunn found his landmarks and then tried to locate Professor Sutherland's cabin. He couldn't find it. As their wagon drew nearer, a tight knot started to grow in his belly as expectation was replaced by a deep sense of foreboding and then shock.

"The cabin is gone!" Kate whispered. "My God, it's burned down!"

"And look," Christopher shouted, leaping from the wagon and racing on ahead. "The professor's cornfields have all been flattened."

Kate gripped Dunn's arm hard. When he turned to look at her, he could see his own fears mirrored in her eyes. "Bill, what could have happened!"

"I don't know," he said, whipping their wagon team into a trot and covering the last bit of distance. By the time he pulled the team to a halt, Kate and the Indians were all racing forward toward the square of charred wood that marked all that remained of the professor's cabin.

"Professor!" Dunn shouted. "Professor!"

His shouts were swallowed by the deep, silent canyon. Dunn set the brake and grabbed his rifle. He levered a shell into the chamber and fired into the sky. Once. Twice. Three times. If the professor were within several miles of them, he could not help but hear the shots.

Everyone had stopped and now stood frozen against the setting sun. They strained to hear a response but there was none— just the hot rising wind blowing up from the floor of the Grand Canyon.

Dunn looked to his Indians, who pointed toward the many hoofprints. He followed them from the remains of the log cabin to the cornfields, which Sutherland had so carefully tended in the ancient Anasazi way, using their former terraces and irrigated gardens.

"Navajo or Apache?" he asked no one in particular.

One of the Havasupai, a man named Hav-o-ta, knelt beside the hoofprints and studied them all before saying. "No Navajo. No Apache. No Hopi. White men!"

Dunn knelt beside Hav-o-ta and traced the outline of a sharply defined hoofprint. "Yes," he said, "iron shoes."

"Can you tell how many?" Kate asked.

Dunn looked to the Indians but they shook their heads. The gardens were badly trampled and heavy summer rains had rotted the cornstalks and husks. Squash lay smashed everywhere, the rinds already picked clean by scavengers.

They returned to the burned-out cabin and steeled themselves to begin a search for Professor Sutherland's charred body. The cabin had burned so hotly that it had been reduced to a fine white ash that had mixed with rain to form a pasty gray sludge. Dunn was the first to approach what he remembered had been a good cabin, always warm in winter and cool in summer. He could easily recall the little tin stove, the simple furniture, and the many meticulously inventoried boxes of Anasazi artifacts.

Christopher wiped tears from his eyes. He dropped to his hands and knees and began to punch his fingers through the top crusted layer of sludge.

"Maybe you should go off with Kate," Dunn suggested, not wanting him to discover the professor's remains. "Go see what they did to the professor's excavation."

"No."

Dunn dropped to his hands and knees, splayed his fingers and began to sift slowly through the ashes. "Everything you find," Dunn said, as the Indians began to join him in the sifting, "and I mean even the smallest piece of bone or rock, place it in a pile outside, and we'll inspect it later."

Kate hurried off to see if the murderers had razed the professor's beloved excavations. Surprisingly, they were undisturbed, although the heavy seasonal rains had taken their toll. Tears burned her eyes as she recalled the many enjoyable hours spent here working and visiting with dear, eccentric Walter Sutherland. She remembered the way he often hummed ditties and folk songs as he scraped, picked, sketched, and brushed with his long fingers, seeking the hidden keys which he believed would unlock so many Anasazi mysteries.

Every summer, Christopher had spent several weeks here,

learning from and assisting the scientist. And, while Kate had taught the boy to love the written word, it had been the archeologist who had taught him the precision of applied science and mathematics. Taught him reasoning and logic so that he could reach sound conclusions based on facts and observations instead of simply relying on the fickleness of human emotions.

But now, with Sutherland gone, Kate knew that, for her at least, life on the South Rim had lost its mystery and magic and these lovingly excavated kivas, houses, and granaries, so faint and time-worn that only a professional eye had been able to detect their presence, would now be abandoned again to the ages. Rain, wind, snow, and blowing dust and sand would assault the now partially exposed and thus vulnerable Anasazi village until it was lost forever or reburied.

Kate didn't bother to wipe away the tears that coursed down her cheeks despite the possibility that Walter still lived. Kate knew in her heart that the scientist could not have stayed away for as long as it had taken the rains to do their damage. She knew that Walter was as dead as the Anasazi ghosts that had consumed his heart and his once-nimble and fact-filled mind.

"Kate?" Dunn called as he hurried through the twilight to the dig. "Kate, are you all right?"

"No," she confessed, "I'm not. Did you find him?"

"No. We found a lot of bones and pieces of pottery, but not the professor."

"What about the split-twig figurine?"

"It was probably consumed by the fire."

"And the Spanish soldiers' dagger, armor, helmet, and buckles?"

"Gone," Dunn said, sitting down heavily on a fallen tree and staring at the professor's excavations. "That's why I'm holding out a slim hope that he saw approaching danger, stuffed the Spanish artifacts in a sack, and ran to hide before the enemy arrived and burned the cabin down."

"But, if that were the case, he would have returned," Kate said.

Dunn's head tipped down between his knees and he stared at the red earth. "You're right. If he were alive, he would have returned, unless . . ."

"What?"

"Unless he escaped into the Grand Canyon," Dunn said, sitting bolt upright. "Kate, that was *my* avenue of escape. I'll bet the professor fled over the rim and is down in the canyon poking around for more ruins and, once in awhile, thinking he ought to climb back out to water his corn."

Kate took heart. "Maybe you're right. Maybe tomorrow we can find him."

"I'll use a rope at first light and descend into the canyon as far as possible," Dunn promised. "I'm just sure that we'll locate him. He was smart and experienced enough to have figured out a way to reach the Colorado River. And, with water, he would be able to find enough food down there to stay alive."

"But how can you possibly reach the river? Remember Cardenas and his three Spanish soldiers? They couldn't find a way to the bottom even though they were dying of thirst."

"I'll try to figure out something tomorrow morning."

The next morning, Dunn awoke before first light to watch an always-incredible Grand Canyon sunrise. As dawn strengthened, he once again was reminded of the canyon's fantastic size, its amazing rainbow of constantly transforming colors. Professor Sutherland often had remarked that it was quite impossible to really grasp the immensity of the Grand Canyon. Averaging ten miles across, five thousand feet deep, and over two hundred miles long, this abyss could hold every living being that ever existed and would still appear empty. The professors had liked to say that even the Egyptian pyramids would have been lost in its depths.

Dunn's eye tracked downward toward the successive ridges and terraces of stone, trying to recall the names of the separate layers of rock, each marking the passage of millions of years. Several miles out, an eagle soared more than a mile above a river that gleamed like molten crystal.

The profound silence over this canyon, a silence unlike any other, filled him with despair and reminded him that it was foolish to expect to find Sutherland alive. Last night, he had believed that survival was almost possible down there, but this morning, in the clarity of the rising sun, he realized that nothing but a few hardy plants, insects, and animals had ever been at home in those baking canyon depths.

Even to enter them was a fool's folly. Dunn was forced to consider the very real possibility that he might not be able to return once he went over the side. He also realized that he had always been secretly afraid of the Grand Canyon, even when he'd placed great trust in Major Powell. He could feel the fear rising in his gut.

"Stop it," he hissed. "Look at the colors and the beauty. Don't think of death."

He cleared his mind of apprehension. It wasn't hard because the colors were spectacular, almost painfully intense in this early morning light. They were as vivid as any flower, much more so than any rainbow. But, as the sun rose higher, he smiled as the colors mutated into pastels. He knew from experience that, later, after the burning summer sun crossed its zenith, the pastels would darken and become almost somber. Late in the afternoon, the fast-moving shadows of windblown cumulus clouds would play tag with the slowly lengthening rock shadows, creating optical monsters that romped across the canyon's floor.

Dunn thought that the Grand Canyon was most beautiful in the afternoon. It was then that golden mesas, copper-colored buttresses, and jagged crimson spires gouged upward into the hot, blue sky. Then, as the afternoon lengthened, wall shadows softly cloaked the innermost canyon depths while the highest rims burned intensely against the dying red fire of sundown.

"I should like to sit here all day and do nothing but watch," he told himself.

"Father?"

Startled, he turned to see Christopher, and wondered how long the boy had been watching him.

"Father, I want go down there with you to hunt for the professor."

Dunn's first reaction was to say no, to tell his son that it was far too dangerous. But when he looked deep into Chris's eyes, he could see that the boy needed to help find his friend.

"All right. We'd better take at least two canteens each and some food to keep up our strength."

"And what if the professor is not on the Tonto," Christopher asked, using the term that the professor preferred to describe the first huge sloping terrace off the rim.

"I don't know," Dunn admitted. "We'll decide when we get down there."

Christopher nodded, realizing that they would either find a body on the Tonto or return empty-handed to this rim.

A short time later, Kate kissed them both good-bye. Dunn, attempting to lighten the mood, whispered, "If I get back out, will you finally marry me?"

"Maybe."

"At least that's a step in the right direction," he said. They had a couple of hundred feet of rope, insufficient unless they discovered a trail at least partway down the first cliff. That took several hours and, after they finally began to descend, the air turned very hot.

"We'll just take our time and stay roped together," Dunn told his boy as they began to work their way down the cliff.

"If you fall, I'm not nearly strong enough to stop you."

"If I fall, try to wedge yourself between two rocks and cut the rope."

They worked all morning to descend that first cliff, which was nearly a thousand feet high. When they finally reached the Tonto, they were drenched with sweat and trembling with fatigue.

"Now we have an inkling of how those three Spanish soldiers must have felt," Christopher said. "I wonder how the professor ever managed to haul out that Spanish armor?"

"He was a very determined and courageous man. That's why I still think he might be alive. He also knew how to live off this land like an Indian."

"But what about water?" Christopher asked.

"There's been a lot of rain this summer and there might be a spring or at least a stone basin that would have caught enough to keep him going, even in this heat."

"Why don't you shoot your gun and maybe he'll hear that," Christopher suggested.

Dunn fired twice. The boom of his Colt sounded unnaturally loud in the confines of the great chasm. It was some time before the echoes faded enough so that they could have heard Sutherland's call for assistance either on the Tonto or way down on the canyon's floor.

But they heard nothing.

"Maybe the professor made a raft and floated down to Havasu Canyon," Christopher said, trying hard to sound optimistic.

"Maybe."

They tromped to the very edge of the second cliff and peered over its eroding rim but saw only another terrace far, far below. They were over a mile from the river and the air was radiating off both walls as if they were furnaces. Dunn wasn't sure what to do. He was carrying most of the rope, but it wouldn't begin to reach the next terrace, and he wasn't sure that they had the strength to pull themselves out. If they got stuck down there, halfway between the rim and the river, both he and Christopher were as good as dead.

"Father, look!"

Dunn turned to follow his son's gaze back up the slope, almost to the base of the cliff. Lying across the crown of a

flat rock was the professor's broken body, or what was left of
it.

"Chris, stay here!"

Dunn hiked back up to the body, trying to keep himself
between the remains of the archeologist and his son. Scavengers had ravaged his flesh and scattered his shattered bones.
Dunn tried to examine the body for evidence of a bullet hole
in the head or some other proof that he had been murdered,
but there was nothing left to examine. The violence of the fall
had pancaked the skull.

Dunn examined the contents of Walter's pockets. He extracted Josie's old split-twig figurine, a broken pencil, and a
few folded sketches that had been nearly obliterated by the
rain. Hoping that the sketches might provide some evidence
leading him to the killers, Dunn held them up to the sun but
the faint marks related only to archeology.

Gazing back down the slope toward Christopher, Dunn
quickly set about covering the body with rocks. After uttering
a prayer for Walter's departed soul, he hurried back to Christopher and gave him the prized split-twig figurine. "He'd have
wanted you to have it."

Christopher's grubby fingers closed over the little figurine.
He hugged his father and sobbed so loudly that Dunn was sure
that it could be heard from above so that they would know
the professor really was dead.

Dr. Charles Milford, President
American Archeological Society

Dear Dr. Milford:
    *It is with great sadness that I inform you that your
distinguished colleague and our friend, Dr. Walter Sutherland, was murdered sometime early this summer beside
his camp at the South Rim of the Grand Canyon. We have
not yet determined who murdered Walter, but I will not*

rest until the perpetrators of this heinous act have been brought to justice. Dr. Sutherland's beloved Anasazi excavation site has not been violated, but his papers, drawings, sketches and all other writings perished in the cabin fire.

We have been able to salvage many of his artifacts, although the Spanish armor is missing. We earnestly hope that it can be reclaimed. Dr. Sutherland's remains have been consigned to his beloved Grand Canyon. Please inform his friends and associates of his tragic and untimely death. If you wish to reclaim the professor's Anasazi artifacts, or if someone would like to continue his work, we will assist in every possible way.

The scientific community has lost a great man and we all have lost a very dear friend.

> *Sincerely,*
> *William Dunn*
> *Lonesome Valley Ranch*
> *Coconino Plateau*
> *Arizona Territory*

"I'll mail this as soon as we get our sheep and cattle to Captain Benson at Fort Whipple," Dunn promised as he kissed Kate good-bye. "I don't like to leave you with murderers roaming this part of the country."

"You think it's those same four men that Christopher spoke to at Fort Verde, don't you?" Kate said.

"I'm almost sure of it, but I wouldn't want to tell Chris that. He might feel responsible."

"And we've no proof."

"Not until I find them," Dunn said. "And I *will* find them."

Kate said, "The very moment you *know* it was those men, pull your guns and shoot them down. Give them no chances, or they'll kill you and Christopher without hesitation or remorse."

"You're right," he told her. "And when it happens, I'll make sure that Christopher isn't around."

Kate kissed him again and then rushed back into their cabin before her tears began to flow.

Twenty-four

Dunn had fulfilled his annual Fort Whipple livestock contract and posted his letter to Dr. Charles Milford. Afterward, he'd ridden east to Fort Verde for a talk with Sergeant Buck Quincy, that army post's quartermaster.

"Just wanted to make sure that you still intend to buy mustangs next summer, Sergeant."

"Yep. And I'll pay top dollar for the best ones."

"What about beef or mutton?" Dunn asked. "We just delivered to Fort Whipple."

"I'll need a few dozen head of each. And what I don't buy, you can always sell in Flagstaff or to the Mormons making all those railroad ties at Fort Moroni."

"Any chance they'll actually be attacked by Indians?"

"Building that fortress is sheer foolishness. Brother Young, however, has become convinced that the Indians are about to stage an all-out attack on Flagstaff, and he wants to make sure that he and his people are protected."

"Isn't that your job?"

"Sure, but we can't outlaw someone from being a fool, now can we?"

"John Young didn't strike me as a fool."

"Maybe he isn't, in a business sense," the sergeant admitted. "Brother Young is pig-headed and difficult, but he and his church members are hardworking, God-fearing, sober people, which is the main reason why they won that big contract with the Atlantic and Pacific Railroad."

"Mr. Young wants to buy Lonesome Valley Ranch."

"I wouldn't sell it to him."

"Why not?"

"Because, when the railroad arrives, Flagstaff is going to boom. People will be pouring in here and you know what that will do to cattle prices."

"They'll go up."

"Faster'n a rifle bullet," the sergeant predicted. "So that's why John Young hopes to buy you out. He'll send off word to his Mormon friends and, the next thing you know, they will be driving thousands of head of cattle down from Utah and running them all over your range. They'll make a fortune off of Flagstaff."

"Why are you telling me all this?"

"I like competition," the sergeant replied. "If you and a dozen others are all supplying me and the people of Flagstaff with beef, the prices won't get so outrageous, but if it's just John Young and the Mormon Cattle Company, we're in big trouble."

"Makes sense to me. I do have one more question."

"Then ask it. I ain't watchin' no clock."

"Do you remember those four hardcases who rode through here when we first met?"

"I'm afraid so. We fed 'em a few meals and then caught them trying to peddle their damned rotgut whiskey right here in the fort. We ordered them to leave."

"Have you seen them since?"

"No. Why do you ask?"

"My best friend was murdered on the South Rim. His name was Professor Walter Sutherland."

"He *lived* there?"

"That's right," Dunn said. "He was excavating an old Indian ruins."

"Did he find anything of value?"

"Bones. Arrowheads and spearpoints. Grinding stones and pottery. But, to me, the most interesting things he discovered were some armor and other remnants of a Spanish expedition that found the South Rim over three centuries ago. They were missing when we found the professor's body, long after he'd been thrown off the rim."

"Damn," the quartermaster said, "that would be a hard way to die. I hope they shot him before they threw him over the side."

"Me, too," Dunn said. "I believe that those four whiskey peddlers were the ones who robbed and murdered Professor Sutherland. They came by my ranch looking for work and I sent them packing. They said they were going to mustang, but no one has seen or heard of them since."

"Any proof they killed your friend?"

"Not unless we find it on them."

"Well, be careful," the sergeant warned. "I've learned a thing or two about men while serving in this army. Trust me, Mr. Dunn, those four were *all* bad."

"I had the same impression."

"If I see them, there's nothing I can do," the sergeant told him. "Not without proof."

"I know. But if you do see them, I'd appreciate if you could find out where they are going next."

"I'll do that."

"Do you know anyone in Flagstaff who might have some good sheepdogs for sale?"

"Nope. There are sure a lot of barking dogs in town, though. I wish the Apache would come in and roast 'em all! Some go wild and run with the coyotes. They'll pull down calves and sheep. They're nothing but a menace."

"Well," Dunn said, "I've got just one good sheepdog and I need about three more like him."

"Ask around and find some pups," the sergeant suggested. "Take 'em home and put 'em with your sheepdog and see if he can teach them how to work a flock. Most likely, though, you'll raise up some damned dinks that will go bad and eat your lambs."

"You're probably right," Dunn said. "But I'll keep my eyes open for a pup or two."

Dunn excused himself and joined Christopher. As they rode through Flagstaff, it was obvious that the town was growing faster than milkweed in springtime. When they reached the Mormon fortress of Moroni, John Young hailed them.

"Mr. Dunn, have you finally decided to sell me your ranch?"

"Afraid not. I'll stay in ranching a while longer."

"That's a big mistake," Young told him, the friendliness going out of his voice. "I'm even prepared to offer you more money than your rangeland and cattle are worth. I was in Prescott two weeks ago and looked up your ranch boundaries on the government land maps, and I know exactly how much you paid for that ranchland. I'm prepared to make you a very generous offer, one that would earn you a *very* fine return on your investment."

"No thanks."

Young scowled. "When someone has cash and you have product and the price is good, you should sell out. If a few herds are driven down from Utah or up from Texas or New Mexico, I'll guarantee you that beef prices will tumble. Then you'll be wishing you'd sold out to me today."

"Well," Dunn replied, "I'll just have to take that gamble."

"Suit yourself," the Mormon leader said, then abruptly turned his back on Dunn and marched back to Fort Moroni.

"He's a persistent man," Dunn said, "and he doesn't like to take no for an answer."

"I don't like him very much," Christopher said. "Did you ask him about those four drifters?"

"I forgot."

Dunn had to ride back and catch Young's attention and ask him about the cowboys.

"Haven't seen any men of that description."

"Then you're lucky," Dunn said, thanking the man for his

time before riding away with his eyes on a storm front moving in from the north.

"Let's get on back to Lonesome Valley," he said to Christopher as he put his horse into an easy lope.

"We're going to freeze up in the San Francisco peaks tonight!" Christopher shouted as they rode stirrup to stirrup.

"I expect so," Dunn yelled. "Maybe we'll just ride on through the night and get home early."

They galloped on into the cold, biting wind. The aspen were starting to turn colors. Within a few weeks, Dunn knew they'd likely have snow up in this high mountain country. Within a month, they could even get some snow along the South Rim.

But winter never really arrived on the Coconino Plateau. All they had to contend with was a few weeks of freezing temperatures and some brief snow flurries. Juan and Lucio Ortiz appeared that spring, leading a big mule neck-tied to the great liver chestnut stallion their father had so prized and then chosen as his personal saddle horse.

"What happened to Armando?" Kate asked when the pair dismounted. "And why is that stallion tied to a mule?"

"He is a devil!" Lucio spit. "He tricked my father into trusting him, then kicked him with both hind feet! Broke three of his ribs, and this devil would have stomped him to death if we hadn't roped him first."

"We wanted to shoot the horse," Juan explained, lips curling with hatred. "But our father said no, that we should not do such a thing, and that this horse had so much spirit that he could not change his nature. He said that we should bring him back and turn him loose on your range so that he can father more big, strong horses."

Dunn noticed that the stallion's eyes still burned with defiance, and that the vaqueros had muzzled the animal to keep him from biting their mule. He was surprised that the mustang had managed to kick the old vaquero, but that just proved that any man could be fooled.

"We can leave tomorrow for the Warm Springs country," Dunn said. "I don't want that chestnut hanging around this ranch waiting to steal back our mustang mares."

Kate was plenty glad to exchange ranch life for the excitement of a mustang roundup. It had been a sad winter after the professor's death, and she was eager to ride out and see tall grass, bees, blossoms, and wildflowers.

They left early the next morning when the sky was clear and the air sweet with the smell of new life. Right away, the big chestnut stallion became excited.

"He knows he's almost on his home ground," Juan explained. "This is good country and he remembers his mares."

"He will have to win a new harem from another stallion," Lucio said. "But I don't think he is worried."

"What will your father do this summer?"

"Braid reatas," Juan answered. "He can make as much money sitting in a chair as on a horse."

"But it will not be so much fun," Lucio quickly added.

When they reached Warm Springs, they discovered that four mustangs had been ambushed. To make matters even worse, there was no sign of the four hundred head of Longhorn cattle that Dunn had introduced onto his new range the previous fall.

"What is going on here!" he swore, galloping over to examine the nearest mustang carcass.

Kate stayed with the vaqueros and the stallion became very agitated. "Now he smells death," Lucio said. "Let's free him."

Juan agreed. They removed the muzzle and released the chestnut. The big horse went racing toward the Grand Canyon. At a full gallop, he was a joy to watch, with his head held high and his throat bugling freedom.

"Someone shot these mares in the neck!" Dunn said when the others joined him.

Juan dismounted, handing his reins to Christopher. He knelt beside one of the dead mares and carefully examined where the bullet had ripped through the crest of her neck, breaking it instantly. This particular mustang had been young, no more than two years old, a pretty black with two white stockings.

"My brother and I have seen this before," Lucio said, his face darkening with fury. "Fools too lazy to catch the wild ones believe that, if a bullet strikes the neck just above the withers, the animal will be stunned and can then be captured."

"I never heard of such a thing!" Kate exclaimed.

"It can happen," Juan assured her, "but it takes great skill with a rifle *and* much luck. Still, bullets are cheap so bad men are always willing to take the chance, no?"

Christopher reined his horse away, face ashen.

Dunn said, "Lucio, we need to find whoever did this. And when we do, I expect we'll also find our missing cattle. I'm going to see if I can pick up their trail."

"Lucio has already found it," Kate said, pointing to the vaquero who had ridden a short way and was now standing beside his horse, motioning for them to come and join him.

"How many?" Dunn asked when they reached the vaquero.

Juan held up four fingers, pointed off toward Prescott and said, "They've got cattle *and* mustangs."

"It's *them*," Dunn grated. "And I'm going after them."

"Maybe we should go back to the ranch and get our Indians to ride with us," Kate suggested. "Those four are seasoned gunmen."

"No Indians," Dunn said. "If word got out that they helped kill white men—even cattle rustlers—well, who knows what would happen to The People."

"We will go with you," Juan said, getting a nod of agreement from his brother.

"It's not your job."

"But it is our *duty*, Señor. You see, these men shot the wild ones like they were no more than rabbits. Who knows how many more they have killed that we would have corralled and sold? They also take your cattle and kill your friend."

"We don't know for sure that they murdered the professor."

The Ortiz brothers mounted their horses and did not even bother to reply as they reined toward Prescott. Dunn looked at Kate and Christopher. "I wish you'd go back to the ranch and wait."

"We're sticking together," she told him. "We both can handle rifles, and, even with Juan and Lucio, you'll need our help."

Around midday, the wind freshened and the sky boiled dark with thunderheads. By late afternoon, the sky opened and it poured rain. Wary of flash flooding, they sought the higher ground, and no sooner were they across an arroyo than it suddenly was filled by a wall of water churning with uprooted brush and debris. Dunn saw two rattlesnakes entwined in a big uprooted creosote bush heading for the rim of the Grand Canyon faster than an express train. Fortunately, the squall passed in an hour and the heavens made their apology with a stunning rainbow to frame the bright orb of the setting sun.

"What are we going to do to them?" Christopher asked his father as they began to climb into the foothills of the Juniper Mountains.

"Arrest them and take them to the authorities in Prescott."

"I don't think they're going to let us do that without a big fight."

"I expect that they won't," Dunn agreed, "especially if they haven't already sold or butchered all of our branded cattle. Cattle rustling is a hanging offense. Our best hope is to catch them by surprise and disarm them without a fight."

It soon became too dark to ride, so they made a cold camp beside a seep where the horses could drink. Dunn and Kate stood the first watch. As they sat on a rock and listened to coyotes howl, Dunn remarked that he had never seen a more peaceful night.

"I was thinking the same thing," Kate said, laying her head on his shoulder. "And I was wondering if what we are doing is right."

"If we let them get away with it," Dunn reasoned, "others

will do the same until we're wiped out. And, if they murdered the professor, they deserve to die."

"I know, but I'd rather lose everything than have one of us killed, especially you or Christopher."

"I feel the same about you and Chris. And the Ortiz brothers are brave vaqueros, but they're not gunmen. I'd hate to have to tell their father that they were killed on my account."

"But you can't turn back."

"No," he said. "I can't. I couldn't do that and live with myself, and it would set a terrible example for Chris. I've always taught him that we have to fight for what we believe. If we don't, we might as well give up."

"I agree," Kate said, "but I'm scared."

"Me, too, darling. Me, too."

They picked up the tracks easy enough the next morning. If it had been just a horse or two they were following, the tracks might have been washed away by the previous afternoon's fierce downpour, but the rustlers had taken at least fifty head of Lonesome Valley Ranch cattle. They might as well have left a road map. Two days later, the trail fed into what appeared to be a box canyon located in rugged, rocky country about thirty miles northwest of Prescott.

"The Yavapai Indians live in these parts," Dunn said as they dismounted and hid their horses in a dry streambed about a quarter mile from the mouth of the canyon.

"So what are we going to do?" Kate asked.

"We'll wait until they are asleep and get the drop on them. This is an open-and-shut case of cattle rustling."

Dunn took Kate's arm and escorted her away from the others so that they would not be overheard. "I wish you and Christopher would stay here," he said. "Juan, Lucio, and I will have the element of surprise and . . ."

"Bill, you're not a gunman, so you don't realize what kind of men you're up against. They'll *never* surrender. They'd rather die than hang."

"Are you speaking from personal knowledge?"

"I know how Monty would have reacted, and these four are cut from the same cloth."

"But your husband was taken alive."

"Only because he got stinking drunk and didn't wake up until he'd been handcuffed and tossed into jail."

"Kate, we can't just shoot these men in their sleep."

"Yes, you can! Killing them in their sleep would be a better end than they deserve."

"Maybe it would," Dunn agreed, "but I just don't have the stomach for it."

They waited until long after sundown before they readied their weapons and then started following the creek bed toward the canyon. A grinning half-moon bathed the land like candlelight. It took them less than half an hour to reach the mouth of the box canyon. It was no more than fifty yards across and was marked deeply by horse and cattle tracks.

"Listen," Dunn whispered after they'd crept through the narrow opening.

They could hear the restless stamping of feet and the occasional click of horn as the cattle shifted about on their bed ground. Dunn gripped his Winchester tighter. He saw the faint orange glow of a campfire. Up a little higher in the box canyon, the Longhorns and horses caught their unfamiliar scent and began to shift about. Several of the cattle began to bawl and the outlaws' hobbled saddle horses stopped night grazing to lift their heads and stare down at the camp. At the far end of the canyon, a mustang whinnied and other wild horses began to mill.

It seemed as if everything and everybody was waiting. Dunn kept moving ahead because he had decided to make an attempt to disarm the cattle rustlers. He reached the first man and collected his rifle, then tiptoed over to grab a second one. He couldn't see any holstered six-guns and figured that the outlaws were keeping them handy under their blankets. He expected all hell to break loose at any moment. His heart was pounding and his mouth was dry. Seeing no more rifles, he grabbed a piece of wood, took a deep breath, and tossed it squarely into the smoldering campfire. A shower of embers erupted, momentarily bringing the entire camp into sharp focus.

"Hands up! On your feet!"

They sprang off their blankets and started shooting. Dunn dived for cover into the rocks, gun blazing. He emptied his pistol at movement and muzzle bursts. The Longhorns began to stampede, spooked by the rolling volleys of gunfire caroming off the canyon's walls. A tall bay saddle horse, hobbled but bounding like a deer, leapfrogged through the camp. Dunn felt the earth shake as first the Longhorns and then the mustangs charged the canyon's mouth in an attempt to escape.

"Christopher! Kate!"

His words were drowned out as the stampeding animals reached the camp, spraying the last embers of the campfire into the night sky. The outlaws screamed and a thick cloud of choking dust smothered everything.

"Chris!"

"I'm all right!" he answered as the last of the cattle and horses bolted through the mouth of the canyon. "Kate!"

Kate climbed out of the rocks, coughing in the thick dust. "Juan? Lucio!"

One by one, they answered, all fearful that their voices might attract gunfire until Juan called, "They're all dead!"

"Thank God!" Kate said, coughing in the dust.

"Let's get out of this death trap," Dunn said, taking her hand and then finding Christopher and leading them both after the retreating cattle and horses.

They tried to get a little sleep before morning, but Dunn was up an hour before daylight to build a campfire. Kate joined him and they sat together, drinking strong coffee and watching daylight brighten the landscape.

"We had no choice," Kate said. "You know that, don't you?"

"Yeah, but it still isn't something I am proud to have done. And I'm not sure what Christopher is thinking. He was real quiet after the fight was over last night."

"He'll be all right. He's lived all his life on the ranch surrounded by decent, hardworking men. He's never seen the dark side of human nature. It's going to take time for him to come to terms with all of this."

"I expect so, but I wish I could have protected him from knowing this kind of thing happens. It'll change him, you know."

"It will change all of us. Why, it's even changed the way that I'm looking at things this morning."

"How?"

"I'm ready to be your wife," she told him. "Life is too short and precious for us to waste even a minute. I'm going to seek an annulment as you suggested. And then, I want us to be married and have children together."

Dunn swallowed hard. He set his coffee cup down and turned to look into her eyes. "Do you think that I'm snakebit for women?"

"What do you mean?"

"I've never been able to find any lasting happiness with a woman. Cynthia Holloway was more dream than reality and Josie . . . well, you know the sad ending of that story."

Kate put her own cup down and took his hands. "Are you *worried* that something bad will happen to us if we get married?"

"A little," he admitted. "But I want to marry you."

She refilled their cups. "And have more children?"

"I can't promise you that, Kate. But I *can* promise that we'll have a real good time trying."

"Fair enough," she said, blushing in the sunrise.

* * *

They spent all the next morning rounding up the outlaws' horses and their own Longhorn cattle. They knew that the mustangs were probably already halfway back to their own range near Warm Springs.

"Kate, you and Christopher hold the cattle here while we collect those bodies," Dunn said, signaling to the vaqueros that he needed their assistance.

"What are you going to do with the bodies?" Kate asked.

"Take them down to the authorities in Prescott. Then I'll sell their horses."

When Dunn and the vaqueros returned to the bodies, they quickly searched them. He found no identification, but something far more important.

"Look! This one is wearing one of the professor's Spanish buckles. That's all I needed to know in order to put my mind to rest."

"I'll search their saddle and duffelbags," Juan offered.

A few moments later, he found the Spanish dagger but not the helmet or the coat of mail nor any of the other buckles.

They wrapped two of the bodies in their torn bedrolls and the other two in bloody cowhides that bore Dunn's Lonesome Valley Ranch brand, the Rocking L. "In case there are any doubts about what those four were up to," Dunn explained, "this will be our evidence."

That night, they made camp in the beautiful Chino Valley a few miles north of Prescott and, the next morning, Dunn rode into Prescott with Kate and Christopher, leading horses carrying the outlaws' bodies. Their arrival caused a sensation and a crowd soon gathered outside the marshal's office.

A short while later, Marshal Elvin Gant took their sworn testimony, studied the evidence after the bodies had been hauled off by the mortician, then heartily congratulated them on doing a fine and necessary service for the Territory of Arizona.

"Those four were in town selling butchered beef and I had my suspicions," Gant drawled. "I expect they intended to sell your cattle to the army or to some ranch, Mr. Dunn. However, without a bill of sale and because you've already been supplying Fort Whipple, your brand would have been familiar and they realized they'd be arrested for cattle rustling. I'll keep their horses and sell 'em to cover the burying and miscellaneous expenses, but you can keep their saddles, bridles, and other gear."

"I don't want any of it," Dunn told him flatly.

"I understand. I'll sell everything and put the money to good use." Gant clucked his tongue. "I am obliged to point out that you should have come to me instead of taking the matter into your own hands. I'd have deputized you and formed a posse. We'd have brought them to trial and then hanged them inside of a week. We've no tolerance for cattle rustlers in this county."

"If there ever is a next time," Dunn promised, "I'll come to you first."

"That's what I wanted to hear," Gant said. "Now, are you buying any more ranchland this trip?"

"Depends on if I can sell the cattle we recovered."

"There's little doubt that you can. Cattle prices are good, but there are rumors that a big herd of Longhorns is being driven up from Texas. Might give you some competition."

"That's fine," Dunn said. "Any idea where they are going to range?"

"The fella over at the land office might know."

"I'll ask," Dunn said, thinking that he probably ought to buy more range while it was still available.

The next few days proved satisfying. Dunn sold his Longhorns and bought several thousand more acres with the proceeds. As it turned out, the Texas herd had gone to settle somewhere west of Flagstaff after learning of the huge holdings already taken by the Lonesome Valley Ranch. Right after that, Dunn and Kate went to see Judge Westerling over at the courthouse, where they explained their Utah problem.

The judge was nearing retirement but his mind was sharp. He had spent his lifetime enforcing frontier law, and he'd also *written* a good part of the statutes governing the young Arizona Territory.

"What I can do," he said when he had a complete grasp of the facts, "is to write my counterpart, Judge Larimer, in Salt Lake City and ask him to sustain your petition for an annulment."

"Monty wouldn't agree," Kate said quickly. "And I'd rather he didn't know that I was asking."

"He doesn't have to agree," Westerling said, "but the law will require that your husband at least be notified of your action and where it was originated."

"Then let's forget about it," Kate said, rising. "He's a hateful and vengeful man."

Dunn came to his own feet. "Kate," he pleaded, "we've got a chance to become a *real* family. If your husband intends to find us, he'll find us whether you do this or not. I say that we petition for the annulment, get married, and then let the cards fall where they may."

She looked up at him, eyes clouded with worry. "Even if it gets you killed?"

"That won't happen," he vowed. "But we *will* be married. What do you say, Chris?"

"We can take care of ourselves," the boy answered. "Please, Kate. You're already like my real mother, but . . ."

"All right."

They all hugged and Kate even cried a little in the judge's chambers.

"Mrs. Ford, I'll prepare a petition of your annulment for your signature," Westerling promised. "For what it is worth, you are doing the right thing."

"Could you also find out exactly when Monty Ford is expected to be paroled?"

"If such a determination has been made, of course."

As soon as they were outside, a short, energetic man in his

thirties, wearing a brown suit, starched collar, and derby hat hurried up to them and introduced himself.

"My name is Noel Kodish and I'm a reporter on assignment for the *American Gazette* of New York City. I'd like to know what happened to those four dead men you brought in draped across their horses."

"They were cattle thieves," Dunn said quietly. "And they also murdered our friend, Professor Walter Sutherland."

"He was a *professor?*"

"That's right."

"Of what?" the reporter asked, pulling out a notepad and pencil.

"Kate, why don't you and Chris start shopping while I talk to this fella? I'll be along soon."

"Those four were murdering thieves!" Kate said angrily. "And you can quote me."

"We shot them as they were trampled by the Longhorns," Christopher added. "We gunned them all down in the dark."

"My, my!" Kodish said, beginning to scribble. "This is going to be *quite* a story! Can we retire to the saloon where I'll buy you a beer while I hear all about your harrowing experience and lesson in frontier justice?"

"All right," Dunn agreed.

He left the saloon two hours and four beers later thinking that maybe he'd talked a little more than was necessary, especially about the professor's excavation at the South Rim and the man's deep fascination with the Anasazi. He had even told the reporter about his sense of outrage when he'd first witnessed the mares whose broken necks had been "creased."

Dunn did not, however, reveal that he had been a member of Major Powell's first journey through the Grand Canyon. Nor his marriage to Josie and their idyllic time spent in beautiful Havasu Canyon. He said nothing of Kate's involvement with John and Emma Lee at Lonely Dell, preceded by her tragic childhood experience during the Mountain Meadows Massacre.

Kodish must have filled ten pages and was extremely excited about the story, even asking if he could bring a photographer out to the ranch as well as to the professor's burned-out cabin and archeological excavations.

"I think the professor would have wanted his work to be recognized," Dunn said. "And you're welcome to visit our ranch if you don't mind the fact that we're always on the move, especially from April to October."

"That's what I would have expected," Kodish said, pumping his hand vigorously. "Mr. Dunn, you haven't seen the last of me. You've lived an extraordinary life!"

Dunn bit the inside of his lip, thinking that the reporter didn't even know the half of it.

He treated Kate and Christopher to a big dinner in town. During their meal, they were constantly pestered by other people wanting to know the details of the killings.

"If we stay in our usual hotel rooms," Dunn said, "we'll have no peace. What do you say I pay our bill and we ride on back to our cattle camp and join Juan and Lucio, then head for home tomorrow morning?"

"I'd like that," Kate said.

Christopher agreed.

Darkness dropped across northern Arizona long before they reached their cattle camp in the Chino Valley. It didn't matter because they were guided the last few miles by a campfire as bright as any lighthouse beacon. They rode quietly up the broad, grassy valley, each lost in his own reflections.

"Are you happy, Kate?" Dunn asked after Christopher galloped ahead to join the Ortiz brothers.

She reached out for his hand. "When we get home, Bill, let's move some furniture."

"Consider it done." He took a deep breath. "Not to seem too anxious, but I'd like at least one daughter, a girl who will grow up strong and pretty like you."

"And I'd like at least one more handsome son."

That was just fine. In fact, Dunn thought, it was a damn sight better than fine.

Twenty-five

Dunn felt both rich and lucky that October as he pocketed his money from the sale of another consignment of mustangs, sheep and cattle to Fort Whipple. "Captain Benson, I thank you for the business as I do every year at this time."

"It's always been a pleasure to deal with you, Mr. Dunn. I have learned that you deliver as promised. Four hundred head of mustangs that will make mighty fine cavalry mounts. I'll be sending most of them off to the other military posts. It's gotten to the point where they don't want any mustangs except those off your South Rim ranch."

"That's because my partners, Lucio and Juan Ortiz, are careful not to injure our horses during their capture and they take a lot of time and trouble to break them right."

"I also know that your son Christopher is a remarkable rider and roper."

"He's good, all right. Chris boasts that he could ride a mountain lion and rope a horse fly—by its hind legs. And you know something, Captain, when I watch him working horses, I think that maybe he could!"

"He's a fine boy," the captain agreed. "And how is Kate?"

"Quite well, thank you. She sends her regards from Havasu Canyon, where she is visiting The People."

"Those poor Indians sure have gotten a raw deal from Washington, D.C., the last few years."

Dunn nodded, not really trusting himself to speak. His blood began to boil whenever he thought about the recent injustices

committed against the Havasupai people. President Rutherford
B. Hayes had established the Havasupai Reservation, stripping
The People of all their South Rim winter hunting grounds and
confining their lands to the interior of Havasu Canyon. Dunn
and others had vigorously fought this outrageous decision by
writing letters and sending telegrams to everyone in Washington, but their efforts were in vain. The very best he'd been
able to do to offset this terrible wrong had been to give the
Havasupai complete access to the Lonesome Valley Ranch so
they could continue their traditional winter hunting and way
of life.

Sadly, President Hayes's callous disregard for the rights of
the Havasupai was only the beginning. After Garfield's death,
President Chester Arthur had bowed to powerful mining lob-
byists and gone one step farther by reducing the Havasupai
Reservation to a pitiful 518 acres—just barely enough to include Supai and their surrounding cultivated fields.

The captain's brow furrowed. "Speaking of the Havasupai,
I'm sure you know we've had some trouble there with prospectors moving in on your friends."

"So I've heard," Dunn said. "First it was those two fellas
that found pure lead deposits in Havasu Canyon and had all
those big plans to open a mine, then it was that fella that
dropped nearly a hundred feet to his death after being lowered
on a rope over the middle falls."

"The poor devil's name was James Mooney," the captain
reminded him. "They're now calling it Mooney Falls."

"They ought to call it Fool's Falls. James Mooney and his
prospecting friends had no business being in Havasu Canyon.
Thank God the lead discovery proved unreliable, and there
never has been a trace of gold or silver found there."

"If that should ever happen," Benson said, "you and I together couldn't stop the stampede from wiping out the Havasu
Canyon people."

"I know," Dunn agreed. "So what do you hear from your
fellow officers over at Flagstaff?"

"They're having one hell of a time with all the riffraff that's come in since the Atlantic and Pacific Railroad arrived. Flagstaff is booming and the Mormon Cattle Company is always calling on the army to chase after cattle rustlers. I hear that John Young has offered you one hundred thousand dollars *cash* for your Lonesome Valley Ranch."

Dunn had to grin. "It isn't *quite* that much . . . yet."

"You sure have a gold mine, Mr. Dunn. Why, the first year you delivered cattle to us was for . . . what? Ten dollars a head?"

"Fifteen."

"And now they're *fifty* dollars a head, thanks to the arrival of the railroad and all the new settlers in northern Arizona. As far as I'm concerned, I liked things a whole lot better when it was peaceful and quiet."

"Times have changed, and I've been very lucky to profit from them."

"I'll say! I hear that you are building quite a home in your valley."

"We've outgrown the original old log cabin," Dunn told him. "Chris has offered to take it over. He and Tucson could use the space, although I'd hoped to convert it to another bunkhouse."

"And you've never had trouble with rustlers?"

"Not since we tracked down and killed those four up in the Juniper Mountains," Dunn said. "I guess news about that spread far and wide."

"Can you stay for supper tonight at the officers' mess?"

"I'm afraid not," Dunn replied. "I've got to run over to see Judge Westerling. Afterward, he and his wife have invited me to dinner."

"Give them my regards."

"I will." Dunn got up to leave. "I asked Christopher, the vaqueros, and the rest of my cowboys to stay here with the mustangs and cattle until you've expanded your corrals."

"We're still about a week from being finished."

"I have to leave for Flagstaff tomorrow and take delivery of supplies and new glass windows that I ordered from Albuquerque. I expect that, by the time I go there and return, the timing will work out just right. You'll have those new corrals finished and not need the services of my stockmen any longer."

"Why don't you take your son along?" Your vaqueros and Indians can handle the stock this week without him. A kid his age needs to see something besides the south end of a Longhorn. He's growing up."

"That he is," Dunn said, unable to mask his pride. "Chris is six feet tall, but skinnier than a willow switch."

"When are you and Kate going to formally tie the knot?"

"We've been waiting all these years for news from Utah about her former marriage. I'm hoping that the judge finally has gotten either a divorce decree or an annulment."

"You sure make a happy and successful pair. Just let me know when it finally happens and we'll crack open a bottle. I'll be retiring in another three years."

"Where will you settle?"

"Right here in Prescott. Finest little community I can imagine. This will always be our home and the home of our closest friends."

Dunn pushed to his feet and shook the officer's hand. Benson looked far too young to retire, but the news was another reminder that time kept marching on.

"Oh, by the way," Benson said, "that Eastern newspaper reporter. What was his name?"

"Noel Kodish."

"Yes. He stopped by and said that his articles were causing quite a stir back East. Tourists are starting to flock in here, many of them hoping to visit the Grand Canyon."

"It's a free country. I don't even mind them crossing my range on their way to the Grand Canyon as long as they don't mess with my stock or watering tanks."

"I understand Kodish has been out to your ranch three or

four times. Thanks to his series of articles, you're quite a celebrity in the East."

Dunn blushed, for he had received a lot of unwelcome attention because of those articles, even fan letters from the East and people trying to invite themselves out to his ranch. "I tell you this much, Captain, it's time Noel started writing about other ranchers—or, better yet, the town people."

"You really ought to try to cash in on the tourism. I think there is big money to be made from it."

"That's what I keep hearing," Dunn replied with an indifferent shrug. "There already are a few entrepreneurs setting up little cabins and camps beside the Grand Canyon in the hope of catering to tourists. I met a fella named John Hance and another named William Bass, and both of them are talking about tourists and more tourists."

Benson chuckled. "The next thing you know, they'll be building hotels along both rims and hauling boatloads of greenhorns down the whole damned river!"

"That's no joke," Dunn said, looking disgusted as he left and calling back over his shoulder, "Keep 'em the hell out of Havasu Canyon, Captain!"

As Dunn strolled across the parade ground, he noticed quite a commotion over by the army's old horse corrals. He mounted his horse and rode over just in time to see Christopher preparing to swing onto a tall, battle-scarred old paint stallion with a head shaped like a keg of beer and feet as big as dinner plates. It had one blue eye and one white one, and both were rolling around like dice in a cup. The paint was raising so much hell that even the vaqueros were struggling to keep it under control until Christopher could find his stirrups.

"Whose outlaw is that?" Dunn asked one of the soldiers.

"He belongs to some drunken old horse trader who left him behind last week. Ain't he a demon, though! No one can ride him. He's stomped the only two with guts enough even to try!"

"Chris!"

"But that tall kid and his Mexican friends took two-to-one odds from everyone that he could ride that paint horse to a standstill. Must be close to a four hundred dollars bet against the kid. He'd damn sure better have a little extra for the doctor or the mortician!"

"Chris!" Dunn shouted. "Get the hell out of there!"

But Christopher was already vaulting into the saddle. Both vaqueros dived between the rails as the bronc erupted.

Dunn choked his saddlehorn and watched as the big paint stud began to spin like a tall Texas twister. Chris was wearing spurs, but he wasn't really using them. When the spinning didn't work, the stallion began to leap toward the sky, bawling like a bull, then coming down stiff-legged. Dunn knew right then that the animal was a veteran bucker and a damn "pile driver," the very toughest kind to ride. Every time the horse landed, Chris's neck snapped like a whip and Dunn winced. After just a few such landings, Chris's nose started to flow with blood.

"Spur him, son! Fight back!"

The vaqueros had stopped grinning. Their reatas were coiled and ready for a throw that might be needed to save Chris's life if he were tossed to the ground and the stud tried to stomp him to death. On the other hand, the soldiers were going crazy as they rooted for the horse to win so that they could collect their bets.

Dunn yanked the rifle from his saddle boot and jacked a shell into the chamber. Nobody noticed when he raised it, fully prepared to drop the outlaw in its tracks if his boy was hurled to the earth.

But Christopher suddenly had had enough of the one-sided contest; he began raking the horse with his spur rowels. Almost immediately, the big paint started to grunt. Putting its head down, it changed tactics and began swapping ends like a big brook trout. Christopher clung to him like scales on a snake. Around and around the pair went, grunting, fighting and stomping until, finally, the paint suddenly quit.

The big outlaw just froze in its tracks, head down, nostrils flared, sweat and lather dripping down between its big, unshod hooves. Christopher slumped forward until his chin rested on his chest. Then, he reached down and patted the paint's neck before he dismounted. He made only two steps before his legs buckled and he sank to his knees. Dunn saw the outlaw's head shoot up and he jammed the rifle to his shoulder. But the paint was too weak, or maybe its fighting spirit had been broken, because it allowed Juan and Lucio to drag Christopher to safety.

"Damn fools," Dunn muttered as handfuls of wagered army money were shoved toward the Lonesome Valley Ranch horsemen. Dunn jammed his rifle back into its scabbard and reined his mount away. He was going to be late for his appointment to see the judge, and Christopher was certainly in no condition for a social visit.

A short time later, Judge Westerling invited Dunn into his study, pouring them brandies and exclaiming, "Congratulations! I've finally received word from the Utah Territorial Prison. They have forwarded the paperwork I'll need to grant Kate that long-overdue annulment."

Dunn raised his brandy glass in salute. "We owe it to you, Judge. Will you also do us the honor of officiating at our wedding?"

"With great pleasure! But I thought Kate wanted a minister this time instead of just a judge and a civil ceremony."

"Well," Dunn said, suddenly remembering that the judge was right, "then how about being my best man?"

"Now that *would* be a privilege and a pleasure. Of course I will."

"I'm curious," Dunn said a few minutes later, "why has all this taken so long?"

"I was wondering myself," the judge confided. "I kept writing letters to the Utah authorities, but they wouldn't respond. Finally, using the influence of our governor, I learned that Mr. Ford had been involved in a prison riot."

"A riot?"

"That's right. Apparently, Monty Ford was a ringleader. The escape attempt resulted in a riot. Three prisoners were shot to death, many more wounded. There were also several badly injured prison guards and a lot of property damage. The prison officials did not want to reveal any of this, for reasons I'm sure you can imagine. Monty Ford was shot, but finally, and fully, recovered. His sentence has been extended, and he won't be due up for parole until after the turn of the century."

"Good," Dunn said, unable to hide his relief, "though I am sorry about the prison guards."

"Those things are bound to happen," the judge said. "Violent men packed into close company, many with nothing worth losing. What else can be expected?"

"I don't know," Dunn answered, "I'm just grateful that I'll finally be able to marry Kate."

The rest of the evening was very pleasant. Over the past years, Dunn had become close friends with Westerling and his wife. They were all in good spirits and enjoyed a fine meal of roast duck, fried rice, vegetables stewed in sour cream, with peach cobbler and coffee for dessert.

After dinner, when Mrs. Westerling had excused herself to prepare for sleep, the judge and Dunn went back into the study to enjoy a cigar and a nightcap. When they had their brandies and cigars in hand, Westerling kicked his feet up on an ottoman and said, "Living way out in that lonesome rim country, I don't suppose you keep up on national politics."

"No," Dunn replied, "and I doubt I'm missing anything of great importance."

"Not so," Westerling argued, punctuating both words with the orange tip of his cigar.

"All right, what have I missed?"

"Are you aware that a very up-and-coming United States senator from Indiana has just introduced his *second* bill in Congress to make the Grand Canyon a national park?"

"A what?"

"A national park," the judge repeated. "Haven't you even heard the term before?"

"Can't say as I have."

"There is already such a park, and it's called Yellowstone. It was set aside by the government so it can be preserved and used by *all* the people."

"You mean it can't be owned by anyone?"

"Just the government. There's a fellow named John Muir who has helped to found a group called the Sierra Club. They're pushing this 'national park' idea very hard in Congress and it's getting a lot of favorable attention. I've read some of Muir's writings and he's a poet who makes damned good sense. There's little doubt that a place in California called Yosemite is going to be our second national park and it will happen in the very near future."

"Well, I'll be," Dunn said, not sure yet how he felt about the concept. "But what would the public want to *do* with the Grand Canyon?"

"Just leave it alone and appreciate it," Westerling told him. "You won't believe the number of people that will be coming. Thousands."

"No!"

"It's true," the judge insisted.

Dunn smoked in silence for a few minutes, then looked up and asked, "Would the government take ownership of my Lonesome Valley Ranch?"

"If they did, they'd certainly have to pay you for it."

"Even if I don't want to sell?"

"Yes, it's called the power of eminent domain. They're going to have to buy out a lot of people in Yosemite Valley who don't want to sell. But you could capitalize on a national park."

"How?"

"Build a stageline in Flagstaff and start carrying passengers to the South Rim."

"No thanks."

"If you don't, others will. I just thought you might be interested in cashing in on the change."

"I like being a rancher. Last year I sold off most of my sheep, and next year I'll sell off the rest and have nothing but cattle."

Westerling chuckled tolerantly. "You know something I've learned over the years? All through life things happen that we neither want nor expect. Success or failure is directly related to how we adjust to life's unpleasant surprises. I'm telling you right now that it is better to adjust than resist."

"And by that, you mean embrace a bunch of tourists?"

"I do. Give it some thought. I know you've done very well with livestock, but, after the Grand Canyon becomes one of those national parks, I believe the real future is tourism."

"Pour me another brandy, Judge, and let's talk about my wedding."

Westerling grinned. "Now *that*," he said, "will be a real pleasure."

They talked so late that night that Dunn stayed over in one of the Westerlings' extra bedrooms. The next morning, after a big breakfast, he stopped by Fort Whipple to collect Christopher, and they rode off toward Flagstaff.

"Riding that outlaw yesterday was pretty stupid," Dunn said after they'd put the fort well behind them. "You could have been killed."

"Naw! Lucio and Juan were right there with their reatas. They'd have roped that stud's front legs and dropped him like a stone."

"Even they could miss."

"Not likely," Chris said with maddening unconcern. "Did you have a nice evening with the judge and his wife?"

"I did."

"I won four hundred dollars yesterday."

"Congratulations," Dunn said tightly, "but what would you have used for money if you'd been thrown and had to pay off your bets?"

"Heck," Christopher said with a wide grin, "you're packing a lot of cash now, and, besides, I can count on one hand the number of times I've been thrown this year."

"Don't ever again cover your bets with someone else's money," Dunn snapped. "Is that understood?"

Christopher's eyes blazed and he drew his horse up short. "I think I'll just stay with the livestock, Father."

"Suits me," Dunn growled as he pushed his horse into a gallop and hurried on toward Flagstaff.

Dunn didn't enjoy being alone at the fine hotel where he usually dined and stayed with Kate and Christopher. Still, given the news of the annulment and all the money he was able to deposit in the local bank, he was in an expansive mood. He had two drinks before dinner and sat enjoying his ruminations on finally marrying Kate and perhaps even siring more children. Maybe he was getting a little long in the tooth for that, but Kate was still young enough and Christopher was growing up way too fast.

Tony, his regular waiter, came over. "Would you like another drink, Mr. Dunn?"

"Sure, why not," he answered, "but I'd also better order my usual cut of medium well done steak."

"There is someone who wishes to see you."

"Did he say what he wanted?"

"No, but it seemed urgent."

"Send him over."

"Her," Tony said. "And, if I may say so, she is quite lovely."

"That means she's probably from the ladies' aid society or one of the churches looking for a donation. And, Tony, after she leaves, you'd better bring me a *Lonesome Valley Ranch* steak instead of a piece of Mormon meat. You know I can taste the difference!"

Dunn turned back to his drink. He was sorry that he'd lost

his temper with Christopher, but the boy had to realize that only fools wagered money they didn't have.

"William?"

He had raised his glass almost to his lips and then it suddenly dropped from his hand to shatter against his empty plate. Dunn's head snapped up and he croaked, "Cynthia!"

She was as tall and lovely as ever, though not quite as young or as willowy. Everything except the two of them ceased to exist in the dining room.

"Cynthia," he repeated, his mind blank, his heart now racing. "What in heaven's name are *you* doing in Flagstaff!"

"May I join you?"

Dunn jumped up, almost upsetting the table and spilling his water glass and whiskey. Flustered, he groaned and beckoned Tony for help.

"Tony, you'd better bring me a full bottle of whiskey and something for Miss Holloway."

"French white wine, please."

"A bottle, Miss?"

"Why not," she said, staring at Dunn and reading his every jumbled thought as if she alone could create order out of chaos.

When Tony was gone, Dunn took a deep breath, but his mind remained a blank. He just wanted to *look* at her for a few minutes.

"I read all Mr. Kodish's articles about you," Cynthia began. "Until the first one, I had long thought you dead. I wrote Major Powell, and he assured me that you and two other members of his party had been murdered by Indians on the North Rim. I was heartbroken. I couldn't eat or sleep. I wanted to die. For a very long time, I *was* dead inside."

"I'm sorry," he stammered, suddenly overwhelmed by guilt. "I wrote again and again, but never mailed any of them."

"Why!"

"I felt completely unworthy. That I'd succeeded only in justifying your father's . . ."

"He died two years after you left. I wish he were still

alive . . . for my sake . . . but also so that he could see what a huge success you've become in this Arizona Territory."

"How did you get here?"

"It wasn't difficult. There are trains now, you know. I've been here several weeks, asking about you without being too obvious. You are very highly respected in northern Arizona."

She reached across the table and squeezed his hand. "I'm so *very* proud of you."

He shivered at her cool, delicate touch. He hadn't felt hands so satiny in many years. Kate's hands were as thick and hard-callused as those of a workingman. Cynthia's were soft and beautiful. He had trouble taking his eyes off them.

"Cynthia, what about you?"

"I finally married," she confessed. "I have a lovely daughter whose name is Alice. Alice Rebecca Blake."

"Blake," he said. "Then you . . ."

"I divorced my husband five years ago," she told him, sadness altering her face. "George was a terrible drunkard, a cheat, and an habitual gambler. Thank heavens I inherited a very sizable estate. Alice and I are much, much better off without George."

He didn't know what to say.

"I understand from the article that you are married and you have one son?"

"Christopher is fifteen."

"Alice is fourteen."

"My wife was half-Havasupai Indian. She was killed soon after Chris was born."

"Did you ever remarry?"

"No," he hesitated and then added, "but I'm expecting to."

Cynthia waited for further explanation. When it was not forthcoming, she finally said, "Well, I suppose that congratulations will soon be in order. What is your fiancée like?"

"Kate is strong," he heard himself say. "She has been very good for me. She always helps with the roundups."

"I see. The ideal frontier woman."

"Something like that."

"You know, I once was very good for you. Oh, Bill, we were so very good for each other."

Dunn nodded, at a loss for words, almost even of thought. Emotions ruled.

Cynthia leaned back and he heard the relief in her voice when she said, "Here comes the waiter with our bottles, just in the nick of time."

"Your steak will be along in a few minutes," Tony said brightly. "Would your guest like to . . ."

"No," she said. "I'm not hungry."

"Neither am I," Dunn said, spilling liquor into his glass. "Tony, please just . . . just leave us alone."

"As you wish," he said, blinking and then hurrying away.

"Alice will be starting to worry about me," Cynthia said after they had drunk too fast and in painful silence. "I had better go now."

"She's *here?*"

"Of course. She has bronchial problems. The doctors said she would be able to breathe much better in a climate that's dry but not too terribly hot. After reading all about you and Flagstaff, we decided to come for a restful visit."

"It's a fine town," he heard himself say, and realized he was just babbling. "You couldn't ask for a nicer one. There is snow in the winter, but it's not all that bad."

"That is good to know." She forced gaiety into her voice. "Well, I couldn't help but tell Alice all about us and show her the wonderful articles that have been written about you and the Grand Canyon. She really hopes to meet you. However, if that would be . . . uncomfortable, I understand."

"No, no!" he quickly objected. "Come visit our ranch. Ride horses, meet my Indian friends and our vaqueros."

"Are you sure?"

"Absolutely! This is the best time of year to see the Grand Canyon. It'll get cold in a few months and it's quite warm in the summertime. This really is the ideal time, Cynthia."

"But, are you *sure?*"

He tossed down his drink and refilled his glass. "I've never been more sure of anything."

She studied him closely, then nodded her lovely head. "Very well then. When should we come?"

"How about tomorrow? I'll be loading supplies early in the morning and leaving for Lonesome Valley Ranch in the afternoon. We'll camp one night along the way. Would that be all right?"

"It would be heavenly, a dream come true," she breathed, taking his hands and squeezing them once more.

"Then it's settled."

"I hope so," she said quietly. "I certainly hope so."

Dunn didn't sleep at all well that night. Over and over, he recounted the almost-dreamlike evening he'd just spent with Cynthia. He had drunk too much—they both had, and it had been well past midnight when he'd finally escorted her up to her room. Alice had been asleep, and he'd wisely chosen not to awaken her and introduce himself in his somewhat-intoxicated state.

This morning, his life was still turned upside down. Instead of going back to the ranch with the wonderful news that he and Kate could finally be wed, all he could think about was Cynthia. Did he *still* love her? Yes. Did he still love Kate? Of course! But how could he love them both? And how could he be so confused, weak, and stupid? How could he not fail to see that it was Kate who had stood beside him these past years? Kate who had raised his son and helped to give his life meaning and purpose?

Dunn's mind and heart were at war. He had never felt as wonderful and alive as he had last night when he'd been with Cynthia. He'd never felt as gay and giddy. Her mere presence addled his brain like Zack's mescal. Cynthia smothered his senses just as she had so many years ago when he had vowed he would never love another.

Dunn was joyously miserable. Again and again, he asked

himself what else he could have done last night other than
invite Cynthia and her daughter to his ranch. They were alone,
thousands of miles from family and friends. They *deserved* his
support and protection. Kate would understand that, wouldn't
she?

Perhaps not. Probably not.

"Good morning, William!"

He was unshaven and his head throbbed painfully as he
stood beside his big freight wagon while the last of the ranch
supplies were being loaded. Dunn took a deep, steadying
breath and pivoted to see Cynthia and Alice standing in the
street with satchels in their hands. As dull as his senses were,
he could see that they also were anxious and unsure. Perhaps
they were even wondering if his invitation stood, or if accepting it was proper.

"I am pleased to meet you," Alice said, stepping forward
and extending her hand.

When they touched, all Dunn's reservations evaporated.
Alice mirrored her mother. Slender, gentle, and lovely, she had
those same China blue eyes and fetching sprinkle of freckles
across the bridge of her nose. Her hair glistened like spun gold
and competed with her mother's dazzling smile.

"Alice," he said, wishing he had shaved and worn his suit
so that he could have made a better first impression. "I'm
pleased to meet you, and I hope that you and your mother will
enjoy your visit to my ranch and trip to the Grand Canyon."

"Mother told me that you were tall, handsome, and very
nice," Alice shyly confessed. "She said that you had dimples
and were a real Western cattle rancher."

Dunn blushed. "The men will need another hour or so to
finish loading. Why don't we have some dinner at the hotel
and then we'll just get in the wagon and go."

"Are we going to actually sleep outside?" Alice asked.

"That we are."

"What about Indians, snakes, and scorpions?"

"Tonight, we'll be camping in the high San Francisco peaks.

There are no snakes or scorpions at that elevation. However, if it would make you feel safer, we can fix a bed in the wagon for you and your mother to sleep. I'll make sure we have plenty of extra blankets so that you don't get cold."

"But the Indians would still be able to find us in the wagon, wouldn't they?"

"These days, they're pretty friendly," Dunn assured the girl. "In fact, the only people I hire on the ranch are our friends, the Havasupai and Hualapai Indians. They're very good people and I promise that you'll like them."

"Can't you find any real cowboys?" Cynthia asked.

"My Indians are 'cowboys,' " Dunn said. "I mean, they're as good as any cowboys you've probably read about. I also have two vaqueros who sold a ranch in New Mexico to come up here and go in partners with us in mustanging. The Ortiz brothers have taught Christopher just about everything there is to learn concerning mustangs, riding, and roping."

"And he is fifteen?" Alice asked.

"Yes." Dunn leaned closer and lowered his voice to speak confidentially. "But I must warn you that he is . . . rough."

"Rough?"

"Uh-huh. Compared to the young gentlemen that you've probably known back East, Christopher is going to seem pretty wild and woolly. He's a lot better with horses and cattle than he is with people, and he's never really been around a young lady."

"Is he mean?"

"Alice!"

"It's all right," Dunn said, realizing that he was really enjoying this wide-eyed girl. "To answer your question, Chris is not mean. He's a fine young man, but Kate and I have probably been a little lax concerning his manners."

"Kate is Mrs. Dunn?"

"No," he said, needing to explain. "We are not married but she is my very good friend and partner. When Christopher's mother—who was half-Indian—died in an accident, Kate raised him from the cradle. They are just as close as any mother and son."

Alice glanced up at her mother, then back to Dunn. "How long will we stay at the ranch before we go to see the Grand Canyon?" she asked.

"I don't know. We can decide that after we get there."

"I really want to meet Christopher and your Indians, Mr. Dunn. I've never done anything so exciting before in my life."

"I hope this climate agrees with you."

"Of course it does." Alice giggled. "And why wouldn't it?"

Dunn looked to Cynthia but she had glanced away. He turned back to Alice and replied, "I can't imagine there would be any reason at all."

They camped that night on the northern slopes of Humphreys Peak, which Dunn proudly informed them was the highest promontory in Arizona at just over 12,600 feet.

"It's mantled with snow almost year-round," he said. "It is one of three San Francisco peaks and was recently named after a man who just died. I'm told that Andrew Humphreys was a pioneer railroad surveyor, an authority on river hydraulics who later became a chief army engineer."

"And all that flat country to the north," Cynthia said, pointing into the vast Coconino Plateau, "is just desert and wilderness?"

"Nope," he said, disguising his amusement, "most of it is our Lonesome Valley Ranch."

"Oh, I'm sorry! I didn't mean to . . ."

"It's all right," Dunn said, understanding the basis for her question. "When I first arrived from the East, much of the West seemed wilted and like a desert. And when I joined Major Powell and saw this Grand Canyon country, I was *sure* it was a desert. But you'll soon learn that what first appears to be an arid wasteland is really excellent ranching country. The grass is rich and livestock thrive on it. The problem is water, but only during late summer and early fall. We've had to dig some wells and reservoirs and expand and protect our natural springs. It's all part of improving the range, making it more productive for both livestock and wildlife such as the deer, antelope, and mustangs."

"Will we see them?" Alice asked.

"I expect you will, starting tomorrow."

That night, Alice elected to sleep beside the campfire rather than in the protective coziness of the wagon. Dunn fed a fire and sat beside Cynthia on the mountainside, staring out toward the Grand Canyon, which was distinguishable only because of the thin, shadowed edge of the higher North Rim.

"I barely escaped off the Kaibab Plateau with my life," he confessed after telling her how he had abandoned the Howland brothers and then been saved by the Havasupai. "I've had to carry that guilt for a lot of years. I've tried to live my life since then as if I had a debt to repay. I've worked hard and been a good friend to the Indians, and I'll never stop fighting to restore their traditional lands."

Cynthia drew her knees up close and rested her chin. "I remember the day when you and I said good-bye, William. I thought you would return for me from the West dressed in buckskins and loaded with bundles of beaver pelts and sacks of gold. Every night I fantasized about how you would stand over my father and demand his permission to marry me. And how he would tremble and then give us his blessings and a beautiful wedding. But you never came back, and I finally lost the dream."

"I should have written you long, long ago," he said. "I guess it would have changed both our lives."

"Why *didn't* you ever write?"

"I did, but I never sent my words. They seemed unworthy. I *felt* unworthy. Then I met Josie. We were as happy as I ever expected to be."

"But she died and you found this Kate woman?"

"Yes. I won't even go into her very complicated and tragic

past," Dunn said. "Suffice to say, Kate is a very admirable person."

"Do you love her?"

"I do. But, to be honest, you've sort of muddied the waters, Cynthia."

"Maybe they will become as clear and bright as those stars in the heavens," she told him. "Actually, I'm a little confused myself, and I know that Alice is, too."

"Let's just play it one day at a time," he suggested. "First the ranch, then the Grand Canyon, and then we'll see what happens."

"To what? Our hearts?"

Dunn stood up and walked over to his blankets. "Good night, Cynthia."

"Good night, William."

The next day they rolled out of the mountains and across the Coconino, arriving at ranch headquarters late in the afternoon. Kate and Christopher, along with the vaqueros and Indians, were standing in the ranch yard to greet them.

Dunn smiled at Kate, nodded to Chris, then set the wagon's brake, telling everyone, "I got the windows and most all the supplies. I guess you've all heard that I sold our cattle to Captain Benson."

Kate dipped her chin, but she wasn't paying any attention to him. Her eyes, like everyone else's, were fixed on Cynthia and Alice, who were perched up on the wagon seat trying to take in everything at once.

"This is Mrs. Cynthia Holloway Blake and her daughter, Alice," he said, loud enough for everyone to hear. "Cynthia is a very old friend and I want you all to make her and Alice feel at home."

"Kate, you have a very beautiful ranch," Cynthia said.

"Thank you."

Cynthia studied the almost-completed two-story frame house. "I hope we are not intruding."

"Not at all," Kate replied, managing a smile. "You and your

daughter must be very tired. Please come on inside, and I'll fix you some refreshments and we can get acquainted."

Dunn tried to catch Kate's eye, but she wouldn't look at him. And, after he had helped Cynthia and Alice down and the three women had gone inside, Christopher sidled up to him and said under his breath, "We'll, you've really stepped into it this time, haven't you."

"What do you mean?"

"You *know* what I mean," Chris said. "It'll be interesting to see how you're going to handle things now."

"No more interesting than it will be for me to watch how you handle Alice," Dunn answered.

Twenty-six

"Are you taking Cynthia and Alice to visit the Grand Canyon this morning?"

"Yes. Have you enjoyed them, Kate?"

"Very much. Christopher has become quite smitten with Alice, though I can't quite imagine why. They've absolutely nothing in common."

"She's a lovely girl. She likes it out here. So does Cynthia."

"I wonder."

"Look, Kate . . ."

"Christopher follows Alice around like a lovesick calf."

"It's *puppy* love," Dunn replied. "Just a bad case of puppy love."

"Some men never get over 'puppy love,' do they."

"I wish you'd come with us."

"No thank you."

"All right. I'll take Cynthia and Alice over to the rim and show them around for a few days, then return them to Flagstaff."

"And then?"

"I'll be back, Kate. I'll be back and everything will be the same as it was before."

"We'll see. And, Bill?"

"Yes?"

"Please take Christopher with you."

"I thought you weren't pleased about him spending so much time with Alice."

"I'm not, but that's not why he needs to go with you."

"I see."

"No, you don't, Bill. But *I* do."

"There it is!" Dunn said, drawing the buckboard to a stand-still. "The Grand Canyon!"

"Oh, my Lord!" Cynthia whispered, hand flying to her lips.

"Oh!" Alice exclaimed, jumping to her feet. "It's even bigger than I'd dreamed!"

"It's a piece of work, ain't it!" Christopher said, throwing his right leg up and curling it around his saddlehorn while his spirited mustang danced in the sage. "Damn biggest hole in the world!"

"I just can't wait to stand beside it!" Alice cried.

Christopher uncocked his leg, jammed it back into the stir-rup and extended his arm. "Then hop on behind me, Miss Alice, and I'll get you there in a hurry!"

Alice jumped off the buckboard onto the back of Christo-pher's horse, and they shot ahead, both whooping as the animal raced for the rim.

"My heavens," Cynthia cried in alarm, "can he stop that runaway before it plunges over!"

"You bet," Dunn said. "Relax, Cynthia. There's nothing to worry about."

He slapped the reins against the rumps of the team and Cynthia grabbed his arm as the buckboard began to bounce ahead. By the time they reached the rim, Christopher and Alice had dismounted and were standing at the edge of the Grand Canyon, neither saying a word.

"Well, Cynthia, there it is," Dunn said, swinging her down from the wagon. "What do you think?"

It took a while for her to say, "It's . . . it's beyond descrip-tion!"

Dunn felt an immense sense of proprietary interest as he began to point out the various landmarks. "We're standing at

Yavapai Point overlooking Granite Gorge. That's Bright Angel Canyon and Bright Angel Creek across from us and, off to the east along this rim, is Hopi and then Pima Point. I understand that most of these landmarks were named during Major Powell's second expedition. The professor told me that that big point across from us was named Cape Royal. I stood there many years ago with him, Josie, and a flock of bleating sheep."

"How far away is it?"

"At least ten miles."

"The air is so clear it appears less than five."

"I know. Distances in this canyon have always been deceptive. The first Spaniards badly underestimated the distance down to the Colorado River."

"Who was 'the professor'?"

"It's a long story, Cynthia."

"We've time."

Dunn supposed that was true. He unhitched the buckboard and hobbled their horses. Then he and Cynthia began to stroll along the rim while he told her all about Professor Sutherland.

"He was like a brother to me," Dunn confided, "but it seems like I've lost every good friend. Seneca Howland, then Zack, then the professor. It's gotten so that I'm afraid friendship is a curse."

"But Kate is your good friend."

"Yes. But she's a woman."

"Quite obviously."

"I mean, that's why she hasn't been snakebitten."

"And what am I?"

The sun was low on the western horizon, setting the canyon ablaze with fiery colors. Dunn stopped and jammed his hands into his pockets.

"William, what *am* I to you?" she asked softly, pressing close.

He tried to keep his eyes riveted on the majesty of the canyon but, suddenly, Cynthia was in his arms and he was kissing her mouth, swaying on the very brink of the abyss.

"Cynthia, no," he rasped, easing her away. "I can't have you. I can't do *this.*"

Cynthia wouldn't let him go. "Why! Because you're still in love with me? Because we were *meant* for each other! William, we are as inevitable as . . . as this Grand Canyon!"

"Why?" he repeated. "Because it's wrong! I do love Kate! She *needs* me. Someone is coming to *kill* her!"

"I'm truly sorry," she said after a long, agonizing moment. "William, forgive me. I had no right to say those words. Let's pretend we're just old friends."

"Friends?"

"Yes. Because we are, you know."

"Did you really come out here just for your daughter's health?"

"No. I lied shamefully. Alice is in perfectly good health. But the articles written by Mr. Kodish did cause me to dream of a new start and even of *us.* I see now that it never can happen."

"I want you to stay in Flagstaff. I want to see you whenever I visit town. It's important to me to know that you and Alice will be safe and well taken care of."

She allowed herself a thin smile. "Am I to be your *kept* woman?"

"Of course not! But I want to help."

"We can take care of ourselves, William. Remember, I have that nice inheritance. But I still want to do something useful."

"Such as?"

"Such as work in a millinery or dress shop."

"You? Work in a shop?" The idea seemed ridiculous.

"What's wrong with that?" she demanded. "I am very well qualified and have excellent taste in clothes."

"I didn't mean . . ."

"And I enjoy serving people," she added with indignation. "What do you think I'd do with myself in Flagstaff? Sit beside a window every day, pining for the mere sight of you?"

"Well, of course not, but . . ."

"I'm not afraid to work. It would keep my mind occupied."

"Fine," he said, just wanting to change the subject, "go ahead and work."

"Thank you, William. I am certainly glad that you've given me permission to do that."

He felt like a fool. "I'm sorry. You'd do a wonderful job in a women's store of some kind, even though there aren't a lot of women in Flagstaff."

"Not *yet*. But there is one store in town owned by a Mrs. Bartlett."

"Oh, yes," he said, shaking his head, "I know Willa Bartlett. I've been in her store a time or two to buy Kate something nice, but she's a very unpleasant woman. I always come out of her store feeling depressed."

"You shouldn't. Mrs. Bartlett is honest and well intentioned, although she knows nothing about fashion and her inventory is extremely limited. It's just that she constantly complains about her aching back, her feet, and her general health. She'd be tedious and depressing to work for, but I could turn that store into a very popular and profitable business."

"Then why don't you consider buying Willa out and do the women of Flagstaff a big favor?"

"I suppose I could do that," Cynthia replied. "But so much is happening so fast that I've had no time to make any plans. And, of course, everything I dreamed might happen for us is now impossible."

They walked a while longer, Dunn trying to imagine Cynthia behind a counter, trying to please Flagstaff's tough frontier women.

"Yes, I'll really give that idea some thought," Cynthia mused aloud.

"It might work," he said, trying hard to sound encouraging. "And I want to help."

"No."

"Cynthia, be reasonable! Don't be too proud to accept help."

"Aren't you?"

"No," he told her. "I've had more than my share of help, starting when Josie's Havasupai people dragged me out of the river and saved my life. A few years later, Josie's father gave us the gold to start buying rangeland. People have always helped me, and now I'm finally in a position to start returning favors to those for whom I care deeply."

She took his hand. "Let's walk into the moonlight, William. Maybe it has some magic in it, and you'll kiss me again and we'll fall in love."

"We're already in love."

"Yes, but you're going to marry Kate."

"That's right."

"I see. Actually, I *don't* see. But I'm prepared to accept that and just be friends."

"I'm sorry."

"Me, too. Sorrier than you can possibly imagine."

Dunn took her hand and led her over to the charred remains of the professor's cabin. "It was a nice place," he said. "The professor lived here for many years. And just over there in that thick stand of juniper is where he worked excavating the Anasazi ruins."

"It's so lonely out here. What kind of man could stand this quiet and solitude?"

"A special one, Cynthia. Walt was very happy here. If he hadn't been murdered, he would have been content to spend the rest of his life trying to unravel the secrets of the Anasazi."

"Where did he find the Spaniard's armor and learn the secret of where they'd descended?"

"Just a short way to the east. There's nothing left now to see." Dunn extended his hand, but Cynthia ignored it. "Come on," he said, "let's go join the kids and I'll show you the ancient Anasazi ruins."

The ruins had not been violated since Dunn's last visit. There was, however, plenty of evidence that wild horses and other animals had come to drink and graze at the ancient

Anasazi springs. Some of the mustangs and probably his own Longhorns had trampled sections of the ruins.

"I'm going to buy a couple of rolls of barbed wire when we get back to Flagstaff and fence off this dig," he told Cynthia. "The professor spent too many years working here to just let it all be stomped out by livestock."

"It's interesting," Cynthia said, slowly walking around the excavation. "Did he tell you what the Anasazi did in these places?"

"Some of them." Dunn was able to point out the Anasazi sleeping quarters and the granary storage area as well as the big round depression in the earth that the professor had called a kiva, used primarily for religious ceremonies.

"The professor found a lot of ancient grinding stones, arrowheads, and pottery," Dunn told her. "I've got some of it stored at the ranch."

"Where did you find the professor's body?"

"They threw it off the rim behind his cabin," Dunn said, eyes going bleak. "Chris and I climbed down and discovered it."

"This is a beautiful but *violent* land."

"I don't look at it that way," Dunn told her. "But it does attract hard and desperate men. Out here, you stand or fall on your merits."

"I see." Cynthia walked over to the two-foot-high wall outlining one of the rooms which the professor had uncovered. "Did he ever speculate on what the Anasazi talked about or how they felt about life? Things like that?"

"The professor had discovered enough pictographs to know that they had their own gods. They also had ceremonies for rain and good hunting, for fertility and to give thanks for new life and to ask their spirits to be kind to their dead. I expect that Anasazi mothers loved their children no differently than they do now, and fathers took the same kind of pride in a son's accomplishments."

"Of course they must have," Cynthia said. "Times, circumstances and surroundings may change, but we always have shared the same basic human emotions. Love. Hate. Fear. Envy. Greed. Happiness. Loneliness. Sorrow."

"Yes," Dunn agreed, "but Indians do not worry like whites. They're more . . . more accepting of things."

"I've accepted the fact that I can't have you," Cynthia bluntly told him. "How could any Indian woman be more accepting than that?"

"I don't know," he replied, smiling because he appreciated how she was trying to make light of something very painful.

"Let's go back and make camp before it gets dark," Dunn suggested, taking her arm. "We can spend a day or two here, or follow the rim eastward so that you and Alice can gain some new perspectives."

"I'd like that," she told him. "The cabin's ashes must be a sad reminder of your friend, and these ruins create more questions in my mind than answers. So let's follow the rim."

"Maybe we can even see some wild mustangs, as well as the usual deer and antelope. I'll bet you and Alice would enjoy that."

"We would," she agreed as they began to walk.

The following afternoon they traveled east to a vista point along the rim high enough to be dotted with tall ponderosa pines, and they discovered a thriving homestead. Dunn was surprised and impressed at the sight of a substantial log cabin with an attached porch and several outbuildings, as well as two huge canvas tents. To complete the picture, there was a pole corral, horses, several mules, and even a milk cow.

"Would you look at that," Dunn said with a shake of his head. "Cynthia, this is all a surprise to me."

"Me, too," Christopher said, "but we haven't been through here since we went looking for Kate at Lee's Ferry years ago. Remember?"

"You're right. It's been a good long while."

"Has he settled on your ranchland?" Cynthia asked.

"No," Dunn replied. "We left the eastern boundary of our Lonesome Valley Ranch about twenty miles back. This is open land and, if it belongs to anyone, it would be the Navajo. But my guess is that this homesteader bought legal title before he invested so much in all these buildings. He's got himself a real nice place."

"He's been busy all right," Christopher said. "But I sure can't figure out what anyone would be doing building right beside the rim. I haven't seen any sign of him running sheep or cattle."

"He must be a prospector. And, from the looks of his place, I'd have to guess that he's been pretty successful or else he's got himself a big financial backer."

"But no one has found gold or silver in the Grand Canyon."

"I know," Dunn replied, "but they must figure that, as big as it is, there *have* to be rich ore deposits down there someplace. I'm afraid that we're going to be seeing more and more of them in the years to come. But, for right now, we might as well pay him a social call. But, ladies, I'll warn you that prospectors can talk pretty salty, and it's often a good idea to keep them downwind."

"You mean that they talk badly and never take baths," Alice said, making a face.

"That's exactly what he means," Christopher added, giving his father a wink.

As soon as they were within a mile of the cabin, two big hounds came charging out from under a low porch, barking as though they were trying to tree a bear.

Fortunately, both Cynthia and Alice were in the buckboard because Christopher's horse started bucking when one of the dogs nipped its hocks. Dunn had his own troubles as the team was challenged by the other big dog.

"Dammit!" a tall, bearded man wearing a large, shapeless brown hat yelled as he came flying out of the cabin waving a double-barreled shotgun. Spraying chewing tobacco, he screeched in a high, reedy voice, "You mangy curs, git away from them horses!"

To emphasize his point, the man unleashed a deafening double blast from his shotgun that sent the dogs streaking for the cover of the pines.

"Sorry about that," the homesteader shouted, cradling his smoking shotgun in the crook of his arm and smiling as he advanced in a loose-jointed, long-stepping fashion.

He was gangly and all sharp angles, with a face as long as a horse's and centered with a big Roman nose. His shabby clothes were far too small so that his shirtsleeves reached just halfway down his forearms, exposing knobby wrist bones, while his pants fell only to the middle of his shins. He wore a primitive leather holster in which rested a pistol belted to his narrow waist.

Dunn never had seen bigger ears or hands on a man before and noted he was missing his right index finger. Taken feature by feature, the fellow was extremely homely, but there was little doubt he was genuinely happy to receive them as visitors.

"You folks don't mind them damned dogs! I'll shoot their mangy hides off if they ever greet you that'a way again! Hey, kid!"

"Yeah?" Chris called from the top of his pitching horse.

"You're a pretty fair rider! Too bad you ride such a goosey horse."

Christopher finally got his mount under control. "What's wrong with your *mean* old dogs, Mister!"

"Ah, they ain't mean! When I grabbed my shotgun, they just figured we were going rabbit hunting. Chasing rabbits, coyotes, and varmints is all them dogs live for, and they get real excited. Now tie them nervous horses up and come inside. I ain't seen such pretty ladies in a long, long time. Glory, glory, what a surprise!"

"It'll be all right," Dunn assured Cynthia and her daughter as he helped them down from the wagon and made the usual introductions.

The prospector propped his shotgun up against the side of his cabin and favored them with a wide grin. His hair was mostly gray, matted and plastered to his forehead. He looked about sixty, but he might have been younger.

"Welcome to my new Captain John Hance Ranch and Hotel!" the man grandly proclaimed. "It sure is a pleasure having you guests."

"Hotel?" Alice asked.

"Yep!" Captain Hance exclaimed, turning to make a sweeping bow toward his big log cabin. "She's pretty darned nice, too, ain't she! I'm carvin' some rockin' chairs for the porch right now."

"It's a fine cabin," Dunn agreed. "Are we your first visitors?"

"Golly no! I've had upward of a hundred this past summer and that's only the beginning. After the railroad finally arrives, well, sir, I'll spend all my time countin' my money!"

Dunn appreciated the man's enthusiasm, but thought him somewhat of an optimist. "That could take a while, Captain."

"Yeah," Hance said, pulling on his beard but not looking a bit worried. "But, until then, I've discovered a little mine down in the canyon and it pays enough to keep me in beans between my paying guests. I also got me a nice, sweet spring over yonder in them pines and this is the first and *only* hotel along thus hull beautiful canyon."

Despite Captain Hance's proclamation, Dunn thought it a stretch to call the cabin a hotel. True, it was bigger and finer than most wilderness cabins, and it probably had two or even three rooms, but it was still just a cabin.

"It's nice to have a neighbor," Dunn said. "We run cattle and a few sheep on Lonesome Valley Ranch off to the west."

"Oh, sure! I've heard plenty about you, Mr. Dunn. I heard that you're a good man whose word is his bond. I've also heard that you've no tolerance for horse or cattle rustlers."

"That's true enough, Captain." Dunn turned to look at the tents. "What are those for?"

"Overflow," Hance said, hooking his thumbs in his bib overalls. "Some people might even prefer 'em to the hotel in the summer when it's hot. I'm chargin' just one dollar a day to stay in one of those fine, *waterproof* tents, which includes all the sourdough bread and rabbit stew you can eat."

"That sounds reasonable enough," Christopher said.

"Why sure it is!" the captain exclaimed. "People come here and they got a million-dollar view of the canyon. Best place to see it for fifty miles in either direction. And, as for eating rabbit all the time, sometimes I get lucky and shoot an antelope, a mule deer, or even a few quail or sage hens, but mostly it's rabbit. Mr. Dunn, have you and your fine family come to spend a few days at my hotel?"

"Well," Dunn said, caught off guard by the directness of the man's question, "we've been camping under the stars."

"That's fine and you can do it right here and still eat in my hotel for fifty cents a day. But I got something that you're going to enjoy a lot more than sourdough biscuits and rabbit stew."

"What's that?" Cynthia asked.

Hance grinned even wider. "A mule trip right down to the river!"

"You can reach it from up here?" Dunn asked with surprise that bordered on outright disbelief.

"Yep, I've spent the last two years building a good trail all the way down to the Colorado River."

Dunn looked at Christopher, and both shook their heads because they knew the enormity of that accomplishment.

"Now listen," Hance was telling them, "it'll take us a full day to ride down and another to ride back out. While we're visiting the floor of the canyon, you folks can swim and fish while I work my mine and do a bit of prospectin'. It'll be a trip you'll never forget."

"That's what I'm afraid of," Dunn said, wondering how safe Hance's trail might be.

The old man clearly read his concerns and said, "Ah, it's

safe on my mules! And the weather and water is mighty nice down below."

"But the fishing isn't good," Dunn said. "At least, it never used to be."

"You been down there?" Hance asked with sudden interest.

"I have," Dunn said, choosing not to elaborate. "But it was a good many years ago."

"Who'd you go with?"

"Just some friends," Dunn said, purposely vague. "How much do you want to put the ladies up in the cabin?"

"Three dollars a day . . . for both. Good beds and I promise that they'll find no ticks nor fleas. No scorpions nor rats nor spiders, either."

"How about it?" Dunn asked Cynthia and her daughter. "Would you like to spend the night in a real bed?"

Before she could answer, Captain Hance said, "Spend a night or two here, then let me lead you down into the biggest and most beautiful canyon in the whole world! Best memories of your life. You'll never forget 'em."

"Father?" Christopher asked. "Can we?"

"Cynthia?" Dunn asked.

"I can't think of anything I would rather do," she told him after receiving an enthusiastic nod from Alice. "That is, if you can spare that much time from your ranch."

"I can."

"Then it's all settled!" Captain Hance whooped. "Tomorrow I'll give you the rim tour, the next day we'll ride down and have ourselves a real good time."

"What about our horses?" Christopher asked.

"Let 'em stay and rest in my corral with the milk cow. We can throw 'em enough hay to last until we get back."

"I'm sure not riding any rabbit-eared *mule*."

"Ahhhh!" Hance scoffed, "you'll be glad you did as soon as we start down the canyon side. My mules are as surefooted as mountain goats. First couple of trips down there was a little . . . edgy. But not anymore."

"If we go down, we'll ride mules," Dunn decreed, remembering Josie.

It *was* a good thing they rode mules because Captain Hance's new trail made the treacherous track into Havasu Canyon seem like a city street. Dunn and Christopher clung to their saddlehorns while Cynthia and Alice never said a word but were white as chalk the whole time.

The trail itself was a monument to backwoods ingenuity. It took advantage of every natural feature and probably the work of the Anasazi. Captain Hance had shored it up in the most dangerous places and, if you didn't try to guide your mule, it all worked out just fine. Once on the floor of the canyon, Captain Hance gave them a visit to remember. He was an excellent cook, although his menu would have been monotonous if Dunn had not brought along their own food to supplement rabbit.

The weather was perfect. They all had a fine time swimming, wading, and exploring, and the evening campfires proved memorable because Captain Hance was a lively and gifted storyteller.

"As you know, Mr. Dunn, last winter was real mild," Hance told them one evening after supper, "except for that one humdinger of a snowstorm. It was a January morning when I woke and discovered that the snow was as deep and white as the icing on a wedding cake. Well, I was out of meat and needed to go hunting, so I strapped on my snowshoes and grabbed my trusty shotgun. But damned if it didn't commence to snowin' again. And real hard, too! But my stomach was growlin' so I kept walking and lookin' for somethin' to shoot. The snow kept falling and pretty soon it was real deep and fluffy and soft as Carolina cotton. I couldn't see anything to shoot and finally decided to turn around and head back to my cabin when, suddenly, I noticed that my snowshoes were sinkin' in mighty fast!"

Hance poked at the fire, winked, and said, "Chris, you ever wear snowshoes in snow so soft that you sank nearly to your waist?"

"No, Captain, I don't believe that I have."

"Well," Hance said, "that's what was happening to me. And no matter how I tried, I just kept sinkin' and sinkin' until *finally,* I realized that I'd plumb walked off this South Rim and onto a sea of clouds stretchin' from one rim to the other."

"Aw, Captain!" Alice squealed. "You're fibbin' again!"

"No, Missy, I am *not!* You ask Mr. Dunn if the Grand Canyon sometimes don't fill right up to the brim with clouds. Looks just as white and pretty as a cup full of fresh cream. Ain't that right?"

"It does," Dunn had to admit. "I've seen it happen many times in winter."

"You see!" Hance exclaimed. "I'm telling you the truth. Anyway, just before the clouds blowed away and I was about to drop three thousand feet to the canyon's floor, I saw a big pinnacle of stone a'pokin' up through the thinning clouds. So I jumped, grabbed, and hugged it with both arms."

Hance shook his head. "Of course, it saved my life, but there I was, stuck way up there in the middle of the Grand Canyon with no place to go. It was a bad, lonesome feeling, I'll tell you."

Christopher rolled his eyes. Alice giggled and Cynthia beamed and said, "So how did you escape, Captain?"

"I had to wait almost a week for another snowstorm, biggest one that ever was and it filled the canyon right up to the top with snow—not clouds—but *real* snow, and so I just walked back to my cabin and made do with pancakes and molasses all the rest of that winter."

Dunn thought he'd never had such a happy time in his life as those days on the bottom of the Grand Canyon. He learned a few things, too, like the fact that there were a good many prospectors now exploring the depths of the canyon. Enough of their burros had either escaped or been turned loose that it was not uncommon to hear them mournfully hee-hawing all hours of the day and night.

He and Cynthia managed to act like old friends; neither of them spoke of the future. Instead, they enjoyed their children, and Dunn was surprised at how differently he now regarded the Colorado River and the interior of the canyon. Years before, during Powell's first daring exploration, he had considered it an enemy, or often simply an object of trial and conquest. Now, he saw it in a truer light as simply a great, geological wonder created by a timeless river. And so it was that he left the Colorado River with an entirely new perspective, and with no small amount of regret.

"Did you have a good time?" he asked Cynthia the evening before they departed as they sat close together beside the river, tossing pebbles into the water and watching their golden rings expand in the moonlight while their children were entertained by Captain Hance's humorous, outrageous yarns.

"I will never forget this," she confessed. "No matter where I go, I will never forget."

"But I thought you were going to settle in Flagstaff?"

Cynthia took a deep breath. "William," she told him, "I'm not sure that I can."

"Why not?"

"Do you really need to ask such a question? I'm in love with you! And, when you're in love with someone you can't have, there's heartache. William, every time I saw you it would sharpen my pain. I just don't know if I can live like that."

"Cynthia, I . . ."

"Shhh!" she warned, putting a finger to her lips. "Don't say anything. I'm thinking about going to California. I hear that it is a good place to make a fresh start."

"Dammit, Cynthia, it can't be an easier place to start over than right here."

"I don't know," Cynthia quietly told him as her eyes filled with tears.

"Give it some time," he pleaded. "I can't help you in California. Just promise me that you won't leave without giving it some time."

"All right," she promised.

After returning to the hotel in Flagstaff, Dunn and Christopher set about buying a few supplies for their return to the ranch. Dunn went into Mrs. Willa Bartlett's millinery and dress shop, intending to pick out something nice to bring back to Kate.

"Oh, Mr. Dunn," Willa sighed, "how are you today?"

"Fine, Willa. Do you have any . . ."

"I wish that I was feeling fine, too," the woman whined from a chair behind the counter. "Business isn't good and my poor feet are *killing* me. I don't know how I'm going to get by much longer. My husband's health isn't much better than mine, you know."

Dunn knew Arnold Bartlett. The poor man was a colorless dishrag who earned a meager living doing sign work.

"Willa, maybe you ought to hire someone to help you out."

"Can't afford to pay anyone."

"You just might be surprised. There is a very nice lady in town named Cynthia Holloway Blake. She has a daughter and . . ."

"Oh," Willa said, "I wouldn't hire *that* woman."

"Why not?" he asked with surprise.

"Mr. Dunn, she's really quite desperate, you know."

"What!"

"It's true. But she puts on such airs! Why, she came waltzing into my store with some hatboxes when she first arrived in town and tried to *sell* them to me! Can you imagine! Used hats!"

"No," Dunn said, totally confused, "I cannot."

"And she's pawned her jewelry and then crawled into the bank begging for a loan. I understand she's unable to pay for her hotel room. Of course, the bank won't have anything to do with her. That woman has no money and no visible means of support. I expect that we'll next hear of her . . ."

"Mrs. Bartlett," Dunn said, cutting her off, *"I'll* buy this store. How much will you take for everything?"

"Why . . ."

"A *figure,* Willa! Just give me a damned figure and don't say another word!"

"Two thousand?" she squeaked.

"You can pick it up at the bank before it closes today," Dunn said, spinning around on his heel. "Good day, Willa!"

He found Christopher at the livery and informed him that their departure would be delayed an hour and then he told his son why.

"I'm buying Mrs. Bartlett out, lock, stock, and barrel, and then I'm hiring Cynthia and Alice to run our new millinery and dress shop."

Christopher's jaw sagged.

"You heard me," Dunn said, draping his arm across his son's shoulders and steering him toward the bank. "You see, over at Lonely Dell, John Lee taught me that a smart man never puts all his eggs in one basket. So we're buying us a town business."

"But a *millinery and dress shop?"*

"Yep. Mr. Lee also taught me always to look ahead to the future. How would you like to go into partnership with me on a stageline to deliver tourists to the South Rim of the Grand Canyon?"

"Well . . ."

"Son, tip your hat," Dunn said as they stepped off the narrow boardwalk, "when we pass these ladies."

"But they're *old* ladies."

"All the more reason," Dunn said, setting the example and making sure that Christopher followed suit.

"What is going on," Christopher demanded, long, skinny legs stretching to match those of his father. "Next thing I know, you'll be running for mayor!"

"Might not be a bad idea," Dunn said. "What do you think about Alice?"

"What do you mean?"

"Have you fallen in love with her yet?"

Christopher stopped in his tracks and his face turned crimson. "Geez, what a damned dumb question!"

Dunn threw back his head and laughed. "If you haven't yet, you will. It's inevitable!"

"If I didn't know better, I'd swear you've been drinking mescal."

"Nope. I'm clearheaded now. Never seen things clearer."

After leaving the bank, he stopped by the telegraph office.

"Clyde," he said, "I'd like you to send a telegram to Judge Westerling in Prescott."

"Sure thing, Mr. Dunn," the operator said, jumping up and grabbing a pencil and pad of paper. "Shoot!"

Dunn frowned in concentration and began to dictate.

Dear Judge Westerling. STOP. Please make all the arrangements for a church wedding two weeks from today. STOP. Put all expenses on my ranch account. STOP. Stay healthy and thanks for being my best man. STOP. Thanks. STOP.

"Well, let me be the first to congratulate you and Kate!" the operator said, beaming. "About time you made her an honest woman."

Dunn nodded, turning to leave as he said, "She's *always* been an honest woman, Clyde. The trouble is, I haven't always been an honest man."

Twenty-seven

"I tell you what, Kate," Dunn suggested one warm spring evening as they sat rocking on their veranda. "Let's take Christopher to Flagstaff and celebrate his birthday. And, while we're in town, we can enjoy all the hoopla over the maiden run of the new stageline up to the South Rim."

"I'd like that," Kate said. "Besides, I've been wanting to see what new things Cynthia has in stock. I understand she had quite a time at the big fashion show in Boston."

"She did, but the main reason she went was to visit Alice at her boarding school. I expect she's turning into quite the proper young lady."

"I liked her just fine the way she used to be," Kate said. "And Christopher did, too."

"Alice has her sights set pretty high."

"Higher than our son?"

"She's not the right one for him," Dunn said. "Chris needs a *ranch* girl, someone who would enjoy living out here. That isn't Alice, unless I've read her entirely wrong."

"No," Kate agreed, "I think you're probably right, though I doubt that Christopher would agree with us."

"He's smart enough to find someone more suitable."

Kate allowed herself a smile. "Just like you did, huh?"

Dunn should have anticipated that little dig. Kate had never quite forgotten the past and how close he'd come to throwing everything away and running off with Cynthia.

"Now, Kate," he said, "don't you start that again."

"Well," Kate said, reaching over to pat his hand, "if we're leaving tomorrow, I'd better go inside and start making my shopping list."

"In that case," Dunn replied, climbing out of his rocking chair, "I'll hunt Chris up and make sure that he approves of our plan."

Dunn stretched, pulling his right pants leg down over his boot top. It had caught on the handle of the Spanish dagger again. He'd never heard back from those Eastern archeologists and, over the years, the professor's Anasazi excavations had been eroding away with every passing season. Dunn had bought enough barbed wire to fence off the professor's dig, but he couldn't fence out the wind, rain, or snow. In another few decades, the barbed wire and the cedar posts would probably still be standing, but the Anasazi ruins would have melted into obscurity.

Dunn was getting stiff in the joints but, considering the kind of rough life he'd led, he was feeling well. He had some arthritis in his hands and feet that became vexatious during winter, but he had few physical complaints. Lucio and Juan gimped around nearly as much as he did, and they were a damn sight younger.

Dunn paused as twilight burnished his South Rim rangeland. He could hear guitar music coming from the bunkhouse and see the lights gleaming from the permanent cabins he'd built for the vaqueros and his other married employees. Old Armando Ortiz had enjoyed the final three years of his life on the Lonesome Valley Ranch and was now buried in the family cemetery along with a fair number of Indians. Tucson had surprised everyone and married a Havasupai girl and returned to live with her in Havasu Canyon; he still visited Lonesome Valley every winter, bringing his wife and two children.

Dunn reached into his vest pocket and extracted a letter he'd received the day before. He didn't need to open it to remember that it urged him to run for territorial commissioner of the newly created Coconino County. It was signed by three of

Flagstaff's prominent businessmen and suggested that it was time that he gave serious consideration to entering politics. After all, Dunn was one of the biggest and most successful ranchers in northern Arizona and a sizable stockholder, not only in the Bank of Flagstaff, but also in several local businesses.

Dunn was flattered, but knew he would again decline. The only reason he could think of to enter politics would be to give him enough influence in Washington, D.C., to ensure that a sensible balance was reached between protecting the Grand Canyon without choking its expanding tourism. But, even more important, he desired enough influence to finally convince Congress that they had wronged both the Hualapai and the Havasupai and that their traditional South Rim hunting grounds ought to be restored in totality. *Yes,* Dunn thought as he went to find Christopher, *I'd become a politician if I could have an impact on those matters.*

As usual, he found his son out by the horse corrals, working with a mustang. This evening, Chris was teaching an exceptionally nice mare the finer points of neck reining.

"Hey," Dunn called between the corral poles, "how would you like to go to Flagstaff tomorrow?"

"What for?" Chris asked, riding the mare over and dismounting. He was taller than Dunn now, almost six-foot-four, but still filling out.

"To celebrate our wedding anniversary, your birthday and the inauguration of Flagstaff's new stageline up to Captain Hance's Hotel."

"Sounds exciting," Chris said, scratching the mare behind her ears. "I've heard that Alice is back for a visit, and I haven't seen her yet. Thought she might have come right out to visit the ranch, but I guess she's got more important things to do in town."

Dunn heard the disappointment in his son's voice. He wanted to tell Chris that there were a lot of other pretty girls, but he knew that would not be appropriate. So, instead, he joked, "Maybe Alice has just forgotten that you're such a tall, handsome dog."

Christopher laughed, just as Dunn had hoped.

"Yeah," Chris agreed. "But maybe I'll look pretty rough after the Boston boys."

"Maybe," Dunn admitted, "but you're no rougher than you have to be in this ranching country. You can't be something you're not."

"Did you buy into that new stageline?"

"I invested some money. We're going to be supplying all their horses."

"I can't figure out why you got into that deal," Chris said. "You know that the citizens of Williams are lobbying the Atlantic and Pacific to build a spur line from their town directly up to the South Rim. If they get it, they'll put our stageline out of business."

"Not necessarily," Dunn countered. "Even if Williams does get the new railroad spur line—and I'm pretty sure that they will—there will still be a need for an excursion stageline running along the rim between the new Bright Angel Lodge and Captain Hance's Hotel. We can operate cheaper than the Williams people, just because we've got the advantages of this ranch and an almost-inexhaustible supply of horses."

"I suppose," Chris said. "That big Thoroughbred stallion you had shipped out here sure has upgraded the quality of the mustangs we caught this year at Warm Springs."

"It was a gamble that paid off handsomely," Dunn said. After Pepper had gotten too old to work sheep, Dunn had sold his flock to a Basque sheep rancher and used the proceeds to buy a run-down livery in Flagstaff and to pay for that Tennessee stallion as well as the costs of rail transportation for the horse and a stableman to accompany it on the long journey to Flagstaff. His biggest concern was that even a very strong Thoroughbred would sicken or break down in ranch country or else be killed by another stallion, but that had not happened.

"Are we leaving in the morning?" Chris asked.

"Yes. We'll be taking a buckboard because Kate is working up a shopping list."

"Then maybe I should bring along a few sale horses to cover the bill Kate will run up in town."

"That might be a fine idea."

"You still planning to buy the town's other livery?"

"If I can get it at a fair price," Dunn replied as he turned back toward the house in the rapidly fading light, "either that or Abe Milner's Feed Store and Saddle Shop. He's interested in semi-retirement but he'd stay on part-time for another few years."

"Don't know why you bother with all that," Christopher said. "We already got too many irons in the fire."

"Diversification!" Dunn called back as he strode toward the house. "It's the key to an Arizona rancher's survival."

The next morning, just as they were about to leave, a dusty horseman arrived after having made the crossing at Lee's Ferry several days earlier.

"The Colorado River is running real high," the rider told them as his horse drank its fill at their stock tank, "and the ferry crossing was dangerous. But I couldn't get away from Lonely Dell quick enough, I'll tell you."

Kate and Dunn knew that Emma Lee had married Frank French and had relocated somewhere in Arizona, most likely near Winslow. Lonely Dell's new residents, Warren and Permelia Johnson, seemed like a very nice couple with plenty of young children to help them with their orchard and truck farming.

"What was wrong?" Kate asked.

"Last summer, an emigrant wagon came through Lonely Dell to Lee's Ferry. The family had just lost a little girl to sickness, so they asked Mrs. Johnson if she wanted their daughter's clothes and dolls. I guess they were just too painful to keep. Of course, with six girls of her own, Mrs. Johnson accepted the clothes and gave the family a free ferry ride. They continued south. Four days later, the Johnson's five-year-old son, Jonathan, came up sudden with a sore throat and fever."

"Oh, no," Kate said, dreading the rest of the story.

"Well," the rider continued, "about a day later, Laura Alice and Millie, ages seven and nine, came down with the same sore throat and fever. All three of those Johnson children died the following week. And, as if the Johnson family hadn't suffered enough, the sickness took their oldest daughter, fifteen-year-old Melinda. That family lost four children in less than a month."

"What was it that killed them?" Kate asked, feeling sick at heart.

"It was diphtheria," the rider replied with a sad shake of his head, "and it would have killed even more of the Johnson children but they were attending school up in Kanab. That emigrant family didn't realize they needed to burn everything their daughter had worn or touched, and they never learned of the deadly sickness they'd left behind at Lonely Dell."

"That poor family!" Kate lamented.

"Yeah, their hearts were broken," the rider told them. "Mrs. Johnson looked dead in the eyes. Know what I mean?"

"I do," Kate said. "And as soon as possible, I'm going over there and see if there is anything I can do to help."

"I wouldn't," the rider warned. "You never know about diphtheria. Might still be hangin' around at Lonely Dell. I can tell you this, nobody is going to stop and take their meals with that family for a good long while. Especially anyone with kids."

This tragic news sank their spirits, but they drove over to Flagstaff anyway and arrived just as the first stagecoach out of town came barreling up San Francisco Street accompanied by the cheers and gunfire of a well-lubricated crowd. As the stage flew past, Dunn saw that the stageline had even jammed passengers onto the top of the big coach. They were all firing pistols and waving whiskey bottles.

"I sure wouldn't want to be on that run," Christopher said.

"Someone is bound to fall off and break his neck or get shot." Dunn waved as the stagecoach sped north, leaving a big rooster tail of dust hanging under the canopy of pines. "I'll bet that rowdy bunch drinks and raises hell all the way to the Grand Canyon."

"Captain Hance will know how to handle them," Kate predicted. "And I'll bet he's already preparing big kettles of rabbit stew and pans of sourdough biscuits."

"Kate! Bill! Where have you been!"

Dunn turned to see Mayor Bob Randall hurrying over with his hand outstretched.

"We were a little slow this time," Dunn said before he winked and added, "And dammit, Mayor, we probably missed all the best speeches."

"Mine included," Randall said, slapping Dunn heartily on the back. "Of course, I told our citizens that this occasion marked the beginning of a very special era. And I reminded everyone again what a prize it would be if Flagstaff—not Williams—could snag the spur line up to the Grand Canyon.

"Why, if we could win the spur, I think we'd rival Prescott, Williams, and Tucson all put together! We'd be the front runner to become the first capital of the great state of Arizona!"

"And you'd be sitting pretty for its first governor, I suppose," Dunn said with a wink.

"Ah!" the mayor scoffed. "You ought to be ashamed of yourself for being such a cynic. Dammit, Bill, this hasn't anything to do with personal gain or politics. This is about Flagstaff's *destiny!*"

"Our city will do just fine with or without that spur line," Dunn predicted. "But it sure wouldn't hurt. And we could use some good publicity after that Stanton survey fiasco."

"You bet we could," the mayor said, hailing someone else and then excusing himself before rushing away, hand outstretched again.

"He's still talking about Stanton after two years," Kate said.

"I know," Dunn replied. "It's as if he wants to keep the memory of it alive."

"I very much doubt that."

Dunn knew that she was right. The "Stanton fiasco" had been a harebrained idea hatched by Easterners to build a railroad between Denver and San Diego *via the Grand Canyon*. Everyone in Flagstaff had thought it a spoof until a chief engineer, named Robert Brewster Stanton, actually was hired to survey the interior of the Grand Canyon by the same means that Major Powell had used over twenty years before. The survey was abruptly terminated when three of the party's members, including the president of the newly formed Denver, Colorado Canyon, and Pacific Railroad Company, were tossed from their boats and drowned. Dunn remembered reading about the foolhardy expedition and the bold headlines proclaiming: THREE RAILROAD VISIONARIES DROWN IN THE DEVIL'S GRAND CANYON!

From what he'd heard, those same headlines had been used by newspapers and gazettes all over the country, much to the consternation of northern Arizona's land promoters and public officials.

"There are Cynthia and Alice," Kate said, waving. "Let's go over and say hello."

"Sure," Dunn said, noting the number of young men hovering around Cynthia and her lovely daughter.

"Aren't they something, though," Kate said a little wistfully as they worked their way through the boisterous Flagstaff crowd. "They both look as if they should be sipping mint juleps on the veranda of a Southern plantation."

"I agree," Dunn replied, noting how fine both women looked in their summer hats and long, matching orchid-colored dresses. And, even though Alice had the physical advantages of youth, her mother was still very easy on the eyes. Dunn couldn't imagine why someone in Flagstaff hadn't been able to win Cynthia's hand and heart.

"There you are!" Cynthia called, breaking away from the

circle and coming to greet them. "I was hoping you would bring Christopher to my house for refreshments. And don't tell me that you didn't get my invitation!"

"We're always late," Dunn said. "You know that. Alice looks wonderful. The East must be agreeing with her."

"Yes, she's having a splendid time in Boston, but she does miss Arizona. She is even talking about returning after she finishes school next year."

"That really surprises me," Kate admitted. "I would have thought, with all the young suitors and opportunities she has back East, she would have wanted to stay."

"Please don't say that," Cynthia told her, making a worried face. "I would miss Alice so! And besides, she confided to me that she finds most of the Ivy League boys a little . . . well, stuffy and not all that exciting."

Kate giggled. "And the next thing that you'll be telling me is that she is in love with Christopher."

"I don't know about that," Cynthia said, leaning forward so that she could not be overheard by everyone. "But I do know that she flirts with men she is not particularly interested in, yet seems indifferent to the ones she *is* interested in. Now you go and figure it."

"Chris is a little the same way," Kate admitted. "You should see the way he flirts with the Indian girls when we visit Havasu Canyon. He doesn't give them a minute's peace, but they all know better than to take him seriously."

"Don't be too sure of that," Dunn interjected. "Those Havasupai girls have a way of turning a man's head. Oops, there's my friend Wilbur, and I need to talk to him while you ladies discuss romance."

J. Wilbur Thurber was supposed to have been the driver of this first stagecoach, but he'd broken his arm a week earlier, so reluctantly had remained in town to manage the stageline of which he was part owner. He was about ten years younger than Dunn, of medium size, but a natural-born leader and organizer. In his younger days, Thurber had been a prospector in Montana, a Texas saddlemaker, and a mule skinner driving ore wagons back and forth between Reno and Nevada's famous Comstock Lode.

"How is the arm?" Dunn asked.

"It's mending," Thurber replied. "Did you see our first stagecoach leave town?"

"I sure did. It was packed! And at twenty dollars a head, I'd say we're off to a very profitable start."

"We sure are," Thurber agreed. "Of course, we won't always have a full coach, but for every man on that stagecoach, there were two more that wanted to make the historic first trip."

"Most of them are tourists returning in a few days, no doubt."

"There were all kinds," Thurber said, "but mostly just folks who always have wanted to see the Grand Canyon and finally decided to do it in grand style."

"I kind of wish that I was on that coach myself," Dunn said. "It looked like they were having quite a party."

"Yeah, and you can bet Captain Hance is going to put on a show for them. I expect he'll have plenty of food and spirits—all for sale at a very fat profit, of course."

"Of course!"

Thurber's left arm was in a sling, and Dunn noticed that he held it close across his stomach, probably to prevent some drunken miner, logger, or cowboy from giving him a very painful jostling.

"Oh," Thurber said, "I almost forgot to tell you. There was one fella on that stagecoach that I just couldn't figure. He's a friend of yours and Kate's."

"What was his name?"

"Damned if I can recall," Thurber replied. "You can imagine how crazy it was selling tickets at the stage office. But he said he was an old friend from Utah. Said he'd known Kate when she was young. Asked all about her—and you. I told him you'd probably be in town for this celebration, and he was watching for you both, but then he suddenly decided to get on the stage and go see the Grand Canyon."

"Humph, how old was he?"

"About your age. Maybe a few years younger. Big, tough-looking man. Had a companion just as rough-looking but quite a bit younger. I didn't much care for the looks of either of them, but they had cash and seemed real happy to learn about you and your ranch. Didn't even know where it was located until I told them."

Dunn's palms suddenly went cold and clammy.

Thurber clucked his tongue and said, "Now I remember—the young one called your old friend—Monty."

"Holy Jesus," Dunn whispered.

"What's wrong! You look like you've just stepped in your own grave."

"Maybe I have," Dunn said before spinning around and hurrying away.

Dunn found Christopher with Alice and pulled his son aside to tell him about Kate being in mortal danger. Chris excused himself, and they began to usher Kate out of Cynthia's busy dress shop.

"What is wrong with you two!" Cynthia demanded.

"It's Kate's ex-husband," Dunn explained. "The one she testified against years ago and sent to prison. He's back to even the score."

"Then find the marshal and have the lunatic arrested."

"On what grounds?" Kate asked as she climbed into their buckboard. "Monty is smart. He'll play the law-abiding citizen until it's time for him to ambush one of us. So what could the marshal do to stop him before it's too late?"

"I don't know. But there must be *something* that can be done. Your life is in danger, Kate. You could take the next train to Albuquerque, or on to California. It'll be coming through tomorrow. We could . . ."

"Absolutely not! We're family. I'm staying and we're finishing this once and for all. No more worrying. I'm *glad* Monty is here for a showdown. I wish he'd come years ago. If he had, I'd either be dead or I'd be a lot happier than I am now."

When Alice rushed up, Christopher told her about his mother's former husband and the man's threat to exact revenge.

Alice surprised them all when she replied, "I think you should find and kill him. And that other one, too."

"Alice!"

"That's the way I feel," she told her mother. "Otherwise, those men will probably ambush and murder Kate, Chris, and Mr. Dunn."

Christopher slipped his arm around Alice's waist, pulled her close, and kissed her lips.

"Christopher!" she protested. "What did you do that for!"

"In case I *am* killed," he answered, "I needed to remember the sweet taste of your lips."

Alice's pretty face crumpled and she hugged Christopher's neck and sniffled, trying to hold back tears.

"This isn't helping anything," Dunn said, taking Kate's arm and assisting her into the wagon. "Let's get back to the ranch. As long as we don't do anything stupid, we'll be safe at the house."

Kate jumped up in the wagon and Chris disengaged himself from Alice and ran for his horse. Dunn took his seat and gathered the lines.

"There must be *something* we can do to help!" Cynthia exclaimed.

"There is," Kate said, looking far older than she had only a few hours before. "Pray for us!"

When they arrived back at Lonesome Valley Ranch, Dunn gathered the few men who had not gone out to start the spring roundup and explained the threat. Lucio and Juan were no longer young men, but they were steady with a gun and agreed that the best thing to do was to ride over to Captain Hance's Hotel and have a showdown.

"I'm coming with you," Chris said.

"We'd like to come, too," Juan said, looking to his brother and getting a solemn nod of agreement.

"In addition to the Indian ranch hands, at least one of us must remain in the house with Kate," Dunn told them.

Christopher stared at the Ortiz brothers, maybe expecting them to volunteer. But they didn't, and so it was left to Dunn to say, "Chris, I want you to stay and help protect your mother. After all, she's the one they're *really* after."

"But . . ."

"I can't make you," Dunn said quietly, "but I'm asking you to please stay here at the ranch with Kate."

Chris turned away for a moment and Dunn noted the tension in his shoulders and felt the tremendous struggle that was going on inside the young man. But, finally, Chris turned back and nodded his head, saying, "You're right. I'm the most likely choice."

"Thanks. And remember, I'll have the element of surprise when we reach Captain Hance's Hotel because they don't even know what I look like."

"But they'll guess when you, Juan, and Lucio come galloping in from the west."

"Then we'll circle around and come from Flagstaff," Dunn decided. "Or even come in from the east along the rim."

"And old Captain Hance will call out your name the moment he sets eyes on you."

"Nothing is guaranteed," Dunn said. "Your job is to keep Kate in the house until we return and tell you that she has nothing more to worry about. Is that understood?"

Chris dipped his chin in acknowledgment.

"All right then," Dunn said, looking to his old friends and mesteneros, "let's get this over with."

He didn't even say good-bye to Kate but instead left on the run, knowing she would try to go with him. They rode all night and approached the hotel when the sun was well off the horizon. As expected, the stagecoach was still in the ranch yard and the stage horses corralled, resting for their return trip to Flagstaff.

"How do we do this?" Lucio asked.

"You two ride in and pull Captain Hance aside. Ask him to point out the pair we're interested in. Then ride back here and we can decide how to handle this without getting anyone else hurt."

The vaqueros quickly rode off. When they reached the hotel, they dismounted and tied their fine horses to the captain's hitching rail. They sauntered into the hotel but reappeared a few minutes later and came galloping back to Dunn.

"Did you see them?"

"They're gone, Señor Dunn! They stole money and horses yesterday and rode off in a big hurry."

"Oh my God!" Dunn whispered, jumping for his own horse, "they've slipped past us on their way to Lonesome Valley!"

Kate heard the howl of coyotes just before midnight. She lay half-asleep with a loaded six-gun resting under her pillow, willing to bet that a very anxious Christopher was still wide-awake in the parlor, likely braiding a pair of rawhide reins or a beautiful bridle. He might even have lugged in one of the many old stock saddles that he was constantly repairing for their crew. J. Wilbur Thurber had gotten Christopher interested in saddlemaking several years ago, and the boy had quickly exceeded the skills of his tutor and begun to study leatherwork from the best men he could find in Flagstaff.

Kate must have fallen back asleep because the very next thing she knew, she heard gunfire coming from the front of the house and then her door crashed open.

"Hello, Katie darlin'!"

Monty Ford stood, framed by the glow from the hallway

lamp, filling the doorway. Even as Kate tried to gather her wits, she heard another thundering volley of gunfire.

"Christopher!" she screamed.

"I'm sure he's dead," Monty announced, striding into the room. "Was he your only son, Kate? The son *we* always talked about?"

Kate's hand stabbed under her pillow and dragged out the pistol. Monty jumped back into the hallway as Kate fired into the open doorway. She climbed to her feet, still firing as she burst into the hallway, thinking that Monty had run for cover.

Instead, he was waiting—just as he'd been waiting all those years in prison. Kate tried to swing her smoking pistol around to line up on his broad chest, but his rifle boomed and she felt herself lifted and then hurled backward to land and skid across the hallway carpet.

"Dammit, Katie," he said, tromping forward to gaze into her eyes, "I was hoping we could have us a real good time before I finally had to kill you."

Kate tried to curse. Failing that, she twitched her fingers to locate the pistol which had spilled from her hand. She heard more gunfire from inside the house and struggled to sit up.

"Christopher!" she gasped as Monty spun around and fired back down the hallway.

Just as her vision went blank, she saw Christopher pitch forward and then felt the floor shake beneath her.

Christopher awoke when the big man dragged him to his feet and down the hallway into Kate's bedroom, then slammed him down into a chair. His chest was tightly bound with a bloody bandage and the sun was well up, their ranch yard drenched with bright morning sunlight.

"You tell your men that if they rush the house, I'll kill you!" Monty raged. "You tell 'em I want two fast horses and two pair of empty saddlebags and that, if anyone tries to stop me when I come out, I'll kill you, then I'll kill all of them!"

Chris couldn't focus. He was weak from the loss of blood and in danger of losing consciousness. Suddenly, the window shattered and Monty was bellowing into the ranch yard.

"The kid wants to talk to you!" Monty dragged Chris up to the window and held him erect, face pressed to the shattered opening. "Tell 'em what I said!"

He told the men, somehow. Told that he was shot. That Kate was dead. Then, struggling to break from Ford, he screamed, "Shoot! Don't let him . . ."

Out of the corner of his eye, Chris saw the shadow of Monty's gun barrel descending an instant before he spun back into total darkness.

Dunn and his vaqueros galloped back into the ranch yard only to have the few remaining ranch hands leap from cover to drag their winded mounts into the deepest shadows.

Dunn listened carefully as both Hualapai and Havasupai Indians explained the night's events. How the two killers had murdered one of them and then managed to enter the ranch house. And how Christopher had spoken from Kate's window and then had abruptly been silenced.

"Are they both dead?"

The Indians didn't know.

"Dunn!"

The shout came from his house and Dunn twisted around, hand slapping for his gun. "Yeah?"

"Your son is alive. I found your office safe, but I can't find the damned combination. I want all your money!"

"What happened to Kate!"

"She tried to kill me. I had to kill her instead."

Dunn covered his face and rocked back and forth on the balls of his feet as waves of grief washed over him.

"If you want your son to live, you'll do as I say! Come in unarmed. Open the safe and I'll let you *and* the boy live—if you let me get away!"

Dunn choked back his tears. He felt Lucio's steadying hand on his shoulder, heard the vaquero's whisper. "My brother and I will sneak around to the back of the house and shoot him through your office window, Señor."

"Good," Dunn said, taking several deep breaths. "Just don't let that man go free! Comprende?"

"Sí." The brothers slipped away into the darkness and Dunn knew that they would separate, circling in opposite directions around the house. They knew the interior layout, knew that his office was located on the east end and that it had windows that would afford them a clear line of fire.

"Dunn!" Monty Ford bellowed.

"Yeah?"

"Are you coming or does the kid die with me!"

"I'm coming!"

Dunn started across his ranch yard. When he was within thirty feet of the front door, Ford called, "Hold it! Unbuckle that gun belt!"

Dunn did as he was ordered.

"Now take off your coat, then your shirt. No tricks. Not if you want the kid back alive."

Dunn removed his light canvas jacket, then his shirt and tossed them away. He wasn't carrying a concealed gun but that old Spanish dagger was resting inside his boot top. He prayed that Lucio or Juan would be able to kill Monty Ford with a clean shot through a window and that he wouldn't have to make a grab for the dagger.

"Come on ahead!"

Dunn continued forward. His legs felt like rubber; his breathing was light and rapid. He didn't know if Kate was really dead or not, but he did believe that Chris was still alive. Without Chris, Ford was a walking corpse—he had to realize that he'd never leave the house alive.

"Come on inside, and let's see what kind of a man my dear Katie threw me over for!"

Dunn climbed the steps of the veranda and went through

the doorway. He halted, searching for the man who had haunted Kate all these years and then had fulfilled her worst nightmare.

"Over here," Ford said, emerging from the shadows with a pistol clenched in his big hand.

His hair was shoulder-length and streaked with silver. His face was very pale with few lines, but Dunn didn't notice that as much as he did his eyes, which were black, deep-set, and closely spaced. His nose had been broken and was badly off center. He wore silver Navajo jewelry and a bowie knife strapped around his narrow waist. His jaw was square and he was still quite handsome in a dark and twisted way. But, to Dunn, Monty Ford most nearly resembled a feral animal, one cornered and ready to rip out an enemy's heart, or throat.

"Sorry we had to meet under such sad conditions," Ford said in a dry, rattling voice. "Just raise your hands and start moving toward the study. Once I get the money, we'll walk back out—you in front. We'll lead the horses into the shadows, and I'll leave you there to mourn poor Kate's death."

"You'll kill me just like you killed her," Dunn choked with bitterness and anger.

"Now, now," Ford said, smiling. "Just keep remembering that your son is still alive."

"I'll see him before I open my safe."

"No!"

"Then shoot me," Dunn said, lowering his hands, knowing that the man couldn't afford to do that and have any chance of escape.

"All right," Ford agreed. "He's been roughed up a bit, but he's going to survive—if you don't try to become a hero."

When Dunn entered the hallway, he suddenly pulled up and had to lean against the wall as he stared at Kate's bloodstained, pale, and lifeless body. Tears sprang to his eyes and he twisted around, insane with rage and ready to attack Ford.

But the man had anticipated this and was smart enough to say, "Take a look at the boy! Check his pulse. He's unconscious, but alive. As you can see, I've even bandaged his wounds so he wouldn't bleed to death."

Dunn reached for his son's pulse. It *was* there, but Chris was in rough shape.

"Now then," Ford said, "let's get that safe opened. I'd like to put some miles between myself and this ranch before daylight."

"You'll never make it."

"I will if you value the kid's life. Maybe he's worth saving. After all, he managed to kill my friend, Harvey, who wasn't half-bad with a gun though he was reckless."

Dunn remembered the dagger. What better time than now while his hand was so close to his boot top? Leaning over Chris as if to inspect his wounds, Dunn slipped his hand down his leg, tugging up his pants just enough to reach into his boot top and clench the old Spanish dagger.

"Come on, come on!" Ford snapped impatiently.

Dunn bent his wrist so that the blade pressed against the inside of his forearm. Had the light been good, Ford would have seen the long, double-edged weapon.

"Let's go!" Ford shouted, stepping back into the hallway so Dunn could move past.

At that moment, Dunn pivoted sharply, then drove his blade upward, impaling Ford as he slammed the man against the wall.

"Ahhh!" Ford screamed, clawing at Dunn's eyes and trying to raise his pistol.

A shot exploded between them, causing blood to well up through Dunn's boot, but he kept ripping upward with his blade until it came to rest under Monty Ford's sternum.

"May you roast in hell!" Dunn shouted, lifting Ford up on his toes. Dunn staggered back, leaving the dagger embedded in Ford's chest. The killer's pistol spilled from his lifeless hands and clattered to the hardwood floor. The outlaw slid down the wall like a clod of mud. Dunn reeled around and hobbled back to his son, scooped him up, and somehow carried him into the parlor, laying him on a couch.

"Juan, Lucio!" he called frantically.

The vaqueros burst in through the back door. Dunn heard the pounding of their boots as they charged through the house.

"Vaqueros!" Dunn yelled, his voice thin and strained. "Relay horses into Flagstaff and bring back a doctor. And the marshal, too!"

Juan and Lucio took one good look at Christopher and ran out the front door to saddle fresh horses. Dunn knew that they would reach Flagstaff in record time and that a doctor could be expected back in less than twenty-four hours.

What he *didn't* know was if his son had that much time.

Twenty-eight

Lonesome Valley Ranch, 1901

Dunn sat bent before an enormous rolltop desk, toying with his ink pen and struggling to begin a long-overdue letter to Alice. There had been a time when words had come easily to him, when he'd even thought of himself as a writer. But now, after years of ranching and working outdoors, his fingers were thick and his mind was far from nimble.

His eyes came to rest on an ancient split-twig figurine. Pen slipping from his hand, he reached out to grasp the ancient artifact, remembering how precious it had once been to Kate. Dunn sighed deeply. For several years after her murder, he had wanted to shut himself off from the rest of the world. He had even rebuilt the professor's old cabin and lived as a hermit for a time on the edge of the South Rim and might have stayed there indefinitely, had it not been for Cynthia. She had come often to visit, usually staying for several days before she needed to return to the dress shop in Flagstaff. Cynthia had been his salvation—then, and now. They had been married five years ago, and that was when he had regained his spirits.

But there were still times in this ranch house, times like right now, when Dunn keenly felt the aura of Kate's quiet strength and presence. Without her, he knew he would never have accomplished so much in his lifetime.

Dunn could hear his wife moving about the house, readying

for their trip to Grand Canyon Village. He had promised Cynthia he would write a letter to Alice and post it at the Grand Canyon. And so, gently returning the split-twig figurine back to its privileged notch in his desk and forcing his thoughts back from Kate and the past, Dunn began to write.

My Dear Alice:

    I join your mother in hearty congratulations on the birth of your son, Michael and agree that you should take this next school year off from teaching. It is also good to learn that your husband's Boston law firm continues to prosper.

    Cynthia and I are about to attend another of Arizona's historic events—the arrival of the first train at the Grand Canyon. It will have an enormous and long-lasting effect on the economy of northern Arizona as more and more tourists arrive. Of course, we were very disappointed that Flagstaff didn't win the spur line, but Williams is about twenty miles closer to Bright Angel and that was the critical factor. At any rate, as Senior County Supervisor, I have been asked to be present when the first railroad arrives, but I have already told our Governor that I will not make a speech. There will be enough long-winded Arizona politicians as well as Santa Fe and Grand Canyon Railway Company officials present to fill the entire Grand Canyon with hot air.

    Your mother and I are extremely happy living in Flagstaff. We visit the ranch every few months but, since advancing years prohibit me from mustanging or even being very useful on the roundups and cattle drives, I devote my remaining energies to the administration of Coconino County. I recently had the great privilege of meeting and hearing a very well known wilderness preservationist named John Muir, who spoke eloquently about his struggle to save Yosemite from private exploitation. He has captured the ear of President Theodore Roosevelt and as-

sured me that the President will declare not only Yosemite, but also the Grand Canyon, national parks before he leaves office. I am going to do all that I can to see that this becomes a reality. You would not believe all the miners, schemers, and outright thieves that are swarming around attempting to exploit the canyon.

You asked if Christopher has ever found a woman that he could marry. I'm afraid not. He has completely taken over the operation of our ranch and works extremely hard. As you know, he loves the ranching life and especially working with horses, the Indians and the vaqueros. His bullet wound can plague him at times, as mine does when I am on my feet too much, but we both manage reasonably well. I cannot believe that my son will soon be thirty years old and that I am on the sundown side of my sixties. Where did all the years go?

I know that you remember that old character—Captain John Hance—who once led us down into the Grand Canyon on his surefooted mules. Well, he sold his ranch and hotel to my friend, J. Wilbur Thurber, whose stageline was no longer needed with the completion of this railroad spur up to the rim. Wilbur has greatly expanded and renamed the Captain's old guest ranch Bright Angel Hotel, located in the new Grand Canyon Village.

Don't fret about Captain Hance. Our favorite story-teller is now the Grand Canyon's first postmaster and entertains visitors with his incredible yarns—which some people actually believe! Alice, do you remember the one Captain Hance told us long ago about him snowshoe-walking on clouds? It still makes me laugh.

I will soon post this letter with Captain Hance, and your mother and I are very much looking forward to seeing the Grand Canyon's first train arrive. We expect thousands to attend the celebration. There will be a dance, lots of food, beer, and many other activities. Chris informs

*me that there will also be horse racing, which always
draws a big, betting crowd.*

*Well, there is not much left for me to say. My health
remains excellent and I keep very busy. Your mother is
enjoying her retirement and keeps prodding me to cut
back on investments and civic works. At this point in my
life, the only thing that I feel I have been unable to accomplish is to rectify the injustices done to the Havasupai
and Hualapai whose lands still have not been restored.
We very much look forward to having you and your family
as our guests in the years to come. We have many extra
bedrooms in our Flagstaff house as well as out at the
ranch. Give our best regards to your husband and we
wish him continued success.*

Sincerely, Bill

The following day as they neared Grand Canyon Village,
Cynthia exclaimed, "I'm certainly glad that we have rooms
reserved at Bright Angel Lodge. Just look at all the people!"

"Good thing the weather is so nice," Dunn commented. "I
expect that many of the people who arrive on the train will
spill over to the Grandview Hotel at Grandview Point."

"I hope so," Cynthia replied.

"Me, too. Pete and Martha Berry are in for a tough fight
to draw tourists to their place. It's only eleven miles away and
has a spectacular view, but most tourists won't invest the added
time and expense to drive to Grandview unless Bright Angel
is booked solid."

As their carriage drew closer to the new railroad depot,
Dunn saw Christopher galloping out to meet them.

"You're just in time for the first horse race!" he called.

"And no doubt you have already placed bets on it," Dunn
said, not bothering to mask his disapproval.

"Don't worry," Christopher assured him. "I bet only a hundred dollars on the sorrel Thoroughbred from Texas. I feel

obligated to make up for the fact that you *never* bet—even on a sure thing."

"Whose horses are running?" Cynthia asked.

"A Morgan-mustang called Miss Viper out of Santa Fe. She's quite an animal, but I can't imagine her beating the Thoroughbred."

"Where are they racing?"

"A half mile out to circle that lone ponderosa pine, then back across the start and finish line beside the new railroad depot." Dunn saw the two contestants being led to the starting line. It did indeed appear to be a mismatch. The Thoroughbred towered over a short-coupled but very powerful black mare. Dunn could see that both animals were being ridden bareback.

Several whooping and bottle-waving cowboys galloped out just beyond the ponderosa pine to watch the race horses make the turn while the crowd began to form a V-shaped funnel out from the dual start and finish line.

"Go ahead and get a closer view, Chris, we can see it all just fine from here," Dunn told his son.

"All right. See you later!"

He rode back toward the starting line just as the gun fired and the two race horses bolted forward. Chris loved a good horse race. And, if he hadn't filled out to an even two-hundred-pounder, he'd have entered the contest with one of his own fast ponies. But he was too big and heavy to be a jockey, and so he just watched and admired the horses and the skill of their lean, sinewy riders.

The crowd was cheering wildly as Miss Viper shot into an early lead, but it was a lead that the crossbred mare could not hold as the Thoroughbred's long stride steadily closed the gap. The two horses each rounded the pine, but the Santa Fe mare had more agility and the inside track. Like a cow pony, it leaned into the corner with its rider low and tight on its back, then burst into a four-length lead and sprinted back toward the depot and the cheering crowd.

Chris shouted for the faster but much less nimble Thoroughbred to close the gap, but the footing was soft and sandy and the Thoroughbred was losing steam.

"Come on!" Chris shouted. "Run!"

Miss Viper was totally focused on the finish line with her ears flattened back and her tail whipping 'round and 'round. Chris saw fire in her eyes, as well as those of her expert rider, who was clinging to her neck.

"Damn," Chris swore, realizing that the Thoroughbred could not possibly overtake the smaller, gamer mare, who entered the human funnel streaking toward the finish line.

Suddenly, two cowboys standing at the edge of the crowd grabbed a pair of chickens out of burlap sacks and pitched them directly into Miss Viper's path. The squawking, flapping chickens flew directly under the Santa Fe mare, causing her to veer sharply, hurling her jockey to the ground. Miss Viper raced west along the rim. A few seconds later, the heavily favored but badly beaten Thoroughbred crossed the finish line.

Gray-faced with anger at the foul trick he'd just witnessed, Christopher rode over to the fallen jockey and vaulted off his horse. "Kid, are you hurt!"

The rider was lying facedown, groaning. Christopher gently rolled him over, then drew in a sharp breath. "My God, you're a girl!"

"My horse," she said in a dazed voice. "Where did my mare go?"

The girl's cap had been knocked loose to reveal a thick pile of auburn-colored hair. She was about five-foot-five and so boyishly slender that she couldn't have weighed much over a hundred pounds. It was clear she was trying to hide the fact that she was in a great deal of pain.

A man hurried up to join them shouting, "Move aside, I'm a doctor! Young woman, can you move your toes and your fingers?"

"Yes."

"Thank heaven!" The doctor glared back toward the finish line. "Tossing those chickens under your mare was an outrageous tactic! This girl is lucky not to have broken her neck!"

"I know," Christopher growled, eyes searching the crowd for the two guilty cowboys. "And as far as I'm concerned, that Santa Fe mare won."

Now, he saw the two cowboys heading for the beer keg, arms draped over each other's shoulders, both laughing like mad. Christopher glanced once more down at the girl. She was pale and bleeding. Silent tears were streaking the dust on her cheeks. She was tough and she was pretty—or had been until her nasty spill.

"Doc, is she going to be all right?"

"It's immediately obvious that she's broken her left arm and a few ribs. She definitely has a concussion."

Christopher marched over to his horse and swung into his saddle. He took up his reata and shook out a big loop, then drummed his heels against his horse's flanks and went after the offending pair of cowboys. The crowd saw the look on his face and the menacing rawhide reata whirring over his head. They parted as Christopher's reata snaked out and dropped over the cowboys. In one swift, practiced motion, Christopher dallied his rope and reined his horse into a sliding turn, then sent it racing back toward that solitary ponderosa pine. He heard his reata snap like a whip and felt a violent wrench as the laughing cowboys were yanked completely off their feet.

"Yah! Yah!" he shouted, forcing his cow horse to dig hard as it dragged both men away, twisting, screaming, and cursing.

Christopher hauled the struggling pair right on past the doctor and the girl, past the gawking spectators and halfway out to the ponderosa pine, before he figured he might kill them if he didn't rein in his puffing horse.

The cowboys were tangled and scraped. They also were

madder than teased snakes. Christopher didn't care. He bailed
off his horse and waded in, fists pumping hard and fast. He
had the advantage of surprise and outrage, and the fact that
his horse was still backing up and keeping the reata taut so
that the pair's arms were locked helplessly at their sides. Christopher hit them each several times in the face, breaking one
man's nose, opening a deep gash over his companion's eye.
He might even have booted them for good measure if his father
hadn't jumped out of his carriage and interfered by grabbing
him around the waist.

"Chris! That's enough! They're finished!"

Christopher was shaking with fury. The cowboys were down
and making no effort to get up and fight, even after he released
them.

"You *lost* your bets!" Christopher shouted. "All of us did
who bet on the Thoroughbred."

The cowboy with the big gash in his eyebrow blinked. "Did
you bet on the Thoroughbred, too?"

"Damn right! I lost a hundred dollars!"

"Well, we only lost ten each, so I guess we deserved a
whipping."

"That was a *girl* riding the Santa Fe mare and, thanks to
you boys, she's hurt pretty bad."

"A girl!"

"That's right."

The man wiped blood from his eye. "We didn't know *that*.
Honest!"

Christopher unclenched his fists and shook his head in dis-
gust. "That was just a damn foolish thing to do. Some of the
spectators could have been trampled as well."

"We're real sorry."

"Don't you *ever* come looking for a job at Lonesome Valley
Ranch! And don't you ever set foot on our range, either!"

He coiled the reata, draped it over his saddlehorn, and remounted. Then, not waiting for his father and stepmother, Chris-

topher galloped back to the starting line, where he climbed up on a wagon.

"The Santa Fe mare won the race!" he shouted. "We all saw that. I lost money, too, but we don't cheat in Arizona, and we don't do fool things to hurt women!"

There was some grousing from the spectators who'd lost money, but not much. Everyone knew that Christopher was right. The debts were collected and the hat passed around for the girl's medical bills.

"Where is your husband?" Christopher asked when he returned to the injured young woman.

"I don't have one."

"A friend, then. Or family."

"It's just me and my mare. Where is *she!*"

"I'll find her," Christopher promised. "Don't worry."

The doctor had finished his hasty examination. "I need to reset and then splint her arm before there is any more swelling, but I sure don't want to do that out here in the dirt. Young lady, where are you staying?"

She clenched her teeth. "Doc, I've been hurt worse than this before. Bandage me up and get me to my horse."

"You can't ride! Not with broken ribs."

"Just watch me," she gritted, pushing to her feet. But after two faltering steps, her legs buckled.

Christopher caught and then carried her to his father's wagon. "You're going to have to listen to the doctor," he said. "I've had broken bones after being pitched from broncs, and I know how bad you hurt and that you can do even more harm by moving around."

"How many bones have you had broke?"

"More'n I can remember," Christopher said. "Now, just stretch on out in the wagon."

"Where'd you ever learn to rope like a vaquero?"

"Long story."

"I'd like to hear it sometime."

"Just close your eyes and we'll get you to the hotel," Christopher told her. "I'll go find Miss Viper."

"I appreciate that. She's all I got."

"Don't worry. I'll bring her back."

Christopher remounted and galloped west to search for the Santa Fe mare while Dunn and Cynthia prepared to drive the injured girl and the doctor to the hotel.

"Mister?"

Dunn realized she was speaking to him. "Yeah?"

"Is he *really* your son?"

"He is," Dunn replied, proud enough to bust his buttons.

"He married yet?"

"Nope."

"What's his name?"

"Christopher. Christopher Dunn."

"My name is Miss Ginger Kelly."

Cynthia drew a silk handkerchief from her purse. "Ginger," she said, "we've got to get you taken care of, so just lie down and rest easy while we drive to the hotel."

"I must look pretty horrible, huh?"

"Not good," Cynthia admitted.

"That's why he didn't give me a second glance," Ginger said. "But when I feel better and fix myself up a little, I'll bet anything your Christopher will give me *more* than a second glance."

"Yeah," Dunn said, thinking how much this girl reminded him of Kate with her grit, spunk, and determination, "I kind of expect that he will."

Christopher did not return to Lonesome Valley Ranch the next day as intended. Or the next or even the next, because he felt a powerful attraction to Ginger Kelly. There was no question that this wild young woman knew as much about horses as he did, and there was a mystery about Ginger that made him want to learn everything he could about her unusual past.

"My mother and father both died in west Texas," Ginger explained one afternoon as they lazily sunned themselves on the expansive porch of Bright Angel Lodge. "They were pioneer ranchers and friends of the local Comanche, who taught me everything I know about horses and mustanging. The Comanche can ride better than anybody in the world."

Christopher couldn't let that remark pass. "Not as well as the vaqueros . . . or me."

"You don't know that! Comanche can stick to a racing horse tighter than whitewash on a church."

"But you've never even seen me or a Mexican vaquero ride, rope, or catch mustangs. And I'm damned sure that no Comanche Indian ever learned to handle a sixty-foot reata. Why, I can almost rope a bird on the wing!"

"Well aren't you just the amazing one!" Ginger scoffed. "All rich and full of yourself."

Christopher started to jump out of his rocking chair and angrily stomp away, but Ginger reached out and touched his arm, freezing him.

"I'm sorry," she apologized. "Money has nothing to do with the way you stood up and protected me after that horse race. Tossing those poor chickens was a mean and sneaky trick."

"I'd have beaten both of those fool cowboys to a pulp if they hadn't apologized."

"They were probably just drunk," Kate said, studying him closely. "At least you bet on the right horse and won money for all your trouble."

"No," Christopher sheepishly confessed, "I did not."

"You bet *against* me!"

"Yep. Just like most everyone else."

Ginger cast him a stern and a skeptical eye. "Then maybe you aren't such a good judge of horseflesh as you think. My mare has an uncommonly good conformation. I'm surprised that such an expert horseman as you judge yourself missed that entirely."

"I didn't miss anything," Christopher grated. "And the Thoroughbred was purely faster! He just couldn't make a decent turn to get around that big ponderosa. That's where you really won the race."

"Nope," Ginger said, "I just made it all *look* like that's how Miss Viper beat that Thoroughbred. The fact of the matter is, if I hadn't gotten hurt, I'd have let them talk me into another race on a straight track and we'd *still* have beat 'em——then I'd really have won tall dollars."

"You're mighty cocksure of yourself, Miss Kelly."

"And so are you!" Ginger's voice softened. "But I like that. My father was always sure of himself. As best I can remember, he only made one mistake, but it cost him and Mother their lives."

"What do you mean?"

"He mistook some raiding Kiowa for our friends the Comanche," Ginger said quietly, her eyes becoming moist. "He and my mother were . . ."

Ginger couldn't finish and twisted away to hide the tears.

"I'm sorry." Christopher took her hand. "I lost my real mother when I was a cradle-board babe. And now I've lost Kate, who raised me like a son. So I know about how you must feel."

Ginger drew a deep breath. "Tell me how you go about mustanging in this Arizona country."

Christopher spent an hour telling her. When he was finished, he leaned back, folded his arms, and asked Ginger what she thought about his and the vaqueros' methods.

"We do a lot of it the same way, but you didn't mention anything about 'horse hopping.' "

"What?"

"Horse hopping," Ginger repeated. "Down in Texas, the Comanche taught me how to overtake a racing mustang and make a flying jump onto its back. Then how to use a short piece of rawhide to finally bring it under control."

When Christopher gawked at her, Ginger said, "I guess you don't do that in this part of the country, huh?"

"It's crazy!"

"No, it's exciting," Ginger told him. "Especially if you miss the hop."

"If you've been doing something *that* foolish, I'm amazed you didn't break your neck years ago."

"I could teach you when I heal."

"No thanks!" Christopher shook his head knowing that Ginger wasn't fooling. "I'd rather teach you how to rope like a vaquero. It's a lot safer."

"You don't strike me as someone much worried about being safe."

Christopher didn't know how to respond, so he just took Ginger's callused hand and rocked a little faster.

"Have I embarrassed you?"

"No."

"Good," she said, "because what I really know is that you are brave and honorable."

When he blushed, she made things even worse by adding, "And on top of all that, you're a handsome devil."

Christopher's cheeks burned and he went tongue-tied until Ginger started to giggle. Then he got to laughing, too.

After that, Christopher said no more about himself and the vaqueros. But two weeks later when Ginger was fit to ride in a buggy, he took the Texas girl to Lonesome Valley Ranch and gave her the run of the house. Concerned with her reputation, he provided her with a personal maid and chaperone in the form of a Havasupai woman who didn't tolerate any silliness or impropriety—even from her young employer.

With autumn turning the cottonwoods gold, Christopher began to teach Ginger how to handle a reata. It was great fun, and he'd never seen anyone learn so fast. On the very same day that Ginger roped him, using a nifty overhand toss that made him proud, they galloped off to Flagstaff to get married.

It made Cynthia and his father as well as the Havasupai woman very happy. It also made excellent sense because now they could burrow in tight for a long and happy canyon country winter and make exciting plans to go mustanging early next spring.

Twenty-nine

In celebration of his seventieth birthday, William and Cynthia had their pictures taken by the Kolb brothers at their new photography studio in Grand Canyon Village and then spent a few leisure days at the magnificent El Tovar Hotel, which had opened eighteen months earlier in January 1905. The hotel had been built at the insistence of the railroad, which desired first-class accommodations for its tourist passengers. The nearby Bright Angel Hotel was still popular, although it offered much more modest rooms at only seventy-five cents a day. Both South Rim establishments were successfully managed by the Fred Harvey Company, which ran all the hotels and restaurants along the Santa Fe Railroad lines.

Dunn had actually met Mr. Harvey in 1900, one year before his death. The ambitious and visionary English immigrant had amassed a fortune civilizing frontier travel along the Santa Fe line. Dunn judged the Englishman gracious and in possession of an extraordinary gift for organization.

The El Tovar, with one hundred rooms and an architecture that combined the impressive characteristics of a Swiss château with those of a German castle on the Rhine, was the pride of northern Arizona. The hotel was serviced completely by electric lights powered by a generator, while all the water for the huge resort, as well as for the rest of Grand Canyon Village, was hauled in by the Santa Fe Railroad.

Especially pleasing to Dunn, and others who had feared that a big hotel would mar the canyon rim's esthetics, was the fact that the El Tovar seemed to "belong." This was not due only to its appealing architectural design, but also to the generous use of native boulders and massive pines. Constructed at the unprecedented cost of over a quarter of a million dollars, the El Tovar rivaled anything in the West. It had a splendid dining room, where visitors could order everything from sea food to prime cuts of Lonesome Valley Ranch beef. Fresh fruits and vegetables were grown in the hotel's greenhouse, while its fresh milk and eggs were supplied by the El Tovar's henhouse and quality dairy herd.

After a sumptuous dinner with a wine list that would do honor to any hotel in San Francisco or New York City, the El Tovar's pampered guests could relax in a cavernous lobby, read a New York or even a London newspaper, enjoy the talents of musicians and artists, or retire to the Club Room, Solarium, Grotto, or sunny roof gardens with their inspiring views. Best of all, Captain Hance had been offered a full-time position as local historian and storyteller, drawing large and appreciative crowds.

Near the hotel, visitors could stroll through a replica of an Indian pueblo, called the Hopi House. It was here that Navajo and Hopi Indians were encouraged to practice and demonstrate their tribal crafts, put on traditional dances, and wear their native costumes for the throngs of Grand Canyon tourists.

"Why don't we just come over here and live year-round?" Cynthia suggested, only half in jest, after a lovely evening of dining and then dancing. "Wouldn't you like that, my dear?"

"It would get a little expensive."

"We could afford it," Cynthia assured him. "Anyway, the winters would be milder here than in Flagstaff, wouldn't they?"

"Yes, but the ranch is only . . ."

"Just give it some thought," Cynthia said. "Perhaps we could stay at the El Tovar a few months each winter, enjoying the views and their immense fireplace. We could sip brandy and have a marvelous time meeting interesting tourists from all over the world."

"With a sales pitch like that," Dunn drawled, "you ought to be getting *paid* by the El Tovar."

"Not unless you agree to work beside me. After all the years we were apart, I'm never again going to let you out of my sight."

Dunn squeezed his wife's hand. He felt as if his life had been unusually blessed. Christopher had married Ginger and had given him a grandson and a granddaughter who now were the apples of his eye.

"I tell you what I would like to do," Dunn confessed. "Instead of going back to Flagstaff after we leave, I'd enjoy taking you over to the North Rim and showing you Jacob Lake and the Kaibab Plateau. As you know, it was just made a national game preserve, and I haven't seen it for over forty years, but still remember the cool, sweet smell of the pines. I know you'd love the alpine meadows and the views off Cape Royal and Walhalla Point."

"Can you spare the time away from your county work?"

"Don't worry, they'll get along without me. In a few more years, I'll retire from all of that."

"To do what?"

"I dunno," he said with a shrug. "Maybe come over here and tell stories like Captain Hance."

"But, darling, you're a terrible storyteller!"

"And to think I once considered making my mark as a writer."

"When you were with Major Powell and wrote me all those love letters that you never sent?"

"That's right."

Cynthia hugged him tightly. "You can still write me love letters anytime, but I want them so passionate that no one would ever dare put them in print."

Dunn got another chuckle out of that, and then they went about planning on how best to see the Kaibab Plateau.

* * *

On a bright morning in early October, Dunn and Cynthia departed from Lonesome Valley Ranch in a wagon filled with food, a big canvas tent, and camping gear. They headed east toward Lee's Ferry, with Dunn wondering if anything remained of Lonely Dell.

Cynthia had never seen the Little Colorado Gorge and was amazed by its depth. "It's very impressive," she remarked as Dunn drove the wagon down into the canyon where they camped.

"I was with Major Powell's expedition when we rested for three days at the junction of these two great canyons. I recall that Oramel Howland was furious when I dropped his rifle off the South Rim and shattered its stock. But the antelope I killed nearly forty years ago may have saved us from starvation. After we repaired the boats and the major had finally completed taking his astronomical readings, we pushed on down the river."

"Did you write me all about it?"

"Yes."

"I would give anything to have those old letters. I'm sorry they were destroyed."

"Me, too," Dunn replied. "I remember that Oramel and Seneca were already prodding me to take them out of the canyon. I wish that I had refused and not led them to their deaths."

"That's history," Cynthia told him. "No one can predict either good or bad outcomes. You and those brothers did what you thought was best. It was a tragic but innocent mistake."

"The biggest one of my life," he said before drifting off to sleep.

When they finally approached Lee's Ferry, Dunn was pleased to note that the arduous wagon track across Lee's Backbone had been replaced by what people called a "dugway," a road notched into the side of the slope. The dugway made traveling down to the ferry much easier and safer. Dunn was especially glad to see that the ferry was still in operation.

Had it not been, they would have had little choice but to turn back.

"The ferry didn't look anything like this when I saw it last," Dunn said as they reached the southern bank of the Colorado River. "Back then, it was just a big flat-bottomed barge that had to be rowed across. The current would push it downriver so fast that it had to be dragged way back up the Colorado before it could be rowed to the other side. But now, I see that they've finally put it on a cable so that the current will actually push it across. This way, the operator doesn't have to worry about the return crossing."

"It still looks dangerous to me," Cynthia told him. "Are you sure the cable and its anchors will hold?"

"I've no reason to think they'd fail. Besides, the river is lowest at this time of year. In the spring, after all the snow melts on the Rockies and feeds down through this canyon, the Colorado can be very dangerous."

Dunn drew the wagon up and waved across the river. Three men on the other side waved back and soon cast off their ferry lines and started across.

"Look at how slick that ferry moves along its cable!" Dunn exclaimed with admiration. "To appreciate this, Cynthia, you'd have had to see the way we fought the current in the old days."

"I guess I would," Cynthia nervously replied.

But the ferry arrived right where it was supposed to and Dunn, with some coaxing, got his team to pull the wagon on board.

"Name is James S. Emmett and these are my sons!" a huge man with massive shoulders and a shaggy white beard bellowed over the river's swift current. "Be three dollars to cross!"

"And well worth it!" Dunn shouted back, introducing himself and his wife.

Emmett and his boys shook hands with Dunn and nodded respectfully to Cynthia before they cast off the line and the ferry began to surge toward the north bank. Dunn climbed up in the driver's seat and took his lines. The horses were fidgety and he had his hands full keeping them under control until they reached the shore, where he quickly drove back onto solid ground.

"Thank heaven we made it!" Cynthia said, after he'd pulled the team well up on the riverbank and set his brake.

Dunn jumped down from his wagon to have a final word with Emmett. As expected, the man was a Mormon polygamist with two wives and eighteen strong, hardworking children.

"You could stay with the family at Lonely Dell," Emmett offered, "or you got a good four hours left of daylight. Enough to make rim country."

"I think we'll push on," Dunn decided. "Maybe we'll stay overnight on our return. But first, whatever happened to the Johnson family? We heard the tragic news of them losing four children to diphtheria."

"Mr. Johnson sold this crossing to our Church six years ago and took his family to live in Kanab. But he fell off a wagon, paralyzing him from the waist down. He should have stayed among our people, but the fool got a bee in his bonnet and moved his family up to the Big Horn Basin in Wyoming."

"Why would he leave the community if he was paralyzed?"

"Don't know! Nobody could figure it out. Anyway, them awful Wyomin' winters got to him and he died and was buried up there a couple of years ago. His family came back to live among our people. The missus had some good kids and they and the Church will see she don't starve."

"That's good to hear," Dunn said, shaking his head to think about all the grief and misfortune the Johnson family had suffered.

"You from these parts?"

"We live in Flagstaff."

Emmett nodded. "You folks down there ought to give this Arizona Strip to Utah. We're the ones that settled it north of the Colorado and we're still runnin' it."

"That may be true," Dunn said, "but this is Arizona and Arizona it will stay."

Emmett didn't like that, but Dunn did not care. The issue over the right to claim the so-called Arizona Strip had been festering between the people of Utah and Arizona for years. The strip represented Arizona's entire northeastern corner above the Grand Canyon. James Emmett was right to claim that the strip had been settled by Mormons, who still represented the vast majority of its population. Because of that, Utah had first attempted to annex the strip soon after she achieved statehood in 1896, when Arizona was still just a territory. More legislation to annex the Arizona Strip to Utah had been introduced in both houses of Congress again in 1902 and still again in 1904. And, while Dunn saw no reason to get into an argument with James Emmett, as a territorial commissioner, he had joined the united ranks of northern Arizona citizens determined to defeat Utah's repeated attempts to annex. To Arizonans, it was unthinkable to give away the magnificent North Rim of the Grand Canyon.

As Dunn trudged back to rejoin Cynthia, Emmett followed him, arguing about the Arizona Strip. Dunn chose to ignore the man and climbed onto his wagon.

"We're heading to the Kaibab Plateau for a few days of camping, Mr. Emmett. I was once a shepherd for Mr. John Lee up at Jacob Lake. Is his old cabin still standing?"

"Nope," Emmett said, hooking his thumbs in his bib overalls. "The winter snows finally did her under a few years back. But I expect you'll meet 'Uncle Jim' Owens, who will talk your legs off. You tell him he can come down here and hunt mountain lions in Paria Canyon—if he ever runs out of 'em on the Kaibab Plateau."

"All right," Dunn said, taking up the lines.

"And you Arizonans are just plain wrong not to turn this North Rim country over to Utah!"

Dunn drove on, putting the entire matter behind him. As

they passed Paria Canyon, he stood up in his wagon, but he could not see Lonely Dell.

"I thought you wanted to go up there and revisit the cabins, fields, and orchards," Cynthia said with raised eyebrows.

"I guess not," Dunn decided with a frown. "Whatever good memories I once had were stamped out when John Lee was executed, then the Johnsons' four kids died of diphtheria. As far as I'm concerned, Lonely Dell is a hard-luck place."

A few hours later, they passed the fascinating red rock sculptures that Dunn remembered had so delighted Josie. Cynthia was equally amazed at how some of the great pillars of red stone balanced on their tiny bases, or were piled one upon the other like rounded scoops of strawberry ice cream. Then they began to climb up a long, desolate valley as they left the river far behind. By evening, they were camping in a thick stand of juniper and piñon pine.

"By noon tomorrow, you won't believe how much the country will change," Dunn promised as he fed their campfire and roasted a fat sage hen he'd shot just before sunset. "We'll be up in the high country among pines, spruce, and aspen."

"Aspen?"

"Yes. Maybe you've never even seen them because they're only found over seven or eight thousand feet. But the aspen will be turning color about now, and you've never seen a prettier sight. I've never forgotten them or the North Rim country."

"You sound as if you've always been in love with the Kaibab Plateau."

"I believe that I have been," Dunn admitted. "When Josie and I came up here, there were very few people. The Kaibab Paiutes made it their summer hunting grounds, and the few Mormon ranchers we met called it all Buckskin Mountain because this country was so thick with mule deer. We stayed in a cabin beside Jacob Lake and then John Lee introduced us to Professor Sutherland."

"Do you wish you'd founded a ranch up here instead of in Lonesome Valley?"

Over the years, Dunn had given that very question a good deal of thought. "Well," he said finally, "I was real spooky about the Kaibab Paiutes who'd attacked and killed the Howland brothers and almost got me. And North Rim winters are pretty fearsome. Early every fall, I'd have had to drive my livestock down off the rim and winter them along the Colorado River. So, all in all, I think I made the right choice. Besides, Josie was expecting Christopher and it made sense to be nearer to her people on the South Rim."

"I'm glad you bought the Lonesome Valley Ranch down there," Cynthia told him. "If you hadn't, maybe you'd never have become famous and I'd never have learned you were still alive."

"I guess it all worked out for the best," Dunn agreed.

They sat beside the fire long after dark, holding hands, talking about the past . . . and the future. They made love in their blankets and saw a bright shooting star just before midnight. The next day they climbed up in the high Kaibab Plateau country, where Dunn proudly introduced Cynthia to Jacob Lake, still a glittering jewel nestled in deep green forest and ringed by the yellow, red, and orange splashes of aspen.

"This is so beautiful!" Cynthia exclaimed as she hopped down from the wagon to explore the ruins of the old log cabin Dunn and Josie had shared so many years before. "Can we stay here a few days?"

"Sure. And we can take some day trips over to the rim."

"I can see the rim almost anytime," she replied, "but country like this . . ."

"I won't allow you to miss out on the views from Walhalla Plateau and especially Cape Royal and Point Imperial," he vowed.

"All right. But I wouldn't object if we stayed right here until the first snowfall."

Dunn laughed at that because the first snowfall might be five or six feet deep. If that happened, they'd never get their wagon out, and tent camping could get mighty cold.

* * *

They spent two glorious weeks exploring the North Rim country and, while they saw evidence of Indians and Mormon cattle, they never met either. Dunn figured that the Mormons who used this land to ranch had probably already driven their stock to the lower country, and the Paiutes had gone to winter where it was warmer.

On the day they were leaving, they were visited by "Uncle Jim" Owens, the new federally appointed game warden. Owens was of average height, with a slightly humped back and a drooping mustache. He carried a big hunting rifle, a cartridge belt, and a sidearm on his right hip, as well as a sheathed knife on his left hip.

"Howdy," Owens said, then introduced himself. "I'm the new game warden up here. You been hunting?"

"No, sir," Dunn replied.

"Well," Owens said, climbing down from his horse, "if you do, you can kill wolves, bears, coyotes, and mountain lions, but you'll have to skin 'em out and hike their hides up in a tree where I can find 'em."

"I thought a game warden was supposed to *protect* animals," Cynthia said.

"That's what I'm fixin' to do," Owens said, thumbing back the brim of his slouch hat and squatting on his heels. "I mean to hunt out them predators so the deer are always safe. This first summer alone, I already shot thirty-six mountain lions, and that's only the beginning."

Dunn couldn't quite figure this man out. "You've hunted and killed that many lions?"

"I have," Owens said proudly. "And I'll wipe every damned one of 'em out before I'm through. There ain't but a few grizzly left on this rim, but I'll get them, too."

"You ever heard of John Muir?" Dunn asked.

"No, I have not."

"He's a pretty famous fellow," Dunn said. "I heard him talk

a few years back and he says that everything in nature is naturally in balance."

Owens squinted suspiciously. "What is *that* supposed to mean?"

"Well," Dunn answered, knowing he was stepping onto thin ice, "John Muir meant that nature puts predators on this earth so that animals like mule deer don't overpopulate and then starve. In the opposite case, when there aren't enough deer, the mountain lions and other predator populations will naturally decline. Things stay in balance that way. As a cattle rancher, I have to think about that myself and . . ."

"Nobody is talking about shooting any damned cattle! Mister, I don't know what in hell you are talking about," Owens snapped with annoyance. "I've been hired to wipe out the predators, and I mean to do just that!"

"But then the animals they feed upon will overpopulate. That inevitably leads to mass starvation."

"Shoot!" Owens snorted. "You and your missus had best go back to the South Rim country where your kind of folks generally don't know what the hell they are talking about!"

Dunn bit back an angry response. After the game warden had departed, he said to Kate, "Sometimes I have to learn to just keep my mouth shut. I should have known better than to try to explain Muir's philosophy to that kind of man."

"But you were right," Cynthia said. "If he wipes out all the bears and mountain lions, the deer *will* overpopulate and eventually starve during a bad winter."

"Yeah," Dunn said, "but we won't be here to see that happen."

"Why not?"

"Because," he said, "we'll be sitting in front of that huge rock fireplace at the El Tovar Hotel."

Thirty

Grand Canyon Village, South Rim, 1919

"Damn automobiles," Dunn grumbled as he boldly threaded his horse and carriage down the very center of West Rim Drive. "They've just ruined this part of the South Rim."

"Funny," Cynthia said, "that's exactly what Christopher and Ginger always say."

Dunn glanced sideways to see if his wife was teasing and decided that she was not. What could he expect? He was in his early eighties and as much out of time as Professor Sutherland's ancient Anasazi, still preferring horses to the newfangled automobiles. His time was long past. He had boldly, even recklessly, ventured down this canyon with Major John Wesley Powell exactly fifty years ago and was almost murdered by Kaibab Paiutes. Instead, he'd been blessed with three loving wives, fathered a fine son, and enjoyed a half century of ranching, political, and entrepreneurial success. He had no complaints coming—none at all.

"Now that the Grand Canyon has been declared a national park," Cynthia said as another automobile tooted and bumped past their slow-moving carriage, "what will happen here?"

"This canyon will survive. It's taken a hundred million years to form, and it'll take at least that long to wear away," Dunn told her as they drew nearer to the El Tovar, where they stayed every year for a month in the winter and another in the summertime.

"I'm sure you're right."

Dunn *hoped* so. Everything had changed so fast in just fifty short years, and it was changing even faster now—for the better and the worse. For example, old "Uncle Jim" Owens had kept his vow to shoot out all the North Rim mountain lions. And what had happened? Just what John Muir had predicted. The mule deer population had soared from its natural number of around 4,000 to more than 100,000. People visiting the North Rim described a "high line" on all the stripped and ravaged trees where the hordes of hungry deer ate every green thing they could reach and where ground vegetation was almost nonexistent. There would be a terrible famine and die-off one of these bad winters, but Dunn wouldn't take any joy in reminding folks of John Muir's grim prophecy.

Dunn hauled his carriage up before the El Tovar and two uniformed porters rushed out to greet and then assist them into the hotel.

One fresh-faced and somewhat impertinent young man grinned and asked, "Nice horses, Mr. Dunn! We don't get many people arriving this way anymore. When are you going to buy a car?"

"The day this canyon freezes over," Dunn replied, taking Cynthia's arm and carefully ushering her into the El Tovar's grand lobby.

As usual, they were fussed over by the hotel's management. Dunn didn't object because he knew that Cynthia enjoyed a bit of special attention merited by so many years of loyal patronage.

"Mr. Dunn," one of the hotel's managers said, coming over to greet him. "How are you, sir! And Mrs. Dunn! You both look very fit indeed!"

"Thank you," Dunn replied. "Will we have our usual rooms?"

"Of course!"

Dunn gazed around the splendid lobby, feeling the tension of their long carriage journey up from Lonesome Valley Ranch drain out of his still broad shoulders. It might be chaos outside with all the bleating automobiles, but all was peace, tranquillity and refinement in the El Tovar Hotel.

"How's Captain Hance these days?"

The bell captain's smile dissolved. "I'm afraid that he's failing and very weak."

"Where is he?"

"Up in the solarium. We try to make him rest, but you know how much he enjoys our guests."

"Would you excuse me?" Dunn asked his wife. "I'll just visit the captain for a few moments and tell him we'd like to have him join us for dinner."

"Of course. I'll meet you back at our room."

The El Tovar was busy and Dunn carefully threaded his way to the solarium, where he found Captain Hance reclining in a chair surrounded by hotel guests, many with children. As always, the captain was in the middle of one of his yarns about the Grand Canyon.

Dunn stood back and waited for him to finish, needing a few moments to recover and compose himself after the shock of seeing Hance so thin and pale. It was obvious that the captain's health was in rapid decline, but he was equally pleased that the old man still enjoyed putting on a good show.

"Hello, Captain," Dunn said when the tale was over.

"Why, if it isn't my dear friend William!" Hance looked all around. "Where is Cynthia?"

"We'll be back a little later to take you to dinner."

"Then we'd sure better drink it up good tonight! I heard that the United States Congress just passed the law of Prohibition. Come January, there'll be nothing left to drink in this hotel!"

Dunn was about to make a comment when one of the smallest children blurted, "Why, Captain, how'd you lose that finger?"

The old man looked down as if this were the very first time he'd ever noticed his missing index finger.

"Well, I'll be jingoed!" he exclaimed, holding the stub up and turning it this way and that with amazement. "Why, sometime or other I must have worn it plumb off pointing out the Grand Canyon to all you nice folks!"

As Dunn turned to leave, he heard the captain's familiar cackle. Passing a huge north-facing window, he could see a wide sweep of the Grand Canyon already slipping into shadows . . . ever-changing . . . ever-stunning . . . ever reminding him of the yet unseen glories to come after his own gentle passage through darkness.

AUTHOR'S NOTE

Grand Canyon begins in 1540 with the desperate attempt of three thirsty Spanish soldiers to climb down the South Rim, probably very near Tusayan Ruins, and reach the Colorado River. Another two centuries passed before Major John Wesley Powell's historic first journey down the Grand Canyon in 1869. This was one of the most daring and courageous expeditions ever undertaken in the American West. Just imagine for a moment their fear as immense canyon walls grew closer and closer together and the Colorado River ever louder and swifter. Toward the end of the journey, Powell's men were almost certain that they would be cast over some immense waterfall and swallowed up by the mighty river.

In *Grand Canyon,* I chose to focus on William Dunn, the most experienced and least-known of the three men who deserted Major Powell and scrambled up to the Kaibab Plateau just above Separation Rapids. Those three were never seen or heard from again. On his second expedition, Major Powell was told by the Kaibab Paiutes that his deserters had been killed in a skirmish. But what if William Dunn *had* managed to flee and then leap headlong into the Colorado River, later to be rescued by the peaceful Havasupai Indians? Wouldn't such a man, badly injured and hundreds of miles from his own people, have remained and possibly married into a tribe that had, for untold centuries, enjoyed that hidden canyon paradise? I also think it likely that Dunn would have felt extremely guilty over the deaths of his companions, Oramel and Seneca Howland, and initially sought anonymity.

Josie, Zack, Professor Sutherland, and most of the other main characters in this novel are fictitious. But the tragedy surrounding John Lee and his wife Emma at Lonely Dell is historical fact. John Lee really was executed for his leadership role in the Mountain Meadows Massacre and Emma did marry Frank French and leave Lonely Dell. Furthermore, the heartbreaking loss suffered by the Johnson family owing to diphtheria is true. The carefully tended graves of their four children can be visited at the old cemetery near Lee's Ferry where, today, modern rafters depart to begin an exciting river journey through the great canyon of stone.

Grand Canyon chronicles the tremendous changes that took place in northern Arizona between 1870 and 1920. In that relatively short time span, the Grand Canyon became world famous thanks to John Wesley Powell, the gifted artist Thomas Moran, and many others. Its popularity was also enhanced by Fred Harvey's genius at creating the magnificent El Tovar Hotel and Grand Canyon Village.

In what might well be considered the classic case of wildlife *mis*management, the vastly overpopulated Kaibab deer herd was decimated during the severe winter of 1924-25 when tens of thousands died of famine, thus validating John Muir's conclusions about the natural balance of nature. Because of its isolated location, the North Rim developed much more slowly. The first automobiles did not arrive at Point Imperial and Cape Royal until 1928, when the spectacular Grand Canyon Lodge was completed.

Because this novel ends in 1919 when "Captain" John Hance actually died and the Grand Canyon received its national park status, I was unable to cover its fascinating modern history. William Dunn would have had a very long fight ahead of him on behalf of the "people of the blue-green water" to restore their native hunting grounds. After having their reservation reduced to a mere 519 acres in 1882, it would take nearly a century of struggle before the Havasupai could reclaim their beautiful waterfalls and winter hunting lands. Today, their reservation occupies over a quarter of a million acres along the western part of Grand Canyon's South Rim. The Havasupai now rely heavily on summer tourism and their sleepy village of Supai is the only United States Post Office where all the mail is still delivered on horseback.

I would like to close this story with a quote from John Muir who, in 1898, eloquently pleaded for a Grand Canyon National Park with these timeless words:

No matter how far you have wandered hitherto,
or how many famous gorges and valleys you have seen,
this one, the Grand Canyon of the Colorado,
will seem as novel to you, as unearthly in the
color and grandeur and quality of its architecture,
as if you had found it after death,
. . . on some other star.

GRAND CANYON CHRONOLOGY

2000-1000 B.C. Ancient Anasazi culture leaves behind cliff dwellings, kivas, pottery, pictographs, and split-twig figurines.

A.D. 1000 Prehistoric Pueblo Indians live in canyon, mostly farming although doing some hunting.

1540 Members of the Coronado Expedition enter canyon country. Garcia Lopez de Cardenas discovers Grand Canyon and sends three soldiers down to fetch water from the South Rim. They fail and barely manage to escape the canyon.

1776 Francisco Tomas Garces, a Franciscan missionary, visits the Havasupai Indians in Havasu Canyon. He is well treated by the friendly "people of the blue-green water."

1826 An American fur trapper, James Ohio Pattie, sees the Grand Canyon.

1863 President Abraham Lincoln creates the Territory of Arizona. One year later, under the protection of Fort Whipple, Prescott named territorial capital and its first permanent structure, a two-room cabin, later becomes a boardinghouse called Fort Misery.

1866 Fur trapper James White claims to have escaped Indians by rafting completely through the Grand Canyon. Most historians doubt his account.

1868 The name "Grand Canyon" first appears in print and on maps.

1869 Major John Wesley Powell departs at Green River, Wyoming, and is the first to journey through the entire Grand Canyon. William Dunn, as well as brothers, Oramel and Seneca Howland, desert expedition at Separation Rapids . . . never to be seen again.

1871-72 Major Powell makes second and much more "scientific" expedition ending at Kanab Canyon, about halfway through the Grand Canyon. He explores and surveys Kaibab Plateau.

John and Emma Lee homestead Lonely Dell in Paria Canyon.

1872 John Lee and Mormons launch first ferryboat named "Colorado" and establish historic Lee's Ferry, the only Colorado River crossing for hundreds of miles.

1874 Hualapai Indians defeated and relocated to reservation at La Paz on the Colorado River south of Parker, where they die by the hundreds.

1875 Major Powell's outstanding report, The Exploration of the Colorado River of the West, illustrated by the famous artist Thomas Moran, is published, creating great excitement about the Grand Canyon in the East and arousing first major tourism interest.

1876 Flagstaff is given its name on July 4, when a tall pine was stripped of its bark and branches, then adorned with an American Flag raised by boisterous celebrants.

1877 Mormon leader John Lee was executed by firing squad at Mountain Meadows, Utah.

1878 Charles T. Rodgers, cattleman who ran the 111 Brand,

homesteads what is now Williams, Arizona. The Atlantic and Pacific Railroad arrives four years later putting it on the map.

1879 Emma Lee leaves Lonely Dell for Arizona and marries Frank French. Warren M. Johnson and his large Mormon family take over operation of Lee's Ferry.

1880 Prospector James Mooney plunges to his death in Havasu Canyon at the falls named after him.

President Rutherford Hayes, bowing to ranching and mining interests, signs bill creating the Havasupai Indian Reservation, stripping all of The People's winter hunting grounds.

1882 President Chester A. Arthur further reduces the Havasupai Indian Reservation to only the village of Supai and The People's cultivated fields, totaling just 518 acres.

Senator Benjamin Harrison of Indiana unsuccessfully introduces a bill to create Grand Canyon National Park.

Atlantic and Pacific Railroad (later called Santa Fe) reaches Flagstaff. John Young, son of Brigham Young, has railroad tie contract and constructs Fort Moroni against possible Indian attacks.

1883 Surviving Hualapai Indians are given back their lands along southwestern rim of Grand Canyon and the huge Hualapai Indian Reservation is created.

"Captain" John Hance becomes the first white settler, miner, and farmer in the Grand Canyon.

Farlee Hotel, the first Grand Canyon boardinghouse, is located near the bottom of the canyon.

1885 William Wallace Bass established a camp near Havasupai Point, offering tourist accommodations.

1886 "Captain" John Hance offers mule rides into the Grand

Canyon down Old Hance Trail and accommodations at his hotel located on the South Rim near Grandview Point.

1889-90 Engineer Robert Brewster Stanton completes his survey under harebrained illusion that a railroad could be built *inside* the Grand Canyon. Three on his expedition are drowned.

1890-91 Bright Angel Trail is built by prospectors along an old Havasupai Indian trail.

1891 Four of Warren and Permelia Johnson's children contract diphtheria from an emigrant wagon passing through Lonely Dell. All are buried side by side at historic Lee's Ferry Cemetery just above the homestead in Paria Canyon.

1896 J. Wilbur Thurber erects the Grand Canyon Hotel at Grand Canyon Village.

1897 "Captain" John Hance becomes first postmaster at the Grand Canyon. It was officially called Tourist, Arizona.

   The Grand View Hotel first opens for business on the South Rim at Grandview Point.

1898 John Muir, founder of Sierra Club, visits the Grand Canyon and champions its designation as a National Park.

1901 First passenger trains arrive at Grand Canyon Village from Williams.

1902 First automobile, a steam-powered Toledo Eight, reaches South Rim of the Grand Canyon.

1903 The Kolb brothers open their photographic studio at Grand Canyon Village.

   President Theodore Roosevelt visits the Grand Canyon and urges its preservation as a National Park.

1904-05 El Tovar Hotel is built and operated by the Fred Harvey Company.

1906 Bright Angel Hotel is sold to the Fred Harvey Company.

"Uncle Jim" Owens is appointed first game warden of the new Grand Canyon Game Reserve. He lived on the North Rim. Before retirement in 1918, he claimed to have killed 532 mountain lions.

1908 President Roosevelt proclaims Grand Canyon a National Monument.

1909 First automobiles, a Thomas Flyer and a Locomobile, reach the North Rim.

1910 Disastrous flood sweeps through Havasu Canyon. Fortunately, most of Havasupai are still wintering up on the South Rim.

1912 Arizona becomes forty-eighth state.

1913 President Theodore Roosevelt visits the Grand Canyon for the second time. He hunts mountain lions with "Uncle Jim" Owens on North Rim and also takes a mule ride down to what is now called Phantom Ranch.

1914 Mary Elizabeth Jane Colter, architect for the Fred Harvey Company, designs Hermits Rest. She will design the beautiful Bright Angel Lodge as well as the famous Watchtower at Desert View.

1919 Automobiles are first allowed to drive on West Rim Drive.

"Captain" John Hance, famous storyteller, dies and is buried in the cemetery at Grand Canyon Village.

President Woodrow Wilson signs the bill establishing Grand Canyon National Park!

About the Author

Gary McCarthy has written ten American historical novels as well as twenty-two western novels. His highly-regarded THE GILA RIVER won the Western Writers of America Spur Award in 1993 and his most recent work, YOSEMITE, has received widespread critical acclaim for its historical accuracy.

The author is an accomplished horseman and thoroughly enjoys poking about in the scenic American West while gathering research for his exciting novels. Mr. McCarthy has more than two million books in print and lives with his family in the beautiful Ojai Valley of California.

GREAT GIFT IDEAS FOR THAT
SPECIAL SOMEONE!